ROSCOE'S SERIES.

———

THE

WIDOWS' WALK;

OR, THE

Mystery of Crime.

TRANSLATED FROM THE FRENCH OF CHARLES RABOU.

LONDON:

PUBLISHED BY E. APPLEYARD, 86, FARRINGDON-STREET;

AND SOLD BY ALL BOOKSELLERS.

THE WIDOWS' WALK.

H.CARTER

PROLOGUE.

CHAPTER I.

LATE in the evening of a cold day in the month of January, 1804, a fiddler and a clarionet-player, attached to the

* The Champs-Elysées is a vast tract of ground planted with trees in various avenues, and containing within its precincts many buildings. In some parts it borders on the Tuilleries, and the most frequented quarters of Paris; in others, on remote and comparatively deserted suburbs. The WIDOWS' WALK (*Allée des Veuves*) is an avenue of trees in the Champs-Elysées.

orchestra of the celebrated Café des Aveugles,* turned their steps towards the home afforded them at the public expense, in the national hospital of the Quinze-Vingts.†

The fiddler was called Michel, and the name of the clarionet-player was Corniquet.

Arm in arm, and supporting each other, their sticks in their hands and their heads in the air, they started with

* This is a subterranean coffee-house, chiefly for the lower orders, situated in one of the galleries of the Palais-Royal. There is music every evening, and the orchestra is entirely composed of blind persons of both sexes. Hence its name: *Coffee-house of the Blind.*
† This hospital was founded in 1220, by Saint-Louis, for the reception of three hundred blind, who, according to the manner of counting at that period, were termed *Quinze-Vingts* (Fifteen-Twenties). At present it contains a greater number of blind persons. None but those absolutely blind and indigent are admitted.

1

a swaggering though somewhat unsteady gait, for the other end of Paris. They were without a guide, but they trusted in Providence, who for many years had preserved them from all accidents during their nocturnal rambles, and likewise in the instinct common to blind people, who, when once upon a road to which they are accustomed, are much less likely to lose their way than many clear-sighted persons would be.

On leaving the Palais-Royal, or Palais du Tribunat, as it was then called, the path of the two *virtuosi* lay in the direction of the Rue Saint-Honoré, which they had to follow in its whole length; thence, keeping a straight line, they would arrive at the Place de la Bastille, and at the distance of a few steps was their abode, No. 38, Rue de Charenton.

Connoisseurs in snuff, the two worthies never quitted their musical den without stopping at the celebrated tobacconist's shop, the " Civet," which was already at that time in high repute.

On the present occasion, having filled their boxes, and addressed sundry compliments to the shop-girl, whilst they did not forget to desire her to give good measure, our travellers again set off, and, arriving at the Place du Palais-Royal, soon perceived that it presented a scene of most unusual bustle and confusion.

They heard a distant and uncertain rumour; people passed hastily by them, all taking one direction; and, nearly at the same moment, a sound resembling the sonorous echo of a train of artillery passing over the pavement, fell upon their ears. Soon after, their progress was arrested by the approach of a considerable armed force.

"So, so," said Michel, "the Faubourgs are up again!"

"They're wrong perhaps, eh?" replied Corniquet, who was a zealous democrat; "the people have so much to be pleased about, haven't they?"

But, from a conversation that was being carried on at a little distance, they soon found that this was a false alarm, and their field-pieces proved to be simple fire-engines: the fact was, a fire had just broken out at a liquor-shop in the Rue Saint-Honoré, at the corner of the Rue Pierre-Lescot.

The burning house was precisely in their line of road, and, judging by the consternation manifested in the neighbourhood, the flames were very rapidly spreading. The Rue Saint-Honoré was probably blocked up; and besides, if they ventured too near the scene of the conflagration, they might be forcibly detained to assist in *forming the chain.**

Under these circumstances, prudence suggested the propriety of changing their course. Now, it is no slight matter for blind people to alter a route familiar to them from long habit, and these two held deep council together on the matter. At last, Corniquet proposed to hire some vehicle, which would take them home; and this certainly appeared to be a very reasonable plan.

But Michel was stingy, and would never agree to spend until the last extremity. He was conceited too, and always asserted that he knew Paris so well, that he should never be puzzled to find his way; and these pretensions, so singular in a blind man, formed a prominent feature in his character.

He therefore proposed to turn into the Rue Saint-Thomas du Louvre, which would take them from the Place du Palais-Royal straight down to the river.

"Let us once get to the Seine," added he, "and we shall do very well! The parapet of the quays is as straight as a line; we have only to follow that, and to count the bridges. After we have passed the fourth, the Pont-Marie, all the streets to the left lead into the Rue Antoine, and when we get there, we're at home, as one may say."

This plan was really well conceived, and Corniquet, who was very much in the habit of yielding to Michel, made but few objections.

Unhappily, the sagacious leader began by making a great blunder.

The Rue Saint-Thomas du Louvre is joined at its extremity by the Rue de Chartres, with which it forms an acute angle, and, by a mistake which is easily understood, Michel just took the wrong turning.

The consequences of this mistake may be imagined; for a whole hour did these poor devils wander about, and when they made inquiries of a chance passenger, they found, to their inexpressible disappointment, that they had left the river behind them, and were in the Rue Saint-Honoré, near the church of Saint-Roch.

Even the intrepid Michel felt discouraged, and he no longer refused to hire a coach, provided one could be found; but this, considering the lateness of the

* In France, when a fire takes place, long rows of individuals are formed, from the burning pile to the nearest supply of water, and buckets are passed along the line with wonderful rapidity. This is called the *chain.*

hour, it being long past midnight, appeared a very doubtful matter.

Before many minutes had elapsed, however, to their great joy, a hackney-coach rumbled past, driving furiously down the Rue Saint-Honoré, towards the stable where it put up, which was outside of the Barrière de l'Etoile.

Being called to by the wanderers, the coachman stopped, and asked where they wanted to go.

But when they began to talk of the Rue de Charenton and the Place de la Bastille, not feeling disposed to undertake such a journey at that hour of the night, he prepared to drive on again.

To induce him to take them, and at the same time hoping to obtain some reduction in the fare, Michel appealed to his humanity, and set forth the wretched plight of two poor blind men, who had lost their way at night, in the middle of Paris.

Corniquet thought it best to appeal to his love of gain, and roundly offered to give him three francs.

Unfortunately, this offer touched the only sensible chord in the heart of the worthless driver, and he suddenly formed an infamous plan for making sure of the proffered gain, without leaving the road which led to his home.

He pretended to have some doubts of the solvency of his customers, who in truth did not look as if their affairs were in a very flourishing condition, and insisted upon being paid beforehand.

Having accomplished this imposition, he made them get into the coach, and turning his horses several times, as if he found great difficulty in making them take the contrary direction from that which led to the stable, he effectually prevented all suspicion in the mind of his dupes.

When he arrived at the Rond-Point* of the Champs-Elysées, he calculated that the drive had been long enough for the poor fellows to think they had reached their destination; so he stopped, opened the door, and then, whipping his horses into a gallop, left the musicians in the middle of the road, without caring what became of them.

The blind men were not immediately aware of the trick that had been played them; for, as Corniquet got out of the coach, he dropped the mouthpiece of his clarionet, which protruded from the pocket of his great coat, and had not been properly secured. A considerable

* A circular space, on one side of which opens the Allée des Veuves.

time was spent in searching for this important part of the instrument, and it was not till they had at length regained possession of it, that the two friends thought of ringing the bell to rouse the porter, who probably, said they, had given them up for that evening.

But they could neither find the bell nor the door to which it ought to be attached ; and having advanced eight or ten steps, without meeting with any resistance at the ends of their sticks, Corniquet said : "It's very odd ! a man may lose his way in no time."

"Nonsense," replied Michel; "I feel the wall on the right. You don't know your bearings, I tell you !"

Corniquet, whose arm his companion had again taken, followed without making any resistance ; but suddenly displaying great sharpness : "Michel," cried he, "for certain, we're not in our street !"

"What makes you think so ? " asked Michel.

" Just feel this a bit," said Corniquet, striking the ground with his stick ; " that's not pavement, any day."

"Bless me ! but, in fact, I *see*, by my feet, that we are on bare earth ; precious hard it is too: it's been a famous sharp frost."

" Ah, well ! we're in a pretty pickle," said Corniquet, in a lamentable tone.

"Stay," returned Michel; "I see how it is: they're making a drain at the end of the street; the coachman did'nt care to risk his neck among the rubbish, and he has left us on the Place de la Bastille, where I feel quite at home."

"Oh ! you're never at a loss, you're not !"

"I'll bet you anything I take you straight to the guard-house, which is not fifty steps before us," said Michel, confidently: and, forcing Corniquet to follow him, whilst he neglected to guide their steps with his stick, he advanced to the edge of one of the ditches which run along the side of the footpath, and rolled into it, together with his friend.

"My violin is safe !" cried Michel, getting up, for his first care had been for his means of livelihood. Then turning to Corniquet, who was complaining that he had bruised his elbow : "You've nothing broken, have you?" asked he.

"Might as well," said Corniquet. "You're a nice one to lead the way !"

"I tell you, we're just at the beginning of our street," replied Michel. "Only feel the wind that's coming right in our faces !"

And, in fact, when they had managed to scramble out of the ditch, a strong current of air, which met them, revealed the neighbourhood of some cross-street, or alley. Besides, the pavement began again within a short distance, and this was a fresh inducement to follow the road which offered itself to them, for to blind persons the pavement tells of the abodes of men, of civilization.

The poor fellows were far from suspecting what was the formidable locality into which chance had conducted them.

The Allée des Veuves, where, even at the present day, a merely relative security has been obtained by the establishment of two guard-houses, and by the vigilance of an improved police-service, was, at the period referred to in this history, a place of the worst repute.

This lonely cross-road opens at one end into the frequented part of the Champs-Elysées, but still at a considerable distance from the great carriage-drive, the centre of life and movement; at the other, it joins the high road to Passy, close to the Seine. This road, upon which there is much traffic during the day, begins at dusk to be deserted, and, on account of its dangerous proximity to the water, has itself the reputation of being unsafe.

In 1804, unlighted, and rendered still more obscure by a double row of centenarian trees, which, even when the winds of autumn had despoiled them of their leaves, partially concealed the sky, the long avenue to which we have introduced our readers, could boast but of a few small and isolated habitations, diversified with gardens and waste ground. No attempts had as yet been made at building speculations in this remote quarter. And most of the habitations in question had remained closed and deserted, since the aristocracy, of whose secret pleasures they were the asylum, had been scattered and despoiled of their opulence by the fury of a revolutionary mob.

From time to time, some fortunate son of the new *régime* found his way to these *petites maisons*, thus left without an owner; and sometimes too, the walls, which had witnessed the elegant profligacy of the old monarchy, echoed the boisterous mirth of popular orgies. But this remote and solitary place was especially favourable to a grosser licentiousness; to those frightful and monstrous vices, which, even amid the corruption of a great city, cower under the shade of night and solitude. It was therefore

carefully avoided by the most courageous—by those who, in any other place, would have faced with intrepidity a ruffian demanding their purse or their life.

Thus adapted for the perpetration of every crime, and the accomplishment of the darkest mysteries, the Allée des Veuves had frequently been the scene of bloody outrages, and of mournful tales. But just on account of its detestable notoriety, many false reports were in circulation respecting it, and the fears of the public made them look upon it as a sort of accursed spot. It was the reputed locality of a host of tragedies, palmed upon popular credulity by the newspapers or the lovers of the marvellous; and we may suppose what would have been the terror of our blind friends, if some inspiration or officious warning had revealed to them their alarming situation. Fortunately for them, they were ignorant of their danger, and quietly pursued their way, in the feeling of full security.

Persuaded that they were really in the Rue de Charenton, they went on till they thought they had reached No. 38, the house at which they resided; then, turning to the right, they felt for the great gates, but to their utter amazement they ran against the trunk of a tree, and found that they were once more at the edge of a ditch.

"I tell you what! the devil has a hand in it," said Michel, who would not give up the idea of being close to his abode.

"Be quiet a moment, that I may listen," said Corniquet, suddenly; and with that exquisite sense of hearing, which is given to the blind as a compensation for their infirmity, he soon distinguished the murmur of voices at some little distance.

Having thus ascertained that there were still some persons up in the neighbourhood, of whom they might ask their way, Corniquet proceeded in the direction from which the voices appeared to come.

Michel, at first, protested vehemently against what he called *letting themselves down;* but as Corniquet would not give way, he ended by following him, and they soon found themselves close to a wall. They groped along it, until they came to a wooden door; and the mouldings, which they felt, together with the elegant iron knocker, would have convinced them that it was the entrance to a house, even if the noise of the conversation which had first attracted them, and which now became more distinct, could have left them in doubt as to the place whence it issued. They listened for a moment, but could not distinguish the words, though they remarked that the speakers were animated, and appeared to be quarrelling.

Sure that he was not breaking any one's rest, Corniquet seized the knocker, and gave three or four heavy strokes; but the only effect produced by this noisy mode of announcing his presence was a sudden pause in the conversation, so that perfect stillness reigned throughout the house.

"They must be confoundedly taken up with what they are saying," remarked Corniquet; and, resolved to make himself heard, he knocked more loudly than before; but the most profound silence followed this new attempt, broken only by the sighing of the wind among the trees, and the distant barking of a watch-dog.

It was evident that the tenants of the house did not intend to open the door, and Michel tried to dissuade his companion from making any further efforts, declaring that he could do very well without the assistance which had been refused to them in so inhospitable a manner.

Corniquet, however, would not listen to this; his blood was up, and as the knocker had been productive of no favourable result, despair inspired him with a brilliant idea.

Taking his clarionet from his pocket, he adjusted the different pieces, and said to Michel, "Wasn't *Morpheus* a famous musician in old times, who tamed the brute-animals by his music?"

"Yes, so it's said," replied Michel; "and my opinion is, as how he'd be very useful here, to break in these other brutes with his harmony."

"Well! take your violin, and we'll give 'em a tune in their den."

"What! you're going to give a serenade to these surly wretches?" asked Michel, rather surprised at this singular project.

"Why, if it does no good, it can't do harm," replied the adventurous musician. "They'll say, it can't be rogues, because it's musicians. Well, come now! are you ready?"

"After all," thought Michel to himself, "the thing's droll enough."

"Are you ready?" said Corniquet, repeating his question; "now for it, begin boldly, let us charm them with our crack tunes!"

Michel opened with a full chord, and the surrounding echoes, no doubt sufficiently startled by this nocturnal harmony, were soon awakened by the famous air, "*Où peut on être mieux qu'au sein de sa famille?*"* The performers standing a fair chance to pass the night in the streets, this air, naturally so expressive, was peculiarly appropriate and touching.

It would not be correct to say, that nothing resulted from the execution of this strange plan for a musical invasion. The musicians had scarcely completed the first few bars, when they became aware of some movement within the house; but as, after repeating the piece three or four times, no disposition was shown to open the door: "It bites," said Corniquet, "it bites! They've stirred, which proves they hear us; but I see, we must rouse 'em with something more brisk:" and Michel having taken the hint, the sentimental music of Grétry was succeeded by the more lively and not less popular air, *The Tartar March*, from the opera of *Lodoiska*.

At this move, it was impossible to hold out any longer, and a small window in the roof being opened, a voice, which betrayed very great impatience, called out: "How now! what rascals are making such a confounded noise at our door?"

"You see," said Corniquet to his companion, "what harmony does! I was sure of it." Then, changing his natural voice for the most whining and pitiful tone: "I ask pardon, sir," said he, "for disturbing of you; but we're two poor blind men, who have lost our way, and we wish you'd be so good as to put us in the right road."

"Devil take you!" said the speaker, who did not seem satisfied with this explanation; "did ever any one choose such a way to announce himself!"

"Sir," answered Corniquet, "we knocked, and no one came. I says to myself, at this time of night, perhaps they take us for ugly customers, so I think we'd best give 'em a little music; for you know, sir, rogues don't meddle with music."

"Well, well! but who are you?"

"Why, don't we tell you we're blind men!" replied Michel.

"But is it true that you are blind?"

"Ah! merciful God! if we are blind!" said Corniquet, dolefully; — "but too blind! from our birth we've never seen the blessed sky!"

* " Where can one be better, than in the bosom of one's family? "

"We belong to the hospital of the Quinze - Vingts, close by," continued Michel, with great simplicity; "you can make inquiries about us."

"Wait a bit," was the answer given them; "I will come down."

A considerable time elapsed between this promise and the execution of it, so that Corniquet lost all patience, and threatened to try the music again, talking of a decisive attack by means of the overture to the *Caravan*. But the door opened at last, though with much caution, and a man appeared, with his face nearly concealed by the raised collar of a large top-coat; he held a light in his hand, and told the blind men to draw near, that he might convince himself of the reality of their infirmity.

Michel passed muster first, and his eyes, which, with their sightless balls, bore a strong resemblance to those of an antique bust, appeared to carry conclusive evidence to the mind of the examiner.

"And I'm still in a worse plight," said Corniquet, advancing in his turn; but this was pure boasting, for really, neither could claim any advantage over the other.

"All right! you may come in," said the man in the great-coat; "I see you are honest fellows, and that there is nothing to fear from you."

Corniquet was already seeking for the entrance, glad to profit by the invitation; but Michel who persisted in believing that he was close to his home, observed that the slightest direction would enable them to regain the Rue de Charenton, near which they must now be.

"The Rue de Charenton!" exclaimed the man; "is that where you are going?"

"Yes," rejoined Michel, "to the establishment of the Quinze-Vingts, to which we belong."

"Well then, my good fellows, that's a long way behind; you are here at the Avenue des Triomphes, near the Barrière du Trône."*

"Now, what did I tell you?" cried Corniquet, whilst his companion was speechless from surprise.

"You've been really very fortunate," added their wily and provoking new acquaintance, "to have met with nothing unpleasant on the road; robberies and murder are quite common in this out-of-the-way place."

* This would have been quite at the opposite extremity of Paris, from the Champs-Elysées.

"Well, but come, sir!" said Corniquet, in alarm; "be a little charitable, and help us out of this. Couldn't you send some one with us, to show us the way, if we paid 'em?"

"Impossible, friend! I am alone in the house, with my wife; I am in great trouble about her. But yet," continued he, "to be sure, I might hit upon a plan."

"Well! what is it?" said Corniquet.

"No, no; all things considered, it would be very difficult to manage; so, good night, my fine fellows! it is not at all pleasant to stand talking here."

"But, sir, we might understand one another," urged Corniquet, not at all liking the idea of being again left to the guidance of Michel.

"Why—to be sure—I might tell you what it is, but a little explanation would be necessary; so come in, at all events, and if we can't come to terms, that need not prevent me from offering you a glass of wine to warm you."

"That's what I call sense," said Corniquet; "you seem to be a *good 'un*, after all!"

Michel felt an instinctive reluctance to venture within this unknown house, and appeared to hesitate at the entrance; but Corniquet, taking his arm, asked him what he was afraid of.

The fear of ridicule triumphed; deciding against his secret presentiment, Michel followed his friend without making any further resistance, and the door was closed behind them.

———

CHAPTER II.

AFTER traversing a small court-yard, they were introduced into a spacious and lofty apartment, and their host invited them to sit down; then addressing them, and raising his voice in a marked manner: "You must know, my friends," said he, "that, at the moment you knocked at the door, I found myself in a very awkward predicament."

"Indeed! what was it?" replied Corniquet.

"Just fancy. My wife, who is in the next room, had been suddenly taken with the pains of labour."

And, at that moment, as if to confirm the assertion, a woman's voice was heard to utter stifled and plaintive groans.

"Is that all?" exclaimed Corniquet. "Ah! well! that didn't bother me much, when my good woman was alive! I just used to send off for the midwife, when those miseries took place."

"It is very easy for you to talk," rejoined the host; "but in the first place, I am alone with the sick woman, and the nearest midwife lives a good distance off: and then, that's not all; I, who speak to you, am only the porter of the house in which you are."

"I," said Corniquet, "have never been anything but a poor musician; but when things came, why, they came, and if I had not *blunt* to pay the needful, I made up for it later; a child is not killed for being born on *tick*."

"You do not understand me," replied the porter; "I have wherewith to pay for my wife, but my master has strictly forbidden that she shall lie-in here."

"Well! that's a good 'un!" cried Corniquet; "has a master anything to do with that? Isn't a woman at liberty to ——"

"How you talk!" said Michel, impatiently; "can't you let the gentleman speak?"

"I tell you what it is," continued Corniquet, striking the ground with his stick, "and I'll always say it, and stick to it, a master has no right to prevent ——"

But Corniquet was here interrupted by the husband, who reminded him that they had no time to lose in idle words.

"I listen," said Corniquet, doggedly pursuing his idea, notwithstanding; "but if, after the revolution, masters will meddle with such like things, where's liberty? that's all."

"I was going to say," resumed the husband, after a short silence, finding that Corniquet had exhausted the expression of his comic indignation, "that my master receives in this house, his friends of both sexes, and gives them gallant entertainments, so that he does not care to be annoyed by the presence of a sick-woman or the cries of a child. He has made me understand that matters must be managed away from here, or he will discharge me."

"Then, that man is a tyrant! and I say it!" cried Corniquet. "And you gave in to it?"

"Not to lose his place," suggested the prudent Michel.

"That is the very thing; I have good wages and plenty of perquisites, without speaking of the place itself, which is very light, for my master often does not come above twice in a fortnight. Besides, his whim does not put me to great inconvenience; at the hos-pital of Saint Anthony, near here, there is a nurse who is from my part of the country, and I am sure my wife will be as well taken care of as if she were at home."

"Well, if you all agree," said Corniquet, "there's no offence."

"Certainly, but here is the difficulty. In order to transport the patient more commodiously than in a hackney coach, and more decently than on a stretcher, I provided myself with a sedan-chair. One of my friends, who is a coach-maker, has bought up a number of them since the revolution. With the assistance of a cousin, who is gardener here, I could have carried the poor woman very comfortably, but she is before her time, and my fool of a cousin has gone to spend the night at a wedding party; so I am left with her on my hands. I don't know what I shall do!"

"I hear you, master, clattering along with your wooden shoes," replied Corniquet; "it's not difficult to guess what you are going to say."

"What do you understand?" asked the porter, feigning to be surprised that his thoughts should be so easily guessed.

"Why, to be sure! you want us to help you in removing your wife."

"As you so frankly offer me your services, I will not deny it; the assistance of worthy people like you, would be very valuable to me just now."

"Well, but I say, old boy," rejoined Corniquet, in a tone of friendly reproach, "you made us kick our heels at the door a pretty long time, eh?"

"In the first place, when you began to knock, I was occupied with my wife; and then, in these lonely parts, we are cautious about opening the door at night."

"Yes, but when we struck up the air from *Lodoiska*, you said to yourself:

"Et vous saurez que les Tartares
Ne sont barbares
Qu' avec leurs ennemis."*

"I confess," replied the porter, "that the music reassured me very much; but when you informed me that you were blind men who had lost their way, it seems, said I, as if Providence had sent them to me."

"Ah, well! all for the best!" said Corniquet, gaily.

* Well-known words in the *Tartar March*:

"And you know that the Tartars
Are barbarous
Only to their enemies."

"I thought, in the first instance, blind people are naturally handy and obliging. These men have a service to ask of me, and I, on my side, shall be glad of their assistance; they can help me to remove my wife, and I can conduct them home. It will be a capital arrangement."

"But how are we to fasten ourselves to your *machine?*" objected Michel, who was not very well pleased with the plan; "we have quite enough trouble to find our way, without having a load upon our arms."

"That need not be an obstacle," replied the husband; "I might be the front bearer, and then the one behind would only have to follow me; or suppose you both take it, so as to leave my hands free, in case of necessity, to use the weapons with which I shall provide myself; if I hold the arm of the vanguard, can I not guide the caravan with perfect ease?"

"Certainly! that's clear enough," said Corniquet.

"Besides, if after I have seen you home, you think I am still in your debt, you can name your price."

"Ah, now, Mr. Porter! that's not friendly of you," exclaimed the good-natured Corniquet; "don't you say so again, or we shall fall out!"

"Well, at all events, you'll take a glass of something to refresh yourselves."

"Oh, as to a glass, I don't say; that's another thing. Eh, Michel?"

"I'll be with you again in a moment," said the husband to the two friends; and he went into the next room. As soon as he entered, his wife began to moan heavily, and when he returned with a bottle and some glasses, he declared that no time must be lost, for she was getting worse every moment. Having poured out the wine: "Here's your health, my good friends," added he; "it's the real stuff, from my master's cellar."

Corniquet pledged him, and taking a mouthful, tested it after the fashion of a connoisseur, then pronouncing it to be *prime*, he tossed off the glass.

Michel, who had all along appeared to submit to what was taking place around him, rather than to take any part in it, now refused to drink, and pressed them to make haste.

"I am sure I am anxious to do so," replied the husband; "and if you will come with me, we will get out the chair."

The blind men rose immediately, and their companion opening the door of the room which contained his wife, said to her: "Do not lose patience, my dear; we shall come for you in a moment." He then gave his hand to Corniquet, and Michel, holding by his friend's coat, followed with a discontented air. Thus disposed in a bunch, if we may be allowed such a comparison, they reached a coach-house, and the porter placed the poles of the sedan-chair in the hands of these *impromptu* bearers.

They carried it to the bottom of a flight of steps, which led up to the house, and the man told them to wait a few minutes, whilst he fetched his wife. "I must wrap her up well, in blankets and a good cloak," said he, "for I think the cold is increasing."

He soon returned, bearing his burden in his arms, and apparently with some effort, for he observed: "I expect you mean to present me with a famous boy; you are none of the lightest to carry, I can assure you"

The patient made no reply, but by continuing her groans; and this pattern of a husband, having placed her as comfortably as he could on the seat of the chair, and consoled her by the assurance that in half-an-hour she would be in a good warm bed, turned to the blind men, and exclaimed with energy: "Gunners, to your posts!"

He then assisted them to secure the leathern straps upon their shoulders; the outer gate was opened, and the escort set forth at a good round pace.

We will not affirm that the sick woman was particularly well satisfied with her bearers, for, unaccustomed to the office, and urged on by the husband, they gave many rude shocks to the chair and its contents; the leader of the band seemed to think they could never go fast enough, and would willingly have increased, not diminished their speed. They went through that portion of the Allée des Veuves which the two friends had already traversed, and arrived at the Rond-Point; when Corniquet, wishing to display the acuteness of his perception, remarked: "We're crossing a square; I know that by the wind, which blows rather fresh."

"Yes, the Place du Trône!" replied he whom we must call the mystifier; for our readers have, doubtless, long ago guessed, that a fresh plot was being practised against our friends of the Quinze-Vingts.

However this may be, the leader of

the party caused it to move very quickly, so long as they continued in the open space which separates the two plantations of the Champs-Elysées, or in the frequented part of the Faubourg Saint-Honoré, but as soon as they reached the labyrinth of deserted streets which give such a dull, melancholy aspect to this quarter of the town, he slackened his pace, and appeared to be in no hurry to reach his destination, for he commenced what might be aptly termed a *Penelope's* walk. He went up one street, and down another, retracing his steps, doubling and turning, so as to create an inextricable confusion in the memory of his companions, in case they might afterwards wish to point out the course which he had pursued.

Just as they came to a solitary lane, which ran into the Rue de la Pépinière, and which they had already visited several times in the course of their perambulations, they heard the measured steps of the night-watch advancing in that direction. The moment their leader was aware of this, he, without saying a word, let go the arm of Corniquet, and stealing away on tip-toe, so as not to attract attention, turned into the lane; when he had got to some distance, he laid aside this precaution, and starting off at full speed, soon effected his escape.

His dupes were some little time before they could persuade themselves of the reality of this new mishap. A few minutes passed in doubts and suppositions on the part of Corniquet, and in reproaches and curses on that of Michel; and whilst they were trying to disengage themselves from the strap and fastenings, the watch came up to these unlucky wanderers.

We have not yet mentioned, that it was a bright moonlight night, for to the two actors who have hitherto filled so prominent a part upon the scene, this was a matter of no consequence; sun, moon, and stars, were alike a blank to them. But, in point of fact, the sky being remarkably clear, in consequence of the sharp north wind, the *star of night* (to use the words of a romance which attained to great celebrity some years later) had every facility to shed *its peaceful splendour* over the scene of this meeting.

The street was not at that time built up, but was bounded by the walls of some neighbouring gardens, and the light of the moon fell full upon the group formed at the moment by the sedan-chair and its perplexed bearers.

Now, this was a singular spectacle at so advanced an hour of the night, and could not fail to command the attention of the officer of the watch. He advanced towards the forsaken pair, and demanded what they were about.

"How should I know?" replied Corniquet. "It's another trick that's been played us; I think we're bewitched to-night!"

"A trick?" returned the officer; "explain yourself."

The explanation was necessarily long and confused; Michel and Corniquet spoke together, and made a sort of *olla podrida* with the Café des Aveugles, a fire, a wicked coachman, the Avenue des Triomphes, a woman in labour, a rascally porter who had led them about, and a hundred other details. The only thing which appeared clear to the leader of the watch, was, that he had to do with blind men, and thinking it strange that they should have been chosen to convey the singular vehicle before him, he immediately conceived strong suspicions as to its contents.

The door being opened, he saw something seated, and ordered this something to get out and answer for itself; but no word or movement followed this intimation, and he then commanded two of his men to bring it out by force. They obeyed, and lifted out of the chair apparently a human form, enveloped in a large cloak laced with gold.

The curiosity of the bystanders was now still more excited; the cloak was opened, and instead of a woman in the *delicate* situation stated by the blind men, they found a man of about fifty or sixty years of age. At first they thought that he had fainted, but soon, from the blood which saturated his linen, and a large wound in the left side, they discovered that he was the victim of assassination. This time, the Allée des Veuves had not belied its reputation.

Pressed with questions, the blind men could only give a detailed account of what had passed in the house they came from. Their infirmity, and the calmness of their demeanour, did not allow suspicion to attach itself to them; and the most natural solution of the difficulty appeared to be that which they themselves gave, namely, that they had fallen into the hands of a dexterous villain, and had unconsciously assisted in removing the body of the victim. Still, it was prudent to detain them in custody, so that they were first taken to the house of the magistrate for the district, and then sent to the police-depôt, to await the conclusion of their harassing nocturnal Odyssey.

Next day, justice having received information of the affair, its officers used every exertion to establish the identity of the murdered man; but there was nothing to indicate his name or quality, and the exposition at the Morgue remained without result. Corniquet and Michel, interrogated separately or together, never varied in their evidence, which agreed in the minutest point. Inquiries had been made concerning them, at the establishment of the Quinze-Vingts, and the answers being very satisfactory, no one entertained the slightest suspicion that they might be the guilty parties. But as Corniquet was positive he should recognise the voice of the man who had placed them in this unpleasant position, if he heard it again, the magistrate, before he set them at liberty, formed a plan which might have had some chance of success, if it had been executed on the night the crime was discovered.

The blind men were taken to the spot where they were arrested, and requested to try to find out the road they had followed on that memorable occasion. But the assassin had so effectually taken his precautions, that such an attempt could not be productive of much success. Besides, the unfortunate friends were still so confused and alarmed at finding themselves in the hands of justice, that they had not sufficient presence of mind, or clearness of recollection. Michel, proceeding pretty much by chance, notwithstanding his pretended skill in being always able to find his way, led the police agents who accompanied him, to the place where the slaughter-house of the Roule now stands, a lonely spot, without houses or trees, not in the least resembling that whence the funeral procession had set forth.

Corniquet was somewhat better inspired. He took the direction of the Champs Elysées, and succeeded in finding the Rond-Point; but then, instead of turning into the Allée des Veuves, he went down the Avenue d'Antim, and at once indicated, as the scene of the outrage, the house of an aged member of the Conservative senate, who lived there with his wife, a cook-maid, and a man-servant. The social position of this individual acquitted him of all connection with the crime, and justice would not even examine into the pretended discovery of Corniquet. The man-servant alone was confronted with him, and when he spoke, the blind man immediately declared that his voice was not at all like that of the murderer.

Once it was thought that a very important clue had been discovered. On the same night that the two members of the Quinze-Vingts were arrested, a patrol going the rounds in one of the most solitary streets of Chaillot* had met a young man in a state of great excitement, who spoke of murder, of a dagger, and of a man who wished to take his life. But the incoherence of his expressions soon proved this young man to be labouring under mental derangement. A letter was found on him, addressed to a most respectable party in Paris; and it was ascertained that a few days before his insanity had declared itself, he had suffered severe domestic calamities, which might easily account for the presence of the disease. He was closely watched for some days, and being duly pronounced by the doctors to be of unsound mind, was conducted to the lunatic establishment at Charenton.

The only result of the investigation of justice, was therefore the experiment which had been tried with the blind men. The press drew public attention to this fact, and it gave rise to a controversy between several learned men, which was not peculiarly remarkable for either courtesy or utility.

The numerous plots which at that time menaced the safety of the state, and the life of the first consul, Buonaparte, gave by degrees an almost exclusively political direction to the police-service; and when the first moment of interest was passed, the crime, the discovery of which we have related, was forgotten, like many other outrages committed and left unpunished about the same period.

But the hand of Providence was still there, to bring to light, in its own good time, the dark business, of which as yet we have but a confused hint. Happy is it for mankind, that Providence is always patient, always watchful, and fruitful in expedients! We may confidently trust to it for the detection of this black mystery.

Besides, he who reads will learn !

* A village in the environs of Paris, very near the Champs-Elysées.

END OF THE PROLOGUE.

PART I.

CHAPTER I.

AT the period of the outbreak of the Revolution of 1789, one Joseph Lebeau was at the head of a first-rate establishment, in the mercery line, situated in the quarter of Saint-Denis, Paris. The concern had been in the hands of his family for several generations.

He was not a zealous partisan of the new doctrines, but he felt convinced that they would ultimately triumph; and, considering in a commercial point of view the inevitable consequences of this general overthrow of the past, his first thought was how it might affect the interests of his business.

The changing circumstances which marked this eventful time, never found him unprepared. When the green cockades were mounted, as the revolutionary symbol, he was instantly ready with a considerable quantity, and he sold them off with a rapidity which is the privilege of any trader able to meet the wants or the whim of the moment. But the green cockade was a transitory fashion, and was succeeded by the *tricolour*, destined to a more enduring and glorious career. On this occasion likewise, Joseph Lebeau was provided with the necessary materials to satisfy all demands for the great national demonstration; besides supplying the civic decorations for an immense number of hats, he had an ample assortment of scarfs and rich ribbons, to be used as sashes and other ensigns of authority; and when, descending from the political sphere into that of fashion, the *tricolour* was adopted in ladies' attire, this skilful man of business produced a succession of tempting novelties, unrivalled in the perfection of the tissues, the elegance of the patterns, and the freshness and variety of the shades.

So much activity and tact could not fail of their reward, and at a crisis which was fatal to many in the commercial world, long before the end of the *Constituent Assembly*, Joseph Lebeau had realized a handsome property. He was not ungrateful to the noble colours which had brought such good fortune to his house; he placed it under their special patronage, and exchanged his former unmeaning sign of the "*Clouded Ribbon*," for that of the "*Tricoloured Prism*," under which latter denomination his establishment was thenceforth known.

But during the calamitous days of the Reign of Terror, Joseph Lebeau suffered in common with his brother traders, from the stagnation of business, and vainly exercised his ingenuity to discover some favourable opening for speculation. When luxury again flourished under the Directory, a slight amelioration was perceptible in his affairs, and his hopes rose with the edict of the 29th Floréal, 10th year (19th May, 1802), which created the *Legion of Honour.** It was at first a purely civic institution, but the clear-sighted tradesman soon discerned a future widely-diffused order of knighthood under these quiet commencements, and he already calculated the splendid profits he should make upon the ribbon required for the decoration. This flattering dream was, however, suddenly arrested by the hand of death. In the month of July, 1802, Joseph Lebeau was seized with a malignant putrid fever, which carried him to the grave in the course of a few days.

When his premature end was known in the neighbourhood, and especially on the day of the funeral, the numerous assembly of commercial men expressed, as with one voice, respect for the upright character and high capacity of the deceased. A sad reflection accompanied their flattering testimony to Lebeau's worth; it was the general impression, that the establishment which had been raised to so high a degree of prosperity by his talents, would be ruined by his death.

"For," continued the talkers, "though there have been examples of young women placed at the head of large establishments, who have managed them with much credit to themselves; yet, there is a great difference in women, and the exceptions had been brought up to trade; before they put their hand to the work, they had some idea of what is meant by keeping books, having a connexion, bills falling due, &c."

"But was this the case with the young Annette Lebeau? Her father, who had singular opinions on that subject, had brought her up like a princess; she never appeared in the shop, she was always dressed in the height of the fashion, and, in her whole life, had never taken down a bandbox for a customer. As to ribbons, did she know anything about them, except to select them for her waist or her hair?"

All these things were indeed rigorously true; and when some friends of

* This was not at first an order of knighthood, but it became so under Napoleon.

the family ventured to observe, that Mademoiselle Lebeau was a very superior person, and possessed of a good understanding, "Oh, yes!" was the reply, "witty and agreeable in conversation, she may probably be; but business does not require wit; strong common sense, activity, and solid qualities, are wanting:" and, encouraged by the general assent and approbation, the speakers went back to their first position, declaring that the *Tricoloured Prism* had sustained a terrible blow by the death of its principal, and that it must be plain to every one, it could never recover the shock.

It happened, however, that these predictions were not so well founded as their authors supposed. Mademoiselle Lebeau undertook the management of her late father's affairs, and in her hands they did not fall into the rapid and complete decay with which they had been threatened. We may account for this fact by presuming, either that the young girl, who had been so hardly judged, found in the powerful reaction of self-love, sufficient strength to accomplish the difficult task which had devolved upon her; or, that in her case was exemplified the consoling doctrine, that human intelligence is full of resources, and may be applied, by energetic will, to the most various pursuits.

Assisted in the first instance by the advice of some old friends of her father, and afterwards guided by a sound and instinctive perception of the true principles of commerce, she was soon enabled to meet the difficulties of her position; and as she went on with her arduous undertaking, her frank and open temper, her modest self-possession, and the charm of her manner, won for her general sympathy, so that all were emulous in their expressions of goodwill, and in the endeavour to lighten her labours. The success of her courageous attempt was not long doubtful; before many months had elapsed, not only had the evils which menaced the future prosperity of the establishment been averted by her skilful and steady management, but a fresh impulse had been given to the concern, and it had never been in a more flourishing state.

There were some, however, who would not allow that they had been mistaken.

The fact was there, as plain as if it had been stated in black and white, and could not be denied; but they tried to find some plausible explanation for it. Now, in the time of old Joseph Lebeau,

a certain clerk, named Chevillard, stood high in his employer's confidence, and had the exclusive care of the cash and accounts; these reasoners therefore declared, that they saw nothing so very surprising in the sudden commercial vocation of the fair mercer; for, said they, "The thing is simply this: she has been sensible enough to place her inexperience under the guidance of a *long head*, who leaves her all the apparent merit of the result, whilst in reality he supplies all the study and intelligence necessary to its attainment. In this way, there is no great wonder she should be successful; any petticoat could have done as well."

Unfortunately for our theorists, many persons were well acquainted with the extent of Chevillard's capacity. He was indisputably a worthy young man; he had all the required qualities for a good accountant—exactitude, integrity, application to business; but so far from being able to direct a large concern, he was essentially a man of details, whose ideas fell into confusion at the slightest attempt to interfere with his usual routine, and who, every year, when required to take stock, make up the accounts, and strike a general balance, evinced the most comical distress that can be imagined.

Besides, this pretended leader was, from his character and habits, very inferior to the part assigned him; ardent in the pursuit of pleasure, Chevillard, whenever his occupations would permit, dressed himself with the most scrupulous care, to display to the best advantage, a person which, in many points, had been favoured by nature: and we may here remark, that he expended upon the gratification of his vanity, a larger portion of his yearly revenue than was strictly consistent with prudence. Devoted to the fair sex, and treating every passing fancy as a serious passion, if he had fallen into the hands of certain heroines, he would have been easily led to commit the most imprudent excesses. Good-hearted, generous, and desirous to oblige his friends, he was, like all people of that stamp, careless of money; and though he had always been in the receipt of a fair salary, at the age of twenty-six years, he had not, to use a popular expression, "saved a single penny."

It must be confessed, that, with these qualities and defects, he was not particularly fitted for a commercial career; and, in fact, the accountant had em-

See p. 18

braced it from the force of circumstance, rather than from inclination. All things considered, we may regard him as a man who had more weakness than strength, more frivolity than reflection, more agreeable accomplishments than solid acquirements — as one who himself needed a severe mentor, and was in no condition to act in that capacity towards Mademoiselle Lebeau.

It is certain, however, that Chevillard had at one time aspired to exercise the influence which was attributed to him in the affairs of that young lady. When she took the direction of the establish-ment, she was naturally inclined to avail herself of any resources which might offer themselves, and had sought the officious guidance of a man, whom she supposed to be skilful and ex-perienced. He, on his part, was quite ready to manage for her; but soon per-ceiving that his advice was not judicious, the pupil had quietly resumed the helm, and consulted no one but herself on the course she pursued.

Notwithstanding the extreme delicacy with which the young girl effected this transition, the hard necessity of a forced abdication was far from agreeable to the dethroned monarch. As far as he was able, he had shown no outward marks of vexation, but his deposition had left a feeling of ill-will, and he frequently gave way to fits of envy and railing against his young *patroness*, which he would have found much difficulty in justifying.

Kind by nature to all who surrounded her, Mademoiselle Lebeau appeared to take peculiar pains and pleasure in lavishing on this sulky gentleman continual marks of her goodwill. In so doing, she followed the steps of her father, who had always treated Chevillard with affectionate consideration; and perhaps also the consciousness of the severe disappointment she had inflicted by discarding him from her royal council, had some influence on her demeanour towards him. Besides, who can tell. Although Mademoiselle Lebeau must really have perceived that Chevillard was inferior to her in every respect, the habit of seeing him every day, a familiar and constant association with him, the care he bestowed upon his appearance, which is never unpleasing to a woman, the good qualities he really possessed, and even his whimsical fits of ill-humour, and his desponding airs, were probably quite sufficient to interest a young person, who was the sole mistress of her actions, and in whose position a speedy marriage was in some sort an imperious necessity.

We will go further: the moral and intellectual inferiority which we have noticed in our account of the clerk's character, rendered this supposition still more probable. Superior and privileged natures frequently experience a strong sympathy for inferior organizations, which they feel called upon to complete by governing them. Women, whose affections are proverbially capricious, are constantly affording us examples of this phenomenon, which might be denominated, the *sympathy of contraries;* and in the case under consideration, may not a similar predilection be supposed? And the fact once admitted, need we seek for any other explanation of the favour and attentions shown to Chevillard?

* * *

Independently of a large connection in Paris and the provinces, Mademoiselle Lebeau's house had important transactions in other countries. To keep up and extend these foreign relations, a travelling-clerk was indispensable. We must say a few words of the individual who held that responsible situation in the executive of the *Tricoloured Prism.* He was called Chabouillant.

Like the generality of commercial travellers, this Chabouillant was a jovial fellow, full of fine phrases, and *wide awake*, though without any great pretensions to real wit. He had little elevation in his feelings or ideas, but was gifted with the most imperturbable self-possession. In person, he was short and thick, with an impudent, red-face, and stiff hair, of a rather fiery auburn. His robust frame appeared to have been formed expressly for the wearing life of a commercial traveller, accustomed, as every one knows, to seek forgetfulness of the annoyances and fatigue consequent upon his perpetual motion, in a turbulent abuse of the pleasures of the senses.

Such as we have sketched him, Chabouillant would not have been exactly vexed at finding himself in the world, if he had but entered it in a more straightforward manner. But his register of birth stated, with most annoying frankness, that he was born of *unknown parents*, and he had never been able to make up his mind to submit to this anonymous relationship. He asserted, that the mystery concealed opulent kinsfolk and a noble origin; and he was possessed with a singular passion to establish his identity, or, as he jocosely termed it, *legalize* himself.

Not that his heart was lacerated after the furious fashion of modern *Anthonys.** He did not belong to that unfortunate class of bastards, to whom some unknown personage brings, at the end of every three months, their quarterly allowance; so he had no leisure time for meditation, for hoarding in his *manly bosom* the wild tumult of inconsolable grief, or for flying from this to the innocent recreations of murder and violence. Afflicted in a less impetuous style, he might be said to *smile at grief;* and the persevering and active search after his lost family, which he gave out as the principal and true object of his journeys, of itself placed him in a very amusing position. But it was especially diverting to hear him, when laying at the feet of the fair mercer (or, as he gallantly called her, the *Tricoloured Fairy*), the homage of a conditional passion, he declared that he only waited for the appearance of his noble parents, to *insinuate* the offer of his heart and hand.

* Alluding to a modern French work of that name, belonging to the ultra-romantic school.

As this *casus matrimonii* did not appear very imminent, and the whimsical admirer acquitted himself of his commercial duties to the entire satisfaction of Mademoiselle Lebeau, she good-humouredly smiled at the pleasantry, which Chabouillant never failed to repeat with periodical exactness, whenever he came to take leave before setting out on a new expedition.

CHAPTER II.

In the month of November, 1803, Chabouillant was on the point of starting for Germany. He had come to receive Mademoiselle Lebeau's instructions, when Chevillard entered the private room, to get her signature to some letters which were to be despatched by that evening's post. Whilst the young lady was, according to her constant and laudable practice, perusing the correspondence before she signed it, and at the same time attending to the applications of twenty customers, and three or four shopwomen, Chabouillant took the accountant on one side, and addressing him in the peculiar style that he had adopted: "Chevillard, prop of this honourable house," said he, "may I, with the consent of the reigning powers, make a proposal to you?"

"What is it?" said Chevillard.

"You are doubtless aware," replied the traveller, "that, in a few hours, a rapid car will bear away your comrade and friend, towards the frontiers of the Rhine?"

"Ah! do you go this evening?" observed the book-keeper, in more sober prose.

"Yes, my dear fellow."

"Well, I wish you a pleasant journey!" said Chevillard, mischievously. "Don't forget to bring back the *family papers!*"

"No joking upon that subject, I beg," replied Chabouillant, laying his hand upon his heart with a melancholy gesture. "I have a presentiment, that during this journey —— but, enough; I come back to my proposal."

"Speak, man! what is it about?"

"It is, that the stage, which carries me away this evening, will not stop before eleven o'clock to-morrow morning, for breakfast; so that, until that moment, I shall be prohibited from taking any species of sustenance——"

"The deuce! that will be a long fast."

"Too long for a stomach naturally delicate. So I have some thoughts of going, when I leave here, to the Palais du Tribunat, to Février's,* where the cookery is not to be despised, and of furnishing myself with an agreeable and nourishing repast."

"By Jove! not a bad precaution!"

"Undoubtedly; but I do not wish to dine all alone, like a hermit; I should like for us two to make a little civic banquet, if you feel inclined."

"Thank you," said Chevillard, "I intend to work all the evening; I must make up some arrears."

"You can do that to-morrow; a day more or less, what does it signify?"

"No, I assure you, I would rather not go out to-day."

"Chevillard!" replied the traveller, in a sententious tone, "I think I have had sufficient experience of life to affirm, that it is not natural for man to refuse a good dinner; there must be some superlative reasons for your squeamish scruples, which you do not impart to your friend."

"What reasons should I have?" said the book-keeper.

"Ah! ah! perhaps we're afraid of displeasing our charming employer."

"Oh, indeed!" returned Chevillard, with great dignity; "I should like to see her find fault ——"

This declaration of independence was interrupted by Mademoiselle Lebeau, who had remained a stranger to the foregoing conversation, but who now, looking up from her letters, said to the accountant, as if she had just remembered the fact: "Mr. Chevillard, you know that Madame Foubert did not pay the draught for three thousand francs this morning; she promised to be prepared to settle this evening, without fail; you had better call there yourself, after dinner, and then if she does not pay, you will be able to have it protested early to-morrow morning."

"Well, now," said Chabouillant, addressing Chevillard, "I think you are *hooked* this time. Here is Mademoiselle, who plays my game for me!"

"What game?" asked the latter, who had heard the concluding words.

"The case is this, fair lady: our friend Chevillard, here present, peremptorily refuses to dine with me, for fear of incurring your celestial indignation."

* A well-known eating-house of the period. It was at this house that, in the time of the Convention, Lepelletier de Saint-Fargeau was assassinated.

"I never said such a thing!" cried Chevillard.

"Really, I should have felt astonished if he had," replied Mademoiselle Lebeau, with a slight degree of asperity, "for it is not my custom to interfere with things which do not concern me."

"Oh, certainly!" said Chabouillant; "but as you usually profess no very great respect for my patriarchal virtues, Chevillard imagines you would prefer his being with any other host."

"If you take it in that point of view, to be frank with you, my dear sir, you have never appeared to me a model of discretion and temperance; and between ourselves, as bachelor dinners do not always suit Mr. Chevillard very well, it would perhaps be more prudent for him to dine here as usual, and to refuse your invitation; but I must beg to remark, that he is *old enough* to act for himself, and he must do just as he pleases in the matter."

"Very lucky!" said Chevillard, in a low tone; whilst Chabouillant exclaimed: "You see, my dear fellow, Mademoiselle Lebeau will not be angry if you accompany me, especially if we promise to behave well; so, as you must go out about this money, you can have no possible reasons to refuse my invitation."

"At all events," said the book-keeper, who had now made up his mind, "I cannot go out as I am."

"Well, well; that's soon settled! I will go up-stairs with you, and you shall have half-an-hour's grace for the duties of the toilet. At the same time, I can see your room, which I am told is a perfect little palace."

"Have you any other commands for me?" said Chevillard to Mademoiselle Lebeau, with a kind of mock humility.

"Oh, no!" replied she; "only, I should advise you to present the draught before dinner."

"Now, that is too bad," said Chabouillant; "I could never have supposed such insinuations ——"

Mademoiselle Lebeau did not give him time to finish the sentence; without precisely turning her back upon him, as soon as she had made this severe remark, she rose, and approaching the fire, began to stir and arrange it. Perhaps she wished to avoid observation.

Chevillard, on his part, had looked very black upon receiving this palpable hit, and, going out first, exclaimed with some temper to his companion: "Do you mean to come or not?"

Chabouillant staid, however, to address a chivalrous farewell to Mademoiselle Lebeau, and insinuated something relative to the speedy and inevitable discovery of his family, which would allow him to indulge in flattering hopes! But his pleasantry was on this day received with the most chilling reserve, and the only answer vouchsafed, was a short and imperative request to write, as soon as he reached Strasburg, concerning the "shaded ribbons." Seeing that laughter was not the order of the day, and that the *Tricoloured Fairy* was in no mirthful humour, he made his obeisance with the most elaborate assumption of politeness, and hastened after his guest, who, tired of waiting, had gone on first.

When the two friends were again together, and whilst they were climbing the ninety-five steps that led to Chevillard's room, the latter said: "Did you notice how high Mademoiselle Lebeau was, merely because I talked of going out?"

"Why, you know, my good friend," replied Chabouillant, "that I have the reputation of being a very dangerous fellow, and people are reluctant to trust innocence in my wily hands."

"That's not it. It is pure tyranny. All employers are so; they think one ought not to stir. But it was just the ill-will that was displayed, which induced me to accept your invitation; I am determined I will not be led like a child?"

"My good friend Chevillard," said the other, pompously, "you understand nothing about women; this charming creature looks sweet on you, take my word for it. She trembles to see me your associate: it's quite natural; you are a tender plant that she wishes to shield from the storm."

"You dream," replied Chevillard, opening the door of his room.

The commercial traveller did not for the moment continue the conversation, so much was he surprised at the almost sumptuous elegance that met his view. Being the sole heiress of her parents, Mademoiselle Lebeau found herself, at their death, mistress of a quantity of furniture, for a great part of which she had no use; under the specious pretext of keeping it in good condition, but in reality to prepare an agreeable surprise for Chevillard, who at the time was absent on family business, she had caused a complete alteration to be made in the arrangements of his room. When

the fortunate clerk returned, he found, instead of the former scanty furniture in humble walnut, a bedstead wardrobe, and other useful articles, of solid mahogany, enriched, according to the fashion of the day, with a profusion of gilded bronze ornaments, among which were conspicuous, the eternal sphinxes, so universally adopted as decorations, since the Egyptian campaign.

The bed, soft and downy as that of a prebendary, was shaded by curtains of a light texture, supported on a gilded pole. The pattern was large yellow rosettes, on a red ground, and the window was hung with draperies of the same material, and with worked muslin, surmounted by rich silk fringe. The chimney-slab was adorned with an alabaster clock, and two vases of artificial flowers, protected by glass shades; and at the corner of the fire-place, a blue velvet easy-chair *extended its arms* (to use a then common expression) to invite to drowsiness and listless reverie. Add two corresponding arm-chairs, a few other seats of highly polished cherry-wood, with straw bottoms, and a washing stand of classical shape, and we shall have an accurate inventory of Chevillard's effects.

By a rare piece of good fortune, in that close and populous neighbourhood, the room faced the east, and being situated in a back part of the premises, had before it a vast open space, and enjoyed all the advantages of free air and light. When, on a fine spring day, the morning sun darted its bright rays on the carefully waxed floor, shining like a mirror, it seemed to bring with it a host of pleasant thoughts, and the heart of the young man sung for joy.

While gazing round the apartment, Chabouillant suddenly espied a pair of elegant watch-pockets in blue flowered satin, edged with pink *chénille*, hanging by the side of the chimney-glass. "Ah! ah! you sly fellow," said he; "it seems you are in favour with the fair sex!"

"That! Oh, that was a birthday-present from Mademoiselle Lebeau."

"Well, now, what did I tell you?"

"No, no, you are mistaken," replied Chevillard; "Mademoiselle Lebeau does not think of me—and for that matter, I have no thoughts of her," added he, with a shade of foppery in his manner, as he arranged the bow of an enormous cravat, like those which Mr. de Talleyrand wore to the last.

"Why are you so difficult to please? The girl is very good-looking, my dear fellow."

"Pooh!" said Chevillard, disdainfully.

"How now! as fresh as a rose, an engaging air, fine eyes, beautiful teeth, a charming hand; what more do you require?"

"Do you admire the colour of her hair?" said the book-keeper.

"To be sure! Splendid hair, as black as jet."

"Well! that does not suit my taste; I am for the fair girls."

"I am not like you," cried the other; "fair or dark, I love them all: if Dame Nature produced any tri-coloured beauties, I should love them too, dear creatures!"

"I confess," continued Chevillard, "that I should be capable of committing any folly for a fair woman, but a brunette has no charm for me; and then, between ourselves, even if I could make up my mind to marry a person engaged in business, I should think twice before addressing the lady in question; she has a very pretty little will of her own. You saw a sample of it, just now."

Whilst the two clerks were thus chatting together, Chevillard had put the finishing touch to his toilet, by investing himself with what was then called a *spencer*; it was a winter-garment much resembling a jacket, from beneath which the tails of the coat peeped out in a very ludicrous style. Having informed his companion that he was now at his commands, they started for the before-mentioned eating-house. The book-keeper had been so hurt at the ironical advice offered him by Mademoiselle Lebeau, that he resolved not to attend to it, and to assert his independence by leaving the draught unsettled until he had packed the virtuous Chabouillant into the stage-coach; but the latter, who, notwithstanding his levity, looked upon business as a serious matter, insisted that the money should be received before dinner.

"No one," said he, ingenuously, "when he sits down to table, can tell *how* he will leave it."

As Madame Foubert's residence was in the same direction as the eating-house, whither the two friends were bound, Chevillard at last yielded to the remonstrances of the other, and called upon the defaulter, who, without any more delay, paid the amount of three thousand francs in bank-notes.

"Now," said Chabouillant, "we have nothing to think of, and may proceed at once to our little gastronomical operation."

They were soon after comfortably seated at a table; not at Février's however, as was their first intention, for the rooms were full, but in a superior establishment, the celebrated Robert's, which had been opened near the Palais-Royal, in the early days of the Convention, in a style of true republican simplicity, but which had already acquired a reputation for splendour. The dinner offered nothing worthy of particular remark; Chabouillant was noisy and familiar with the waiters, whom he summoned by ringing with his knife upon a glass, and endeavoured to show off as a man accustomed to good society, by being very difficult to please, and by finding fault with almost every dish that was brought in. He also took care to give all possible publicity to his conversation, by pitching it in a key that might be heard at the further end of the room; and laboured to fascinate a modest-looking young woman, who sat opposite to him, by staring at her in the most impudent and pertinacious manner. But he did not obtain a glance in return. As for other matters, he prided himself upon doing things handsomely; neither wine nor good cheer was spared, and if Chevillard had not resisted the increasing warmth of his generosity, the chances are that they might have drained the cellar.

The bill being paid, they went to take coffee in a place of no very good repute, which was in those days crowded to witness the performances of a learned dog, and a ventriloquist named Fitz-James. The coffee was, of course, succeeded by every possible variety of *liqueurs*, and when Chevillard, who was nearly *done up*, cried mercy, Chabouillant declared that he should not consider him as his friend, if he refused to join him in a bowl of punch! The result of all this friendship was, that when the two revellers left, to take a stroll in the galleries, they had very nearly reached the highest pitch of excitement.

When Chabouillant had indulged in wine, he was gay and communicative; Chevillard, on the contrary, was not outwardly excited, and for this reason was not much the worse for these sort of excesses. Silent and abstracted, as the fumes mounted to his brain, his thoughts took a rapid and tumultuous course; and whilst his companion flirted with the easy beauties who thronged the Palais-Royal, or manœuvred to obtain a bow from the second consul Cambacérès, who was taking his accustomed walk with his acolytes, Grimod de la Reynière, and d'Aigrefeuille, *he* thought of the little dispute he had had two hours before with his employer, and asked himself if he was in a social position worthy of his superior talents. At a period of revolutionary movement, when he had seen so many splendid fortunes rise from obscurity, was he to aim at nothing higher than an obscure existence in a shop of the Quartier de Saint-Denis? Thus following each the bent of his humour, the two friends arrived before a house of disgraceful celebrity, which was closed only a few years ago. This haunt had taken its name from the number which was above the door, and was commonly called No. 113, without any further explanation.

It happened that Chabouillant, the day before, had read in a newspaper some curious observations concerning this disreputable place; and as commercial travellers are very fond of *speaking* the articles they read, our hero resolved to appropriate the remarks in question. He dragged Chevillard into the middle of the garden, and placing him in front of the suspicious-looking house, exclaimed in a doctoral tone: " Chevillard, my friend, be so good as to consider that edifice!"

" Well! what about that?" said Chevillard, who perceived nothing remarkable.

" Why, man, are you not struck with the strangely philosophical connection of the divers callings sheltered by that roof?"

" Upon my word, I am not," replied the other, looking more narrowly.

Now, Chabouillant had passed many hundred times before this very place, and, truth compels us to state, had even frequently entered it, without having been more quick-sighted than the bookkeeper; but, full of his newly-acquired experience, he continued in the words of the newspaper: " Look there! On the first-floor, a gambling-table;

" On the second, a pawnbroker's;

" On the third, a harem;

" A dram-shop in the porter's lodge;

And lastly, on the ground-floor, a gunsmith's shop.

" So that, within these narrow limits, a man finds all that he wants to live merrily and die badly."

" Well, that's certainly odd enough!" was all Chevillard's reply.

" By the way," said his friend, struck with a sudden thought, " have you ever been in a gambling-house?"

Chevillard, having confessed his innocence in this respect, the other exclaimed: " Oh! it's worth seeing, and since we are close at hand ——"

" But the stage will leave without you!"

" I have full three-quarters of an hour to spare," said Chabouillant, after consulting his watch.

" And the money I have about me?"

" The money? No one will take it from you. There are excellent police regulations in these places, and a thief had better not venture there, I can tell you."

Chabouillant either deceived, or was deceived. Some years later, government turned its attention to the subject of providing for the security of those who frequented gambling-houses; but, at the time of which we write, scandalous scenes were of frequent occurrence. To give an example in point, some blacklegs tried one day to blow up the bank, by placing fire-works under the roulette-table; these exploded, and wounded several of the persons who were present.

Since this event, the directors of the place had adopted the strangest expedient to protect themselves from the attempts and turbulence of the gamesters. They had taken into their pay a band of ruffians called the *Infernal Band*, who constantly awaited their orders at a neighbouring tavern, which they had converted into a species of arsenal. These men not being invested with any public authority, would not have attempted to arrest a disturber of the peace—they had too much respect for the liberty of the subject; but if any one complained of the game, or expressed discontent, the *supporters* of the establishment were instantly summoned, and after they had sought a quarrel with him, they carried him into the Rue de Valois, and exhorted him not to make so much noise. Then, leaving him the choice of weapons, they contrived by chance or design to inflict some hurt, to cool his blood, as their phrase was. If death ensued, and justice made inquiries into the affair, it passed as a meeting resulting from a quarrel at the gaming-table, and nothing more was said.

These things considered, the amusement proposed by Chabouillant was of a rather dangerous nature, and Mademoiselle Lebeau was happily inspired, when she opposed a pleasure party, which was to end by initiating Chevillard in the mysteries of this den of iniquity. But the latter was not in possession of his cool judgment; besides, he intended merely to take a hasty glance, and then to accompany his friend to the coach; so he followed him without any objection, and, in a few minutes more, entered the gambling-establishment on the first-floor.

CHAPTER III.

CHABOUILLANT was well acquainted with the usages of the place, and at once deposited his hat with an individual who was stationed in the antechamber for that purpose, and who was called the *hat-man*. But Chevillard, thinking that this was an optional proceeding, declared his intention of leaving in a very short time, and that it was perfectly unnecessary to trouble any one to take charge of that part of his attire. His companion then explained to him, that what he supposed to be a mark of

courtesy, was in reality one of mistrust; the custom of exchanging your hat upon entering, for a card bearing a number, was adopted, in order to oppose a check to the escape of any enterprising thief, who might endeavour to rush out of the place, with the money belonging to the bank, or the players. This had been really effected several times, but the precautions now taken greatly facilitated the pursuit and arrest of the audacious pilferer, even if he managed to elude the vigilance of the attendants, and to venture out bareheaded.

On entering the sanctuary, Chevillard was first struck with the solemn silence which reigned in the numerous assembly before him. Only the monotonous voice of the banker was heard at intervals, pronouncing the sacramental words: " *Make your game, gentlemen!* —*The game is made!*—*All is done!*" (that is to say, the stakes are on the table, and cannot be withdrawn); and soon after proclaiming the decrees of fate: " *Number* 25, *black, odd and wins;* —*Number* 12, *red, even, and loses;*" according to the number, colour, and combinations which had turned up.

The altar erected by these worshippers of Chance, was an oblong table, rounded at the ends; in the centre was fixed the *roulette*, a sort of hollow cylinder, turning on an axis, and fitted with alternate red and black divisions, each marked with a number. This cylinder having been previously set in motion, the *tailleur* threw from his hand, in an inverse direction, an ivory ball, which, after bounding several times from side to side, lodged in one of the divisions, and thus decided the successive chances. At the four corners of the *roulette*, facing each other, after the fashion of the cardinal points, were four *tailleurs* or bankers, who presided at the game. Before them was a sum of forty to fifty thousand francs, in silver, gold, and bank notes: this was the *bank;* from it the gains of the players were paid, and it was replenished from their losses, which were quickly gathered up by attendants armed with long maces. The table was covered with green cloth, printed with various designs: first came a pattern of red and black lozenges; then three longitudinal rows of twelve numbers, surmounted by *nought and double nought*. By placing money upon the devices or the numbers, any person secured a share in this lottery in action.

The players, or *pontes*, as they were termed in the jargon of the place, crowded round the table in various attitudes, and displayed the most opposite emotions. Some manifested a real or affected indifference, others laid no restraint upon their feelings and expressions; several tried to calculate chances, and followed with eager solicitude the capricious fluctuations of the game, pricking them down upon cards prepared for the study, and generously provided by the establishment; a few were seriously occupied with algebraical computations, by which they were *certain* to foretel the number to be drawn; others were gravely taking notes to establish an infallible system which they were on the point of discovering; and finally, some exhibited the strongest superstitions, such as stopping their ears with great care, so as not to *hear* the banker call out the numbers, which they nevertheless *saw* quite plainly.

Chabouillant allowed his friend to examine all this for some time without interruption; then, having briefly explained to him the theory of the game, he added: "Well! shall we court the fickle goddess?"

"Where would be the good of it?" asked Chevillard.

"Oh! it's one way of trying a man's fortune. And the experience thus gained may be useful in many other affairs of life."

"I know all that I desire on that subject," replied the book-keeper, in a melancholy tone; "I have no luck in any thing."

"Well, you can but try; for the best of these places is, that, in a single turn, a man may ride to the top of the tree. I do not aim so high; I only wish the bank to be civil enough to defray our dinner expenses."

So saying, he placed a five-franc piece upon a single number; the number was called, and he received thirty-five times the amount of his stake. He then tried a few other turns, and won each time. Turning to Chevillard, he exclaimed: "You see, my friend, people don't ruin themselves quite so often as it is asserted they do, at this noble game!"

Chevillard had been silently making the same remark. "Come," said the other, "risk two francs."

The lowest amount of the stakes had been fixed at this limit, *in favour* of the indigent working-classes, the habitual frequenters of the house. Chevillard was ashamed to hesitate at so trifling a sum, and threw down a two-franc piece upon the table, but he awaited the result with marked anxiety. He felt as if this trial of his fortune would open to him a vista into futurity.

The response of the oracle was very encouraging. Without any clear notion of the intricacies of the game, Chevillard had placed his money upon two numbers; this move brought him seventeen times the amount that he had staked. The first step having been attended with so much success, he resolved to go on. We will not enter into the detail of all his lucky hits, but, at the end of another quarter of an hour, Chabouillant and he had realised about a hundred crowns.

"Confound it!" then exclaimed the commercial traveller, looking at the clock, which would soon point to the hour fixed for his departure;" it is unfortunate, that honour and duty call me hence! This was not a bad beginning. But will you *marry?*"

"How, *marry!*" asked the book-keeper.

"Yes, throw our winnings into one heap. You can continue to court Fortune, and, at my return, you will give me an account of the profits of this partnership concern."

"Oh, no! I will leave with you," replied Chevillard, startled at the idea of remaining in that place without his companion.

"What are you thinking of? Will you throw up the run of good luck which is evidently before you?—What shall we gain by ten minutes more of each other's society?—Why, my good fellow, it will be much better for you to make your own fortune and mine; so shake hands, and good bye for a time! I hope that when next we meet, you will have a good round sum to pay over to me."

The fact is, the neophyte was already under the fascination of gain, and Chabouillant had not much difficulty to persuade him. The two friends shook hands very cordially, and Chevillard immediately returned to the gaming-table; he even advanced a step further in his noviciate; continuing to play standing, he took a seat which had just been vacated by a fortunate gamester. Thus conveniently placed to study the mechanism of the different combinations, and with the aid of his skill in figures, the accountant soon made himself acquainted with what might be termed the *mysteries* of the game, if all foresight and calculated probabilities were not continually frustrated by the freaks of chance. He then began to combine a plan, and placed his money with more thought and method; but this system did not prosper, and he lost several moves in succession. The joint capital was already seriously diminished, when Chevillard, who had become superstitious at the same time that he became a gamester, took up a strange notion, but one which would not have appeared extravagant to the most experienced frequenter of the place.

Opposite to him, and taking no part in the game, stood a man of commonplace appearance, who appeared to regard him with a steady gaze. Whenever he met the eye of this stranger whilst staking his money, it seemed to the book-keeper that chance was favourable to him; and on the contrary he thought it turned against him, when the sympathetic glance was in any other direction. A man will soon learn to risk boldly when he thinks he has found a hold upon fortune. Encouraged by the remark he had made, Chevillard began to put forward more considerable sums, and being still favoured by chance, the joint-stock concern of Chabouillant & Co. found itself, at the end of an hour and a half, in possession of a capital of six thousand francs, of which three thousand would go to the share of the lucky novice.

Those who have not visited the haunts of gamblers, can have no idea how much their determinations are influenced by *round sums*. A player, having made large profits, feels inclined to retire from the table; but something is still wanting to complete the cypher he intended to attain, and in pursuing this fraction, he loses all that he had before gained. Another appears to be in a fair way of breaking the bank; he is in what is termed a formidable *vein;* nothing, neither his mistakes nor his address, neither his hesitation nor his boldness, appears to affect it; he wins because he *does* win, that is the only reason. But he had settled in his own mind: "I will not exceed a certain sum;" and that sum in his possession, he retires—thus evincing, doubtless, much wisdom and fortitude, but missing nevertheless the fortune that was within his grasp.

Chevillard was one of these prudent players. Finding himself master of the unexpected amount of six thousand francs, he changed it into gold, divided it into two equal shares, which he placed separately in the pockets of his waistcoat, and gaily left the apartment. When he arrived in the antechamber,

he found that the individual to whom he attributed an influence over his destiny, was already there; and, while waiting for his hat, the stranger approached, and in a low and expressive tone, addressed him thus: "Sir, if I were the partner, who parted from you a short time since, confiding his interests to your care—decidedly, I would never forgive you."

Surprised at this speech, Chevillard looked at him without returning any answer.

"Yes, sir, I should be mortally offended; for it is incredible, that a man who has but to stretch out his hand to secure a fortune, should so unskilfully let it slip from his grasp."

"But I have gained a pretty sum," replied Chevillard; "and you know the old maxim, *do not make too free with fortune.*"

"Nonsense !" said the stranger, with an impatient gesture; "when you are in such a lucky vein, and with your genius for play (for I watched you, you did not make a single false move), you ought not to give over till you had broken the bank two or three times."

"How you talk !" said Chevillard, not at all offended however at being tutored in this fashion.

"Well, well," replied the other, lowering his tone, "I am perhaps in the wrong to interfere in your affairs, but I feel so confident that you are missing an opportunity——"

"Do you often play ?" asked the book-keeper.

"Sometimes; but I more often look on, and if, like me, you had observed the countenances of the bankers, you would have seen that they followed your play with considerable anxiety, and your departure must have been a great relief to them."

"Well, sir, if you counsel me, I will make another attempt," said Chevillard, who had, as we know, private reasons for listening with deference to the opinion of his adviser, and returning his hat to the attendant, he re-entered the room.

"Now, if I might presume to direct you," continued the stranger, who accompanied him, "I think it would be desirable to increase your stakes; a vein, you see, is a thing which wears itself out, and you should make the best of it while it lasts."

"Perhaps you are right," said Chevillard; "but would you have any objection to place yourself opposite to me ?

I have more confidence if I am looked at."

"Willingly," returned the officious stranger; and he took his post at the other side of the table, facing Chevillard, who commenced operations by placing ten pieces of gold upon one number.

This stake of two hundred francs, multiplied by thirty-five, brought a return of seven thousand francs, and the timid young man, who, two hours before, trembled as he threw down a coin of small value, now, flushed with success, risked still higher sums with increasing boldness, till he created quite a sensation among the surrounding gamesters, most of whom were men of small means. The bankers, disquieted by the proceedings of their formidable adversary, sent for supplies to be ready to meet any emergency; and the interest excited by this *duel* was powerful enough to suspend all other hostilities. It was like one of the combats in an epic-poem, when two generals meet, and their armies stand motionless to witness the encounter.

The object of general attention, dazzled by the piles of gold before him, and moreover encouraged by the glances of his mysterious protector, Chevillard, whose reason was still disordered from the effects of the wine and spirits he had taken, advanced to the extreme limits of temerity, until at length fortune seemed to take a turn. This was certainly a warning that it was time to leave off; but as his stakes had been high, the first losses made a considerable hole in his profits; and, considering this to be but a momentary check, he applied himself with fresh ardour to recover his advantages, staked larger sums, and began to play like a man who had lost his self-possession. The fall was still more rapid than the rise had been; in less than half an hour, the imprudent young man had restored all his winnings to the bank, and had lost even the money which he had risked in the first instance.

"*Cleaned out!*" said one of the bystanders, rudely, meaning to express by this slang phrase that Chevillard was completely ruined.

"Do you think so?" replied the latter, his self-love deeply wounded by these words, and casting a disdainful glance upon the ill-bred speaker; then taking a pocket-book from his coat, he drew from it one of the three notes he had received a few hours before for the house to which he was cashier. He passed this to the nearest banker, saying in an imperious tone: "Gold for this note."

"He has still some notes," said the spectators among themselves; and the struggle became doubly interesting.

The banker soon handed over forty-nine pieces of gold, worth twenty francs each, and the odd money of the fiftieth piece, out of which he kept the value of the exchange. Chevillard divided this sum into four parts, and began to play. The first move was favourable; he might have repaid the money he had taken, and have retired with a slight profit; but he was already a gambler in every sense of the word, and viewing this lucky chance as a definitive return of fortune, he risked at one stake the whole sum that was before him; announcing his intention, according to the established formula. The *mace* swept everything away. Without manifesting the least emotion, but with the cool decision of a man who has made up his mind, he again opened the pocket-book, and handing its contents to the banker: "Change," said he, "for these two notes."

Ninety-nine gold pieces were counted out to him, and they only passed through his hands. When he had but five louis left, he thought he would wear out the run of ill-luck by procrastinating the result; he changed his gold into silver, and began to play five francs at a time, with a miserable alternation of loss and gain, the former greatly preponderating. Resolved to maintain the struggle to the last, he submitted to change his last five-franc piece into smaller coin. He first staked three francs, which were immediately swept away in the vortex. Before risking the two francs which remained, his last hope, he appeared to pause and murmur some inarticulate words, perhaps a prayer; the number was announced, the unhappy man had lost!

Then affecting a calm demeanour, but pale, with haggard eyes, and the cold sweat standing upon his forehead, he left the apartment where his ruin had been consummated, and which an hour earlier he was quitting with a joyous heart. The fatal individual, to whom this unfortunate young man had attributed an influence of which circumstances had clearly proved the fallacy, presumed to follow him, and, expressing his regret and sympathy, placed his purse at Chevillard's disposal, and advised him to make a fresh trial of fortune. But the victim of his dangerous counsels would not even look at him, and, desiring him to leave him, rushed from the fatal spot. He descended the stairs rapidly, but, struck with a sudden idea, he stopped; and retracing his steps, went up to the floor above the gambling-establishment, where the pawnbroker's was situated, which being a *charitable* institution, never closed until after its neighbour. He deposited a gold watch, received an advance of five louis, and, impelled by despair, soon reappeared at the roulette table. It seemed as if the man who had exercised so disastrous an influence upon his actions had some interest to watch the event, for, almost at the same moment, he likewise returned to the room. But he took care to keep out of sight, and mixed with a group in the background; either because prudence was necessary to his plans, or that he feared the pertinacity of his attention would at length lead to some dispute with its object.

Chevillard's last struggle with the bank was of short duration. If chance has no rules, it has nevertheless its precedents, and when it has once decidedly turned against a man, it rarely changes in his favour, during the same sitting. This fact was so well known to all present, that the entrance of the actor, who a moment before excited so much curiosity, was scarcely noticed, and he lost sixty francs of the sum he had just raised, without awakening interest or sympathy. His fatal destiny had already led him to two floors of the house, the distribution of which had been pointed out to him by Chabouillant; he was in no humour to seek consolation in the upper story, but he remembered that below was sold the terrible resource of those who have no other resource left; and having kept enough for this gloomy acquisition, he descended to the gunsmith's shop, and without giving any explanation of the use he intended to make of it, he bought a pistol, which the man very obligingly loaded in his presence.

Thus armed, he entered the tavern, and swallowed several glasses of rum, whilst writing a letter, which he sealed, directed, and placed carefully in his pocket-book, in the place of the notes he had fraudulently taken. Having concluded these preparations, he went out into the Rue de Valois, and walked up and down for some time, in all the agitation of a man who pauses at the brink of an irrevocable resolution; then,

drawing out the pistol, he placed it to his forehead. At that moment, before he had time to pull the trigger, a vigorous hand seized his arm; surprised, he turned round, and, by the pale light of a lamp, recognised the stranger of the gambling-table.

"Are you the demon?" exclaimed Chevillard, enraged; "can you not leave those, whom you have urged to the last extremity, to die in peace?"

"For shame!" was the reply. "At your time of life, does a man kill himself for a miserable sum of a thousand crowns! I know your case; it has happened twenty times before. You staked money that was not yours, and now a false sense of honour drives you to commit suicide."

"And if that *were* the case, how can it concern you?"

"I tell you again, a man does not kill himself for three thousand francs. With a little perseverance, he may always find some one willing to lend them to him; and if you like to call upon me to-morrow, they are at your disposal."

Chevillard could not fail to attend to this abrupt offer of service, which drew him back to life, and gazing at the stranger: "Sir," said he, "who then are you, to trouble yourself thus about my fate?"

"A friend of humanity, young man," replied the stranger, solemnly; "and, above all, an enemy to gambling-houses."

"Singular! I should have thought rather——"

"That I am one of their abettors. Speak your mind frankly."

"Why, you cannot deny that your conduct to me——"

"My conduct," interrupted the other, "is explained by my knowledge of the human heart. When we have to deal with any passion, we should never openly oppose it."

"It would be as well not to stimulate it."

"Come now, young man, if I had left you to yourself, what would have been the result? This evening, you were successful; to-morrow, the love of gain would have induced you to return; the day after to-morrow, perhaps, you would have become an irreclaimable gamester. I wished to stop you on the descent; everything happened as I had foreseen; I confess that the lesson has been a rude one, but I am sure it will be of use to you. You are not the first

whom I have thus served: I visit almost every evening the fatal house you have just left, and whenever I meet with an imprudent and inexperienced youth, I act towards him as I have done this evening towards you."

"If you have often to advance sums to this amount, I should think your lessons must cost you dear!"

"Less than you may think, because I know how to discriminate, and address myself only to young men of sound integrity; I give them their own time, and they repay me. How many have since told me, that they owed me their

honour and the tranquillity of their life! I have even been enabled to establish some of them advantageously."

"Possibly so; nevertheless, you are a singular man."

"Yes," answered the philanthropist, "I have my little eccentricities; but when we are better acquainted, you will find me a devilish good fellow. Here," added he, tearing a leaf from a memorandum book, and writing a few words in pencil, "here is my address; tomorrow, I shall be at your service."

Chevillard did not think himself justified in rejecting this means of escape, for, after all, it was the instigator of his fault who now offered him the means of repairing it.

"Could I see you rather early?" asked he. "You are aware, that the money I lost must be accounted for in the course of the morning."

"Your hour shall be mine," replied the officious stranger.

And thereupon, they parted.

CHAPTER IV.

WHEN Chevillard found himself alone, he felt a natural curiosity to know who was the man that had connected himself in so singular a manner with his existence. He stepped into the Palais-Royal, which was not quite so badly lighted as the Rue de Valois, and succeeded in deciphering these words upon the paper which he had given him : *Legros, Law-Agent, Rue des Moulins,* No. 12.

In our days, the title of *law-agent* is nearly obsolete; it is rarely adopted except by some old civilians without diplomas, who practise in the country or the suburbs. At the period of which we are writing, it corresponded with that of general agent, and served as a cover to that questionable calling, which embraces within its wide limits the business of investing money, negotiating marriages, liquidating old claims, and clearing up doubtful successions and musty credits, with the addition, when times permit, of a little dabbling in usury.

We must however state, that in consequence of the great changes of property resulting from the revolution of '89, an immense number of conflicting interests and rights had arisen, the administration of which might afford an opening for a profession of that nature, as there was then a reason for the existence of the calling, it was not regarded with the suspicion and discredit under which it now labours.

Chevillard therefore saw nothing discouraging in the social position of his new acquaintance; confidence rather than mistrust was excited by the information he had obtained, and he returned to his home with a more tranquil mind; that home which he had been on the point of never seeing again. He hastened to retire to bed, and the fatigue of body and mind produced by the strong emotions he had experienced, soon procured for him a sound and unexpected repose. When he awoke the next morning, the remembrance of all that had taken place

the preceding evening, presented itself in a confused manner to his mind; so many strange events had been crowded into a few short hours of his existence, that he was obliged to reflect for some time, before he could persuade himself that he was not still under the impression of some frightful dream. But his empty pocket-book, the letter he had written to justify his suicide, and the address left in his hands by the man who had arrested the execution of his design, did not permit him to doubt the accuracy of his recollections, and impelled by the urgency of his position, he dressed quickly and went out. For the world, he would not have faced Mademoiselle Lebeau, before he was able to produce the sum which he had wrongfully appropriated.

On his arrival in the Rue des Moulins, he found a house of respectable appearance, in which lodged the individual he sought. The porter pointed out the floor, and a lackered escutcheon with the words, *Legros, law-agent,* inscribed in gold letters, indicating the door of his apartments. Chevillard rang the bell, and an old servant soon made her appearance, demanding if he were the young man her master expected. The visitor answered in the affirmative, and was ushered into the parlour, and requested to sit down till Legros came; he had been obliged to go out on business, but would soon return. The appearance of the room into which the book-keeper was introduced, was singular enough. Modern furniture of small value was intermixed with a quantity of rare and costly effects, such as pictures, bronzes, sculptured ivory, jewellery, and other precious productions, which seemed to bear evidence that their owner was a passionate admirer of art. But upon looking more nearly, this collection was heaped together in such strange disorder, and formed so unseemly an incumbrance, that it appeared to be placed there merely as a temporary thing, and made the apartment resemble an auction-room or a curiosity-shop. For some time, Chevillard examined, with feelings of interest, all that surrounded him; but the lengthened absence of his host made him begin to feel anxious; the usual time for repairing to his office would soon arrive, and he would have to present himself before Mademoiselle Lebeau, subject to reproof for neglecting hours, a fault which she viewed with less indulgence than any other. Still Legros did not come, and every one knows how long the time appears, and how impatient we get, when waiting for any one with whom we have important business to transact. At the end of three quarters of an hour, Chevillard began to feel the most serious fears as to the success of his negotiation. "Evidently, Legros had forgotten the appointment; or he had not at his disposal the sum for which he had come forward; or else, he had never seriously intended to oblige him." For in such a case, what will not a person suppose?

Soon, the inward agitation to which the poor young man was a prey, rose to the highest pitch; he walked with hasty steps through the apartment, speaking aloud, and evincing all the symptoms of feverish excitement. He was once more entertaining the idea of suicide, when the peremptory ring which in every house announces the return of the master, was at length heard, and Legros made his appearance.

"Ah! ah! so you are here, my young friend," said he; "well! how are you this morning?"

"Pretty well," replied Chevillard; "only I was beginning to fear that you had forgotten me."

"No danger of that, I am a man of my word; but I have business to transact with others as well as with you, you understand."

So saying, Legros opened the door of an adjoining room, and motioned Chevillard to enter, observing: "Let us go into my study."

This singular individual had beyond all doubt an inveterate mania for collecting; for rich stuffs, clocks, Chinese ware, ancient weapons, specimens of natural history, musical instruments, and even an Egyptian mummy in its case, were scattered pell-mell in this second apartment, in the same admired confusion as in the parlour. Seeing Chevillard surveyed all these odds and ends with some astonishment, Legros remarked, as he seated himself at his desk to enter some notes in a register: "You perceive, I have something of a mania for collecting curiosities!"

"So it appears," replied the other; "I could fancy myself in a museum."

"Yes, this is my chief expense; sometimes I feel angry with myself, when I think how many poor wretches might be relieved with the money which I squander away, but the passion is too strong for me, I cannot resist it."

Whilst our antiquary was talking, he had finished the writing upon which he had been engaged, and throwing himself back in his arm-chair with the air of a minister giving audience: "Well, now, my dear fellow," said he to his client, "let us speak about your affairs; you say you want a thousand crowns?"

"Alas! yes," replied the book-keeper; "I must account for that sum this very morning, and you have permitted me to hope ——"

"It is here at your service," interrupted Legros, drawing forth a pocket-book. "But first be so good, my young friend, as to inform me of your name and station, with which I am not yet acquainted."

Chevillard having declared his name and the situation he held in the establishment of the *Tricoloured Prism*, the law-agent signified his entire satisfaction. Then taking a huge pinch of snuff from a richly carved gold snuff-box, he observed: "The money you lost yesterday in so imprudent a manner, had been intrusted to you, as cashier; is it not so?"

Chevillard, with some confusion, allowed that this was the case.

"It is doubtless unnecessary for me to remind you of the magnitude of the fault you have committed?" said Legros, with great dignity.

"You saw what I was going to do; I think that testifies sufficiently for my repentance and remorse."

"Right!" resumed Legros; "you doubtless then belong to a family of repute?"

"Before the Revolution, my father was a merchant at Auxerre. He was ruined by the calamities of the time, and he and my mother both soon after died, leaving me quite unprovided for. I had an uncle, a notary in the same town; I lost him a short time ago, and have some claims upon the property he has left; this little inheritance is now in the course of being settled, and out of it I intend to discharge my obligations to you."

"Well! —— and in the house where you are employed, your salary is to the amount of ——"

"Of about a thousand crowns, reckoning a small share I have in the business."

"Not a very brilliant position; is there any chance of its improving?"

"That is doubtful; a clerk, you know, is dependent upon the pleasure of his employer."

"Oh! there is no counting upon the generosity of mercantile people, or upon their gratitude for faithful services ; you ought to seek to establish yourself on your own account, and not remain a clerk all your life."

"Establish myself! —— that is no easy matter: and besides, I have no great inclination for trade."

"Undoubtedly those who are engaged in it make their way but slowly, and I clearly saw yesterday, that you would like to rise rapidly to wealth. After all, we live at a time when plenty of opportunities are to be found, if we can but avail ourselves of them. So now I have been satisfied on all these points, and I hope you will excuse my asking you about them, but ——"

"No excuse is necessary, it is quite natural you should inquire," interrupted Chevillard.

"By the way, how do you propose to arrange our little conditions of repayment?"

"Unfortunately, I have no security or mortgage to offer you ; I can only give you my note of hand for the sum, and I would request that it should not fall due too soon; but naturally, we shall reckon the interest."

"Humph!" said Legros, as if this proposition did not exactly suit him ; "then you propose to sign a bill to my order?"

"To your order, well, let it be so ;" replied the book-keeper, who had expected that his creditor would be satisfied with a simple acknowledgment; but he could not possibly object to this additional precaution.

Legros appeared to reflect for a moment, playing at the same time with a pinch of snuff; then he said to his client : "You will think me a strange mortal ; of course I place the fullest confidence in your honour, since I spontaneously offered you my assistance, but I confess to you that in matters of business I like to take my precautions."

"No one can object to that," returned Chevillard, with a degree of restraint, for he began to be alarmed at the delay.

"I think therefore, that having no personal security to offer, and being yourself engaged in trade, you can have no objection to the formality—the purely commercial formality—of a bill of exchange, that I shall draw upon you, and that you will accept."

Chevillard had certainly not expected so rigorous a proceeding. If a bill of exchange is not met when presented, the party, who has been imprudent enough to subscribe to it, may be committed to prison in a very summary style ; for this convenient reason, it is in high favour with that respectable body, the usurers, and the preference which Legros had so openly expressed, taken in connexion with the strange array of moveables with which his apartments were crammed, suggested certain ideas of a money-lender covering his transactions with the cloak of Philanthropy. Without manifesting any such suspicion, the luckless applicant had nevertheless some thoughts of the kind when he replied: "A bill of exchange is always a serious thing, and in the first place, I must clearly understand when it is to fall due, and what will be the rate of interest."

"As to the latter clause, you will find me very tractable : I do not claim any intere‚t."

"But that is not at all my wish," replied the book-keeper, his anxiety increased by this disinterested offer, for money-lenders are to be mistrusted in proportion as they make a display of liberality and frankness.

"Then we cannot come to any arrangement; for it is my intention to oblige you as a friend, and not on another footing."

Chevillard was completely puzzled ; this man was a mixture of exaggerated delicacy and suspicious rigour, which he could not reconcile.

"Indeed, sir," said he, "you make me feel extremely uncomfortable ; the interest on a thousand crowns is a considerable sum, and I cannot think of your giving it up to oblige me."

"To be sure, young man," replied Legros, " I know your self-love must suffer a little by my resolution ; but this will be the punishment for your folly."

The scruples of Chevillard were necessarily overruled by this obliging and ingenious speech ; but the moment after, his doubts returned in full force, when Legros began to speak of a bill payable eight days after sight.*

"That is a very short term!" exclaimed the book-keeper.

"Or it may be a very long one," returned the other; "suppose I advance my claim six months hence?"

"Certainly, in that point of view, and if you would guarantee a delay of that period ——"

---

* That is to say, payable eight days after it has been legally presented to the debtor, who establishes such presentation by affixing his signature.

" I promise nothing," interrupted Legros; " my patience will depend upon your conduct; for, to explain to you what may appear singular in my proceedings, know that I have but one end in view, that of keeping you in order. If ever you re-enter a gambling-house, I shall know it, and the very next day the bill will be presented; I give you fair warning."

" And if I did not pay?" said Chevillard, laughing.

" Oh! my dear fellow! to prison, without mercy—you may depend upon it."

" Come, I see I shall have plenty of time"—and the young man settled in his own mind that his creditor was a sort of crabbed philanthropist, whom he should be able to manage so long as he kept from the sin of gambling—an offence for which Legros appeared to cherish an aversion almost amounting to monomania.

" At all events," resumed this singular personage, " I promise you that your signature will not be circulated; the bill you subscribe shall remain in my hands."

Viewing matters in the worst light, even if payment were to be demanded immediately, Chevillard would still have eight days to consider what must be done, and, as these thoughts passed rapidly through his mind, he resolved to accept Legros' conditions. He had just announced his intention, and they were preparing to conclude the transaction, when they were interrupted by the arrival of two ladies, who entered familiarly, without being announced. At sight of these visitors, Legros exclaimed: " Ah! my fair friends! what can have procured me the favour of your presence this morning?"

" We came early to Paris to make some purchases, and, as we were in your neighbourhood, we have taken the liberty to come to breakfast with you," replied the eldest of the two ladies, a short woman, somewhat advanced in life, and of large proportions, but who, nevertheless, retained an air of youth and attractive freshness.

" Well, that was a delightful idea! and I am infinitely indebted to you. I am only afraid that, as I was not aware of this pleasure, I shall not be able to receive you as I could wish."

" Ah! you know that Esther eats no more than a bird," returned the lady who had before spoken; " and as for me, a cup of tea is quite sufficient."

" Permit me at least to go and give some orders." And the law-agent immediately withdrew, leaving Chevillard in very agreeable company.

From the moment that the ladies had entered the room, our friend the book-keeper had been gazing with fixed attention at the younger of the two, and, as we are in the secret of his predilection for *fair* beauties, we need not wonder at this, for never could there have been a more enchanting impersonation of his romantic dreams. Large blue eyes, beaming with that humid splendour which gives so much expression to the countenance, a dazzling complexion, a skin admirably fair, luxuriant tresses of the brightest auburn, a graceful figure, and an air in which there was an indescribable mixture of voluptuousness and dignity, combined to render this charming creature an object worthy of general admiration. He fancied, too, that the young girl regarded him with a certain degree of curiosity, and this discovery increased his prepossession in her favour. He was not, however, so completely absorbed as not to feel that it was incumbent on him to endeavour to relieve the awkwardness of the situation by an attempt at conversation. He wished to commence by something sprightly and agreeable, but he was so long thinking about it, that the matron forestalled him by asking " if she had not already had the honour of meeting him at Mr. Legros'?"

Chevillard replied that he was there for the first time.

" That is very singular," continued the lady; " you bear a strong resemblance to a person for whom Mr. Legros was negotiating a marriage. But now I look more attentively, I think that the person alluded to was older, and less gentlemanly in his manners."

Surprised at this compliment, the clerk could only bow his acknowledgments.

" Well, sir!" continued the lady; " as you have come once to consult Mr. Legros, I am sure it will not be the last time. He is extremely clever in business, and a man of such high integrity that he makes friends of all his clients."

Chevillard had just replied that he had every reason to congratulate himself upon having made the acquaintance of Mr. Legros, when the latter entered, exclaiming: " Well, well, fair ladies! I am more fortunate than I had thought; Margaret declares that I shall be able to offer you a presentable breakfast, and it will be served up in a few moments."

Then, drawing his client apart, he said in a low voice: "You must join us, for you see we cannot possibly conclude our little affair now!"

"That will detain me too long," returned Chevillard; "I am already late, and a signature is so soon given."

"But, my good fellow, you would not have me draw out a bill and pay over money before these ladies! what would they think? And then I am not sure that I have here paper with the proper stamp; I must send for some."

"Well, if that is the case, I submit," said the book-keeper.

"I'd advise you to complain!" resumed Legros; "to be forced to breakfast with one of the prettiest women in Paris!"

Taking the clerk by the arm, and leading him forward a few steps, he next said: "Madame de Saint-Martin, allow me to introduce to you Mr. Chevillard, one of my clients."

"I have not the pleasure of knowing this gentleman," replied the lady who was thus addressed; "but just now I thought I recognised him; I took him at first to be the person for whom you arranged that splendid match; you know whom I mean?"

"Well, there is really some faint resemblance. But my present business with Mr. Chevillard is not of that nature; another time perhaps—I don't say."

"The servant now came to announce breakfast, and as Legros led out Madame de Saint-Martin, Chevillard was left to escort her beautiful companion. The impression she had made upon him must have been very strong, for though neither a novice nor a schoolboy, he trembled with emotion at the light touch of her hand. If Legros' impromptu breakfast had been prepared with the most elaborate care, it could not have been more *presentable*; and, though Madame de Saint-Martin had declared that *a cup of tea* would be quite sufficient, and now cried out against the unnecessary profusion, she nevertheless managed to do it ample justice. The young lady, on the contrary, scarcely touched that which was set before her. Chevillard was seated opposite to her, and, as at first he thought that he had attracted her attention, he was much disappointed when he observed how carefully she avoided looking at him. A sad and listless, almost a disdainful, manner marked the bearing of this beautiful girl, and the few words that she uttered were formal and constrained. Madame

de Saint-Martin liberally compensated for this, her natural loquacity being apparently increased by the presence of the *stranger*. Her conversation did not denote any very high degree of polish or intellect, but Chevillard, to whom she addressed a vast number of polite and obliging speeches, was not disposed to be hypercritical. He might, without vanity, consider that he had made a favourable impression, and though it was not exactly in the right quarter, it encouraged him to exert all his powers of pleasing, in hopes of overcoming the reserve of his opposite neighbour, in whom he every moment discovered some new charm. But his efforts were unavailing; though he really made himself very agreeable, the young lady did not appear even to notice his attentions, and her coldness destroyed the pleasure he would otherwise have derived from this unforeseen meeting. Madame de Saint-Martin was much more sociable, and she seemed to have taken such a violent fancy for the person and conversation of our friend, that, when the repast was over, and she prepared to depart, he would not have felt surprised at receiving an invitation to visit this new conquest at her own house. However, her favour was not carried to that extent, and the interview was terminated by a very gracious farewell from the lady, and a rather stiff bow from her young companion, who, indeed, was not much more affable in her demeanour towards Legros.

The gentlemen, when left alone, returned to the study, and Legros at once asked Chevillard what he thought of Madame de Saint-Martin.

"She appears to be very amiable," replied he; "but I think her daughter may be called a perfect beauty."

"That is not her daughter, but a young orphan whom she has brought up."

"Indeed! this accounts then for the melancholy look of the young lady."

"Oh! there are many things to be said on that subject. You must have seen that Madame de Saint-Martin still likes to be admired. This orphan was confided to her charge when very young, and so long as she was a child, she treated her with the greatest kindness; but now that Esther is grown up so charming, the good lady regards her as a rival, and is no longer the same."

"So she is jealous of the poor girl, and does not make her happy?"

"Yes; there is something of this kind."

" But why not get rid of this rival, by disposing of her in marriage?"

" That is under consideration," replied Legros; " and one would think the thing were easy enough, for the girl is a good match. She has not a fortune, strictly speaking; but she has a guardian, who takes a deep interest in her. He is a man of great influence; he has just been appointed commissioner of stores for the navy, and could place the husband his ward might choose in a very good situation."

" I should think then, that this beautiful young lady must have a crowd of adorers."

" Why, in the first place, she goes out but little. Madame de Saint-Martin does not see much company, and lives in a very retired part, almost like the country; and then any one who wishes to win the daughter, must suit the fancy of her adoptive mother, who insists upon having a son-in-law of her own choice, as if she were the person he is to marry!"

" But the good lady did not seem very inaccessible," said Chevillard, in a tone approaching to fatuity.

" In truth, she appeared to be quite *taken* with you, and I can assure you I was astonished at it; not that I mean to question your merit, but so few persons are able to please her."

" If I were sure these favourable dispositions would last, do you know that, after all you have been telling me, I should feel half inclined to place myself on the list of aspirants?"

" My dear fellow!" replied Legros, " you don't seem to me steady enough to get married; and besides, just now, we have something more serious to think of. Let us see about this bill;" and he drew a sheet of stamped paper from a box, in which there appeared to be a good store, notwithstanding the assertion he had made before breakfast.

" You are right," said Chevillard; " I am talking here, and forgetting how late it is, and I shall have a fine lecture when I get back."

" Let me see," resumed Legros, seating himself at his desk, and repeating in an undertone, as he wrote them down, the following words:

" Rouen, November 27th, 1804.
B.P.F. 3000.

" Eight days after sight, please to pay to our order, the sum of *Three Thousand Francs*, value received, which carry as advised by   " LEGROS, Agent.

" To MR. CHEVILLARD.

" No. 7, Rue des Deux-Portes-Saint-Sauveur, Paris."

" Now, will you accept this?" said he, presenting the pen to the book-keeper.

Casting his eyes over the paper, Chevillard wrote across the bill, in a perpendicular direction, *accepted for the sum of three thousand francs*, and affixed his signature. Legros then drew from his pocket-book bank-notes to the amount named, and gave them to his client, who immediately asked permission to retire.

" Certainly, my dear fellow, never neglect business; but I shall hope to see you soon, and—beware of a relapse!"

" Believe me, sir, I shall never forget the service you have rendered me," said Chevillard; and, cordially shaking the hand of his new friend, he left the room.

CHAPTER V.

AT all seasons of the year, Chevillard was at his books before nine o'clock, and this morning, noon struck as he entered the *Tricoloured Prism*. He expected to be reproached for this unauthorised delay, and had therefore already determined upon the course to be pursued: he resolved to offer no excuses, and if called upon for an explanation, to reply in the most firm and dignified manner. Full of these magnanimous sentiments, he entered the presence of Mademoiselle Lebeau, and without further preface, presented the bank-notes, saying as he did so: " Mademoiselle, here is the money you desired me to receive."

" So you did not go till this morning?" observed Mademoiselle Lebeau, somewhat drily, and as if she connected this question with the slight altercation of the day before.

" I beg your pardon, the money was paid to me yesterday evening."

" Indeed! how is it then that you are so late in the counting-house?" asked the fair mercer.

" Mademoiselle, I had some business which obliged me to go out this morning; I think that such a circumstance might happen to anybody."

" Certainly; but you might have taken the trouble to let me know, and to leave me the key of the cash-box. There was a payment to be made just now, and if I had not happened to have sufficient funds in my private purse, I should have been obliged to ask for credit."

" That would doubtless have been very unpleasant: but as you were able to meet the demand, no great harm is done."

"It was quite a chance that I was able to do so," returned Mademoiselle Lebeau, with some warmth; "and the credit of a house should never be left to *chance*."

"The credit of a house is not compromised by such a trifle," retorted Chevillard, in a light and indifferent manner.

"Yes, sir; for *less* than a quarter of an hour's delay is sufficient to cast a doubt upon the solvability of a trader; this is a fundamental principle in business, and I am surprised that I need to remind you of it."

"Oh! Mademoiselle, I have many other things to learn from you," answered Chevillard, alluding to the absolute control that his employer exercised in the establishment. "A clerk cannot be expected to know more than the rough work; it is the heads alone who are versed in the niceties of trade."

Mademoiselle Lebeau had often passed over ironical expressions of this nature, without appearing to notice them; but this fresh ebullition was so very ill-timed, that she lost all patience, and said with much dignity: "Mr. Chevillard, favour me with your attention for a moment; you have for some time displayed much uncalled-for petulance; to-day, when you are so evidently in the wrong, I think you might have refrained from this. You take everything amiss, and are displeased and discontented with all around you: when people are living in the same house, this is exceedingly unpleasant; if you have any complaints to make, state them, but let us have done with this enigmatical and capricious displeasure."

Chevillard forgot the moderation he had intended to maintain, and replied hastily: "Mademoiselle, if my character and services no longer suit you, you have only to signify it, and I will not stay in your house against your wishes. Nothing can be more simple."

Notwithstanding this rude speech, Mademoiselle Lebeau said with much calmness: "Mr. Chevillard, this way of looking at the subject is hardly in good taste."

"It is my undoubted opinion," continued the book-keeper, growing still warmer, instead of appreciating the forbearance and kindness of her reply, "that when people are tired of living together, they ought to part; they need not be the worse friends for that."

"Let us say no more," replied the young lady; "you are angry, and you cannot see at this moment how unjust and unreasonable you are. Here is an account-current that I want presently; will you be kind enough to attend to it at once?"

The separation which Chevillard had proposed was too sudden and unpremeditated a design for him to insist further. He took the papers, and though he did not testify the slighest compunction for his inconsiderate expressions, he seated himself at his desk, and gave his attention to the required task. Arithmetic and book-keeping have usually a very sedative effect upon the imagination, but on this occasion Chevillard could not recover his equanimity, and during the whole day, he was disturbed by conflicting ideas and feelings. He had frequently before, in calmer moments, asked himself if he could always quietly submit to this obscure and dependent existence, and on the preceding evening, he had for a full hour lived in a golden vision, which had vividly excited his desire for a more brilliant and influential position. This dream had been dispelled by a bitter reality; but his wishes for a change of fortune had been revived in full force, by his meeting with the beautiful orphan in Legros' study. For might not the happier destiny, which by the chances of play had for a moment been within his grasp, might it not now be fully realized by the possession of this lovely girl, who brought as her portion a place and powerful protection—in a word, every opportunity for the rapid advancement of an active and clever man?

Our dreamer had probably as yet no very decided plan as to this matrimonial speculation and the manner in which Legros had received the vague hint he threw out on the subject was not calculated to encourage him to proceed; but though his projects were thus cloudy and undefined, he felt as if a distant horizon had risen upon his life. It is therefore not surprising if, in the evening, when Mademoiselle Lebeau and all the members of her household met at dinner, Chevillard should appear singularly preoccupied and silent.

Always disposed to judge of others by her own amiable disposition, Mademoiselle Lebeau thought this constrained manner proceded from the regret he felt for his unseemly warmth in the morning. She harboured no resentment, and, anxious to efface all traces of past differences, she showed herself as kind and affable to the supposed penitent, as if he had given her no cause for

complaint. But ambitious desires harden the heart. The proud book-keeper imagined, that the friendly advances of the kind-hearted girl were inspired by her fear of losing his services, and he was not in the least touched by them: on the contrary, he thought his dignity required him to receive them with marked coldness and asperity, and he put so little restraint upon himself, that his sullen humours at length exhausted the patience of the fair mercer. Woman's pride triumphed, and she ceased to notice this sulky being, though her innate generosity prevented her from treating him with the sharpness he deserved. Full of engrossing thoughts, and discontented with himself, for his conscience reproached him with his behaviour to a person who might have had a serious reckoning to demand, Chevillard, when his evening duties were concluded, felt no inclination to retire to rest; and, hoping that the air would calm the tumult of his mind, he went out to walk.

He had besides an object in view. The night before, he had left his watch in a place, where, for many reasons, he was unwilling it should remain; he therefore directed his steps towards the dangerous house which had been so nearly his ruin, redeemed the property he had pledged, and as he was descending the staircase, which likewise led to the gambling-table, he met his friend Legros. There was nothing in the meeting to cause him much surprise, for that singular individual had himself declared that his eccentric and ardent philanthropy induced him to pay frequent visits to such haunts; but Chevillard had not the same excuse, and his unlooked-for appearance on the staircase of No. 113, seemed to indicate a decided relapse.

"How, sir!" said Legros, with severity, "*you* here, this evening, after your solemn protestations ——"

"You are mistaken, my kind benefactor; I came to obliterate the last traces of my indiscretion. You know where I obtained the supplies for my last campaign; I have just been to redeem my watch, upon which I had raised five louis, and you may see that the ticket is still attached to it."

"Oh! that is all right!" returned the monitor; "otherwise, I should have been down upon you to-morrow with the bill. Well, I am delighted to see you, and if you are not in a hurry to return home, we will take a turn through the galleries together."

Nothing could have been more acceptable to Chevillard than this proposal. He wished to have some conversation with Legros, concerning Madame de Saint-Martin and her adopted daughter, and it suited admirably with his plans, that this should appear to be brought about by chance, and thus enable him to dispense with the significant step of calling upon his friend for the express purpose of making enquiries.

"Well!" said Legros, commencing the conversation in the manner the book-keeper could have most wished, "how did things go off this morning?"

"Very badly, indeed! We have been on very uncomfortable terms all day."

"How! did she suspect anything?"

"No; but your breakfast delayed me terribly, and as she is a very precise person, and loves to domineer, she reproached me in a manner to which I was not inclined to submit."

"So you, like a hot-headed young man, lost your temper?"

"Not exactly; but I intimated to her, in civil terms, that I might possibly give up my situation."

"I do not absolutely blame you; my opinion is, that no one should allow himself to be trampled on; but pride is a fine thing when we are certain of another place."

"Ah! that is the thing," said Chevillard, with a sigh; "that is not to be found every day."

"Do you know," observed Legros, negligently, "I have been thinking—since I saw you this morning—and, as I said before, I am glad we have met, for I can mention it to you ——"

"What is it then?" asked Chevillard, repressing as much as he could his impatient curiosity.

"It is really strange," continued the other, "that though you are almost a stranger to me, I feel so lively an interest in your welfare; but I don't know how it is, I have taken a fancy to you, and as I am aware you are not in a very suitable position, I shall have much pleasure in assisting you to improve your prospects in life."

"You are really too good!" returned Chevillard, warmly pressing the hand of this devoted friend.

"I have an idea, to be sure; but I am afraid my project will meet with many difficulties in the execution!"

"But once more, what is it?" said the young man, with increasing impatience.

"Have you ever thought of getting married?" asked Legros, looking as if the subject had never before been mentioned.

Immediately following up the hint, the clerk replied: "Never, before this morning——"

"And since this morning?" said the other, archly.

"Why, really," returned Chevillard, "I should not speak the truth, if I did not say I have had a vague idea of such a thing."

"Come now, do not let us play at mysteries; confess, that Esther's pretty face has made some impression upon you."

"Why, my dear sir, there are not many whose beauty can be compared to hers."

"And then, my young friend, she is as good as she is beautiful; and considering the positive advantages with which the connexion will be attended, believe me, I think you could not do better."

"But when I had an inspiration of the kind, this morning, you appeared to discourage such an idea."

"Yes, at the first moment; but when I came to reflect, it did not seem to me so impracticable. You have certainly gained the favour of Madame de Saint-Martin. I, on the other hand, possess some influence with the guardian, and to speak frankly, I foresee no serious obstacle but on your part."

"How on my part?" exclaimed Chevillard; "when I say a thing, I mean it."

"Undoubtedly; but you know that even the sun has spots, and if Esther were like those fine apples at whose core there is a worm—in short, if you were a man who cared for prejudices——"

"*Prejudices!*" said Chevillard, rather alarmed at this speech; "I must know what you understand by that expression."

"I mean the greater or less degree of fastidiousness, with which you might view a certain informality of birth; in short, to come to the point, would you marry an illegitimate child? That is the question."

"This little informality, as you call it, is in itself nothing very terrible, and then much depends upon circumstances."

"Oh! there is nothing to object to there. Esther is well born; she is the daughter of the *ci-devant* Marquis de Brevannes, who acknowledged her."

"Then the obstacle might rather be on her side; for, after all, I am nothing but a poor clerk."

"No, there will be no difficulties in that quarter. Her father emigrated, and died abroad, leaving her totally unprovided for, his property having been confiscated and sold by the nation. The Marquis entrusted Esther to the care of Madame de Saint-Martin, and this lady has brought her up in habits of strict obedience. Her will is law to her adopted daughter."

"But perhaps the guardian, of whom you spoke, will not think me a suitable match."

"In the first place," replied Legros, "let me be clearly understood. This guardian is not a legal guardian; he was formerly steward to the Marquis, and has extended to the daughter some of the attachment he felt for the father. He wishes to see this young girl happily married, for he has known her from her infancy, and received the parting injunctions of his former master to watch over and protect her. He has made a large fortune in commercial speculations, but, having a family, he does not consider himself justified in giving a portion to his ward, and intends, as I have already told you, to dispose of a lucrative and honourable situation in behalf of the husband she may choose; but he claims no right to influence her determination."

"The situation would probably be connected with the stores in his department?" said Chevillard.

"Yes; and I assure you, that even supposing the salary to be a matter of six thousand francs only, the *protégé* of so prosperous and influential a man must be an awkward fellow, if he did not get on famously in a short time."

"Well, my dear sir," said Chevillard, "see if you can arrange all this; I put myself entirely in your hands."

"The line to be followed is plain enough," resumed Legros; "to-morrow morning, I will go to Madame de Saint-Martin, and propose you as a husband for Esther. But reflect well upon it first; in plain terms, it is a bastard you are to marry."

"Come, come; in this enlightened age, and with our republican ideas, is a question of birth deserving of serious consideration? My intended is charming, and, as you tell me, endowed with numerous good qualities ——"

"Oh! you may be quite easy on that score. As to you, my dear fellow, I hope you will fully justify the good character I shall give you; for do you know, from the manner in which our acquaintance commenced, I am taking a terrible responsibility upon myself."

"I was led away by the persuasions of a friend, and I swear to you, that I then played for the first and last time."

"I am willing to believe you," returned the law-agent. "Well, to-morrow in the afternoon, you shall hear from me one way or the other. Where shall I address my letter?"

"I shall be in the counting-house all day."

"To-morrow then," said Legros; "but now don't have any misgivings, and draw back, after I have committed myself with my friends."

"Be easy," answered Chevillard; "I am not a child."

Everything being now settled, they parted; and from that moment the aspiring clerk gave himself up to the hope of a new existence, and resolved that, even if his marriage did not take place, he would not remain in the obscurity in which he had vegetated too long already; so that the establishment of the *Tri-coloured Prism* was at all events menaced with no less a calamity than the loss of its cashier.

————

CHAPTER VI.

In Chevillard's present disposition of mind, his intercourse with Mademoiselle Lebeau was anything but cordial. That young lady had made, the evening before, as many advances towards a reconciliation as could be reasonably expected from her, and these having had no effect upon her angry clerk, she now observed the greatest coolness and reserve in her demeanour towards him. On the other hand, the book-keeper, who had made up his mind to leave, was glad to keep up this state of misunderstanding, as it would facilitate the execution of his design.

Nothing therefore had taken place to shake his conviction of the propriety and wisdom of his matrimonial project, when on the following afternoon, he received a letter written in a hand which he immediately recognised. He opened it with anxious feelings, for it seemed to him as if those few lines contained the solution of his destiny. There was no signature, and the communication ran as follows:

" The affair takes a favourable turn. Your pretensions were well received, and I am authorized to present you to-day, on the footing you could wish. Wait for me this evening, about seven o'clock, at the Palais du Tribunat, near the Montansier theatre; we will start together for the place in question. Be punctual, and believe me,

"Yours truly."

This rapid result augured well for the definitive arrangements; and Chevillard felt so happy, that he could not control the outward demonstrations of his joy. At the dinner table, he was full of animation, but as he took care to address none of his conversation to Mademoiselle Lebeau, and indeed seemed scarcely to notice her presence, this change of humour was peculiarly offensive. She could not but suppose that it was assumed purposely to brave her, and at length she gave Chevillard to understand, that she thought his proceedings were in exceedingly bad taste. The book-keeper made an angry reply, and thus the breach between them was still further widened. He soon after announced, in a very off-hand way, that he had some business that evening, which would oblige him to absent himself, and added: "If you think you shall want the key of the cash-box, I will leave it."

Provoked by this irony, Mademoiselle

Lebeau replied: " You had better do so, if your affairs, which appear to me to increase very fast, are to detain you till noon to-morrow."

" Oh !" returned Chevillard, " I don't suppose they will occupy quite so much time; but, at all events, there is the key !"

Mademoiselle Lebeau took it without making any reply, but this slight altercation must have had a strange effect upon her; for, soon after, forgetting the admirable good-temper which was her characteristic quality, she scolded one of the shopwomen for a trivial fault so harshly, that the poor girl burst into tears. Chevillard was at the time in his room, dressing with the most scrupulous care, for that eventful visit.

Legros was punctual to the appointment, and, getting into a coach with his *protégé*, said to the driver: "Allée des Veuves."

" Does Madame de Saint-Martin live there ?" asked Chevillard, surprised.

" Yes; I told you she lived in the country, or nearly so."

" What a very strange place to choose !"

" Why ? It is a place like any other, only rather remote from the crowd."

" A place like any other, do you call it ! Why, it is said to be a regular den of cut-throats."

" Surely you are not afraid !" said Legros, laughing.

" No, but I think it odd for women to live there alone."

" My dear fellow, we must never trust to a name, be it good or bad; besides, Madame de Saint-Martin retired to this unfrequented spot, during the Reign of Terror, because in the neighbourhood where she lived, she was subjected to much annoyance on account of her royalist opinions."

" That explains the matter," said Chevillard.

" I persuaded her to buy this property; it had belonged to an emigrant, forming what, before the Revolution, was called *La Petite Maison*. Madame de Saint-Martin made a capital hit, for the house, with its pretty garden, is a little Paradise, and she got it for a mere trifle."

Chatting in this way, our travellers arrived at their destination. As they alighted, they observed a brilliant equipage standing before the door of the house, and Legros said to the man who sat upon the box: " Ah ! Anthony, is it you ? Then your master is here ?"

" Yes, sir," said the coachman; " my

master dined here, and he told me to return at eight o'clock, to take him to the opera."

"This is fortunate," observed Legros to Chevillard; "we shall kill two birds with one stone: that is the carriage of Esther's guardian, and as, during dinner, Madame de Saint-Martin will probably have informed him of our plans, this meeting may considerably abridge the negotiation."

Whilst this short dialogue was taking place, a country-looking girl had opened the door, and, after traversing a small court and ascending a flight of steps, Chevillard was introduced into an elegant vestibule, adorned with statues and painted stucco. From hence a staircase led to the upper rooms, for the house was a low building of one story. Legros led the way, and opening a door on the ground floor, which was richly inlaid with foreign woods, they entered a saloon, built in the form of a rotunda, and with two windows looking upon a garden. This apartment was fitted up in the luxurious and coquettish style of the century that had just closed; but the furniture must have seen long service, for the hangings and carpet, of a most delicate hue, and the gilding of the mirrors, seats, and cornices, retained but few vestiges of their former splendour. Chevillard saw at the first glance that his destined bride was absent, which he accounted for as dictated by propriety, considering the preliminaries which were to be discussed on this eventful occasion. By the side of the fire, sat Madame de Saint-Martin: she rose upon the entrance of her guest, and received him very graciously; whilst, standing with his back towards the chimney, was a man about fifty years of age, who acknowledged by a slight inclination of the head the respectful bow addressed to him by the book-keeper. As soon as they were seated, the matron commenced the conversation with a phrase which led directly to the object of the meeting; but Legros, whose ideas of propriety were rather more enlarged, felt that some further preamble was necessary, though it were only for the sake of appearances. Taking the first subject that presented itself, he began to relate Chevillard's astonishment at hearing that Madame de Saint-Martin lived in the terrible Allée des Veuves, about which so many startling tales were daily circulated in Paris. Afraid of appearing ridiculous, Chevillard hastened to ex-

plain, as he had already done to Legros, that his observations referred to the danger to which ladies might be exposed who resided alone in so retired a spot.

On her part, Madame de Saint-Martin repeated the explanation that Legros had given. "And besides," added she, "we scarcely ever go out in the evening; occasionally we may go to the play, but then, this gentleman" (and she looked at the commissary) "is kind enough to accompany us, and to bring us home in his carriage. As for the security of the house itself, we have strong shutters and fastenings; and, during the many years we have lived here, we have never heard of anything to justify the bad reputation of the place."

"It were to be regretted, madame," said the commissary, taking this opportunity to give a *profitable* turn to the conversation, "that the gentleman should be prejudiced against the Allée des Veuves, for, from the communication with which you have favoured me concerning his wishes and intentions, it appears to me that he is destined to visit it sometimes."

This remark was an allusion to the projected marriage, but there lurked in it an irony far from agreeable to Chevillard, and indeed, to say the truth, the man pleased him as little as his words. He did not like the way in which this person measured and scrutinised his appearance; for though such curiosity was natural under the circumstances, it might have been exercised in a more discreet and reserved manner. He, in his turn, had glanced furtively at this rude inquisitor, in whose presence he experienced an unaccountable sensation of uneasiness. A bald forehead, a complexion of unhealthy paleness, thick, bushy brows, and eyes which gleamed darkly in their deep orbits, formed a physiognomy which was by no means prepossessing.

He would have found it difficult to repress a slight degree of sharpness in his answer to the expressions which appeared to cast an imputation on his courage, but Legros hastened to interpose, by saying to Madame de Saint-Martin: "I see, fair lady, that you have spoken to our respected friend of the ambition of Mr. Chevillard; an ambition which you have authorized me to encourage."

"Yes, my dear Legros," replied the lady, "I am so fully persuaded of your prudence and sincere friendship, that the proposals this gentleman has made, through you, could not be otherwise than acceptable to me; I wished to tell him so myself, and Esther's guardian having called in the meantime, I communicated the circumstance, for he certainly has a right to be consulted on so important an occasion."

" Well! Mr. Guardian, what is your opinion?" asked Legros, in a tone which indicated that he was on very familiar terms with that gentleman.

" Why, I say as Madame does, that from your hand I would unhesitatingly accept a husband for Esther; and, besides, this gentleman appears to be, in every respect, deserving of the high opinion you have expressed in regard to him."

This compliment was so wholly unexpected, that Chevillard was sensibly touched by it; and, to show his gratitude, he commenced a phrase of most intricate construction, which he with difficulty brought to a close.

" But," continued the commissary, " I have to speak with this gentleman of some — I will not say *conditions*, connected with the marriage, for they are dictated by circumstances rather than by my wishes—but of some unfortunate obligations."

" Before we proceed any further," said Madame de Saint-Martin, " permit me to ask Mr. Chevillard, if he is fully aware of the family circumstances of our dear child?"

This time the book-keeper was more happily inspired, for he replied: " Yes, madam; it is sufficient for me to know that Mademoiselle Esther is a charming person, educated by a virtuous lady, who has acted towards her as a mother."

Every one, and Madame de Saint-Martin in particular, appeared touched by the delicacy with which the young man had avoided all unpleasant explanations; and the guardian hastened to resume: " In the first place, sir, we shall be obliged to conclude this marriage with some degree of haste and precipitation, and this will perhaps not exactly suit you."

" That is not a very hard condition," returned Chevillard.

" Pardon me; it is true, that I am not of an age to have any great predilection for love-matches; but still, it is my opinion, that when two persons have had time to study, and know each other, they are more likely to be happy in their union."

" Certainly," said Chevillard, " that is always the best."

" Yes! but in this case circumstances are stronger than our will. You have been told, sir, that it was my intention to dispose of some employment in favour of Esther's husband. Now, I have just undertaken the supply of provisions for the navy, and, as I am forming the establishments necessary for that service, I should never have a better opportunity of procuring you a good place."

" I perfectly understand," replied Chevillard.

" I am on the point of entering upon an undertaking, the importance of which you will comprehend, when I tell you that it is expected to bring a profit of five or six millions. I foresee that my time will be much taken up in various ways, and I should wish first to see this child happily established, for, from my former connexion with her father, I feel as much interest in her as if she were allied to me by the ties of blood."

" Sir, your reasons are undeniably just."

" Now," continued the commissary, " I come to what may be called the bitter part of my requisitions. The place which I destine for you, sir, is that of superintendent in the town of Rochefort; the emolument is about two thousand crowns, with the expectation of a speedy preferment, so that Esther may be said to bring an income of six thousand francs to her husband."

" Well, sir," said Chevillard, " I see nothing very *bitter* as yet."

" No; but listen: as my superintendent will have to attend to numerous details and orders, he must, especially at first, be continually moving about, and have every moment of his time occupied. Now, his wife could not accompany him in this wandering life, and I cannot have our interests neglected whilst he is making love; so I must stipulate, that, during the first six months at least, Esther is to be left under the safe care of Madame de Saint-Martin, and that he is to go, like a poor hermit, to the residence assigned him."

" I must confess this is a harsh measure," said Legros; " and when I was a fiery young man, I don't think I should have put up with it."

" But, sir," observed Chevillard, " is my widowerhood to cease at the end of the six months?"

" Oh! undoubtedly; either you will

be permanently settled, and your wife will be able to join you, or, as is infinitely more probable, I shall recall you to Paris."

"But is this the only pill, at least?" said Legros, facetiously.

"Not quite all," returned the commissary. "If the thing had been possible, I should have wished Mr. Chevillard to be at his post within a week from this time."

"Well!" said the law-agent.

"Well! if we set about necessary preliminaries, without a moment's delay, nearly a fortnight must elapse from the publication of the banns, before the marriage can be celebrated."

"From which you conclude——"

"From which I conclude, that, if I extend the honeymoon to three days, I shall act very generously, and shall put myself to great inconvenience besides."

"Go to the devil, you and your place!" cried Legros, falling into a fit of comic anger; "never was a poor husband so tantalised!"

"Come, come, my dear sir," said Madame de Saint-Martin; "don't be more refractory than Mr. Chevillard, for I think he sees the force of these reasons, and will submit."

"Certainly," replied the poor book-keeper; "I am not so foolish as to think that a position in life is to be attained without some sacrifices."

"Then you formally accept all these conditions?" asked Esther's guardian.

"Say, that he *suffers* them," cried the law-agent.

"Yes, sir," said Chevillard; "let everything be settled as you wish."

"Seriously, you have made up your mind?" interposed Legros.

"I have indeed; and it would be ungrateful in me to make any objections."

"Well, my dear fellow," said Legros, getting up, and shaking him by the hand, "you are a more sensible man than I took you for, and I do not repent of my good opinion. Now, I must tell you, that you are in the hands of a man who knows how to requite good services; and upon my soul, if he does not give a lift to such a youngster as you, I tell him beforehand, that he and I shall quarrel."

"Why, sir," said the commissary, addressing Chevillard, "ten years ago, I commenced my career with certainly less assistance than I offer you to-day, and now I am reputed to be worth more than a million."

"Yes, I wish I had the odd sum!" observed Legros, as if thinking aloud.

"And Esther?" said Madame de Saint-Martin; "she must be heard in the business."

"Allow me," replied her guardian; "this is the plan I have arranged. To summon the poor girl to a sort of official appearance, in order to give her consent, seems to me rather abrupt. Without communicating my intentions, I told her to go and dress for the opera, and I hope Mr. Chevillard will join our party; when they have thus spent an evening in each other's company, Esther will be better prepared to receive his visit to-morrow, in the presence of her mother only. In this way, her intended husband will not appear to have dropped from the clouds."

"Not a badly devised plot!" said Legros, gaily.

"Excellent! if Mr. Chevillard is at liberty," added Madame de Saint-Martin.

"I had devoted the whole evening to you," replied the young man.

The commissary rung the bell, and said to the servant who answered his summons: "Let Esther know that we are ready."

In a few moments, the young lady entered, and if she had appeared charming to Chevillard, in her simple morning dress, she made a still stronger impression when he saw her attired in an elegant evening costume, which revealed her beauty to an extent authoriezd by the very *uncovered* style then in fashion.

The Helen of antiquity found old men not insensible to her charms, and Esther, thus adorned, inspired even Legros with a feeling of warm admiration, for, approaching Chevillard, he whispered: "Egad, my dear fellow! what a lovely creature! I have given you a treasure!"

The eyes of the commissary flashed fire from under his dark brows, as he contemplated her with a paternal pride.

"Well, shall we go?" said Madame de Saint-Martin, tired of this general ecstacy.

"Offer your arm to Madame de Saint-Martin," said Legros to Chevillard.

He did so, and the guardian conducted his ward. As they were getting into the carriage, perceiving that Legros was preparing to depart, the commissary exclaimed: "Do you not come with us?"

"No, I have an engagement," replied the other, and he wished the two ladies good evening; then, pushing Chevillard upon the step, he whispered: "I wish you success; come and see me as soon as you can, we have a thousand things to arrange."

The door was closed, and the carriage rolled rapidly away.

CHAPTER VII.

THE incidents which, during the last few days, had followed each other in quick succession in the life of Chevillard, were so rapid and striking, that it would have been difficult for him to stop in the descent, down which he had been hastening since the fatal dinner of Chabouillant. Everything was calculated to turn his head. A sumptuous equipage set him down at the entrance of the theatre; the door of a handsome box opened to receive him, and he seated himself on its aristocratic cushions, instead of mingling with the crowd on some obscure bench in the pit, as had been heretofore his custom; the beauty of his intended attracted all eyes; and when, in addition to these things, we consider that, in her company, he experienced for several hours the magnetic influence of music, dancing, and splendid scenery, can we wonder that more was not wanted to disturb the reason of so light and susceptible a character, and to rob him of his free will?

As soon as the ladies were seated in the box, Esther's guardian left them (doubtless to give Chevillard an opportunity to pay his court, unrestrained by his presence), and directed his steps towards the saloon, at that time the place where men engaged in politics or finance congregated by mutual and tacit agreement. Without allowing the change in her manner to be too marked, the young girl, who was the object of Chevillard's attentions, received them that evening with a gentle courtesy, very different from the cold reserve she had manifested at their first meeting; so that when our friend took leave of his beautiful intended, his passion had increased to such a height, that if anything had occurred to break off the marriage, it would have been a very long time before he acquired sufficient fortitude to submit to the disappointment with reasonable calmness.

This delightful evening was followed by a stormy morning. One of the book-keeper's friends, like him employed in a commercial house, had business to transact with Mademoiselle Lebeau, and Chevillard happened to be present when he came in.

He was so anxious to bring out his malicious and indiscreet pleasantry, that, with a hasty bow to the mistress of the house, he turned to the clerk, exclaiming: "Why Chevillard! since when, pray, do you associate with ambassadors' ladies?"

"Ambassadors' ladies!" replied the book-keeper, rather surprised at the question.

"Ambassadors or bankers, I don't know which; but, in short, ladies who take you to the opera, in a fine carriage, with grey horses and two footmen!"

Mademoiselle Lebeau's surprise at this speech was beyond the power of description; she looked anxiously at Chevillard, who grew very red; but, instantly making up his mind to what was inevitable, he replied: "Ah! so you saw me? Where were you?"

"Why, I was in the pit, whilst you were seated in such state by the side of that charming creature; I can tell you, her beauty caused quite a sensation in the house."

"Oh! so that was the business that obliged you to go out last night?" exclaimed Mademoiselle Lebeau, hurried on this occasion out of her usual reserve.

"Upon my word, mademoiselle," said Chevillard, confused, like a man who has been detected in a glaring falsehood, "you would be in the wrong to attach any importance to this visit to the theatre. The persons I accompanied are old friends of my family, who have come to spend some time at Paris."

"And who tells you, sir," returned the lady, with a warmth which betrayed her secret thoughts, "that I attach any importance to the society you may please to frequent; is it any concern of mine? Only I think it is very ridiculous, that you should make a mystery of these things, as if I were a person likely to refuse you leave of absence, when you ask it."

"Certainly," answered Chevillard, "I might have told you the plain fact; but I recollected, that, only a week ago, you appeared displeased because I went to dine with Chabouillant."

"But, Mr. Chevillard, you know why I object to your intimacy with that person: he is a man of no principle, and there is everything to lose in his society. But as I suppose the lady, *whose beauty made such a sensation*, is not, as a woman, what Mr. Chabouillant

is as a man, you need not have made a secret of your engagement."

Chevillard was in an awkward position; he saw one way to escape from it, by getting angry; so, assuming a serious and dignified tone: "Mademoiselle," said he, "I likewise think it strange, that you seem to direct unpleasant insinuations against a person, with whom you are not acquainted. I beg to assure you, that the ladies, in whose society I was seen yesterday, are most respectable women."

"Upon my soul, I should think so!" cried the loquacious originator of the dispute; "with such a slap-up turn-out!"

"As to you, my good fellow," continued the book-keeper, "I shall thank you another time to keep your own counsel: you see what your thoughtless chattering has occasioned."

"Oh, indeed!" retorted the other, angry at being thus reproved; "you need not make such a fuss about the matter; I think it is very ridiculous, for you to be lecturing everybody in this way."

"Come, come; quite enough has been said!" interrupted Mademoiselle

Lebeau, in an authoritative tone, thus preventing some angry retort; and turning to the visitor, she asked him for the invoice he was to bring. Upon receiving the paper, she requested Chevillard to go and verify the amount by his books; and, anxious to avoid any further chance of collision between the parties, immediately dismissed the indiscreet babbler, with a promise to send the money in the course of the day.

By losing his temper at the right moment, Chevillard had got out of this scrape pretty well; nevertheless, the inopportune discovery that had been made, caused him considerable embarrassment. He had an engagement for that evening at the house of Madame de Saint-Martin, when he was to be formally accepted by his fair intended, and after what had just passed, it seemed almost impossible that he could ask leave to absent himself.

This same discovery had deeply wounded Mademoiselle Lebeau, and had completely changed, for the moment, her usually kind and obliging temper. During the whole day, she was captious and arbitrary, and after dinner (thus, without knowing it, anticipating his wishes), she said with *apparent* good-nature: " Mr. Chevillard, if you have any engagement for this evening, with *the old friends of your family*, pray do not stand upon ceremony; I can spare you without inconvenience."

Chevillard felt the irony; but he pretended to think that no more was meant than met the ear, and cordially thanking the fair mercer, he hastened to profit by the permission he had received. The meeting with his intended was a matter of form rather than a serious interview, and therefore any detailed account would not afford much interest to the reader; but there was one circumstance connected with it which is worthy of remark. The young lady who, the evening before, listened to her admirer with the most graceful affability, had now resumed the constrained and absent manner which had struck him so forcibly when he first saw her at Legros' house. But he was not alarmed by this change of demeanour; a well-educated girl always feels, on such an occasion, a diffidence which is easily understood and accounted for.

As for Madame de Saint-Martin, she evidently considered, that her adopted daughter had given a definitive consent, for she immediately treated Chevillard

on the footing of a son-in-law, and began to discuss domestic arrangements. She suggested, that, as his wife was to remain with her during his absence, it would be quite unnecessary to think of furniture, &c., and that her house could serve as his temporary residence after the marriage had taken place. She added, that as circumstances obliged them to an unusual degree of precipitation, she thought it best that everything should be conducted as privately as possible, to prevent the comments and questions which this peculiarity might occasion. Instead, therefore, of inviting a numerous company, or giving a grand entertainment, she proposed merely to offer a breakfast, after the ceremony had been performed, to the wedding party and their witnesses. For the same reason, she advised Chevillard not to make his approaching marriage generally known, for that people were always ready to give their advice on matters which did not concern them, and to object to arrangements of the propriety of which they were often not competent to judge.

Chevillard assented without hesitation to all these arrangements, which appeared to him very sensible; and declared that he should speak to no one but the two friends, whom he proposed to invite as the witnesses to his union with Esther, and the mistress of the house in which he was employed. He must of course inform her of his intended marriage, that she might have time to engage some one in his place, and also, that she might enjoy the facility of paying a daily visit to his intended.

Wishing probably to ascertain, if the last mentioned person was deserving of the confidence Chevillard intended to repose in her, Madame de Saint-Martin (who being, as she said, a woman of noble family, regarded any one engaged in trade with considerable contempt) asked in a disdainful tone, *what sort of woman* she was to whom he wished to communicate his plans.

" Oh! she is a very superior young lady," replied Chevillard, " to whom I may entrust them with perfect safety."

" How, sir!" said Esther, much interested; " a young lady is at the head of the large establishment in which you hold a situation?"

" Yes, mademoiselle, and I must say she manages it very well; only she is rather too fond of doing everything herself, and of asking no one's advice."

" But then, sir," continued the fair

girl, "what I have so often heard repeated is absolutely false, that it is impossible for women to maintain themselves honourably by their own exertions?"

"I can only say, that there are a great many women who succeed extremely well in trade; but I would not venture to affirm, that they are among the most amiable and pleasing of their sex: they have in general limited understandings, cold hearts, and vulgar manners."

"But at least, sir, they are most estimable," returned Esther, with singular animation. "It is a noble thing to owe no one anything, and to attain by one's own exertions, to an independent and honourable existence!"

"Certainly!" said Chevillard, much surprised at the excited manner of his intended, whilst making this remark. But he immediately recollected, that Madame de Saint-Martin was said to treat her adopted daughter with some degree of harshness, and therefore he could have easily accounted for the admiration which the latter expressed for those, who have attained independence by the successful exercise of their talents, even if that adroit lady had not quickly observed: "You see, my dear sir, there is a certain tendency to romantic ideas, and I am glad you should know of it beforehand, because it is a little defect which you will have to look after when you are married."

Viewed in either of these lights, Esther's sudden animation could not be displeasing to her lover; on the contrary, the elevated sentiments she had so spontaneously expressed, gave him a still more advantageous opinion of her to whom he was soon to unite his destiny. Nothing more passed worthy of being recorded; Chevillard left soon after, promising to call on Legros the next morning, to make arrangements for the speedy termination of the necessary preliminaries, and reached home more satisfied, and more in love than ever.

CHAPTER VIII.

WHEN Chevillard presented himself at the law-agent's on the following day, he was told by the servant, that her master was engaged on important business with a client, but that he begged, he would call again in the course of the morning. Now the clerk, who, the day before, had occasioned so much mischief and sorrow by his indiscreet communi-

cation, did not live far from the Rue des Moulins; he was one of the book-keeper's particular friends, and from the first, our lover had thought of asking him to be one of his witnesses. Having therefore some time upon his hands, he resolved to pay a visit to this young man, partly that he might prefer his request in proper time, and partly because, like all happy people, he felt an irresistible desire to speak of his good fortune.

Upon seeing him enter at so early an hour, his friend at first thought that he might have come to call him to account for his babbling the day before; he was therefore agreeably surprised, when, instead of the reproaches he expected, he heard that a favour was to be solicited. As Chevillard did not mention the altercation which he had occasioned, he felt bound to offer some excuses for his apparent indiscretion, and frankly confessed that his real motive had been to verify certain reports which were prevalent in the trade, relative to the particular favour with which Mademoiselle Lebeau was said to honour her head-clerk. He added, that from the way the poor girl had *fired up* at the mere mention of the ladies in whose company Chevillard had been detected, he could no longer doubt the truth of these rumours, and he warmly congratulated his friend on the excellent match which was at his disposal.

"It is a very strange thing," replied Chevillard; "everybody talks to me of this wonderful passion, of which I have really never seen the slightest indication. But, at all events, my dear friend," continued he, with a confident air, "I have something better than that in view."

"How! better than that? I think, if you marry such an agreeable woman, and become the master of an establishment like the *Tricoloured Prism*, you may consider yourself a confoundedly lucky dog."

"Perhaps so; but I aim at higher things. And it is to ask you to be one of the witnesses to this union, which I must say will be rather a cut above the common, that I have come here this morning."

"Why, bless my soul! what princess *are* you going to marry?"

"What did you think of the young lady with whom you saw me at the opera?"

"Charming! on my honour. But tell me, is she the person in question?"

" Yes, my dear fellow, that's the sort of girl for me ; nothing less would do."

" And where the deuce did you meet with such a treasure? You must give me the address ; I have been thinking for some time of putting my head in the noose."

" Oh! it was all chance, and by means of a friend."

" Of course, the kernel answers to the shell ; the fortune is worth stooping for?"

" No, there is no fortune in the case," said Chevillard, assuming a contrite look, as if he were confessing a fault."

" Ah! that's another story; the sun's shorn of its beams!"

" Yes, she is a portionless girl, whom I marry for her beauty alone," continued Chevillard, in the same tone; " only, as a sort of encouragement, she procures for me a situation worth six thousand francs."

" What did you say?" returned the other, in great surprise.

" I said a situation worth six thousand francs, and perhaps the prospect of making a large fortune in the commissariat-department; you see, this may be considered quite as an imprudent love-match."

The witness elect asked for some further particulars of his friend's singular good fortune, and Chevillard put him in possession of the general bearings of the affair, omitting some details which it appeared to him unnecessary to mention, such as Esther's illegitimate birth, and the widowhood and prompt absence by which his marriage was to be followed.

" Well, my dear fellow, I congratulate you," said the confidant of these brilliant prospects; " but would you wish to hear my candid opinion?"

" With whom should you speak freely, if not with me?" replied Chevillard.

" Well, then, if I were in your place, I should have contented myself with Mademoiselle Lebeau; this match would have been more suitable for you than the other."

" Come, come, my good fellow, you don't say what you think."

" I beg your pardon; the more I think about it, the more it seems to me that you are leaving gold for tinsel."

" So you think nothing of a salary such as not one house in the trade would give, and the chance of making a

fortune like a nabob, with a little skill and perseverance."

" Oh, certainly, that is all very fine; but you will enter a family of which you know nothing, and who may one day taunt you with your mercantile origin ; instead of being at the head of a flourishing establishment, you will be dependent upon a contractor, and such men often promise more than they perform. They make use of others to serve their own ends, and then forget them. Besides, their business is a very hazardous one. If I were you, I would think twice of it."

" Why don't you tell me too, that I am wrong to marry a pretty woman, whose beauty may expose me to a thousand troubles !" said Chevillard, ironically, for he imagined that a secret feeling of jealousy dictated these remarks.

" Well, faith! you would not be the first; such things have been, you know."

" So then," returned Chevillard, " you refuse to be witness to a union, which according to you must inevitably lead to my ruin?"

" I said no such thing; and as for my advice, make what use you please of it."

" Then I depend on you, my dear fellow," said the book-keeper; and wishing to escape from a conversation which annoyed him, he was preparing to depart, when his friend the *damper* exclaimed: " But, I say, man, have you plenty of ready cash, that you are going to marry in such style?"

" On the contrary, I make a stylish marriage, because I was never so hard-up in my life."

" Indeed! and the *corbeille*,* who is to pay for that?"

" The deuce !" exclaimed Chevillard, who had not thought of this difficulty; " that's true enough, what you say!"

" My dear fellow, I wish I could assist you ; but I myself am out at elbows."

" Ah! I know some one who will manage that matter," said our hero, after some little reflection ; " we shall not make shipwreck for such a trifle as that."

Then begging his prudent friend not to mention the circumstance of his intended marriage to any one, as it might excite a great deal of envious feeling, and put in commotion the *whole silk-market*, he wished him good morning.

* The usual presents offered by the bridegroom to the bride.

The friend promised inviolable secrecy, and Chevillard set off once more to seek Legros, judging that he must be by this time disengaged. As soon as he entered, the law-agent exclaimed : " Well, Mr. Lover, was last evening's interview satisfactory ?"

" Perfectly so," replied Chevillard ; and he related all that had passed and been agreed on. He even mentioned Esther's enthusiastic sally on the subject of women engaged in trade, whose position she appeared to envy ; and Legros concurred with him in the supposition, that the young girl had taken that opportunity to protest against the somewhat despotic sway of Madame de Saint-Martin. Many necessary formalities were then discussed, and everything being satisfactorily concluded, Chevillard, after some hesitation, addressed Legros as follows : " My kind protector, we have forgotten one very important point."

" What is that ?" said the law-agent.

" It is impossible for me to think of marrying in my present position."

" What ! impossible for you to marry !" cried the other, in the greatest amazement. " Are you mad ?"

" My dear sir, you are better acquainted than any one with my straitened means ; and I ask you, how can I provide suitable marriage presents ?"

" Oh, is that all !" said Legros, as if relieved from a load of anxiety.

" Why, it is *something*, to have to purchase a *corbeille !*"

" My dear fellow, do you wish to offend Esther's guardian ?"

" Certainly not."

" Then be so good as to abandon all such extravagant notions. Morizot is a practical man ; he is aware of your position as to fortune, it was my duty to inform him of everything (always excepting the gambling-adventure, you know), and if he saw you incur useless expenses, and reap before you sow, I can assure you, he would be quite capable of breaking off the marriage."

" But yet, this is a customary thing, and ——"

" My dear fellow, your marriage is a thing quite out of the common way, and therefore cannot be judged by ordinary rules. Besides, Esther is loaded with presents by Madame de Saint-Martin, who has always supplied her with everything suitable, as well as by Morizot, who is as proud of her as if she were his own daughter, so do not conjure up difficulties where they do not really exist ; to tell you the truth, the question has been already considered, and it has been settled that nothing is expected from you."

" Well," said Chevillard, " if that is the case, I will say no more about it."

" Yes, yes, my boy," continued Legros, accompanying him out, " make your mind easy ; try to gain the affections of your intended, and in twelve days' time—for I hope there will be no longer delay—you will tell me what you think of the treasure and the angel I have helped you to."

———

CHAPTER IX.

EVERYTHING seemed to smile on Chevillard ; there was only one drawback to his satisfaction, and this was the thought how Mademoiselle Lebeau would receive the confidence he intended to repose in her.

As he had never given any credit to the reports which had been circulated respecting her affection for him, he did not suppose that the announcement of his approaching marriage could awaken any painful emotions in the heart of this amiable young girl. But in a commercial point of view, he was persuaded she *must* regret extremely the loss of such an intelligent and experienced clerk, and he therefore anticipated a storm of remonstrances and advice, or at the very least a cold acquiescence, which held out no very agreeable prospect for the short time he should remain in the house. In fine, he felt this interview to be a regular bore ; but as he could not avoid it, he resolved to get it over as quickly as possible. As soon therefore as he reached home, assuming a gravity which he considered befitted the important revelation he was going to make, he requested to have some private conversation with Mademoiselle Lebeau. The amiable and single-hearted girl imagined, that Chevillard was weary of the sort of latent hostility which had existed between them during the last few days, and as sullen and resentful feelings were completely foreign to her nature, she not only complied instantly with his request, but secretly resolved to be very placable, and to forget and forgive at the first word of conciliation.

" Mademoiselle," Chevillard began, " I have too constantly experienced the kindness of your excellent father and yourself, not to feel profoundly grateful."

"Mr. Chevillard," replied the young lady, "if you have been satisfied with our conduct towards you, I can assure you we have always been perfectly satisfied with your services, and I take with pleasure this opportunity of expressing as much to you."

"Nevertheless," continued the accountant, "and though I must say that my position in this establishment is in every respect desirable, I am bound to think of the future; and that which is well suited to a young man, may be no longer so as we advance in life."

The conversation appeared to be taking a turn not unpleasing to Mademoiselle Lebeau, as it accorded with certain plans of her own. So she answered, gaily: "Fortunately, you have still some years before you."

"True; but our determinations are often influenced by circumstances. I beg you to believe, that nothing but a very peculiar and unexpected occurrence could have induced me to leave this house."

"Leave!" exclaimed Mademoiselle Lebeau; "you surely cannot intend to do that!"

"I beg your pardon; my resolution is taken, and I have entered into engagements from which I cannot recede."

"Then decidedly, Mr. Chevillard, you have not the good disposition for which I gave you credit. I should never have thought, that the little disagreement which has taken place, would have led you to form a determination like that which you have just announced with so much indifference."

"You mistake, mademoiselle, when you suppose me influenced by the slight misunderstanding to which you allude. I assure you, I too sincerely regret this separation, to have resolved upon it for a trifling cause."

"Well, then!——" said Mademoiselle Lebeau, very kindly, for she thought he wished to retract.

"I think, mademoiselle, you will appreciate the importance of my motive, when I tell you, that I only leave you—to be married."

At these words, the fair mercer changed countenance; but the impression passed away with the rapidity of lightning, and the force of emotion was repressed by the force of will.

"Ah! you are going to be married! ——that is a different thing, sir——that is all very well!" said she, with a voice which trembled almost imperceptibly.

Chevillard was certainly aware, that his words had produced some degree of agitation, but as he was morally incapable of comprehending the energy with which a strong mind represses all outward manifestations of emotion, he judged from these slight appearances, that the *commercial cuticle* alone (so to speak) had been touched, and therefore proceeded boldly to give a more detailed account of his prospects. "Yes, mademoiselle," said he, "it is a very desirable connexion, and one much beyond my expectations. The young lady is gifted with great personal charms, and places me in a position as to fortune——"

"And when is this marriage to take place?" abruptly interposed Mademoiselle Lebeau, who did not conceive herself obliged to listen with unwearied patience to the long account of his good fortune, which Chevillard appeared disposed to inflict upon her.

"In about a fortnight's time."

"That is well!" said the fair mercer, in as indifferent a tone as she could assume; "I will immediately make inquires for some one to replace you;— and indeed, as it is not difficult to meet with a book-keeper, and I can take charge of the cash-department in the interim, I beg you will consider yourself as at liberty from this time, if that suits your views better."

Chevillard had not imagined, that Mademoiselle Lebeau would receive his communication in so chilling and careless a manner; he would have greatly preferred a sharp opposition, for this had at least enabled him to talk of his happy prospects, and to flatter himself that his services were regretted. However, he would not allow himself to be thus put on the shelf without ceremony.

"Mademoiselle," said he, "I think you are in a great hurry to get rid of me, and yet you allow that you are quite satisfied with my services; how is this?"

"I assure you, that you are most welcome to remain here so long as you find it convenient; but I know there is always a great deal to be done on such occasions, and I thought it would be agreeable to you to be at liberty as soon as possible."

"You must be aware, mademoiselle, that I cannot treat your residence as a lodging-house: if you dispense with my services, I can certainly not remain."

"Well, Mr. Chevillard," said the fair mercer, gently, "if you think you can still, without much inconvenience to yourself, give a little attention to my affairs, I am far from opposing your wishes; so do exactly as you please."

"It is very strange!" resumed the mortified book-keeper; "I imagined, from the marks of kindness with which you have so often favoured me, that you would take more interest in the happy event which I have just communicated to you."

"Ah! my dear sir," replied Mademoiselle Lebeau, "it is so difficult to know whether he who enters into the marriage-state has a chance for happiness or for misery. He can never expect unqualified and warm approbation but from himself."

"But I consider, that I am acting prudently and advantageously for the future," said Chevillard, much piqued.

"I fervently hope it may be the case," replied Mademoiselle Lebeau, without however infusing much *fervour* into her tone; and rising as she said this, she went into her bedroom, leaving Chevillard sufficiently disappointed by the manner in which his confidence had been received. Here she was soon interrupted by the principal shopwoman, who afterwards informed her companions, with an air of great mystery, that she could not tell *what ailed Mademoiselle*—that she seemed to be quite upset, and her eyes were red and swollen, as if she had been crying.

The mortified clerk, meantime, deliberated for a moment, whether he would leave the house immediately or not. But he did not much like the idea of settling elsewhere for a few days, and as he felt that a precipitate departure would look like a decided rupture, he quickly abandoned all thought of so intemperate and improper a proceeding. He went to his books as if nothing unusual had occurred, but his thoughts wandered from the task before him, for his self-love had been deeply wounded; and though his heart and head were engrossed by the thought of his beautiful intended, Mademoiselle Lebeau's discouraging remarks had awakened a vague feeling of doubt, such as is often felt on the eve of a decisive resolution.

When Mademoiselle Lebeau had paid the first tribute to female weakness, she roused all her energy, and so effectually subdued the bitterness of her grief, that it would have been difficult for the most vigilant eye to penetrate her feelings.

Exposed during dinner to the general observation, she was grave without being sad; and though her mind was visibly preoccupied, no one would have guessed that it was by any deeper interest than matters of business, as had often been the case before. Her strong good sense preserved her from the common error of wishing to appear gay. A secret grief is never so near betraying itself, as when it strives to assume the mask of thoughtless mirth.

The morning's conversation had been so abruptly terminated, that Chevillard neglected to recommend secrecy to his fair employer, and he now took an opportunity to do this, with the hope of resuming the account of his felicity and grand prospects. But the young lady, who had not the same reasons for taking pleasure in the subject, dexterously parried his attempt, and briefly promising inviolable discretion, she left home to visit a friend in the neighbourhood, though it was quite contrary to her usual custom to go out during the week. But Chevillard was far from suspecting what passed in the heart of this young girl. To him, the whole proceeding seemed to indicate that sordid, mercantile egotism, which cannot forgive any one who deprives it of valuable services. He had unconsciously inflicted a severe wound, at the very time he was accusing her of being, like all people in trade, thinking only of her own interests, and utterly devoid of sensibility. When he compared her with his charming and adorable Esther, his love for the latter seemed to increase, and he surrendered himself to the thought of passing a delightful evening in her society.

Having provided himself with a splendid nosegay to present to his betrothed, he reached the house in the Allée des Veuves, just as the commissary was leaving it. He was received by Esther with a commencement of affectionate familiarity; and his good looks, cheerful temper, and especially the sympathetic influence of a sincere and ardent passion, bid fair to increase rapidly the favourable impression he had made. He was now admitted into the intimacy of the family, and during the long hours he passed with this amiable girl, he discovered fresh proofs of that impulse towards everything noble and estimable, which she had manifested at his first visit on the footing of a declared lover. Notwithstanding the faults of which Chevillard had been guilty at no very distant period, he was of an honourable nature, and could sympathise in her enthusiasm without hypocrisy, and without effort. This interchange of sentiments increased their mutual attachment; we say *mutual*, for Chevillard's affection soon found an echo in the heart of his intended, and harmony and confidence reigned between them. The lover did not fail to question Esther concerning the suspected harshness of Madame de Saint-Martin's maternal sway; and, though she at first denied that it was so, she was afterwards less anxious to conceal the traces of the secret misunderstanding, which evidently existed between them. As for Madame de Saint-Martin herself, she continued to overwhelm Chevillard with attentions; but as, in his character of a lover, he considered himself bound to espouse all the supposed grievances of his beloved, he cordially disliked the poor lady, though, in regard to himself, he could make no complaint against her, for she had always treated him with the greatest cordiality.

It is impossible to go frequently to a house, without seeing a little behind the scenes. Chevillard often met Legros at the Allée des Veuves, and he could not help thinking that there was something more between him and the matronly lady of the dwelling, than the Platonic friendship they professed. This discovery gave him some doubts as to the propriety of leaving his young wife under the care of a woman whose conduct was not irreproachable, and at the same time it threw light upon the grievances to which Esther was subjected, and afforded an explanation for the fits of musing which he had remarked at their first interview, and in which she still frequently indulged. He supposed, as was indeed very likely, that aware of the real state of the case, the virtuous girl was pained and shocked by the irregularities of those around her; and if he had dared to ask her the plain question, his supicions would, doubtless, have been fully confirmed. But he feared to alarm her innocence, and resolved to postpone, until they were married, an explanation of all that now appeared obscure. Upon mature consideration, Esther's prolonged residence with Madame de Saint-Martin did not appear to him open to very serious objections; for, if, when a young girl, abandoned to the guidance of her own excellent nature, his betrothed had so evidently preserved herself pure from the habitual contact of her companion, how much more capable would she be of doing so, when protected by his advice, and the experience of her married life.

There was an additional security too, when he considered the character of Morizot. He had, at first sight, taken a strange prejudice against this man, but as he became better acquainted with him, he soon learned to alter his opinion. Morizot came very rarely to the house, and his visits were always short, but he evinced a truly paternal affection for Esther—an attachment in which warm devotion was blended with the most becoming reserve. Certainly, if he had thought that his ward was not in sure hands, he would not have left her in so dangerous a situation, but would instantly have given every attention to the subject. The confidence of the guardian ought to give confidence to the husband.

By this brief exposition of the posture of affairs in the house of the Allée des Veuves, and in that of the *Tricoloured Prism*, we have made the reader acquainted with the situation of the various personages of our tale, down to the day before the wedding, which, thanks to the zeal and activity of Legros, had experienced no other delay than that which was commanded by the law.

CHAPTER X.

ON the morning of the day alluded to in the last chapter, Chevillard was dressing to go out, with the intention of calling on his witnesses, to inform them of the hour fixed for the ceremony, when he received a message from Mademoiselle Lebeau, who wished to speak with him.

He had not seen her for two days, and was struck with the alteration visible in her countenance, which, nevertheless, retained its usual mild and sweet expression.

" You have anticipated my intention, mademoiselle," said Chevillard, as he, entered, " for though my marriage is apparently, not so agreeable to you as I could wish, I should certainly have made a point of informing you, that it will take place to-morrow, and begging you to honour me with your presence on the occasion."

"Indeed," replied Mademoiselle Lebeau, " I am afraid that will not be possible; the weather is extremely cold, and I have not felt well for some days."

She then arose, and going to her desk, took out a little note-case in green morocco, garnished with steel ornaments, and turning to her former clerk: " Mr. Chevillard," said she, in a tremulous voice, "now that we are going to part, I thought you would allow me to treat you as one of the family, and to present you with this slight token of remembrance of *those* you leave behind."

As she spoke, she presented the portfolio to the young man, who received it with thanks, and praised the elegance and good taste displayed in its construction.

Politeness required that he should glance at the inside, and on doing so, he found that it contained several banknotes.

"Permit me, mademoiselle," said he immediately, "to keep the case—but to leave its contents."

"Mr. Chevillard," returned the lady, "I quite expected that you would object to my putting anything into this portfolio; but allow me to explain to you the right which I have to leave it as it now is. For a long time, I have wished to mark my sense of your excellent services, by raising your salary to a more suitable amount, and this is only the arrears of a large debt of gratitude which I have purposely allowed to accumulate. You will surely not deprive me at the same moment, of your valuable co-operation and of the pleasure I feel in acknowledging the good effects it has had on my interests; it would be too selfish in you to wish me to remain in your debt, just as you take from me all opportunity of acquitting myself in future."

"Certainly, mademoiselle, you turn this in the most delicate manner; but it is raising a painful source of discussion at this moment, and I must beg you to accede to my wishes, and not say anything more on the subject."

"Listen to me," said the young girl: "there were certainly many ways in which I might have made you accept, without hesitation, a proof of my gratitude; for I presume you do not question my privilege, as mistress of this establishment, to offer you a wedding present. Well! I had a reason for choosing this form of conveying it, though I foresaw your present resistance. Shall I tell you that reason?"

"No one should be condemned without being heard," replied Chevillard, rather happily inspired.

"I know that you have not saved much——"

"You may say nothing; you have often remonstrated with me about it."

"I believe you are going to contract a wealthy alliance——"

"A very eligible one at least," interrupted the triumphant bridegroom.

"Well, in such a case, you will be expected to incur certain expenses, which can only be met by contracting ruinous loans. I am sure you would not wish to act differently from others; and why, when this little capital is strictly yours, should you have recourse to any other purse? I am your debtor, and you call in the debt to meet a pressing emergency."

"Mademoiselle, you are ingenious in your kindness, but I assure you, that nothing of the kind is expected from me; I have been expressly desired to avoid such expenses."

"Take care; in such cases people often like to be disobeyed, and are sometimes internally much vexed by a strict adherence to their requests. Besides, this will not enable you to transgress very far."

"No, I beg, mademoiselle, you will excuse me——"

"Then I take back the portfolio also!" exclaimed Mademoiselle Lebeau, with great vivacity. "It shall not be said, that you left this house without carrying with you the shadow of a remembrance. Indeed, if you did, it would be a restraint upon you; you would not be able to forget us quickly enough!"

"Ah! mademoiselle, do not think that; I can never forget the kindness I have experienced in this house."

"Yes, sir, you will. He who knows not how to receive has a bad heart, and a bad heart has no memories, especially in friendship."

"Well, mademoiselle, I yield to your wishes," returned Chevillard, who began to be much affected by this scene; "but do not say again, that I am in haste to prove myself ungrateful."

"That is right; I thank you," said the noble-minded girl, deeply moved by the sacrifice Chevillard had made of his feelings. "But, indeed," added she, trying to smile, "I did not really think as I spoke; after passing ten years under the same roof, and in daily intercourse with *people*, the thought of them will sometimes return to the mind."

"I trust," replied Chevillard, "that we shall do more than remember each other. You must allow me to introduce my wife to you; she will be delighted to make your acquaintance, and I hope we shall often see you."

"Do not deceive yourself," returned Mademoiselle Lebeau; "there is such a thing as distinction of classes; you enter a rich family, and you must not expect that they will either wish or condescend to visit a shopkeeper."

"Mademoiselle, you are mistaken; persons like you must be well received everywhere."

"Well, no matter!" resumed the fair mercer; "I only wish you may be happy."

"There is at least every prospect ——"

"Well, do not let me detain you any longer; on such a day as this, you must have much to attend to."

"I cannot venture again to solicit your presence at the ceremony, as your health might suffer from it," said Chevillard, rising, "but I shall be deprived of a great happiness."

"I do not say no; I will endeavour to go," returned the young girl, trying to conceal all traces of the struggle that was passing within. "Adieu, Mr.

Chevillard," added she; "think of us sometimes."

These words were spoken in so sad a tone, that they were a tardy revelation to Chevillard of the pain he had inflicted on the heart he had so cruelly misunderstood. When he looked at the noble-minded and courageous victim, he saw that she was pale, and that her eyes were filled with tears; and on taking her hand, he found it cold and trembling. As the truth rushed upon his mind, he seemed to lose all power of expressing his feelings, and it was with a faltering voice, that he replied: " Adieu, mademoiselle."

" Adieu !" repeated Mademoiselle Lebeau, with an expression that disclosed her whole heart; and Chevillard too must have been deeply affected, for, as he left the room, he stopped to wipe the tears from his eyes.

CHAPTER XI.

WHEN movement in the open air had in some degree restored our hero to calmness, he began to reflect on the singular disclosure which had taken place. The question was now among the *might-have-beens*, and he asked himself if it would have been better for him to have known, while it was yet time, that which had just been revealed *in extremis*.

He was painfully affected, certainly, to find that he was the involuntary cause of the grief to which the poor young lady remained a prey, but time and another attachment would doubtless bring consolation; and with regard to himself, he had really no reason to regret that he had not been undeceived before it was too late. Reason would have urged him to accept the alliance, if it had been proposed to him in time; but then he would have bound himself to trade for life, while he felt an irresistible impulse to enter upon a wider and more elevated sphere; and besides, notwithstanding the many excellent qualities which Mademoiselle Lebeau indisputably possessed, could he be sure that the imperious and domineering spirit she had sometimes shown, would not have disturbed the harmony of their union?

" Well," thought he, dismissing these now useless reflections, " Providence orders everything for the best;" and recurring to the most material interest he could think of, in order to dispel the sentimental mist which clouded his faculties, he resolved to ascertain the contents of the portfolio, which had been pressed upon him with such ingenious delicacy. He found in it four bank-notes of a thousand francs each; that is to say, a gratuity equivalent to more than a year's salary. If Legros had not so positively signified that he was to resist the dictates of his generosity, he would have found an immediate use for this sum, and indulged in one of the most delicious pleasures of this world, namely, that of giving to those we love; but this satisfaction was denied him, and he therefore thought of another useful and honourable destination for the money; it would serve to free him from his gambling debt, and cancel the bill of exchange.

In pursuance of this design, he repaired to the law-agent, and after some desultory conversation, announced his intention of coming to a settlement with him.

Legros did not meet this overture with the satisfaction which would have been natural in a creditor, and observed drily: " So then, you have been playing again, notwithstanding your promises ?"

" You are mistaken, my dear sir," replied Chevillard; and to remove all suspicion as to the source whence he had obtained the money, he added: " My employer, when I took leave of her, obliged me to accept this acknowledgment of my services."

" You ought not to have taken this present," interrupted the law-agent with great asperity; " from the day on which you announced to this person your intention of leaving her house, all connexion with her should have been at an end."

" My dear Mr. Legros, allow me to observe, that you don't know how the thing took place. I was so situated, that it was impossible to refuse."

" I tell you again, you ought not to have taken this money."

" And I tell you, that in doing so, I acted rightly and wisely. I should have singular notions of honour, if I threw away the means offered me to discharge so sacred a debt as mine is."

" This debt seems to weigh heavily upon your mind," said Legros, bitterly.

" Not so, for I have to do with an indulgent creditor; but still, it is a debt, and I wish to clear myself, now that I have the means in my power."

" It is incredible people should have

so little perception of these niceties of sentiment !" cried the law-agent, as if thinking aloud.

"How! niceties?" said Chevillard; "I do not know what you mean."

"As soon as you have this money in your possession, you come to insult me by an offer of repayment."

"My dear friend, you take things as they are not meant."

"It is you, on the contrary, who have no perception of what is proper. Is it possible you do not feel, that in your peculiar position there is but *one* way of appropriating the money?"

"I am not sure that I understand you," said Chevillard; "do you mean to say that I ought to expend it in wedding presents?"

"You pretend to be in love," returned Legros, "and you ask such a question!"

"Why, devil of a fellow that you are!" cried the good-natured young man, with an impatience that had nothing very serious in it at bottom, "you told me, yourself, that by appearing extravagant, I should get into disgrace with Mr. Morizot."

"I believe you!" replied the law-agent; "you wished to play the gallant at the expense of my pocket!"

"What an odd being you are!" said Chevillard, laughing at this ingenuous confession; "you will not take your money when I wish to return it, and you invent tales to avoid lending any."

"My dear fellow, you cannot comprehend anything; I tell you again, that Morizot knows your debtor and creditor account to a penny, and that the balance is exactly—nothing."

"Well, what then?" said Chevillard.

"To launch out into expenses would have been to tell him you had been bleeding my purse; whilst on the contrary, having money of your own, you employ it as custom dictates, and you act only in a becoming and generous manner."

"So we come back to my original idea. Ah, well! it has not been without trouble. But, tell me, what purchases would you advise me to make with the thousand crowns I had brought you?"

"A thousand crowns, is that the sum at your disposal?"

"I have four thousand francs, but I keep back a fourth part for unforeseen expenses; you cannot say I throw money out of the windows."

"Humph! with a thousand crowns you might get some pretty trinkets, some shawls, or — I really don't know exactly. But," continued he, with assumed indifference, "you doubtless mean to make some little offering to Madame de Saint-Martin?"

"It would perhaps be proper; what do you think?"

"I think, my dear fellow, that a present is always agreeable to a woman, unless it be offered as an insult to her virtue."

"Certainly; but what sort of present would be best?"

"Ah!" cried Legros, impatiently; "I see there is no making you understand things. Come now, you must suppose that a curiosity-hunter like myself has some acquaintances in the trade;" and he glanced round at his immense collection.

"Yes, but I will not buy anything shabby."

"On no account; I should not wish you to have old rubbish, but if you think that a man who has some taste and great experience in buying, can assist you in any way, I am at your service, for the day will soon slip away."

"Really, my dear sir, your offer is very acceptable, and here is the money."

"Very well," said Legros; "at what time this evening do you intend to be in the Allée des Veuves?"

"Seven o'clock at the latest," replied Chevillard.

"Then I will be there about that time; and as we have not funds sufficient to furnish a regular *corbeille*, the presents must be offered in a quiet way, without ceremony."

"All is settled then," said Chevillard. "Select the best you can find for Esther, and something pretty for Madame de Saint-Martin, but not so as to take too much from the other present."

"I will do my best, and I think you will be satisfied," returned Legros.

Upon this, the lover took his leave, having done, as is too often the case in life, exactly the contrary of that which he intended.

———

CHAPTER XII.

THE eve of Chevillard's marriage might truly be called a day of tears. When he reached the Allée des Veuves, he found Esther more than ever a prey to that vague melancholy the true cause of which was as yet unknown to him, and he even thought that she had been crying. He seated himself by her side, and questioned her tenderly on the source of her grief; but she gave him no satisfactory explanation, and at length his self-love was alarmed; he feared that his intended felt a secret repugnance at the approaching union. When he mentioned his fears, Esther answered in a manner which proved that she was strongly attached to him; but still pressed to discover the reason of her sadness, she at last said: " Perhaps, it would be better for this marriage not to take place!"

" Are you crazy, to talk thus?" cried Madame de Saint-Martin. " Have your inclinations been forced? Could you not say this at first, instead of waiting to the last moment?"

" I did not know at first what I know now," replied Esther.

" What is it that you know? What has been told you, concerning me?" cried Chevillard, with warmth.

" Nothing, sir; and it is because I have known how to appreciate your worth, that I hesitate at this moment."

" Indeed, that is singular; if I were a worthless, unprincipled man, would you then prefer me?"

Esther did not answer; so that, notwithstanding the absurdity of Chevillard's supposition, it was not contradicted. This unpleasantly enigmatical conversation had proceeded so far, when the door opened, and Legros entered. " How now?" said he, seeing that every brow was clouded; —" you all look as if you had been quarrelling!"

" Oh! it's Esther," replied Madame de Saint-Martin, impatiently, " who is making a scene about I know not what, and says that, perhaps the marriage had better not take place."

" The deuce she does!" exclaimed Legros; " but when things are so far advanced, they are not to be broken off so easily; and besides, here I come with my pockets full of ornaments, which Chevillard had commissioned me to buy. Now, how pleasant it will be to have to take all these things back again!"

" How, sir!" said Esther, looking gratefully at her lover; " you have been kind enough to think of me?"

" See," continued Legros, drawing a jewel-case from his pocket, " only look at this set of turquoises, and this diamond hoop, and these clasps in brilliants—and then, for Madame de Saint-Martin, this *solitaire*—and tell me if a man of so much gallantry is one to be discarded?"

" Truly!" said Chevillard, " if that were my only merit in the eyes of this lady, it would not avail me much."

" Do not deceive yourself, my dear fellow," replied Legros, with a very singular expression of voice; " women like such toys—Mademoiselle Esther especially. She is a spoiled girl, and would think it very hard to give up luxuries, and live poorly——and with the game she is now playing, that might come to pass sooner than she thinks."

" I do not understand you," said Esther, with much dignity.

" And I know very well what I mean," replied the law-agent. " You ought to be aware, my dear young lady, that Morizot is a positive man, who does not like caprices. When you were spoken to about this marriage, you did not offer any objection; and upon that consent, a positive engagement was founded. The situation to which Chevillard has been appointed, has been left open for him during the last fortnight; and if now, from a whim, you overthrow all these arrangements, take care—it may not be merely a marriage which is broken off! The protection to which you have been indebted for an existence which thousands would envy, may perhaps fail you at last!"

" As for me," said Madame de Saint-Martin, " I am not in a position to make perpetual sacrifices for other people; and whatever Mr. Morizot thinks proper to do, I shall conform to."

Esther made no reply, but she threw upon the woman who had spoken with so much harshness, a look of profound contempt.

" Mademoiselle," Chevillard then said, in a tone which showed that his feelings were deeply wounded, " this marriage would have made me the happiest of men; but I find it is not so agreeable to you as I had hoped. Under these circumstances, I can no longer think of it; but you shall not have to account to Mr. Morizot for your refusal; *I* now withdraw my pretensions, and when I reach home, I will write to him on the subject."

So saying, he rose, looked for his hat, which on such occasions is never to be found immediately, and was preparing to leave the room, when Esther's voice arrested his steps.

" Mr. Chevillard!" cried she, in accents which expressed the affection she had conceived for him.

" No, no!" replied the lover, again

turning to withdraw; " I am the source of trouble to you; we had better part."

" Come now, let us have done with this comedy," interposed Legros, taking him by the arm, and forcing him into the seat he had quitted. " It was only a whim of Esther's; I was sure that when I showed her the consequences of her conduct, she would be more tractable, for she loves you at bottom."

" But how can I have displeased her," said Chevillard, dolefully, " that she should so suddenly wish to break off an alliance which appeared to be quite decided ?"

" Oh! all nonsense," returned Legros; " some young girl's fancy! Perhaps, she thought you might one day reproach her with the slight irregularity of her birth."

" If my mother has not thought fit to discover herself," replied Esther, with a pride which disavowed the explanation offered by the law-agent, " I know who my father was; he was the Marquis de Brevannes, and he has not refused me his name."

" Mademoiselle," said Chevillard, " when Legros first mentioned the circumstance, I told him that I considered myself honoured by your deigning to accept me."

" Well now, I tell you what it is," resumed Legros, ready to give another turn to the strange freak of his fair friend; " I think, between ourselves, you know, that Esther is less reasonable than you are. She doesn't fancy her husband's being sent off so soon after the wedding, and I dare say she has had some words with her guardian on the subject, and has threatened to break off the marriage. Women are like that; they would rather give up a thing than not have it just as they please."

" If it indeed be so," cried the delighted lover, " I must scold her for her want of fortitude; but, I cannot be angry at her taking my interests to heart, and I love her the better for it, if that be possible."

" Yes, Mr. Chevillard, love me," said the young girl, in a tone of deep solemnity and feeling, " for I also love you; do not wonder at my frankness in telling you so. Perhaps it would have been better if we had never met."

" Ah!" interrupted Chevillard; " why that odious idea ?"

" I will not recur to it again," replied Esther; " I think that love may indeed compensate for all my deficiencies; and

I now, before God, take the solemn engagement, that from this day forward, I will live but for your happiness, and will be always the wife you hoped to find in me."

" Well, now!" said Legros; " that is something like."

" Yes, sir," continued the young girl, her beautiful countenance radiant with expression, " I know what I am saying; every day of my life shall be devoted to deserve my husband's love."

" You see, my dear son-in-law," said Madame de Saint-Martin, " her young head is full of romance, as I told you before."

But Chevillard heard her not. He had seized the hands of this strange girl, and covered them with kisses and tears. " Esther! my beloved! my wife!" were the only words he could find to express his emotion.

" Well!" said the law-agent; " as we are now all of one mind, do just oblige me by looking at my purchases."

" I am too agitated," replied Esther; " Mr. Chevillard will excuse my leaving him alone with you. To-morrow!" added she, extending her hand to her lover.

Chevillard made no attempt to detain her; he could comprehend that religion of the heart, which seeks solitude to muse over a beloved object, and he would not have contemplated with more ecstatic rapture, an angel who had quitted him to return to heaven.

After Esther had retired, he remained for a few moments to listen to Madame de Saint-Martin's account of a conversation which had passed between Morizot and his ward, in which, as Legros had before stated, the latter had warmly protested against her husband's banishment; then, after receiving the thanks of the good lady, for the handsome present that Legros had just delivered to her, he took his leave. It was still early in the evening; but he too felt the want of solitude, to recover from the agitation occasioned by the varied emotions of the last few hours.

Lovers, in the words of an old comedy, are eccentric animals; so it was nothing surprising, that Chevillard should remain a full quarter of an hour outside the house, gazing at the light which shone from the window of the chamber where Esther was perhaps at that moment thinking of him. He did not contemplate it with the less delight, because he remembered, that on the morrow that chamber would be open to him. During this kind of vigil, as it would have been called in the days of chivalry, he reflected too on the singular scene which had taken place; and the conclusion to which he came, after considering all the circumstances, was not exactly such as Madame de Saint-Martin might have wished. He did *not* think that Esther was a fanciful and romantic girl, as that good lady continually insinuated; but he suspected that she paid dearly for the protection of those to whom her childhood had been abandoned, and he resolved to requite the affection of which she had given him such decided proofs, by making her happiness the study of his life.

CHAPTER XIII.

THE next morning—the morning of his wedding day—when Chevillard awoke in the room which he was going to leave for ever, a strange feeling of sadness stole over him. When we are about to bid an eternal farewell to scenes long familiar to us, notwithstanding the happy prospects which may await us elsewhere, our heart swells with painful emotions; and so it was, that, whilst dressing for the ceremony, Mademoiselle Lebeau's former clerk thought of the years he had passed in that pleasant nook, and the many agreeable associations connected with it. He could not but confess, that if this long period of his life had not been marked by great joys or brilliant successes, yet it had been exempt from bitter cares and serious misfortunes.

The two young men, who were to act as his witnesses, arrived soon after, and their presence diverted him from his melancholy thoughts; and on reaching the Allée des Veuves, they found Morizot, Legros, and a friend of the latter, who was to join him as witnesses for Esther, waiting to receive them. In her wedding-dress, the bride shone with such surpassing loveliness, that Chevillard's friends warmly congratulated him on his happiness. Legros was in excellent spirits, and seemed determined to make merry on the occasion; whilst Madame de Saint-Martin, attired in the height of elegance and fashion, was most agreeably occupied in observing the effect she produced upon the company. Morizot alone was grave and thoughtful; you might have supposed that he was calculating the chances of some great financial operation. Esther's reception of her bridegroom bore no

traces of the singular hesitation she had displayed the night before; her demeanour was that of a person who knew perfectly well what she was about to do, and felt that she had no cause for regret.

The wedding-party first proceeded to the mayoralty, and afterwards to the church of St. Peter's at Chaillot, where the young couple received the nuptial benediction, and then returned to breakfast at Madame de Saint-Martin's house. Chevillard's witnesses had been surprised at first, that there were no *relations* present; but this singularity was soon explained, when the papers which related to Esther's family connexion were read at the mayoralty. As *friends* of the bridegroom, they were not displeased to find that there was some alloy in the almost marvellous good fortune of their former comrade. They likewise commented in their own way upon the absence of Mademoiselle Lebeau; and Morizot's splendid equipage, which conveyed the bride, gave rise to some whispered remarks of very *strange* import, to say the least of them.

But there was something gloomy about the whole affair; the guests, few in number, and for the most part strangers to each other, had met probably for the first and last time in their lives, and the breakfast passed off as heavily as might have been expected. Morizot, who was beyond all doubt the person of most consequence present, did not make the slightest effort to set the company at ease, and exhibited a haughty reserve and absence of mind, calculated to repress any attempt at gaiety and animation.

The only one of the guests that seemed to enjoy himself, was the friend Legros had brought; and he did such honour to the banquet, that, towards the end, serious apprehensions were entertained that he would not be able to rise from table. He gave himself out for one of the heroes of the famous *thirty-second demi-brigade*, and told terrible long stories of his campaigns and exploits; and when they adjourned to the drawing-room for coffee, he had reached such a state of elevation, that he insisted on kissing Madame de Saint-Martin, and even forgot himself so far, as to slap the commissary on the stomach, and call him *Father Morizot*.

Legros was at length obliged to carry off this noisy guest, and Morizot ordered his carriage soon after; but before he left, he conversed for a few moments in private with the lady of the house. His departure was almost immediately followed by that of Chevillard's two friends, and the young couple found themselves, to their great satisfaction, alone, or at least with no one but Madame de Saint-Martin to bear them company. After a conversation of two hours' duration, in the course of which the most tender sentiments were mutually expressed, that worthy matron, who retained all the coolness and authority of an actual mother-in-law, told Chevillard that he had been billing and cooing quite long enough, and that as he was to remain in the house until the time appointed for his journey, he had better see to having his effects brought from his former residence. It would have been contrary to all propriety, to have removed these before the ceremony was actually performed.

This was sensible advice, and although it dragged the enraptured husband from the seventh heaven to the level of most terribly prosaic details, he could not consistently neglect it. Tearing himself with the greatest reluctance from the society of his beloved Esther, he tenderly embraced her, and returned to spend the rest of the day in his room, of the Quartier Saint-Denis. Though he made all possible haste with his arrangements, it was nearly six o'clock before he arrived with bag and baggage, to take possession of his new dwelling. It had been agreed that Legros and Morizot should come back to dinner at Madame de Saint-Martin's, and that, to pass away the evening, the whole party should pay a visit to the opera. Legros was punctual, but Morizot did not make his appearance at the appointed time, and at length it grew so late, that they were induced to sit down to table without him.

In the middle of dinner, or rather of supper, for it was now near upon nine o'clock, the commissary arrived; but he wore so reserved and sombre an aspect, that it was easy to see he had been detained on unpleasant business. He seated himself, however, and addressing Chevillard : "My dear sir," said he, "I have bad news for you, and I much fear you will be annoyed at what I am going to communicate."

"What is the matter?" asked the husband, quickly.

"I have just left the First-Consul, who sent for me in the course of the day. He wished to complain of the manner in which the business of my department is conducted at Rochefort, and intimated that I must put it on another footing, with as little delay as possible."

"Ah! Rochefort?" said Legros; "that is where you are going to send Chevillard."

"Exactly so," replied the other; "whilst we were arranging this marriage, the situation I destine to Mr. Chevillard, has remained open; complaints have been sent to Paris, and now not a moment is to be lost to prevent the consequences."

"Alas!" sighed poor Chevillard; "this is a fresh breach you wish to make in my honeymoon; but I must not be unreasonable. When do you wish me to leave? I am at your disposal."

"Why, my dear sir, as soon as possible," replied Morizot; "every hour's delay aggravates the evil."

"Well! suppose I set out on the morning of the day after to-morrow?"

"The day after to-morrow!" repeated the commissary; "I would go myself, rather than wait so long."

"To-morrow then?" asked the doleful husband.

"No, my dear sir, you must make up your mind to go this evening, at once. In half-an-hour a post-chaise will be at the door, for by the stage you would not arrive in time."

"Confound it!" said Legros; "this is deucedly severe!"

"So severe," returned Chevillard, "that I cannot agree to it."

"You are pleased to observe!" demanded Morizot, haughtily.

"I say, that it is impossible for me to leave this evening; and that it is cruelty to expect it."

"Business before pleasure, sir; and when I tell you, that there is an urgent necessity for the step ——"

"I allow that to be the case; but when I consent to leave my wife to-morrow, instead of remaining with her three or four days, according to the original agreement, I think the sacrifice is sufficiently great, and that no more should be demanded from me."

"And where do you expect this resistance will lead you?" observed Morizot, with much asperity; "you have your way to make, and do you imagine that this is a favourable beginning?"

"By six to-morrow morning, if it is necessary, I will be upon the road; but to leave sooner is out of my power, and I will not do it."

"So, this is my reward for so easily consenting to give you Esther!" angrily exclaimed the commissary; "I must thank Legros for introducing you in this house."

"Come, come, be calm," interposed the law-agent; "I can put myself in the place of this poor fellow, and conceive it is quite natural he should make a face at this bitter pill. But he will hear reason; and besides, he is a man of honour, and when you explain to him that a prolonged absence on his part will expose you not only to the reproaches of the First-Consul, but to heavy losses, I know he will call up all his fortitude, and will sacrifice his feelings to his duty."

Chevillard was an upright and sensitive young man; the consideration of the serious injury he might occasion to the commissary made a strong impression on him, and he was yielding in his resolution not to go, when Esther managed, unseen by the others, to make a sign entreating him to hold firm, and persevere in his original intention. There was certainly something very indecorous in the interference of a young girl on such an occasion, to prevent her husband from leaving her on the wedding-night, but this did not occur to Chevillard, and, struck with the proof of attachment thus given him by his fair bride: " No, decidedly," exclaimed he, " I cannot make up my mind to pass this night on the high-road; you may call me superstitious, if you will, but it seems to me that it would be a bad omen, and I really cannot do it."

" Do you consider, sir," said Morizot, " that your dismissal will be the result of this strange conduct?"

Before Chevillard replied, he looked at his wife, and her eyes telling him plainly not to regard this threat: " I am much grieved," said he, " that you should take up matters thus, but the manner in which our intercourse has begun, will soften the regret I feel at its cessation."

Esther made him a sign of approval, but this time it was observed by Morizot, who exclaimed: " Why, God forgive me, Esther, I do believe you approve of your husband's inexplicable behaviour!"

" Indeed, sir," replied the youthful bride, " how can I see with regret, that he is sorry to leave me?"

" These are fine sentiments!" returned the commissary, with bitter irony; " and I suppose love will defray the expenses of a house and establishment?"

" It is true," said Esther, " my husband has taken me without a portion; but if the promises that have been made to him are not realised, he is young, intelligent, and resolute, and can support his wife, who will work with him, if it be necessary."

" What ingratitude! Is it possible this is said to me!" cried Morizot, striking the table with his glass, which was shivered to atoms.

Legros, who took things more coolly, now again interposed: " Well, my dear young lady," said he, " if you reckon upon your exertions for your support, I can tell you beforehand, that your position will not be a very brilliant one; for with your tastes and habits, you are fit for nothing but to do the honours gracefully in a drawing-room."

At this point of the conversation, which became every moment more bitter, the noise of wheels and the loud cracking of a postilion's whip were heard outside. Morizot rose; and the rest of the party having followed his example, he turned to Chevillard, and said with great solemnity: " You see, sir, I had counted

implicitly upon you. Be good enough to reflect for a moment; the case stands thus: a rupture must ensue between us, or we begin from this day a friendly intercourse, which for you will lead to fortune. In half an hour, just time to get ready a portmanteau, you must be on the road, or all is at an end between us."

" Come, summon courage and reason to your aid," said Legros, taking poor Chevillard by the hand, and exhorting him to submit.

" Mr. Morizot will remember your giving way to his wishes," added Madame de Saint-Martin, putting in her word, " and I dare say he will grant you leave of absence in a short time."

" No, I cannot consent," replied Chevillard, for Esther's silence appeared to urge him to persist in his resolution.

" Very well, sir! very well!" cried Morizot, pale with rage; " we shall see at last what this unjustifiable conduct will lead to. I must go in your place; that alone may tell you of what importance it is; but, by heavens! you shall pay for this."

" Really, Chevillard," said Legros, with an appearance of deep feeling, " after all I have done for you, your conduct is not noble; I should never have believed it of you."

The kind feelings of the poor young man were so touched by this appeal, that he would perhaps have yielded, if Esther had not contrived to whisper: " Stay!"

Morizot had already reached the door; but, pausing before he went out, he turned round, again approached Chevillard, and pressing his arm with violence, whilst his eyes flashed fire, exclaimed: " For the last time, sir, I ask if you intend to play the part of a dishonest man, and violate all your engagements?"

" It is you, sir, who violate yours!" replied Chevillard, incensed by these violent proceedings; " I was to remain here for three days after my marriage."

" It is impossible to be more abominably duped than I have been!" cried the commissary; " but remember, sir, you have in me a mortal enemy!"

He rushed furiously from the room; but he did not apparently leave the house at that instant, for no noise of wheels was audible. Though freed from this violent adversary, poor Chevillard was not left in peace. Legros and Madame de Saint-Martin overwhelmed him with reproaches; especially the latter, who, in the fervour of her indignation, even declared that the hospitality she had offered to the young couple was conditional on the agreement which had been so dishonourably broken, and that she now considered herself bound by no engagement. But Chevillard was not staggered by this threat, and, losing all patience, replied, that this was far from being disagreeable to him, and if she would have the goodness to send for a coach, he was ready to take away his wife and their effects, and he doubted not it would be a much better arrangement.

Seeing the turn that things were now taking, Legros went over to the other side, and expostulated with Madame de Saint-Martin, telling her that she was out of her senses, and altogether wanting in discretion. The unlucky matron, not knowing how to retrace her steps, had no other resource but that to which all would fly when in a dilemma; sinking into a chair, she fainted away, and this real or fictitious swoon gave Legros an opportunity to leave the room, under the pretext of seeking assistance for her.

The servant entered soon after, and while she, with Chevillard and Esther, was busied about her mistress, the post-chaise was heard to drive rapidly away. When Legros returned, he joined his efforts to those of the rest of the party, and at length the lady was pleased to recover. When they were able to resume the conversation which had been so tragically interrupted, the law-agent announced, that Morizot had remained for a short time at the door, to give Chevillard an opportunity to repent, and that he had finally begun to listen to reason. "I have succeeded," continued Legros, "in making him confess, that the trial he wished to impose on our young friend was rather too severe, and I have some hope he may yet relent. At all events, he quite disapproved of the words ——"

"Which were not from my heart!" interrupted Madame de Saint-Martin, in most theatrical style. "But, cruel children, how can you be so unreasonable?"

"Pray calm yourself, madam; all will be well," said Chevillard, good-naturedly.

"I think so too," continued Legros; "I will at once go to Morizot, and prevent him in the first place from foolishly undertaking this journey, and I trust I shall persuade him to accord an amicable delay till to-morrow morning."

He accordingly went out, and was not long before he returned with articles of pacification. When all these comings and goings were at an end, it was about eleven o'clock, and Legros began to complain of the excessive coldness of the weather.

"I do not know if you are like me," he observed, "but I think it is bitterly cold this evening; I got quite numbed in the cab which brought me from Morizot's, and it would be very amiable in you to give us a glass of mulled wine."

"Willingly," replied the lady of the house; and she rang for the servant, to give the necessary orders.

"If you will allow me," said the law-agent, "I will prepare it myself; the girl understands nothing about it."

With these words, he left the room; and the servant soon after came in to say, that Mr. Legros had asked for Bordeaux.

"Ah! how tiresome it is!" cried Madame de Saint-Martin; "now I must go down to the cellar; he can do nothing without such a fuss."

"Will you give me the keys, ma'am?"

"No, I will go myself," replied the lady, rising.

The young people found themselves alone for the first time. Chevillard drew nearer to Esther, who was pale and agitated; after a momentary pause, he said: "How kind you are to encourage me to stay!"

"It was my duty," replied the young girl, much embarrassed, "though my conduct must have appeared to you very strange."

"Strange! no," exclaimed Chevillard; "on the contrary, I am very grateful to you for this; it is a proof that you love me a little."

Before they had time to say anything more, Madame de Saint-Martin, who must have been extremely quick in her movements, appeared at the door of the saloon, and, addressing her adopted daughter: "Esther," said she, "come with me."

Esther obeyed, and Chevillard, instinctively certain that their conference related to him, followed the two women on tiptoe; they went up to the bride's room, and he entered it almost at the same moment. When she saw him penetrate into this sanctuary, Madame de Saint-Martin exclaimed against his proceedings, as absurd and indecorous to the last degree; but the bridegroom did not care for anything she could say. Then begun a little struggle, conducted however with all due courtesy, between them; the mother-in-law tried to turn out the son-in-law, and the latter did his best to remain; until at last it chanced, that the lady was so near the entrance, that with a very gentle push she found herself in the passage, and the door was instantly closed against her. For a few moments, she knocked loudly with feet and hands, but finding it was in vain, she hastened to Legros for assistance. He had by this time finished his cookery, and did not appear so much affected by the incident as she had expected he would be. He poured the contents of a silver saucepan into a glass, and merely said to the servant: "Here, take this up to the bridegroom from me, and tell him to drink to my health."

The servant knocked at the door much more discreetly than her mistress had done, and her voice being soon recognised, Legros' offering was received into the fortress without any difficulty. The last named personage had apparently forgotten the desire he had expressed for mulled wine, as he kept none of the mixture for himself: he remained for a short time in close conference with Madame de Saint-Martin; then bidding her good night, the most profound quiet soon reigned throughout the house.

CHAPTER XIV.

It might be about eight o'clock the next morning, and at that season of the year as yet scarcely daylight, when Legros stopped in a hackney-coach at the door of the well-known house. He did not ask for Madame de Saint-Martin, who was still in bed, but walked up stairs to the chamber of the newly married pair, and was admitted the instant he named himself.

Chevillard was busied with a somewhat prosaic occupation; he was kneeling before a portmanteau, filling it with necessaries for his journey; but still his whole appearance had in it something of the brilliant and happy bridegroom, who rises joyously from the nuptial couch. The fair bride, fresh and blooming as a rose at early dawn, and attired in an elegant morning dress, which set off her beauty to the greatest advantage, was cheerfully assisting her husband in his preparations. The most affectionate confidence appeared to subsist between them; it was easy to see, that their attachment had greatly increased in a short time.

"Ah! is it you, Mr. Joker?" said Chevillard, as Legros entered.

"How do you mean? What joke?"

"Yes, yes; you who send people draughts spiced with ginger and cinnamon."

"Oh! by the by," said Legros, as if he just remembered the circumstance; "how did you like the cordial I prepared?"

"Do you think I drink such stuff?" returned the other; "I threw your cordial out of the window, its fumes were enough to stifle one."

"You are hard to please," replied the law-agent, looking rather disappointed. "But," continued he, "to talk of more serious matters, when do you think of starting?"

"You see, I am getting ready——"

"You do right; for Morizot sent for me this morning, and we had a stormy debate about you; he cannot stomach the resistance you opposed yesterday to his wishes. However, he has sent your credentials and these written instructions, but you will have great difficulty in regaining his confidence, I can tell you."

"Pshaw!" said Chevillard; "Esther will appease him, and you may be sure I shall set to work in famous style, when I once get there. Well," continued he, "is the post-chaise to take me up here?"

"No," replied the law-agent; "one of Morizot's secretaries was sent on in the post-chaise, yesterday evening, to keep things quiet till you arrive. A place has been taken for you in the stage, which starts in half-an-hour, and I have promised not to leave you till I saw you fairly off."

"Well, my dear fellow, my packing is finished," said Chevillard, submissively; "I have only to kiss my poor little wife, and then I follow you."

"My love," said Esther, "you had better take something before you leave."

"No," answered the doleful husband, "it would be impossible; my heart is too full."

"Come, come, time is going on," observed Legros; "let us make an end of this."

Esther turned away to conceal the tears that sprung to her eyes, and Chevillard, perceiving this, put his arm tenderly around her, saying: "Take courage, dearest Esther; our separation will not be for long."

The young creature wept for a moment in silence, her face bent down upon her husband's shoulder; but suddenly looking up with great vivacity of expression: "Oh, my love!" cried she, sobbing, "pray take me with you."

"Esther!" said Legros, in a severe tone, "this is too much; it appears that you wish to break through all your engagements with your guardian."

"Do not speak so harshly to her," said Chevillard; "her desire is very natural. And you, dear Esther, be reasonable; you know we must make some sacrifices for the future; but we shall soon meet again."

Esther shook her head doubtfully.

"Yes, certainly," continued Chevillard; "it was agreed, that as soon as I got things a little in order ——"

"Chevillard, we shall lose the stage," interrupted Legros. The poor fellow pressed his wife once more to his heart, and hastened to collect together his packages; but in his agitation he would have forgotten half of them, had it not been for Legros' officious zeal. At length all was ready, and Chevillard about to step into the coach, when he remembered he had not taken leave of Madame de Saint-Martin. He wished to repair this negligence, but Legros stopped him, saying: "It is no matter, she is not yet up; your wife will make your apologies to her."

The impatient law-agent did not gain much by this move; for the enamoured pair had still a thousand things to say, and he had almost recourse to force, to tear them away from each other. Esther stood at the door, and followed with her eyes the coach which carried away her husband, until it was lost to sight; then she went sadly to her room, and gave way to the most painful reflections.

*   *   *

She had remained thus for nearly an hour, when some one knocked imperatively at the door.

"Who is there?" she asked.

"I," roughly answered a voice, which she knew to be that of Morizot.

"If you will go down into the drawing-room, I will be with you in a moment," said the young wife.

"Open the door," replied Morizot, in a tone of feverish impatience; and he shook it violently, as if to enforce his demand.

Esther wrapped herself hastily in a large shawl, and reluctantly admitted this imperious visitor, who entered with his hat on, saying in a menacing manner: "You will probably explain to me what you mean by these novel proceedings towards me?"

"I asked you to go into the drawing-room," replied Esther, "because this room is still in confusion ——"

"Yes, a sweet confusion," said Morizot, with marked emphasis; "I do not wonder that you feel somewhat ashamed in my presence."

"I do not understand you," replied the young lady, with much dignity.

"Oh! I suppose not; you are innocence itself, and practise the greatest duplicity without being conscious of it!"

"Sir, I have not been guilty of any duplicity; and I intimated to you last evening, as clearly as possible, that I meant to be in very earnest my husband's wife."

"Indeed, I saw that well enough! It seems that this fellow, with his youth and personal attractions, has had a great effect on your imagination. You have done your best to gratify your liking."

"The grossness of your language," returned Esther, "would authorise me to break off this interview upon the instant; but as, after what has passed between us, an explanation must sooner or later take place, it is as well it should be now. I will speak to you with the utmost frankness, and I trust this will preclude all further reproaches of duplicity."

"I listen, madam," said Morizot, in an abrupt tone, lolling insolently in an arm-chair, into which he had thrown himself.

"You wished this marriage to take place," continued Esther; "you arranged it by means of your confidential agent, Mr. Legros. In all this, I have been completely passive, and have followed your will."

"Say rather your own interest," replied the commissary, sternly. "When, not long since, you vaguely suspected you were likely to become a mother, you wearied me with your complaints and tears; you were inconsolable. Being married, I could do nothing in such a crisis; it was necessary to hit upon some such plan."

"My conscience, too late awakened to a sense of the deplorable course forced upon my youth and inexperience, pointed out another remedy; you would have honoured us both by allowing me to prefer it."

"Nonsense!" said Morizot, with an impatient gesture; "to separate from you! to let you enter a convent! Was such a thing possible? do you know *what* you asked?"

"And so," resumed Esther, "a husband was presented to me. He was introduced by Mr. Legros, he had been picked up in a gambling-house, he was doubtless fit to play the disgraceful part assigned to him. I was habituated to do wrong under your guidance, and that of the woman who helped you to ruin me; I let things take their course, and offered no opposition; why should I, a poor, lost, degraded girl, care what was to be my future destiny?"

"It would have been all very well, if you had continued so to the end; but your indifference was followed by I know not what impertinent fancy."

"Sir, for this you must blame your unskilful agent. You required a libertine: Mr. Legros, who does not usually make these mistakes, was unfortunate enough to meet with an honest man ——"

"Say, rather, a fool, whose brain has been turned by your charms, and therefore he has flattered you in a manner no woman's vanity can resist."

"You are mistaken; in the short time I have had to become acquainted with the man you destined for my husband, I discovered in him many estimable qualities, which first made a favourable impression on me; and then his love was sincere, disinterested; it seemed to restore me to virtue."

"For which reason, you made him your dupe. A singular mode of amendment, truly!"

"It is surely not for *you*, sir, to make me this reproach, though my conscience has upbraided me far more keenly than you can do. After many struggles, on the evening before the ceremony, I was about to confess all, and had it not been for the interference of your confidants, I ——"

"Yes, they told me of that scene," replied the commissary, contemptuously; "and I know, that to gild the pill for the poor devil, you, in theatrical style, swore to him a boundless and eternal love!"

"Theatrical or not," courageously returned Esther, "I took that engagement, and I will keep it."

"Well! but, allow me, my charming creature; I don't exactly see what becomes of me in this felicitous arrangement," said Morizot, insolently.

"You, sir!" replied the young wife, in a tone between entreaty and command; "after leading me astray, you cannot wish to oppose yourself to my living like an honest woman; you surely will keep the promises you have made this young man, and not suffer everything in the affair to prove a deception?"

"That is all excellently arranged," returned Morizot; "only your promises are not quite just; you think I love you with a calm affection, and that nothing would be easier than for me to renounce you."

"Sir, when you gave me to another, you could not but understand it thus."

"You do not believe a word of what you are saying. You know I love you madly, and you must have very little acquaintance with the human heart, not to know also, that the obstacle which impedes my passion, is of a nature to inflame and augment it still more."

"Oh! your words are horrible," said Esther, with disgust.

"Come, girl!" continued Morizot, rising; "I certainly ought to resent the trick you played me yesterday; but you look so beautiful this morning, I must pardon you, whether or no."

"Leave me, sir!" cried his victim, retreating in alarm; and finding that he continued to advance, she ran towards the door, exclaiming: "If you come a step nearer, I will leave the room."

"The deuce!" said Morizot; "decidedly we are acting *Lucretia*; but, my pretty love, you must learn to know, that all these grimaces are as useless as they are ridiculous."

"I tell you, sir, I am no longer the lost creature of whom you disposed at pleasure; yesterday, I swore before God, to be faithful to my husband, and nothing shall make me break my vow."

"But have you considered, foolish girl, that your destiny is in my hands? If, to-morrow, I were to withdraw my protection from the poor devil I have taken into my service, nothing but poverty awaits you."

"Well, sir, I shall accept it as an expiation."

"Ah, you are very much mistaken; you could not support indigence for a single week. Accustomed to ease and luxury, believe me, you would soon be tired of your stern virtue; and besides, remember, that a word whispered in your husband's ear, may dash down at one blow his dream of happiness, and cause him to regard you with scorn and contempt."

"If you did so infamous a thing," replied Esther, greatly excited, "I would kill myself. But take care; my husband would have a terrible reckoning to demand !''

" Very well, madam !'' said Morizot, rather disturbed at this threat. " Such then is the reward of all my kindness to you !''

" What kindness ?'' cried Esther ; " my youth confided to the care of a worthless woman, that you might triumph the more easily over my innocence !''

" Enough !'' said Morizot; " this wedding has turned your brain, and I must let your virtuous fire cool down a little. I will see you again in the evening, and then, more calm and composed, you will probably listen to reason. But remember one thing; I will not be duped with impunity, and I would not advise any one to make me his enemy.''

These words were pronounced with apparent calmness, but there was something so hideously menacing in the expression of Morizot's countenance, that poor Esther was filled with terror. She did not however seek to detain him, and as soon as he had left the room, she ran to bolt the door, for it seemed to her she was no longer in safety in that house.

CHAPTER XV.

GLOOMY and perplexed were Esther's reflections after the interview we have just related. One sad truth was but too apparent : she found, that once in the path of evil, it is not, as might be thought, always at our option to return, for insurmountable obstacles frequently force us back into the track we may have firmly resolved to abandon. And, besides, it must be owned, that the source of the virtuous determination of this repentant Magdalen was far from being blameless ; it was precisely to the deception practised on the kind-hearted Chevillard, and to which, with good intentions, she had been a party, that she at that moment owed her worst troubles. Unmarried, it would have been easy for her to regain her independence, by renouncing the comfortable existence assured to her by Morizot; but now, to remain faithful to her husband, and at the same time preserve the material advantages he had expected from their union, was a matter of impossibility.

Before this interview with her seducer, Esther had flattered herself with many fond illusions on the subject of conciliating these two interests, and the strong attachment she felt for Chevil-lard, had contributed to blind her to the perception of the dangers which menaced her in the future. But her dream of happiness and virtue had been rudely dispelled. The words and well-known character of Morizot allowed of no doubt ; her favours were to be the price of her husband's prosperity, and she must perforce choose. In the terrible struggle of conflicting duties she had created for herself, she for a moment deliberated if, by a sort of conjugal heroism, she ought not to submit, provisionally at least, to the horrid alternative of a connexion, upon which all the welfare of her married life depended. But even if her moral sense had not warned her that this was in fact a shameless sophism, so complete a revolution had taken place within a short time in the ideas of this poor, fallen creature, who had lived for several years in heedless guilt, that she shuddered at the bare thought of again entering on a course of profligacy. She looked upon her marriage as a baptism, which had restored to her the robe of innocence, and death itself was less fearful than this fresh pollution.

After mature consideration, she decided that she would try to gain time, and see whether her supplications and tears might not eventually soften Morizot's heart. If, on the contrary, this bad man continued to claim what he called his rights, she resolved to quit the house, write to her husband to join her, and consult with him on the means of supporting themselves, independently of the assistance and protection which were valued at so detestable a price. Having thus made up her mind to the line of conduct she would pursue, when Madame de Saint-Martin came up soon after, and, faithful to the part she had always acted by her, reproached her with absurd prudery, and tried to convince her of the mischievous effects of such conduct, Esther refrained from expressing the contempt with which the abominable zeal and advice of this woman inspired her. Without positively committing herself, she pretended to regret that her first impluse had led her to repulse so harshly Morizot's advances, and seemed to intimate that her scruples might be conquered, if not too roughly dealt with.

It was still early in the day, when Legros again made his appearance in the Allée des Veuves ; he had been to the commissary to inform him of Chevillard's actual departure, had heard of Esther's contumacy, and being, as we have already seen, a skilful meditator, had undertaken to bring her back into what he was pleased to term *the right road*. He found her apparently much more disposed to err than he had thought, so, instead of remonstrances, he had recourse to felicitations and encouragement, and cited twenty examples of husbands, who, to his own knowledge, were deceived like Chevillard by powerful protectors, whose *useful* attentions they were frequently the first to encourage. In the evening came Morizot, as he had threatened; but, having been informed by his confidants of the more *reasonable* frame of mind manifested by his victim, and, advised to use gentle means at first, he contented himself with tender attentions, and held in check, for that day at least, his ardent desire for the forbidden fruit.

But several days passed, and he was no nearer the attainment of his wishes; he again gave way to violence and threats, and the unhappy Esther was exposed to persecutions which she felt she could not long endure with patience. One evening, when Legros and Morizot had dined at the house, she went up to her room for a few moments, and was surprised by the entrance of the servant, who appeared to have been on the watch to speak with her. This girl was attached to Esther, who treated her with gentle kindness; whereas Madame de Saint-Martin was extremely harsh in her deportment and expressions towards her, and almost impossible to please.

"Madam," said the servant, "there is a plot against you: Mr. Legros, who sent some drugged wine to Mr. Chevillard on your wedding-day, is going to put something in the tea you take every evening; so be on your guard." Then, as if afraid of being discovered, the cautioner immediately left the room.

This last blow was decisive; it was impossible to remain in such a place. Having foreseen the probable occurrence of a similar necessity, the poor thing had already packed up some clothes, and the few valuables she possessed, including the jewels her husband had presented to her at the time of their marriage, and the half of the thousand francs (his sole property!) which he had insisted upon sharing with her before he left. She therefore threw a cloak over her shoulders, shaded her face with a deep bonnet and veil, and, taking the parcel in her hand, slipped down stairs, and was out of the house before her persecutors, still busy with their odious

design, could be aware of her disappearance. When she gained the avenue, the fugitive hesitated for a moment, doubtful whether to direct her course towards the Champs-Elysées or the high road to Passy. The last mentioned direction was in point of fact the least secure; she would have to traverse the most lonely part of that ill-famed and dangerous quarter, and was exposed to unpleasant rencounters. But to her there were no villains more formidable than those from whom she had just escaped, and, by a happy inspiration, she judged that the most unfrequented road was also that by which she was the least likely to be pursued.

The event justified this prudent foresight, for in a very short time she heard, in the direction of the house she had left, loud and animated voices, and presently after the sound of hasty steps testified that search was being made for her; but instead of approaching nearer, the noise gradually receded, and was at length lost in the distance. Having escaped this danger, the courageous young woman was fortunate enough, soon after leaving the Allée des Veuves, to meet with one of the coaches which then plied between Paris and Versailles, and to find a place in it. This coach set her down at the Quay d'Orsay, at the foot of the Pont-Royal, where its office was situated. Giving herself out as a lady from Versailles, who had business which would detain her for a week at Paris, Esther enquired of the woman at the office for some respectable house in the neighbourhood, where she might take lodgings. She was directed to one in the Rue de Beaune, kept by very decent and worthy people, and was soon installed in a neat apartment. When asked for her name, that it might be inscribed on the police register, of which the entries were, at that æra of plots, examined with scrupulous care by the authorities, she gave that of Madame Lefèvre, so as to divert the inquiries which would doubtless be made for her.

After the extreme resolution she had taken, Esther felt that Morizot would not keep her husband in his situation; she therefore immediately wrote the following letter:

"My very dear husband,—Most painful events have occurred since your departure, but it is useless to detail them here. It is sufficient to say, that I could not *decently* remain in the house where you left me; and being detained there

almost by force, I was obliged to effect my escape, and take refuge in the place from which I write. Even if I had not the most ardent desire to have you with me, as my protector and best friend in such trying circumstances, I think it would be a loss of time to remain in a situation, of which you will certainly be deprived ere long by a man who has become our mortal enemy. Start, therefore, as soon as you receive this letter, and come to me without delay. I often ask myself, whether the unfavourable aspect that our affairs have taken from the first, will not make you one day repent having taken me as your wife. I am already deeply affected by the misfortunes which have overtaken us, and it would be hard indeed if they were to diminish the affection you have shown me until now, and which, I trust, has not found me ungrateful. I look forward to our reunion, and in the meantime, I embrace you tenderly, and am your affectionate wife,

"ESTHER CHEVILLARD.

"P. S. My address is Rue de Beaune, No. 11."

CHAPTER XVI.

WHEN Chevillard received his wife's letter, he was not so annoyed as might be imagined; he thought principally of the pleasure of so soon seeing her again. Besides, he was far from satisfied with the situation, in which his supposed patron had placed him. He had been led to expect that he should be the principal in the office, instead of which he found himself appointed to a subaltern employment, that in nowise explained the great necessity alleged for his departure. This, together with some obscure hints, dropped by his fellow-clerks, had raised strange doubts in his mind, and he was full of impatience to question his wife, and *good friend* Legros, on the subject, when the letter of the former reached him. The information it contained solved the mystery he had longed to penetrate, and sure of the love and fidelity of Esther, he at first scarcely gave a thought to his ruined prospects. His position called for promptitude and decision, and the same evening he started for Paris, leaving a letter for the head of the office, in which, without precisely resigning his situation, he stated that he was obliged to absent himself on important business. Ere many days had elapsed, he was once more with his beloved Esther; and when the first tumult of happiness had a little subsided, he anxiously questioned her on the meaning of the communication she had made to him. She could not tell him all, but he learnt, that, immediately after his departure, Morizot, who had apparently his own views in bringing about their marriage, had insulted her with the avowal of his love, and that she had repulsed him with indignation; that Legros and Madame de Saint-Martin were the accomplices of the commissary in his guilty schemes; and that she had thought it expedient to temporise, until finding herself no longer safe from violence, she had made her escape, and taken refuge in her present asylum. She added, that since the night she left the Allée des Veuves, she had heard nothing of the infamous trio who had conspired to ruin her.

Chevillard thanked his wife for the proof of affection she had given him, and at the same time did not conceal from her the suspicions he had conceived during his absence. He asked if the melancholy she had so frequently shown before marriage, was not caused by some foreboding of the passion her guardian entertained for her. Esther was obliged to allow that this was the case; and her husband then told her, that she had been wrong not to place more confidence in him. " I loved you for yourself," said he, " not for the advantages our union might assure to me; and I should still have wished to make you my wife. Thus, at least, we should not have appeared to connive at such degrading assistance and patronage."

When poor Esther heard her husband express these noble sentiments, she felt a poignant regret at the deception she had practised, and once more her secret was on her lips. But again she reflected that her frankness would be rather gratuitous cruelty, for it would reveal what was *irreparable*, and again she quieted her conscience by resolving to efface the guilty antecedents of her married life, by the most devoted faith and affection.

At the present time, it was the future that more especially called for the solicitude of the youthful pair.

Chevillard wished, in the first instance, to seek out Morizot and Legros, to *deal with them as they deserved*. But Esther opposed this desperate step, as only serving to increase the enmity of influential and determined men, who had it in their power to cause them serious injury. This remark came with peculiar force to the understanding of the young man, when he thought of the bill of exchange he had so imprudently signed, and of the scrupulous care with which his perfidious creditor had refused his offer of settlement. The more he reflected upon this, and upon the use which might be made of that dangerous engagement, the more uneasy he became, until he could no longer refrain from informing Esther of the circumstance, and she fully participated in his alarm.

To discharge the debt as soon as possible, appeared to them imperiously dictated by their position; but when they reviewed the state of their finances, they saw the apparently hopeless difficulty of extricating themselves from this emergency. Chevillard had not received any part of his salary, and he had been obliged to pay for his living, and the expenses of the journey from Rochefort to Paris. Esther, on her part, although she had restricted herself to absolute necessaries, had unavoidably encroached upon the note left her by her husband at his departure. So that the contents of their two purses did not amount together to a thousand francs. They thought of parting with the jewels, presented by Chevillard to his bride; but when they offered them for sale, a fresh infamy of Legros' became apparent. He had either kept part of the money intrusted to him, for his own use, or he had expended by far the largest share on the present intended for Madame de Saint-Martin; so that Esther's trinkets, though disposed with great art to take the eye, were of very little intrinsic value, and it was with much difficulty they found a jeweller who consented to estimate them at forty louis. This money added to the small sum mentioned above, did not cover the amount of the bill, and until Chevillard could find employment, they must draw on it for daily expenses. Under these circumstances, the unfortunate young man saw but one resource; this was to go to Auxerre, to hasten the settlement of his claims on the succession of his uncle, the notary, about which he had spoken to Legros. He even resolved to dispose of his claims at a loss, in case the partition with the other heirs should still require much delay.

When Chevillard arrived in his native town, his self-love was highly gratified by the admiration his wife's beauty excited. Every one congratulated him; they were universally courted and caressed, and spent there several pleasant weeks in a continual round of gaieties, for it was the time of Christmas and the New Year. Those festivals, that of Twelfth-day, &c., were just then celebrated with peculiar zest, for republican institutions had suppressed or suspended these domestic feasts during several preceding years.

But whilst he was living so luxuriously, the liquidation of the succession (which the lawyers had an interest in prolonging) came to no satisfactory conclusion; and when at length, seeing his purse growing empty, and wishing at all risks to return to Paris, to obtain some situation in a commercial house, Chevillard brought matters to a close, he found that the costs had absorbed the greater part of the inheritance. As for what remained, the liquidation had been so managed, that disputes arose between several of the co-heirs, and after three or four ruinously expensive law-suits, they might perhaps hope to get enough to pay the lawyers. When Chevillard found the resource upon which he had counted, so completely fail him, he was quite discouraged, and his wife was obliged to exert all the influence his strong affection had given her over him, to prevent his giving way to despair. They returned to Paris after a month's absence, and took modest lodgings in the Rue de la Jussienne, and then the poor young man immediately set to work to seek for some employment, in which his aptitude at accounts might avail him. But the times were ill-adapted for such a research; rumours of plots* were every day increasing, and the anxiety thus created in the public mind, caused a great stagnation in trade, so that commercial houses were inclined to diminish rather than increase their establishments.

Chevillard's applications were everywhere declined or postponed; and as his slender means were rapidly diminishing, the future began to appear to him under the darkest hues, and for the first time since his marriage, he was angry with his wife, because she asked him why, instead of applying to strangers, he did not try to regain his former situation.

"You do not know what you are talking about," said he; "you speak like a fool. I tell you, I would rather beg my bread in the streets, than ask Mademoiselle Lebeau for anything."

Esther could not comprehend this repugnance, but as her husband had received her advice so ungraciously, she did not dare to ask him for an explanation. The reader will however understand Chevillard's feelings, and appreciate his delicacy. About a week after his return to Paris, and when he was almost disheartened by his fruitless exertions, fortune appeared disposed to relent. He had called upon a banker, in whose establishment he was told there was a vacancy, and as he appeared likely to suit, was desired to look in again the next day, when the banker would have made inquiries of some respectable parties to whom his applicant had referred him, and would then give his final answer.

Chevillard did not doubt that the references would prove satisfactory, and went home to his wife with a heart full of hope and joy. The next day, he bade her farewell more gaily than had been his wont for some time, and set off to ascertain the banker's decision.

* Alluding to the conspiracy of George Cadoudal.

He had not been gone many minutes, when the mistress of the house entered Esther's room with an alarmed countenance, and told her that her husband *was down stairs*, and wished to see her. Terrified by the woman's agitated manner while delivering this message, the young wife hastened to descend the stairs, and as she did so, the landlady prepared her for some misfortune, by observing: "It seems that the gentleman is in difficulties."

A hackney-coach was before the house, and the unfortunate young man was seated in it, accompanied by several ill-looking individuals, while a person of better appearance, of whose features Esther had a confused recollection, stood at the door of the coach, as if to guard it. As soon as Chevillard saw his wife, he said: "Do not be alarmed, my love; these gentlemen are the bearers of a judgment, obtained in consequence of the protest of the bill of exchange you know of. I must accompany them to the Tribunal of Commerce to explain."

"Oh!" cried Esther, "you are deceiving me. You always told me, that fatal paper might affect your liberty. My husband is arrested, is it not so?" added she, turning to the person who appeared to have the chief authority.

"Not exactly," replied the bailiff, who, affected by the look of despair which accompanied these words, wished to-spare the feelings of the distracted wife. "But even if it be necessary for your husband to accompany us to Sainte-Pélagie,* it will doubtless not be for long; the sum with all costs is not to a very great amount, and with the assistance of friends, you will most likely be able to pay it at an early period."

"But at least, sir, do not hide anything from me; you are taking him to prison, I am sure of it."

"I am obliged to do so for the present; but if you apply to Mr. Parisot, head of the eighth division of the prefecture of police, you will be admitted to see him without any delay."

"Ah! the wicked wretches!" cried Esther, in an agony.

"Compose yourself, madam," said the good-natured bailiff. "Sainte-Pélagie is not such a bad place to dwell in."

"Come, my love, be courageous," said Chevillard, making a movement to reach her hand, which the bailiff's men

* A prison for debtors, and suspected persons.

instantly checked, by holding him back by the skirts of his coat.

"Did you not say, sir, that I must apply to Mr. Parisot, at the prefecture of police?" demanded Esther of the officer.

"Yes, madam; he is a very polite and obliging man, who will readily grant your request; and if you make a little haste, you may be admitted into the prison almost as soon as the gentleman."

"I will run to get the permission," said Esther, rushing towards the house, to regain her room and put on a more suitable dress, for she had come down in a morning-gown; then immediately retracing her steps, she wished to bid her husband once more farewell, but the officer had already entered the coach, and ordered the man to drive on. Esther stood for a moment, looking after them with despair depicted in her countenance; then, perceiving that she was stared at by a crowd of idlers, who had been collected by this scene, she took refuge in the house, followed by the mistress, who, moved with compassion, would not leave her alone at such a time.

CHAPTER XVII.

ON applying to Mr. Parisot, Esther easily obtained permission to be admitted into Sainte-Pélagie, and soon joined her husband there. She found him a prey to feverish excitement, and before she could ask how their last misfortune had occurred: "The plot was of long standing," he exclaimed; "the infamous Legros sought an opportunity to lend me the money, for the express purpose of entangling me in this marriage."

"Good heavens! my dear husband," said Esther; "it seems as if you regretted it."

"All is now clear," continued Chevillard. "They wished to find a husband of whom they could easily get rid, and I can understand why they wanted me to start in such a hurry on the very evening of the wedding-day."

"But you saw how I aided you to frustrate their perfidious design," returned the unhappy girl, trembling, lest her own duplicity should be suspected.

"I do not accuse you, Esther. But see the infernal dexterity of these wretches; at the very moment they were engaging to open to me a prosperous career, they were already plotting against my liberty. The bill was presented the day after our marriage."

"How is it then," asked Esther, " that you knew nothing of it?"

"Oh! everything was well managed! The house I had quitted was my residence in the eye of the law, and as I had not left word where I was going to live, all the legal notices were served at the porter's lodge, without my being informed of what had taken place."

"But how did they find out where we lived?"

"Legros knew that I had some money-claims at Auxerre; he judged that our straitened circumstances would induce me to go there, to see if I could bring things to a speedy termination; that wretch Morizot, who grudges no money to achieve his wicked plans, sent off a bailiff to trace us, and watch our movements. This man in fact followed us everywhere, and returned to Paris in the same coach as we did."

"How! the gentleman who was so polite to me during the journey? But indeed, when you were arrested, I fancied I had seen him before."

"He is not a bad man," resumed Chevillard; " he follows his profession in a humane manner. He answered very readily all the questions I put to him; but he says Legros is one of the worst of characters—a shameless usurer, capable of filling this place by his unassisted manœuvres. Ah! I was in luck when I fell in with him!"

"My love," said Esther, timidly, "do you think I had better see him? perhaps he might relent."

"Can you think of such a thing? To make advances to these wretches, when evidently they have caused me to be arrested, only that they may the more easily triumph over you, and when my anxiety is chiefly for the machinations to which you will be exposed!"

"But," replied Esther, "I shall leave the house where we were, and come to lodge somewhere about here, that I may be near you."

"Do you think they will not find you out? They have only to follow you when you leave this place."

"What does that signify? when I was in their power, I was able to escape from them."

"Ah! when we have to do with people, who are stopped by no scruples, is there not everything to fear?" cried Chevillard; " only to think of it, I could dash my head against these walls."

Chevillard uttered these words with an accent of the deepest despair; and though his wife exerted all her powers to console him, she found she was not successful. In truth, his situation was dreadful, and apparently hopeless; for, among all his connexion, he could think of no one able to advance the sum for which he was detained. The agitation and anxiety of the prisoner increased as the hour for their separation drew nigh, and when it came, he earnestly entreated his wife to observe the greatest caution, to be very careful what house she went into, and to place herself immediately under the protection of a magistrate, if any attempt was made upon her by Morizot or his agents. Never had the weakness of Chevillard's character been more apparent; he was quite overwhelmed by his misfortunes, and incapable of exertion or energy.

The next day, Esther, having taken a lodging in the Rue Copeau, near the prison, where she thought she should be safe, and terminated all necessary arrangements, again visited her husband in his confinement. Sad news awaited her: poor Chevillard had been seized during the night with a violent fever, and had been carried to the infirmary, by order of the doctor attached to the establishment. The sight of his wife appeared to cheer him a little, but he soon manifested how intense and absorbing was the fixed idea which tormented him, by asking with trembling anxiety whether she had heard of the people whose pursuit she feared. Esther positively assured him, that she had not been annoyed in any way; but he received this statement with incredulity, and declared he was sure something was kept from him. At length he appeared to be more satisfied, but a great languor succeeded to the late violent attack of fever, and during the rest of the day he was in a sort of stupor. It was with difficulty a few words could be obtained from him, and he scarcely appeared sensible that his wife was seated by his bedside.

When night came, Esther in vain begged to be allowed to remain with the sick man; and as she was leaving the prison, her husband's apprehensions were verified. She was accosted by Madame de Saint-Martin, who, guessing she would go to see the prisoner, had made inquiries as to the hour when visitors were obliged to retire, and had placed herself on the watch in time. The young wife refused to listen to this infamous creature, and ordered her to leave her; but the matron persevered in following her to the door of the lodging, and during the walk, tried to convince her of the folly of sacrificing an easy and pleasant life to a ridiculous flight of virtue, which could lead to nothing but misery.

"Do not deceive yourself," said this wicked woman, with the utmost effrontery; "even if your husband find means to pay the debt, he may not recover his liberty for all that. Morizot is greatly incensed at your conduct in all this affair, and intends to push things to extremity; so I should not be surprised, you see, if he were to lodge a complaint against *your* Chevillard, for having left his post without permission. Such a proceeding might lead people to suppose, that there had been some dishonesty in the management of the business intrusted to him."

"What you say is infamous!" cried Esther, led by a feeling of indignation to break the silence she had intended to maintain towards this odious creature.

"There is nothing infamous, my dear little thing," replied the Saint-Martin, unblushingly, "except in your ingratitude! After my being a mother to you, and the kindness you have experienced from Morizot since your earliest childhood, to act towards us as you do, proves that you have no proper feeling."

While Morizot's confidant had the impudence to talk of the gratitude Esther owed her, they had arrived at the lodging-house, and the latter had laid her hand upon the knocker. "One word more," said the Saint-Martin, holding back her arm. "Men are such fools when they are in love! Notwithstanding the wrongs he has sustained, and which he certainly ought not to pardon, Morizot has loaded me with fair words for you. I can tell you, your fate is still in your own hands: he is half distracted at your loss, and if you would consent to look on him with favour, not only would he set your husband at liberty, but would give him a much better situation than the one he has left. I advise you to think over it, and if you come to any *wise* determination, you have only to write to me under cover to Legros, who will transmit me the letter. Since your departure, I no longer live at the Allée des Veuves; I found it too dull."

Esther made no reply, but, knocking hastily at the door, escaped from a woman whose presence and discourse were alike odious to her. When she entered the infirmary next day, before Chevillard could perceive her, one of the nursing-sisters took her apart, and, without further preamble, asked if her husband was a religious man.

"My husband is not a saint," replied Esther; "but why this question?"

"Oh! because, my dear lady, the doctor has just been here, and does not find him at all well," said the nurse, with indiscreet zeal. "It seems, his arrest has been a terrible blow: he has been delirious all night, and raving about a Mademoiselle Lebeau, promising not to leave her house, making calculations, and giving orders as if he were in a shop."

"But is he worse this morning?" asked Esther, with great anxiety.

"No," replied the sister, "he is calm enough; but the doctor says, if he stays here long, either his life or his reason will be in danger; so, you know, if you are not able to get him soon released, it might be as well to call in the chaplain."

"Ah! my sister, I trust it is not so bad yet," said the unhappy young woman, breaking off the conversation to approach her husband's bed. She was immediately struck with the great change visible in his countenance, and to her extreme grief was received by him with coldness; for the sick man had already reached that state of dull indifference, when physical weakness appears to deaden the feelings, and nothing is left to the soul but a sort of jealous anxiety for self. The unfortunate prisoner was nevertheless still under the influence of his ruling idea, and his first words were to ask if the people in the Allée des Veuves had not been heard of. Esther naturally kept back her meeting with the woman Saint-Martin, the night before.

"So much the worse, that they have not sent to you," said Chevillard, coldly; "I think you would do well to listen to their proposals, and leave me; this marriage has brought sorrow into your life, and it can cause you nothing but misery."

When Chevillard spoke thus, did he not disguise in part his thoughts? When he expressed regret for Esther, did he experience none for himself? And was not this feeling discernible even in the words that had escaped him during his delirium, and which seemed to indicate remorse at having quitted Mademoiselle Lebeau's house? Though

Esther clearly perceived this dreadful truth, she would not show how cruelly it wounded her; in her husband's state of weakness, all agitating explanations were to be avoided. She therefore concealed her grief, but it was only the more bitter from the effort.

From the moment she suspected that Chevillard looked to the past with regret, and that she could no longer hope to work out his happiness as she had intended, she could no longer excuse to her upbraiding conscience the deception of which she had been guilty, and it seemed to her that her punishment had commenced. But it was the fatal sentence pronounced by the doctor, when he declared he would not answer for Chevillard's recovery, if his captivity were prolonged, that especially awakened her remorse. As she sat during that long morning by the bedside, scarcely exchanging a word with the patient, one only thought occupied her mind: How could she restore her husband to liberty?

Suddenly, a resource occurred to her; for a moment she weighed the chances, and success appeared possible: that was enough. The prisoner had just fallen asleep. She looked at him tenderly for a short time, pressed her lips to his forehead, and, rising gently, left the prison. She did not waver before the difficulties of the enterprise, but hastened to try this last forlorn hope.

CHAPTER XVIII.

NEARLY two months had passed away, since Chevillard left Mademoiselle Lebeau's house. The fair mercer found in the activity of her life, a powerful antidote against her secret sorrow, and she the more easily averted her thoughts from the subject, that she had never felt for our hero what might be called a *decided passion*.

She had loved him in some sort *from opportunity*, because he was always there; because she had known him from childhood; because he was blended with all her interests, and the whole tenor of her life; and also, because, as we have said before, she was strong in energy and intellect, and did not fear in him the competition of too bold and domineering a spirit. She was therefore tranquilly enough occupied with her business, when she was told that a young lady wished to speak with her.

Mademoiselle Lebeau immediately repaired to her private room to receive the visitor, and whilst begging her to be seated, could not but remark the strong emotion which appeared to agitate her. The stranger paused for a moment, and then said: "Mademoiselle, my name will in a certain measure explain the liberty I have taken. I am the wife of a person who was in your service for a long time—Mr. Chevillard."

"Mr. Chevillard—certainly—yes, madam—he was a long time here," replied Mademoiselle Lebeau, her thoughts so confused that she could not answer as calmly as she wished.

"He has often spoken to me of you," continued Esther, "as of one full of kindness and amiability ——"

Mademoiselle Lebeau bowed in acknowledgment of this courtesy, but she did not by word or look give any encouragement to the request which seemed likely to follow; she waited for Madame Chevillard to explain the object of her visit.

"Mr. Chevillard's marriage," resumed Esther, "has not turned out so well as was expected ——"

"You surprise me," said the fair mercer; "I should have thought Mr. Chevillard's choice would have made him an object of envy to all."

Under a varnish of flattering politeness, this remark had something of a bitter meaning, and the tone in which it was made, might bear either interpretation.

"If it had depended upon me alone," continued poor Esther, "my husband should have had no cause to regret his choice; but soon after our union, a terrible misfortune came upon us."

"Indeed! in what manner?" said Mademoiselle Lebeau, her curiosity, if not her interest, being now awakened.

"Before Mr. Chevillard was married, he committed a great imprudence; he had borrowed money."

"I am much surprised to hear that; I thought that your husband had not much beforehand, but I did not know he was in debt."

"Such however was the case, mademoiselle; and he had entered into engagements, on the strength of which his creditors have acted in the most rigorous manner."

"They have doubtless instituted proceedings against him?"

"He was taken to Sainte-Pélagie the day before yesterday," replied Esther, making up her mind to tell the worst.

"To Sainte-Pélagie!" repeated Mademoiselle Lebeau, with an accent of no doubtful sympathy; then, after a moment of painful silence, she resumed: "But I thought, madam, from what Mr. Chevillard said, that his marriage placed him in a most advantageous position; how then is it?"

"I did not bring any fortune to my husband," replied the young wife; "but an honourable and lucrative situation was insured to him. Unfortunately, from circumstances too complicated to touch upon now, the very persons who were to provide for him, have become our enemies, and it is at their instigation that we have been so cruelly persecuted."

"I do not wish, madam, to aggravate your misfortune by disobliging remarks; but I am astonished that Mr. Chevillard should not, without renouncing the hope of obtaining your hand, have postponed a conclusion which has entailed upon him so many perplexities."

"It was impossible for my husband to foresee what has taken place; and I, although I was not so completely deceived, had become so attached to him, that I did not calculate the probable consequences."

"This is certainly a sad thing," observed Mademoiselle Lebeau, rather coldly; "but how can my interference avail you?"

"Alas! mademoiselle," said Esther, with tears in her eyes, "I am more wretched than you think for. My husband's arrest has been a terrible shock to him; his health was immediately affected in the most serious manner, and this morning the doctor intimated that a prolonged captivity would be fatal."

"Oh! it is not probable, that, in so short a time, such a result can be anticipated."

"It were vain to deceive myself with false hopes; his life or his reason is menaced. I should myself have judged him to be in a very alarming state, if I had not been warned by the attendants. Besides, mademoiselle, the step I have taken must prove to you my deep anxiety."

"Well, madam, but what can I do? what do you desire?"

"I beg you to believe, mademoiselle, that Mr. Chevillard is not aware of this visit; only a woman fearing for her husband's life, and feeling besides, that she was partly the cause of his misfortunes, could have the temerity to implore your compassion."

"You may command my goodwill, madam," said Mademoiselle Lebeau;

"but of what nature is the service you require of me? Personal interest, or pecuniary intervention?"

"Mademoiselle, no steps would be of any avail with the people to whom I allude; our only resource is to discharge the debt."

"And what sum is necessary?"

"Alas! a considerable sum; with the costs, it must amount to nearly four thousand francs."

This figure of four thousand francs recalled to Mademoiselle Lebeau's remembrance, the way in which she parted from Chevillard, and produced an unfavourable effect. She thought, that with the gratuity she had forced him to accept, he might have cleared himself, and restored order in his affairs; besides, she did not put much confidence in this account of the probable result of his imprisonment. And then to sum up, heroism is not a matter of *strict duty*, and to resolve upon making a considerable sacrifice, at the prayer of a woman who had blighted one of the cherished hopes of her life, was not this passing the limit which separates generosity from credulity? From whatever cause it might be, the fair mercer did not at once rise to the height of evangelical charity expected of her. She even expressed her refusal more harshly than she would have done, if she had been sure of the full approbation of her conscience.

"I am very sorry," she said; "but I really cannot advance so large a sum; it is quite impossible."

"My husband is young," replied Madame Chevillard; "he may look forward; by his exertions, and the great economy I shall exercise in our home, we should perhaps in a short time be able to repay you."

The words, *my husband, we, our home,* unluckily brought together in one sentence, must evidently have grated upon Mademoiselle Lebeau's ear. So that, instead of being touched by this promise of a speedy repayment, she replied, in a decisive tone: "Madam, I repeat, that it is not in my power to render you this service; I have a very expensive establishment; business has been very dull for some time, and I have myself to meet numerous engagements."

"I hope, in that case, you will excuse my importunity, mademoiselle," said Esther, rising.

"Your devotion to your husband is quite sufficient excuse, and I regret I cannot take part in it."

"If you should happen to see Mr. Chevillard, may I presume to beg you not to mention an application, of which he might perhaps not have approved?"

"Oh! madam," replied Mademoiselle Lebeau, "there is very little chance that I shall meet with Mr. Chevillard; but, at all events you may rely on my discretion."

Esther had reached the door as these words were uttered, and taking a ceremonious leave, rapidly descended the stairs. Mademoiselle Lebeau politely accompanied her as far as the entrance of the shop, but the poor young creature did not even notice this attention; and the next moment she was in the street, so absorbed in grief, that she was regardless of all around her. Had it not been for the benevolent interference of a passer-by, who drew her hastily towards him, she would have been knocked down by a coach, and trampled under the horses' feet.

CHAPTER XIX.

LEAVING this unfortunate creature, half crazed with despair, to wander on without knowing what to do, or where to direct her steps, we will return to Mademoiselle Lebeau, who, on the other hand, was far from easy in her mind. To be a woman, and take revenge, especially when a quiet and negative sort of cruelty is in question, appears at first a very pleasant thing; but conscience, which speaks so forcibly to generous natures, will not be long silent, and pleads the cause of virtuous resolutions.

If, thought the fair mercer, it be true that this unfortunate young man is in such distress, am I not very obdurate to abandon him thus to his fate? Of what indeed had he been guilty? Had he broken any promise or engagement? To be sure, he had not seen what he might have seen; but was want of penetration a crime, and could the heart be disposed of at will?

It was, doubtless, singular and humiliating, that the very woman, who had disturbed the happiness of her life, should now try to interest her in *her* misfortunes, and solicit protection from the avenging shafts of destiny. But, when the suppliant became the wife of Chevillard, how could she know the blow she inflicted, or have any intention of injuring another? As she reflected upon all the circumstances, Mademoiselle Lebeau could not conceal from herself, that she had been actuated by unworthy motives, which she would have been ashamed openly to avow. In spite of the ingenious sophistry with which our evil propensities seek to justify themselves, she felt, that when she had to choose between a noble clemency and a harsh resentment, she had decided for the latter.

For some time, the balance remained suspended. She was irresolute and ill at ease. But, after a struggle of several hours' duration, she found she could not silence the upbraidings of her conscience, her native goodness prevailed, and she went to her private safe, from which she took the sum required; then, sending for a coach, in less than a quarter of an hour she arrived at Sainte-Pélagie. She was but just in time, the office was about to be closed, and, if she had delayed a few minutes longer, the matter could not have been settled that evening.

The necessary formalities for effecting the liberation of the prisoner were soon accomplished, and Mademoiselle Lebeau retired, after making the clerk promise, that no information was to be given to Chevillard, touching the person to whom he was indebted for his liberty.

This promise was easily kept by the obliging functionary, for that worthy individual being in a hurry to leave the office to go to a dinner-party, did not himself notify the good news to the captive. The gaoler, who went to tell him that the gates of his prison were open, could give no satisfactory reply to his anxious inquiries.

Since his wife had left him, Chevillard had enjoyed several hours of refreshing sleep, and was considerably better; indeed, the doctor had greatly exaggerated his danger, and the welcome intelligence of his release produced so happy an effect upon him, that it appeared to infuse fresh life and vigour into his languid frame. He insisted upon getting up and leaving the prison, in spite of all the efforts of the nurse to dissuade him from his design. Another motive, besides his desire to breathe once more the free air, instigated him to this imprudent act; he could attribute his unexpected deliverance to no one but Esther, and yet he could not conceive by what means she had been able to effect it. Besides, it was strange she had not come herself to announce the success she had met with: it was more than strange; and Chevillard's jealous susceptibility saw in it the evidence of some unwelcome communication with his persecutors. His anxiety on this subject would of itself have given him strength to stand and walk, and in less than half-an-hour he was on his road to the Rue Copeau. It was already dark, when, accompanied by one of the turnkeys, he presented himself to the mistress of the lodging-house; the man came with him to receive the amount of a small bill, which he had not ready money to discharge before leaving the prison, and this proved a fortunate circumstance, insomuch as it served to identify him as the husband of Madame Chevillard, and to gain him ready admittance into his wife's room.

Esther was absent, and had prudently locked the desk that contained her scanty hoard; but as a sort of omnibus-lock is very much in fashion at lodging-houses, which yields readily to the slightest pressure, Chevillard found no difficulty in opening this one with another key, that he took out of a drawer, and thus obtained possession of the sum required. Having dismissed the turnkey, he had no choice left but to await Esther's return, by the side of a crackling fire he had ordered to be lighted. He was vexed at her absence, but still he felt no alarm, and waited patiently for a considerable time; but as it grew later, and still she did not come, a vague feeling of inquietude began to creep over him. The large, comfortless room, dimly lighted by the flickering flame of one candle, was not calculated to inspire cheerful thoughts, and the deserted husband sought in vain to account for his wife's strange delay, now that the evening had completely closed in. A person, who is waiting for any one, feels the instinctive desire of motion and conversation. Chevillard accordingly repaired to the woman of the house, and made minute enquiries as to the time when his wife went out, and whether she had mentioned the place of her destination, or the hour when she intended to return. He could learn nothing satisfactory; so he sadly regained his solitary room, and began to walk up and down, a prey to countless doubts and conjectures.

Another half-hour had passed in this state of uncertainty, and the unhappy man had reached the last stage of impatience and anxiety; he spoke aloud, pressed his clenched hands to his head, stamped on the floor, and, in short, displayed all the signs of frantic grief, when a servant, who had not been present when he questioned her mistress, came in haste to tell him, that, a little before his wife left the house, she had received a letter, brought by a footman in livery. This information, though sufficiently alarming in itself, was hailed by Chevillard as a favour, for it furnished him with a clue to commence some researches, and he immediately began turning over everything in the room, in quest of the letter alluded to. After a long and tedious search, he found, near the place whence he had taken the money, and where he never thought of looking till the last moment, a note addressed to Madame Chevillard, in a hand that was quite unknown to him. He opened it; though without a signature, the contents left no doubt as to its author; they were as follow:

"My charming creature,—Madame de Saint-Martin informs me, that you have at length determined to be reasonable. That is as it should be. If you will come this evening, at six o'clock, to my *petite-maison*, we shall be alone. I send you the key, and the first come shall wait for the other. I enclose a draft for 5,000 francs, payable at my banker's, *to-morrow morning*. So when you leave me, you can call for the money, and restore your husband to liberty. You see, I deal honourably with you, and sacrifice myself without knowing whether you may not change your mind. But you were always incapable of breaking your word; and besides, my sweet angel, you know I am well able to remedy any mistake, if by an impossible chance you should intend to play me false. So, adieu till this evening."

The reader may easily guess Chevillard's terrible emotion when he read this epistle. The absence of his wife, who must think him still in prison, was now sufficiently explained. Seven o'clock had struck, as he made this frightful discovery, and the assignation was at six! All must be lost, and his dishonour completed!

For the moment, he was overwhelmed by the shock he had received, but soon recovering, he thrilled with the hope of finding the seducer still present. The pistol he had turned against himself on the day of the dinner with Chabouillant, was yet in his possession; he seized it, threw himself into a cab, stopped at a gunsmith's, where he purchased a dagger and some powder and ball, and then, promising to give the driver a handsome fee, ordered him to drive full speed to the Champs-Elysées.

Just before they reached the Allée des Veuves, he got out, and was quickly before the door of the house, which appeared to be so fatally connected with the sad and complicated drama of his life.

CHAPTER XX.

THE infuriated young man deliberated for an instant how he should get in; he gazed and listened attentively, but not a ray of light was visible, not a sound was heard, to guide him in his enterprise. At last, it struck him, that, as he could not possibly be expected by those he came to surprise, it was not likely they should be on their guard; he therefore adopted the simplest and most obvious mode of proceeding, and, seizing the knocker, gave two or three loud strokes. Some minutes passed, and then he heard steps in the courtyard, and distinguished a light advancing towards him.

The door opened; but instead of the villain he expected to see, Esther herself stood before him. On perceiving her husband, the unfortunate uttered a piercing cry, let fall the taper, and silence and obscurity reigned once more around. Chevillard's first thought was to cut off all means of escape from his enemy. He carefully closed and bolted the door; then, without knowing what had become of his wife, he went straight to the steps leading to the vestibule, traversed it with precipitation, and entered the saloon, where he saw candles burning. The apartment was deserted, and he soon convinced himself that the wretch he hoped to meet was not concealed in any part of it; he therefore seized a candle, and returning to the vestibule, was about to visit the upper chambers, when a strange and dismal vision fixed him in terror to the spot. Staggering like a drunken woman, her features pale and ghastly, her eyes dull and fixed, Esther painfully mounted the steps, tottered forwards, and, with a stifled groan, fell heavily at her husband's feet.

All other emotions were lost in a sentiment of pity, and Chevillard hastened to raise the unhappy creature, thinking that she had fainted; but to his great surprise, instead of the usual symptoms of a swoon, he found that her heart and pulse were beating with great quickness and force, though a deep and leaden sleep appeared to have suddenly seized upon her faculties. Alarmed and amazed by this singularity, the distracted husband paused in his schemes of revenge, took the patient in his arms, carried her into the saloon, and placed her on a seat; then, kneeling down before her, and chafing her hands, he asked if she did not know him?

"Yes," replied she, speaking almost inarticulately, and in broken accents; "I know your voice, but I cannot see you; there is a mist between us."

When she had said this, her eyes again closed, and she relapsed into her lethargy. Her breathing was so regular, that you might have supposed she was in a natural and tranquil sleep, had it not been for the convulsive shudder which from time to time agitated her limbs. Suddenly, an idea flashed across Chevillard's mind. "The wretches!" he exclaimed; "they have made her take a narcotic; they are familiar with such abominable practices in this house." This supposition tranquillised him a little, and, at the same time, renewed his rage; he rushed out of the room with a light in his hand, resolved to

search the house till he found the odious Morizot, whom he supposed to be concealed in some part of it. He went through all the upper rooms without success, and was descending the stairs, when a prolonged knocking was heard at the outer door.

"At last!" cried he, running to open it; "it is he! I shall have my revenge, and he has not achieved his crime. Heaven then is just!"

But it was apparently decreed, that, in this accursed house, no one should meet that evening with the person he expected. Chevillard was again deceived; it was not Morizot, but his worthy accomplice, Madame de Saint-Martin. At sight of the husband, against whom she had been conspiring from the first, this depraved woman started back in affright; but he rushed upon her, and seizing her arm, exclaimed: "Come in, come in, honest creature! come and contemplate your work; and afterwards we will settle accounts."

He then dragged her into the saloon, and placing her before Esther, still plunged in a heavy sleep: "What have you given to this unfortunate?" he asked, with ill-repressed indignation. "Come! speak—answer!"

"Pshaw!" replied the woman, without being in the least disconcerted; "there is no occasion to give anything to people to make them sleep when they are weary—the poor child has been waiting here at least two hours, for a person whom she was to meet upon your affairs, and who has not been able to come. She must have fallen asleep, while I was on my way to inform her of this mischance."

"And you do not name the person?" said Chevillard, ironically, and raising his voice in a menacing manner, till the noise appeared to rouse Esther once more from her state of stupor.

"See! she awakes," cried the Saint-Martin; "you can question her, and she will tell you if anything has been given to her, as you suppose."

"Esther! speak to me!" said Chevillard; "do you suffer anywhere?"

The patient opened her eyes, to which the prodigious dilatation of the pupils gave an expression no language can convey, and, putting her hands to her head, as if to intimate that it was there she felt pain, appeared about to relapse into her lethargy.

"Come, do wake up!" exclaimed the woman, shaking her; "here is your husband, who says you have had a narcotic given you."

"No—it is I—have taken——" replied the patient, with great effort, and again relapsing into that unnatural sleep.

"Ah, good heaven!" said the Saint-Martin, suddenly, holding a light towards Esther's face; "do you see those yellow spots round her mouth?"

"Well?" demanded Chevillard, in the greatest anxiety.

"Unhappy girl! she must have swallowed laudanum, to poison herself."

"Oh! pray God it may not be true," cried Chevillard; "for your life shall answer for hers!"

"Be quiet, with your threats! You would do much better to go for assistance. From the time you have let the poison work, it is perhaps too late to save her."

"But where shall I find a doctor in this part?" asked Chevillard, preparing to set off, greatly agitated.

"In the Rue des Gourdes, nearly at the corner of the lane that leads from this avenue to Chaillot, a house with iron gates; but stay—I had better go myself; you will lose time in looking for it."

"But is there nothing that can be done till you return?"

"I don't exactly understand what is proper in her state," replied the woman; "but try at least to shake off this terrible sleep, which ends in death."

Having given this prudent advice, she hurried away. Chevillard, left to himself, tried every means he could think of to combat the stupor which gained continually upon the victim; but the poison had been working for several hours, and was now irresistible in its action. During the short intervals when he was able to rouse her in some degree, the words she let fall showed that the faculties of her mind were affected by the poison. It was vain to hope for any intelligible account of the circumstances that led to the accomplishment of her fatal resolution.

Only a short time had elapsed since Madame de Saint-Martin's departure, but Chevillard's impatience for assistance was so great, that minutes appeared to him like hours; and he began to entertain the horrible suspicion, that, too happy to escape his vengeance, she had left the patient to her fate, when, to his great relief, she entered with the doctor. The symptoms of poisoning by opium were so evident, that the medical man was able at once to make up his mind. A large dose had apparently been swallowed, and the coffee and medicated vinegar, which he had brought with him to administer to the patient, did not produce the slightest effect. For several hours, he tried various remedies without success; and when, towards midnight, he decided to try bleeding as a last resource, it was followed by a final crisis, in which death wore so much the appearance of sleep, that no one could tell when the poor young creature breathed her last sigh. Madame de Saint-Martin had been indefatigable and judicious in her attentions to the unhappy Esther (a proceeding easily reconciled to her past conduct), and so long as there was any hope, and Chevillard and she were so engrossed alike by this mournful scene, an indifferent spectator might have supposed the greatest cordiality reigned between them. But when all was over, the bereaved husband gave way to the frenzy of despair; he threw himself upon the corpse, embracing it, and uttering inarticulate cries; then, turning his fury against the Saint-Martin, it is impossible to say what might have happened, had not the doctor interposed.

Although he did not comprehend the nature of the bitter reproaches Chevillard addressed to this woman, he saw that her safety was endangered, and advised her to retire, as there was no longer any occasion for her care. The matron had come to the Allée des Veuves in a hackney-coach, which was still in waiting; so that it was easy for her to reach her home in perfect safety. When he had seen her drive off, the doctor returned to Chevillard, and endeavoured to persuade him to leave the house. But the unhappy young man declared he would not impiously abandon the remains of the victim, and when the other proposed to send a nurse to assist him in the sad office of watching by the deceased, he peremptorily rejected any such hired interference.

Before leaving, the medical man once more carefully re-examined the body, to ascertain, beyond a doubt, that life was extinct, for the lethargic sleep produced by opium, frequently looks like death, before it has in reality taken place; but he acquired the painful certainty, that Providence had issued its irrevocable mandate, and prepared to depart, more affected than he usually was by similar catastrophes. Night, the lonely spot, all the incidents of the melancholy scene in which he had taken part, were calculated to produce a deep and painful impression upon the most callous mind.

A duty remained to be accomplished: the circumstance of poison always excites suspicion of crime. Although from all he had been able to ascertain, the doctor was morally certain that the deceased had committed suicide, he warned Chevillard, that he should be obliged to inform the authorities of the violent death he had witnessed, and asked if on his side he were prepared to answer the questions, which would undoubtedly be asked by the magistrate who would come to view the body.

Chevillard replied, that, far from fearing the investigations of justice, he was resolved to call down all its rigours on the guilty parties; and thanking the kind doctor, who refused all payment for his ineffectual services, he advised him to go and seek the repose of which he stood in need.

CHAPTER XXI.

WHEN Chevillard was left alone, like all persons who are a prey to extreme grief, he felt a strange impulse to recall everything that could increase the bitterness of his loss. Going back in the past, to the first dawn of the horrid fatality which weighed increasingly upon him, he recalled that joyous evening, little more than six weeks ago, when he dined with his colleague the commercial traveller, of which repast Mademoiselle Lebeau had appeared to foresee the disastrous consequences. From this had proceeded a logical and irresistible chain of events: his imprudent visit to the gambling-house, his fault, his acquaintance with Legros, his love, his marriage, all the misfortunes that had ensued, and finally, the frightful catastrophe which had closed the gloomy tale.

When he retraced the troubles that had overtaken him since the moment he first saw *her*, who now lay before him in death, he could not forbear thinking of the calm and happy existence that would have awaited him, had he been earlier aware of Mademoiselle Lebeau's sentiments, and had he married that lady; but he did not admit that these evils had arisen from his own ambition, vanity, and foolish wish to change the even tenor of his life; he preferred ascribing all to the insuperable decrees of fate, of which he was a melancholy and striking example. Then a thought flashed across his mind: now that his task was accomplished, and he had drained the cup to the dregs, might he not quit this losing game? When she, whom he had so loved, had but just departed, might he not rejoin her in that better world, to which she had preceded him?

But it seemed to him, that he had yet a duty to perform: those who had so mortally injured him, and to whom so precious a victim had been sacrificed, must expiate their crimes. He must live for revenge; he would not rejoice his odious persecutors, by sparing them a terrible retribution.

*   *   *

The long hours of the night passed heavily away; the tapers that had been lighted by the hand of Esther, that hand which they had outlived, were consumed in the socket. To their expiring light succeeded that of the moon, whose pale rays fell mournfully on the face of the deceased. Death had not yet changed her features, and they shone with a celestial beauty, awakening in the heart of the bereaved husband a fresh train of recollections.

He remembered, that in the same room, where she was now stretched livid and icy-cold, on the night when their marriage was decided, he had seen her in the full splendour of her youth and beauty. How often, his heart throbbing with love and joy, had he entered this house, now one of mourning and despair; and but a few steps separated the scene of death from the nuptial-chamber. Suddenly, the idea of a strange source of consolation occurred to the unhappy man. There, where his love had been crowned with felicity, he resolved to celebrate the espousals of death: he raised his beloved wife in his arms, carried the precious burden to the chamber above, and placed it respectfully upon the nuptial couch.

Then he remembered, that those who have departed for eternity, claim from us the garments of the grave; and he took from the drawer, where they had been religiously preserved, the clothes that fair girl had worn on her wedding-day. When she fled precipitately from this inhospitable house, she was obliged to leave them, and almost everything that belonged to her, behind; and now, finding a melancholy pleasure in attiring her with his own hands, the husband restored to his dead bride her white marriage garments, cut a lock of her light hair, and, kissing the cold forehead, resolved that she should sleep in no other shroud.

However rude and prolonged a trial may be, it must find a term. This terrible night, therefore, at length came to an end; and, towards morning, exhausted by fatigue and emotion, Chevillard sunk into a kind of dozing state, which, though it could not properly be termed sleep, gave him a few hours' respite from the consciousness of his situation and his sorrows. He was roused from this stupor, by a knocking at the outer door, and on opening it, admitted the magistrate of the district, who, accompanied by a doctor, came to verify the case of violent death which had been reported to him.

The magistrate interrogated the poor young man, as to the causes which had led to his wife's fatal resolution; upon this, he related the persecution to which she had been exposed whilst he was in prison, and the moral violence to which she must have yielded, to obtain his release; and, not doubting that she had sought in death a refuge for her virtue, he asked to depose a complaint against the authors of her deplorable fate. But he was told, there was not sufficient evidence of positive guilt, to warrant any proceeding at criminal law; the attempt at adultery had, as he himself stated, not been put in execution, and his wife's death, whatever might have been the motives that suggested so rash an act to her despair, could not be placed directly to the charge of those whom he accused.

Besides, there was a still more forcible reason: Chevillard's narrative had a certain air of romance, and many things in it were mysterious and unsatisfactory. The magistrate was not quite satisfied with the explanations offered to him, and, by the inquisitorial nature of his questions, manifested that a vague suspicion had arisen in his mind against the husband, when an unexpected yet perfectly natural intervention, diverted this last stroke of ill-fortune from the unhappy young man.

The reader has doubtless not forgotten the clerk, who was one of the witnesses at Chevillard's marriage, and with whom he was on intimate terms. Whilst the magistrate was pursuing his investigation, this young fellow presented himself at the house of mourn-

ing, saying, he had to give his friend a sum of money and a letter from his wife. The public functionary summoned him to tell all he knew, and being authorised thereto by Chevillard, he stated, that the day before, at about half-past five in the afternoon, Madame Chevillard had come to him, and asked him to render her an important service. Upon his answering, that he should be most happy to do so, she had given him a draft for five thousand francs, payable the next morning, and destined to procure Chevillard's release, whose recent imprisonment at Sainte-Pélagie, he thus learnt for the first time.

" I am obliged to start this evening, on an indispensable journey," Madame Chevillard had added, " and I should esteem it a great favour, if you would call on the banker, and then go to the prison to set my husband at liberty. Be kind enough to give him whatever money may remain over, and also this letter, which explains the motive of my absence." With these words, she had left precipitately, after assuring him of her gratitude.

" She appeared to be full of thought," continued the clerk, addressing his discourse to Chevillard; " and this morning, as soon as I got the money, I hastened to Sainte-Pélagie, but heard with astonishment, you had been released yesterday evening. A man at the prison gave me your address, Rue Copeau; I ran thither, and was told you went out last night, and had not returned. I then supposed you might be in this house, where you were staying after your marriage, so I set off immediately to give you the sum which was deposited with me, and Madame Chevillard's letter, for I thought its contents might be of importance to you."

" And you have that letter?" asked the magistrate.

" Certainly."

" Please to give it to me, then."

The messenger hesitated, and appeared to wait the consent of his friend, when the magistrate observed gravely: " Madame Chevillard died during the night, from the effects of poison."

This intelligence was like a clap of thunder to the young man, and the unfortunate Chevillard confirmed it by throwing himself, weeping, into his arms.

After a short pause, the magistrate resumed: " Some obscurity still reigns over this case, which it is the duty of justice to investigate. The letter you have brought, will, in all likelihood, furnish a positive explanation, and it is to your friend's interest that it should be as complete as possible."

Chevillard manifested no opposition to this intimation, and the letter was given up to the magistrate. He opened it, read a few lines, and then, with a rare sentiment of delicacy, which it were to be wished prevailed more frequently in criminal examinations, handed it to the husband. "The firm resolution to commit suicide," said he, "is expressed in the first sentences. It is not the province of justice to penetrate into family secrets, further than is necessary to inform itself of the truth; I need not read any more. As for us, sir," continued he, addressing the doctor who had accompanied him, "we have only to view the body, before drawing up the *procès-verbal* required by law."

Chevillard showed them the way; then, returning to his friend, he read what follows, with eager and mournful curiosity:

"When you receive this letter, my beloved, my heart will have ceased to beat; I embraced you yesterday for the last time.

"The terrible resolution I am going to accomplish, is not caused solely by the generous motive to which you will attribute it. As a dying woman, I come to confess all to you. Be merciful, as I trust God will be to me, for if I did evil, I did it from inexperience and want of reflection.

"I never knew my mother. My father was among the first who emigrated from his country, and it was afterwards known that he died abroad; he left me to the care of the man who now persecutes us. Instead of compassionating my youth and innocence, this man, from an early period, destined me to perform an infamous part, and he was but too well seconded in his guilty designs, by the woman to whom he confided my education.

"Brought up in idleness and ideas of luxury, you were the first person—perhaps, you will remember the evening—that I had heard mention the honourable resources, which a woman might find in her own exertions; before, it had been impressed on me, that opulent depravity or abject misery was her only alternative.

"Oh! how horrible it is to make the avowal; but when I became acquainted with you, I was already a fallen creature. Still, remember many things which may in some degree serve as my excuse for having deceived you.

"My seducer was continually speaking to me of a husband, partly in the interest of his own pleasures, always troubled and uneasy, partly for another reason, which I have never been able to penetrate. You were presented to me as an adventurer, undeserving the esteem of a virtuous woman; in that case, we were well matched. Besides, we were not to live together. I consented to our union.

"In a short time, I learned to know your worth, and then I did more than esteem, I loved you; but in proportion as your influence over my heart increased, the more unworthy I felt to bear your name.

"My struggles were not unobserved by you, and even the day before the wedding, I had resolved to tell you all; but menaced by the people in whose power I was, withheld by my own heart, which seemed to break at the thought of separating from you for ever, by losing your esteem, I made a base compromise with my conscience, and persuaded myself, that by the most devoted affection I might retrieve my shame.

"I had no merit in keeping myself faithful to you; I loved you with my whole soul; you had made me a new creature. I should even have *rejoiced* at the persecution to which I was almost immediately exposed, as proving the invincible strength of my resolution, had not my resistance affected your interests. The unexpected violence that was exercised against you, showed me the wickedness of our enemies, and also how vain were the hopes I had conceived, that with time everything might be arranged.

"On the second day of your captivity, the doctor declared, that, if it were prolonged, your reason or your life would be the sacrifice. I felt, I must save you at any price. After another useless attempt, I saw that I had no resource but one—that of appeasing our persecutor on his own conditions; but once a guilty wife, I could not live. 'Be it so,' I said; 'I will be his, since such is my cruel destiny; but Death shall be present at our meeting.'

"Do not pity me, my love; I had acquired the mournful certainty, that our happiness had no solid foundation. My secret might escape me at any moment; those to whom it was known, might reveal it to you, as they once threatened; and—from some bitter words that you

let fall, I perceived, that, though you were not aware of everything, you already regretted a marriage which had so soon cost you your liberty.

"Tormented by remorse, having lost the hope of making you happy, as I had thought to do, you see, I must die; and it is best so. Besides, this sacrifice restores me in my own esteem. I am not then quite lost, if I am permitted to die for you. They will not set you free till to-morrow, and to-morrow I shall not be with you, for the poison will soon begin its work. A friend will do what I cannot, and will give you this letter; perhaps, when you read it, you will not refuse to believe that I loved you truly!

"Yes, I loved you, my dearest husband, and now, when I am about to finish with life, my heart leaps towards you; you were my first and only love, and my last thought shall be yours. But I feel my courage fails, whilst I talk with you, and presently I shall need it all to die; and, what is worse, to go with death already in my veins, to meet the man who has my promise, and is now waiting for me.

"Adieu, therefore, dear love; do not

seek to revenge my death; you are poor and friendless in the world, and your enemy is rich and powerful. Only think sometimes of poor Esther, and oh! not to curse her memory; for, if she deceived you, you see how she punishes herself for it. So young, and to die!——Adieu, adieu for ever!"

Here the poor young creature's fortitude had failed; the scarcely legible writing, the traces of abundant tears, all testified to the rude struggle she had sustained with the instinct of self-preservation. But a little after, she had recovered her calmness, and had continued her letter in a firmer hand:

"Who will care for my funeral?—you, or strangers? I should have liked so much to be buried in my wedding-clothes, which I left in the house of the Allée des Veuves! But I am doomed to disappointment, and even this may not be."

When Chevillard read this mournful farewell, he was less affected by the revelation which appeared most likely to interest his self-love, than by the passage in which Esther intimated, that her fatal resolution had taken its rise from the imprudent sally of regret, into which he had launched respecting their marriage. Was not this a proof, that, under a certain levity of manner, he had yet retained a truly generous nature?

"O God! O God!" said he, sobbing; "it is I, who am the cause of her death!"

And, as a great sorrow leaves no room for petty calculations of vanity, he gave the sad memorial to his friend to read, heedless of the ridicule he might incur, as a husband deceived before his marriage.

"See," he exclaimed, "what a treasure she was, what a heart I have lost!"

"Yes," replied his friend, after reading it, "she was a noble woman; but she is right; there was little chance of happiness in your union, and this thought should tend to console you."

"Come," said Chevillard, "come and see, how, in everything, our hearts sympathised!"

He conducted his friend to the chamber of death, and showed him how his grief had divined and executed beforehand, the last wishes of the *lifeless bride.* But the awful stamp with which death marks those that are his, was now frightfully apparent, and the young clerk forced his friend away from the cruel spectacle. He then asked him, if he had been able to think of the necessary arrangements for the last sad offices. Nothing had been as yet attended to, and the friendly questioner having received instructions to order a decent but plain funeral, immediately went to put them into execution. He soon returned, and remained with the afflicted husband for the rest of the day, exerting himself to the utmost to prevent his giving way to despair. By gentle violence or ingenious address, he kept from him many of the sad details which precede the last separation from those we love, and thus many heart-rending scenes were spared the unhappy Chevillard.

The doctor, who had accompanied the magistrate when he came to verify the decease, was struck by the rapid change the poison had effected. He had in consequence ordered the interment to take place the same day, before the twenty-four hours required by law.

About three o'clock in the afternoon, a mean hearse, attended only by two young men, took its way towards the church of Saint-Peter at Chaillot. Informed of the motives for the suicide, the clergy did not refuse their prayers for the martyr-wife; the clergy was then tolerant, it had just escaped from persecution. The funeral-car then followed the line of the outer boulevards, and proceeded slowly towards the northern cemetery,* where it arrived at the decline of day. The winter's sun was setting, and its last rays tinged the misty atmosphere with purple. Such was all the pomp at that dreary funeral; and there too friends and relations were wanting, as, a few short weeks before, they had been wanting at the nuptial benediction of the deserted child, the victim of seduction and treachery.

CHAPTER XXII.

WHEN the last duties had been paid to the unfortunate Esther, Chevillard wished to bid his friend good-bye, but the latter would not consent to this, and, notwithstanding some slight resistance, took him to his own rooms, and persuaded him to remain the night. The next morning, he appeared more calm, and his host profited by this disposition of mind, to give him some excellent advice—as for example, to divert his grief by looking out for some employment; he even hinted at the possibility of resuming his former situa-

* That of *Montmartre.*

tion at Mademoiselle Lebeau's, offering, if agreeable, to undertake the negotiation of that business. Chevillard manifested neither approbation nor impatience at this overture; he merely asked for a few days' delay; but his mind was full of other thoughts, and, as soon as he could elude his friend's officious care, he stole away from his irksome hospitality.

He thirsted furiously for revenge; but he felt, that, to *secure* the punishment of the guilty parties, he must proceed with calmness and some degree of method. Before all things too, he wished to clear up a fact as yet unexplained. Whose benevolent interference had released him from prison? and it was not curiosity alone that gave him so much interest in the question. Supposing that Morizot or Legros had by chance *committed* this good action, in the reckoning he had to demand from them, he must evidently set it down to their account. He accordingly repaired to Sainte-Pélagie, to make inquiries of the clerk attached to the prison.

Notwithstanding the promise he had given Mademoiselle Lebeau, to keep her kindness secret, this functionary made no great difficulty in furnishing the most particular description of the young lady who came to discharge the debt. From the account he thus received, Chevillard could not fail to recognise his former employer, and, whilst the esteem and gratitude with which he already regarded her were thus increased, he saw with some satisfaction, that he need not abate in his hatred and resentment towards others. But now another question arose. The sum that Morizot had sent to Esther, had remained in his possession; ought he to employ it in discharging his obligations to Mademoiselle Lebeau, or restore it to its just owner? There was, however, but a transitory doubt on the subject in his mind. It came from an impure source, it was the price of innocent blood; such money could not be accepted by him, nor employed to discharge so sacred a debt. It must be sent back with contempt to the trafficker in his conjugal honour; or (as it afterwards struck him) to carry in person to the murderer his horrid gift, to throw it insultingly in his face, and provoke him at the same time to a meeting, in which one of the two must lose his life, would be the best plan of vengeance possible for him to adopt. If he perished in the struggle, all was over; if on the contrary he triumphed, he would proceed another step in his retributive justice, and, after chastising the *head* in Morizot, he would strike the *arm* and *instrument* in Legros. As for Madame de Saint-Martin, she had with him attended upon the victim; he would leave her unmolested to her own remorseful feelings.

Having come to this decision, Chevillard returned to the lodging in the Rue Copeau, where he allowed it to be thought that his wife had gone on a journey. Although he felt a strong desire to go and thank Mademoiselle Lebeau, yet at the moment of risking his life, any engagement he might enter into with her, respecting the money she had so generously advanced, would be a hollow mockery; and, all things considered, he thought there would be more nobleness of mind—since his evil fortune imposed so painful an alternative—in accepting the advance as a charity, than in acknowledging it as a debt, when he had the full consciousness of his insolvency. But, in return for the deep interest she had shown for his misfortunes, he owed her an unreserved confidence, particularly as he was ignorant how far and in what manner she had been informed of them. He therefore wrote her a long letter, in which, though he kept back *certain* details, he related all the bitter disappointments of his unfortunate marriage. He finished by stating, "that, being on the point of undertaking *a perilous journey*, he had at present no certainty of being able to discharge the obligations he had contracted; but, if he escaped the dangers to which he should be exposed, he regarded this as a most sacred debt, and, whilst his gratitude to her would be eternal, he should have no rest till he had paid the money so generously advanced."

Having written this letter, Chevillard judged, that the time had not yet come to send it, as the events to which he alluded were not entirely dependent on his will, and might possibly not be realised. He placed it therefore in his pocket-book, intending to drop it into the post, a few hours before the time fixed for his meeting with Morizot. The presence of mind shown in these arrangements, proved the firmness of the young man's resolution, and accordingly he now, without further delay, directed his steps to the Rue de Provence, where Morizot's sumptuous mansion was situated.

A great disappointment awaited him, which at the same time explained the unforeseen presence of the Saint-Martin at the Allée des Veuves.

In the afternoon of the day on which the commissary had appointed to meet Esther, he had been obliged to start, quite unexpectedly, on a journey. He had left at five o'clock in a post-chaise, without saying where he was going, or how long he should be absent, but it was supposed it would not be for a great while. Nothing seemed to prosper with the unlucky Chevillard, not even the design of hazarding his life; but his eager resentment would take no denial. As the master had escaped for the present, he resolved to wreak his vengeance on the confidant, and immediately proceeded to Legros' house. In the true spirit of retributive justice, he thought that, after all, this wretch had perhaps the best right to a priority of punishment, as he had been the first to draw him into the snare. But on arriving at the Rue des Moulins, there was a fresh disappointment. He was told by the servant, that her master and mistress (the Saint-Martin, apparently, who must have come, as it seemed, to lodge with the law-agent) had left that morning for the country. She could not say where they were gone, or how long they intended to stay, because they had left no word on the subject.

Thus Chevillard's evil star was still in the ascendant. Either by chance or prudence, the unworthy adversary he made sure of, had likewise escaped him, and for an indefinite time the cup of his wrath must remain full, without the possibility of overflowing. It is not true, that, by the side of great afflictions, secondary vexations are eclipsed and disregarded; far from it, they irritate and embitter still further the wounded feelings of the sufferer, and are to be lamented as destroying the cold resignation of sorrow, and thus depriving it of dignity. Left to muse over his baffled vengeance, not knowing whom or where to strike, Chevillard felt the cold and energetic despair, which had till then sustained him, give way to a species of frenzy. During the rest of the day, he wandered about Paris, sometimes walking straight onwards like a maniac, heedless of everything that was passing around him; at another, talking aloud with animated gestures. At length, harassed with fatigue, and faint for want of food, for he had taken nothing since the morning,

he went back to his dwelling, where he passed a miserable night, unable to sleep, and consumed by a burning fever, which filled his brain with funereal visions and horrible hallucinations. Towards morning, he became more calm, for he hoped that one of the wretches whose life he sought might have returned home, and he went once more to inquire for them; but neither of them had reappeared. A pious thought preserved him from a fresh attack of the furious delirium of yesterday: he resolved to visit Esther's grave, and, notwithstanding the extreme rigour of the season, passed the greater part of the day in the cemetery, absorbed in grief and tender recollections.

In some degree relieved by the abundant tears he had shed, he felt more composed, and set out to seek his friend the young clerk, for his conscience reproached him with having so abruptly left his hospitable roof. He passed a church on his road thither; and, as grief is naturally religious, he entered the holy place, prayed fervently for some time, and felt comforted.

He arrived about the hour of dinner, and was persuaded to take something, and listen to some cheering intelligence. His friend had heard of a situation that morning, and had great hopes of obtaining it for him. Chevillard warmly thanked him, and seemed disposed to profit by his kindness; then the clerk, who was a complete man of business, went on to speak of the personal effects Madame Chevillard might have left, and asked the husband if he did not intend to take some steps in the matter. Chevillard replied, that nothing could be more simple; that his wife had no portion, and that till she knew him she had lived on the poisoned bounty of the man she called her tutor, so that she possessed nothing of her own. The other objected, that Esther must at least have had wearing-apparel belonging to her, and that he would be a dupe not to claim it. Chevillard agreed that his friend was right, and promising to attend to this little matter, soon after took his leave.

When he was once more alone, the conversation that had passed continued to occupy him; not that he was in the least anxious about the trifling value a few dresses and a small quantity of linen could have in a *material* sense; but he remembered, that Esther had been obliged to quit the Allée des

Veuves furtively, and had left behind a number of things which she had in daily use. He had seen these things still in her room, when he sat watching by her dead body, and the idea that they were left in the hands of her executioners, who might some day make a sale of them, filled him with painful emotion. The key that Morizot had sent to the unfortunate wife on the day of the assignation, had been found on her, and was now in his possession, and he immediately thought of using it to obtain entrance into the deserted house, that he might take away these relics of one so dear to him. The absence of his enemies favoured the execution of this project, which proceeded, let us once more assert, solely from a refined sentiment of conjugal piety; but, as Chevillard had not the key about his person, he returned to the Rue Copeau to fetch it, and then set out for the Champs-Elysées.

The lateness of the hour did not induce him to defer his attempt; on the contrary, he was in no haste to arrive at the end of his journey; for he felt, that to enter a house which was not his, in the manner he proposed, to obtain possession of effects which ought to be legally conferred on him by the intervention of the law, was not exactly a regular proceeding; and he liked better to begin his enterprise in the silence and solitude of night. It wanted therefore about a quarter to eleven, when, provided with a tinder-box and his pistols, he entered the gloomy avenue, and approached the house.

CHAPTER XXIII.

At the moment when Chevillard was going to put the key into the lock, the steps of two persons advancing in that direction fell upon his ear. As he could not have opened the door, entered and closed it again, before the two intruders came up, he judged it would be more prudent to wait till they were gone. Not wishing to be seen, or his design to be suspected, he left the spot, and placed himself in ambuscade behind the trunk of a tree close at hand, which was large enough to conceal him entirely.

The steps, meantime, had become more distinct. Two days before, the moon had shed her pale light over the mournful scene we described. On this night, she shone brilliantly in a clear sky, and her rays fell so brightly through the branches of the tall trees, that Chevillard soon distinguished two men, wrapped up in cloaks, advancing rapidly towards the place where he stood. When they arrived opposite to the house, instead of pursuing their way, they stood still, looked carefully round, as if to make sure they were not followed, and then one of them approached the door. He opened it with a key, and, making his companion pass in first, disappeared with him.

Chevillard was much vexed by this singular coincidence of purpose. But this was not all; for, whilst the strangers were entering in his stead, his heart throbbed violently, as he thought that in one of them he recognised Morizot. It would have been a vain task, had he tried to resist the desire which instantly seized him, to know what these two men came to do, at such an hour, in that deserted house. It was not a fierce curiosity alone; he was impelled by a powerful and imperative instinct, to learn the sequel of this mysterious adventure, in which it seemed to him he was concerned. He cared too little for life to be stopped by the idea of danger, and, if he used some precaution in effecting an entrance, it was on account of the discovery he wished to make, rather than on that of his own safety.

He had opened the door very gently, penetrated into the court-yard, and advanced to the entrance of the hall, with noiseless steps; he heard nothing, and perceived no light, so that the people he wished to observe, were doubtless in the principal apartment, which looked upon the garden. As the localities were familiar to him, he hastily struck into a path which led round to the back of the house, and saw from a distance that the saloon was lighted up; he avoided the walks, for fear the noise of the gravel crushing beneath his feet might betray him, and advanced across the beds as far as one of the windows, through which the light gleamed. There he stooped down, and, looking through an opening that was left between two ill-closed curtains, he was able to observe all that passed in the apartment.

He had not been deceived. One of those he had seen enter, was indeed the commissary; the other was a fine-looking man of a very noble presence. He wore powder, which at that period was not yet regarded as singular, and appeared to be from fifty-five to sixty years of age. Through the closed windows, and at that distance from the speakers, Chevillard could not distinguish the sense of their words; but the expressive gestures of the stranger were significant either of his gratitude for some great service he had just received, or of his joy at finding himself in the company of Morizot. He took his hands, which he pressed warmly, and his whole countenance denoted affectionate kindness. Morizot, on the contrary, though he appeared to receive these testimonies of ardent friendship with great satisfaction, had the same dark and gloomy look which had struck Chevillard at their first interview, and it was the prejudice the young man naturally felt against his enemy, that doubtless made him fancy there was a peculiarly sinister expression of face, which would have made him hate and mistrust the man, even if he saw him for the first time.

Chevillard's patience was put to a severe trial; he wished to see how all this preamble would end, but for nearly an hour nothing particular occurred; only the conversation, which was at first very animated, began evidently to languish. Indeed, the stranger appeared to be struggling in vain against a feeling of drowsiness, and his head from time to time sank heavily upon his breast. But suddenly, amid the profound silence that reigned around, the watcher thought he heard two strokes upon the outer door. At the same time, Morizot arose, and taking from the chimney the only taper that lighted the apartment, went out hastily. In a few moments he returned, and by the red, uncertain light of the fire, Chevillard saw him speak to the stranger in an agitated manner; the latter seemed to share his emotion, and both hurried from the room. Ere many seconds had elapsed, a trampling of feet, followed by a cry of agony ending in a death-rattle, was heard behind the closed door.

A silence of some duration succeeded this fatal sound, which conveyed unspeakable terror to Chevillard's mind. He wished to rush to the assistance of the person in distress, but he was fixed to the spot, and his limbs were as if paralysed; besides, it was no longer time, for the door of the saloon again opened, and admitted first the Saint-Martin holding the light in her hand, and then Legros and the commissary, carrying between them the body of the stranger rolled in his cloak. Throwing open the folds of this shroud, the murderers placed their victim in an arm-chair, just opposite to the window, through which Chevillard could behold this horrid scene. The head of the deceased was thrown back, his face was pale, his eyes fixed and open, his arms hung down by the side of the seat; altogether, he was one of the most lamentable objects that human eye had ever contemplated. His pockets were carefully searched by Legros, who handed over to the Saint-Martin the purse, the handkerchief, and the jewels; to Morizot, the papers and pocket-book; after which, on a sign from the latter, the cloak was again thrown over the bloody remains.

From the moment the death-cry had struck his ear, Chevillard had lost all self-possession; weak-headed by nature, and subjected for many successive days to a series of terrible emotions, he had received from this atrocious murder a shock which affected his whole nervous organisation. The sense of sight alone remained perfect, and in that appeared to be concentrated all his faculties. The aspect of the corpse had exercised a sort of fascination upon him, and now that it was concealed, he fixed his eyes upon the countenance of Morizot, the chief actor in this frightful drama.

The extraordinary tension of nerve, which had sustained the assassin in the perpetration of the crime, was followed by a violent reaction; he sat silent and gloomy, wiping away the large drops of sweat that bedewed his forehead. Suddenly, his look rested on the window, from behind which Chevillard was gazing at him; he perceived that what was passing might be seen from the outside, through the interval between the curtains, and, with a rapid movement, he started forward to close them hermetically.

His intention was misinterpreted by Chevillard; he thought he was discovered, and his brain, already weakened by so many shocks, was completely upset; lifted as it were, by his emotion, he started up, and under the impression of his imaginary danger, rushed through the garden with a sort of mechanical rapidity. He climbed the wall by means of some lattice-work, but, persuaded that he was pursued, and fear lending him superhuman strength, he continued to run for a long time, unchecked by the obstacles that presented themselves. At last, he fell in with a night-patrol that was silently traversing the streets of Chaillot, and to the questions that were urged upon him, he could only answer in the accents of terror, and like a wretched maniac, such as he had now become : " He has his dagger, he pursues me !—here he is, here he is—save me !"

It is here, as the reader may perceive, that we rejoin the series of events given in the *prologue* to this history.

The murdered stranger, the mystification of the blind men, the madman arrested on the same night, all is now explained, and found to be closely connected. The letter addressed to Mademoiselle Lebeau was discovered upon Chevillard, and the explanations it contained, confirmed by the mistress of the *Tricoloured Prism*, completely misled the officers of justice ; and these two facts (so strictly united) were thus considered to be perfectly distinct.

Now, what interest had caused this crime to be committed, who was the victim, and what was the final issue of this dark and bloody mystery ? This is what our readers will learn from the *second part*, if they will but take the trouble to peruse it.

PART II.

CHAPTER I.

OFFENBURG is a small town in the grand-duchy of Baden, situated beyond the Rhine, at a little distance from the French frontier. At the beginning of the year 1804, it was one of the centres of those royalist intrigues, which, under the patronage of England, caused so much uneasiness to the Consular government. An insurrectionary committee was organised within its walls, and a number of emigrants, officers from the army of Condé, and conspiracy agents, met there daily. This state of affairs was likely in the long run to compromise the sovereign of the country, the Elector of Baden, who, two months later, saw his territory cavalierly invaded, when, by a bold stroke of policy, the Duke d'Enghien and several members of the *Offenburg Committee* were seized at Ettenheim ; but, in the meantime, it marvellously answered the purpose of Master Schmidt, the landlord of the *Golden Lamb*, for the constant influx of strangers into the town kept his house well filled.

One evening, about a fortnight after the occurrence of the events we have related in the first part of this history, Master Schmidt had just dismissed with all possible civility some travellers, whom he could not find means to accommodate, when a young man, in travelling costume, entered the public room ; he walked up to the landlord, and shaking hands with the air of an old acquaintance : " Ah ! good evening, Daddy Schmidt," said this new-comer ; " how do you get on ?"

" Thank ye, Mr. Chabouillant, not so bad, not so bad — and you ?" replied mine host, with a sort of constraint in his manner.

" Oh ! I'm as sound as the Pont-Neuf at Paris ; but I've had a famously fatiguing journey to-day, and I mean to sleep like a top, in the snug nest you'll have got ready for me."

" You want a room, I see that plain enough," said the host ; " but there's a difficulty in the way, I must tell you."

" Difficulty ! don't know such a word," returned the other ; " it's not French !"

" But it's German, and means I can't give you a bed this evening, because there's not one unoccupied."

" Allow me ; I am Joseph Chabouillant, traveller in the mercery line, whose custom and usage it has been, from time immemorial, to stop, going and coming, at the sign of the *Golden Lamb*, consuming, I may say, a pretty considerable quantity of *prog*, and having never on any occasion asked for an hour's credit."

" You fill me with regret, my good sir, when you remind me of your claims to a distinguished and cordial welcome ; but, upon my word, I have not a corner that I could offer you."

" Very well, my dear fellow !" replied Chabouillant, with great coolness. " The *hotel of the Palatinate* is at the other end of the street ; I will see if travellers are not better received there."

" Ah ! yes, that's just the thing," said the host, rejoiced at getting off so cheaply ; " be unfaithful to me for once, and I promise you that next time ——"

" No, no !" interrupted Chabouillant, " I don't fly from fair to fair in that way ; when I am well received in any place, I return to it. I am like the ivy ; where I have fixed myself, I perish !"

The commercial traveller was, in point of fact, an excellent customer ; the unlucky innkeeper, finding himself menaced with the loss of his patronage, entered into the most detailed account of the circumstances that dictated his refusal. He urged, that, as it was forced on him by necessity, he ought not to be punished by the total desertion of his guest; but the commercial traveller was inflexible, and quietly resumed his cloak and portmanteau.

"Come," said Master Schmidt, "will you listen to a proposal, which will prove to you my goodwill and attachment?"

"Speak, landlord; I listen."

"Do you snore at night?"

"I!" said Chabouillant; "do you take me for a humming-top?"

"No; but I ask you whether you sleep quietly, and do not start and call out; in short, whether you may be trusted?"

"My dear fellow, I never saw myself asleep; but I should imagine that, to-night at least, my slumbers will be those of innocence."

"Well, this it is. You know the little pleasure-house at the end of the garden?"

"Perfectly!" replied Chabouillant; "I ask for no more; that will be just the thing."

"Yes, but the said house is occupied. I have let it to two of your country-people, husband and wife, who I suspect to be agents for the English government, and persons of superior condition—for they do not mix with the other emigrants, fetch their letters themselves from the post-office, and live shut up like bears."

"From which you conclude——" said the guest.

"I conclude, that the two rooms are occupied; but there is a little closet at the back, fit for a servant, and I might be able to settle you there, if you will put up with it."

"Indeed!" said Chabouillant.

"But if I do, you must promise to be very careful, and not make the least noise that may betray your presence; for these people inquired if I meant to let this little place, which is separated from them only by a slight partition, and pay me for it as if they occupied it."

"A newly-married pair?" asked the traveller.

"No, middle-aged people," returned mine host.

"Well, let us have the closet."

"But you must sup, now I think of it; and, during that time, my lodgers (who are out) may return."

"Not at all, I am as full as a sack. I have been at work at the house of one of our clients, in such style, that I shall not want to feed for the next three days. Only get me a glass of punch, and show me the way to bed."

The innkeeper threw a pair of sheets over his arm, and went himself to prepare Chabouillant's bed, as a degree of prudent caution was necessary; half an hour later, our old acquaintance was sleeping like a lord.

CHAPTER II.

CHABOUILLANT had finished his first sleep, when his neighbours, who, contrary to their usual custom, had been out late, apprised him of their presence by the sounds of an animated conversation. It was carried on in a very high key, particularly on the lady's side; so that the traveller could not help hearing the whole of it. The couple decidedly appeared to be quarrelling, for a female voice exclaimed: "No, I tell you again, nothing shall persuade me to return to France; for I do not even consider myself as safe here, on the frontier, where you will persist in remaining."

"But," answered the husband, "when we are told that everything is quiet and forgotten——"

"Nonsense! such things may sleep for fifteen years, and then, all of a sudden, the mine may be sprung."

"But now, where do you think the danger can come from? Esther is dead, Chevillard has gone mad, and that unlucky incident of the assignation given by Morizot, did not raise the least suspicion."

At the name of Chevillard, Chabouillant's attention was naturally aroused, and it redoubled, when the woman resumed: "That may be, but I don't trust to all this. I have always before me that unfortunate man falling by Morizot's dagger. To murder an old friend in that manner is horrible!"

"If you were to say so for ever," returned the husband, "I should repeat, that this crime was almost unavoidable, though I disapproved of it at the time, and dislike bloodshed. Instead of being dead, as was always supposed, our confounded master writes one fine morning to Morizot, from the Rhenish frontier, to say that he should have already re-entered France, if he had been sure his name was erased from the list of emigrants. Now, when his fortune became national property, Morizot monopolised

GREENAWAY & WRIGHT

it; so he was obliged to adopt some expedient."

"A fine expedient truly!" said the woman, contemptuously.

"I confess it was a harsh measure, but it was cleverly conceived, and carried through with the hand of a master. As soon as Morizot received De Brevannes' letter, he got into a post-chaise, and in forty hours he was at the frontier; the marquis crossed it, by passing as his servant. On his arrival in Paris, before he had time to see a living soul, and on the pretext of being in a safe asylum till his position was legalised,

the said marquis is taken to his former *petite maison*, in the Allée des Veuves, a place cut out for the express purpose, and there he is quieted in a twinkling. If that is not rigorous honesty, you must confess it is skill and resolution."

"Why did he not execute his purpose by himself? There was no necessity to send for us to assist at the murder, and thus make us his accomplices, when he alone did the deed!

"Hang it! it was a good thought to have us with him, for he would have been finely puzzled to get rid of the gentleman ; and had it not been for my bright idea of making use of those honest blind men, that were sent to us by Providence, I don't know how the matter would have ended."

" Ah! that's just like you. If you have an opportunity to display your resources and talent for intrigue, you make up your mind to anything. I do believe, you would mix yourself up in the worst affairs, which did not concern you in the least, merely to show your abilities."

" But I beg your pardon ; the affair did concern us, and deeply too. Brevannes could only demand from Morizot an account of his fortune, and of Esther's fortune, which our worthy friend had made so free with ; but the girl's seduction we had to answer for, and we are too deep in the mire not to be glad to get rid of the marquis."

" You should not have given credit so easily to the report of his death."

" Who would not have credited it? The first account of it was received fourteen years ago, and since then it has been confirmed twenty times. Two months since, a rumour was afloat that the deceased still lived ; we immediately provided for that which was most urgent by marrying the girl to Chevillard, and I will say that the affair of the marriage was skilfully combined."

" Yes, and that odious Morizot spoilt everything by his passion for Esther, and forced her to commit suicide by his importunities. And then what a mean wretch ! after Esther left, not to give us the house in the Allée des Veuves, though he always promised it to me."

" But you see, my dear, he wanted it ; it was deucedly useful to him ! "

" And you, what have you ever got out of this miser, for being his devoted slave so long? All his scurvy affairs, his usuries, his stock-jobbing with the property of the emigrants, you took charge of them, even as I engaged to train that unfortunate creature to his will ; and now, when having become the accomplices of his last crime, our safety obliges us to leave France, he dismisses us with a paltry ten thousand francs, whilst he is worth millions."

" But he is a man skilful in business, and of astonishing abilities, for whom I feel great admiration. That is how he has acquired such an ascendancy over me ; and then what would you have ! he has always had the largest share in all our transactions and schemes, but remember from whence each of us

started. You kept the porter's lodge, at the pleasure-house of the marquis ; I was his valet, and Morizot his steward : the latter had naturally the most of the spoil. Besides, he entered the store-department, and was successful."

" Do revolutions take place then for some to have all, and others nothing ?" said the woman, with amusing gravity. " Why should he be better off than you are? Are you not as good as he ?"

" In some respects, I know I am superior to him. I have more cunning, more resources ; but he has more boldness and resolution. Do not deceive yourself ; he is a profound politician— a man who follows the end he has proposed to himself, without heeding the obstacles that may be in the way. I am a sort of Figaro, he is a man of genius. The truth must be confessed."

" Hold your tongue ! he is a villain, and nothing more—a man capable of ruining us if it served his interest, and that is why I don't mean to risk myself in France, in spite of his friendly invitation for us to rejoin him."

" My dear, you are very dull to-day,'' replied the husband. " Do you not perceive, that our position with Morizot has never been better ? The crime, which we have in our keeping, is a piece of good fortune ; we have our good friend in check without his suspecting it, and don't think I mean to be duped for ever."

" Well ! those are the only reasonable words you have spoken as yet ; not but what I should be as well pleased if his crime were his sole property, because I am sure, that, sooner or later, it will bring us into some mess with the law."

" Make yourself quite easy ; the police have other things to do than to hunt out the murderers of a poor devil, whom no one recognized, and whose family is extinct. You see what is taking place here, and what the English government and the royalists are preparing for the First-Consul ; that now occupies all our official people, and no one thinks of us, you may depend upon it !"

" You will always be in the right," said the woman ; " but I shall not sleep more quietly to-night than I have done lately ; I see either the marquis covered with blood, or his unhappy daughter, continually in my dreams."

" You are a child," returned her husband ; " I shall write to-morrow to Morizot, who cannot do without me, and make my own conditions. But whatever you may say, we will not stay here long; my career lies in France, and my fortune is only begun."

Whilst listening to this conversation, full of horrid revelations, Chabouillant greatly regretted that the darkness would not allow him to assist his memory by taking notes; for the name of Chevillard, which had been several times mentioned, gave him food for reflection, when he remembered his friend's simplicity, and the disreputable place in which he had last left him. To supply in some degree the want of written memoranda, he employed himself during the rest of the night in fixing firmly in his mind the principal circumstances, and the names of the actors in the dismal drama which had been unfolded to him, and, instead of sleeping *like a top* (to use his own elegant expression), he waited impatiently for day, to leave his *bedroom*, and enjoy the free use of his liberty.

CHAPTER III.

THE next morning, having endeavoured to avoid any noise that might betray his presence in the cell into which he had been smuggled, the commercial traveller went down to the public-room, and called for his breakfast. He commenced operations with his usual vigour, and, while thus agreeably employed, the innkeeper, who was acquainted with Chabouillant's *monomania*, after asking him how he had passed the night, observed: "Well, and the family? has it been found this time?"

"Hum, hum!" replied the guest, "I have acquired, during this journey, information that makes me think I am on the point of many great discoveries."

"Ah, indeed! well, so much the better," said Master Schmidt, "provided it will not keep you from coming to see us now and then."

"On the contrary, I shall like moving about better than ever," returned Chabouillant. He soon after paid his expenses, and, getting into a coach, started for the French frontier, to proceed from thence straight to Paris

Whilst he is pursuing his journey, we must beg the reader to accompany us for a time to the establishment of the *Tricoloured Prism*. Mademoiselle Lebeau was as yet scarcely recovered from the shock which Chevillard's dreadful calamity had occasioned her. The letter addressed to her, and found in the pocket-book of the poor maniac, contained a circumstantial but rather confused account of the young man's conjugal misfortunes, and the fair mercer thought she perceived, that her hesitation in complying with Esther's request had in some degree influenced the terrible catastrophe. Although she had redeemed, by her subsequent generous determination, the error she had committed in the first instance, in following a natural and excusable impulse, and although the frightful calamity she deplored could not really be laid to her charge, she had bitterly reproached herself for the mournful fate of the unhappy wife. Like all elevated natures, who think a great deal of the evil and never of the good they may have done, the fair mercer pictured to herself that young and lovely woman, perishing in the flower of her youth, for the want of a little well-timed pity; but she forgot the motives that induced her to receive her request so coldly, and the quick repentance and weighty sacrifice which had followed. It may readily be conceived, that, in such a disposition of mind, the possible consequences of Chevillard's state as a widower never occurred to Mademoiselle Lebeau. If this even had been the case, she would have repudiated the idea as a sacrilege; and, in the afflicted inmate of the hospital at Charenton, she only saw an unhappy being having a peculiar claim to her care and compassion, and she gave them to him fully and heartily, without any personal or interested calculation.

One Sunday, all the members of the household, even the domestic servants, had obtained permission to go out, and the sorrowful young girl was sitting quite alone, more than ever absorbed in her thoughts and recollections, when, at a late hour in the evening, she heard the door-bell ring. Some one might have forgotten to take a latch-key, so she went to open the door without hesitation; but she felt a momentary alarm, when she saw before her a man wrapped in a cloak, which quite concealed his face. She could not altogether control her agitation. Fortunately, a well-known voice soon reassured her: "Do not be alarmed, mademoiselle," said the man in the cloak, "I am Chabouillant."

"I confess you frightened me; your strange way of presenting yourself, and the rather singular hour you have chosen for the visit——"

"You shall know, mademoiselle, the reason of the mystery with which I surround myself; but I wish to speak to you in private, without witnesses."

" Come in, I am alone," replied Mademoiselle Lebeau, who knew how to keep people at their proper distance, and therefore feared nothing from the interview she thus granted. However, she thought fit to receive her visitor in the shop, which had not been heated on that day, thinking that this might abridge a conversation she did not wish to prolong.

" First allow me, mademoiselle," said Chabouillant, " to ask after the state of your precious health."

" It is not very good ; I have not been well for some time."

" In truth, I find you in a slight degree thinner and paler. You are too anxious, and have not assistance enough. And Chevillard, how is he?" added the traveller, wishing to know if he whose name was mixed up with the shocking revelations at the *Golden Lamb*, were the same Chevillard with whom he was acquainted. If Mademoiselle Lebeau could have guessed the terrible influence that the commercial traveller had exercised on the destiny of the poor madman, she would have replied to his question with the most severe reproaches, and indignantly have dismissed him ; but her former book-keeper, in the letter he had written, did not confess the way in which he had abused the confidence reposed in him, and, without stating how he became acquainted with Legros, had dated the commencement of his misfortunes from his first fatal meeting with that wretch. Chabouillant had apparently no connection therefore with this sad story.

" Oh ! Mr. Chabouillant," said she, " you do not know the dreadful calamity that has befallen your friend !"

" What is the matter?" cried Chabouillant, with an anxious curiosity that might pass for interest.

" The unfortunate is at Charenton ; he is out of his mind."

" It is he," thought the traveller, whilst he exclaimed aloud : " Good heavens ! what do you tell me?"

" It is too true," resumed Mademoiselle Lebeau ; " he was seized with this terrible disease about a fortnight ago." Then, taking care not to say anything more than Chabouillant might have learned in the commercial world, where this adventure of the ex-book-keeper was partly known and much talked about, she related with tears in her eyes the marriage and imprisonment of Chevillard, the death of his wife, and his own sad fate.

" Poor fellow !" said Chabouillant ; " I left him in the full vigour of youth and health, and now —— just too as I thought to enchant him with the good news I had to tell !"

" Some good fortune has happened to you?" asked Mademoiselle Lebeau.

" Undoubtedly ; that ardour and fierce longing for domestic joys, that has often exposed me to the imputation of folly, was simply an instinct ; and, such as you see me, I am on the point of laying my hand on my family."

" Indeed !" said the young girl, with a slight expression of incredulity.

" Yes, mademoiselle, seriously ; I have tracked out startling claims and proofs ; only I shall greatly miss the assistance of Chevillard, in the further prosecution of my discoveries."

" How so? How could he serve you in a matter so purely personal ? "

" Ah ! because there are persons, whose interest it will be to thwart my birthright ; and I shall have to sustain a law-suit, a struggle, for which I counted on the precious co-operation of friendship."

" But I think a barrister would be of more use to you than Mr. Chevillard, who understood nothing about law-affairs."

" Mademoiselle, you are ignorant of the romantic and chimerical character of my history ; my right is not doubtful, it is as clear as daylight, but I have to do with powerful opponents, who will move heaven and earth to prevent me from assuming my proper name, and if I am not borne out by the kindness of a friend, who, without in any way committing himself, would render me a slight service, I cannot conceal from you, that my life itself may be in danger."

" You frighten me, my dear sir, and it would be but reasonable to renounce so perilous an enterprise."

" Oh ! I know perfectly well what I am about, I can assure you, mademoiselle ; and when the sword has once left the scabbard, I will fight to the last."

" But tell me, then, of what nature was the assistance you expected from Mr. Chevillard ? "

" Is it with the intention of supplying the place of my unfortunate friend, that you ask the question ? " demanded Chabouillant, abruptly ; " for in fact, you might do so without inconvenience."

" Before I can return any answer, I must know what is the object of your request."

" When I say you *might*, I mistake; you *ought*," returned the commercial traveller, with strong emphasis, " you ought to venture in my cause that which Chevillard would not have failed to do, for is it not true that you felt for him an interest of a peculiar kind? Well! you must know then, that my triumph will be likewise his."

" Mr. Chabouillant," replied Mademoiselle Lebeau, " allow me to tell you that you are in a hazardous path. When a man is governed by a fixed idea, it often creates a dangerous excitement, which may have the most fatal results."

" In other words, Chevillard having gone mad, you think it's contagious, and that, like him, I had better pay a visit to Charenton; but if I were to tell you that I know more of his history than you do, and that the people who so basely deceived him are among my opponents, would you still think that I am indulging in a dangerous aberration?"

" Good heavens!" exclaimed Mademoiselle Lebeau, clasping her hands; " it would be indeed a work of Providence; but what in fine do you require?"

" Nothing can be more simple," replied Chabouillant, with an air of mystery; " I have here," and he took from his pocket a small box securely locked, " all the proofs necessary to *legalize* myself."

" Indeed!" said the fair mercer.

" My opponents have the strongest interest to get possession of these papers, and they would not stand at murder to obtain them."

" Oh, horrible!" cried Mademoiselle Lebeau.

" This box must therefore be deposited in a secure place, and then I can inform my respectable adversaries, that it is impossible for them to extract it from me, and that, if any outrage were committed against my person, justice would be immediately informed of it."

" Then you would wish me to take charge of this?"

" Yes, as Chevillard would have done; and I again assure you, on my honour, that his interests are here connected with mine."

" Give it to me," said Mademoiselle Lebeau, overlooking the mystery attached to the service demanded of her, in consideration of its affecting in some degree Chevillard's interests; " and now, what else is to be done?" asked she.

" Nothing; put this deposit away somewhere, and let no one breathing suspect its existence. I will come here from time to time, with all necessary precaution, to inform you how I am progressing; but if, during a fortnight from to-day, I were not either to come or write, then force the lock, and having read the enclosed papers, you will see what must be done to avenge Chevillard and me."

" Certainly, this is a simple request," said Mademoiselle Lebeau; " and yet I feel quite frightened at all this secrecy."

" It is the effect of mystery," replied Chabouillant, with the air of a profound moralist; " it always strikes the imagination."

" And if, before I see you again, our poor afflicted friend were to recover his reason, should I speak to him of all this?"

" You see him then sometimes?" asked the traveller.

" Of course," replied the fair mercer, with great simplicity; " poor, deserted, and with no relations near, who else would pity him?"

" Is there any hope of a cure?"

" As yet the doctors do not like to give an opinion; but yesterday he was a little better. Ah! Mr Chabouillant, if you could see the dreadful place where he is detained! I always quit it with an aching heart."

" To reply to your question," returned the visitor, rising to take leave, " I think, that, even when restored to his senses, our friend's mind will continue at first rather weak, and the shock of any intemperate disclosure is to be feared; all things considered, you had better not mention this affair, without our consulting together."

" I think you are right," said the young lady; " besides, will his reason be restored so soon, or ever?"

" Let us hope," replied Chabouillant; " and, at all events, a thousand thanks for your generous assistance."

He wrapped himself carefully in his cloak, and left the *Tricoloured Prism* with the same precautions he had adopted on entering.

———

CHAPTER IV.

More lucky than Chevillard, we will now go to the Rue de Provence, and obtain at once admission to the house inhabited by Morizot, the contractor and assassin.

There will appear to us, in its most frightful form, what some believe to be an argument against the existence of a superintending Providence, whilst others, who see further and more clearly, pronounce it to be the strongest evidence of another and a better world—namely, the prosperity of the wicked here below.

For it was not only by the possession of a large and plentiful stock of *material* comforts, that this murderer seemed to insult the justice of God and man; to his sumptuous apartments, his rich equipages, his portfolio stuffed with good and valid securities, his pictures, his bronzes, his town and country houses, must be added, in the account of his scandalous happiness, the blessings and joys of a family, which alone might have made him an object of envy, had he been able to appreciate or understand them.

Come from afar, and fallen one knows not how into the hands of this wretch, a mild, devoted, amiable woman, of cultivated mind and elegant manners, had made him the father of two charming girls. Attractive, both by their beauty and their fortune, these young persons seemed destined to make brilliant marriages, and, in the imperial aristocracy that was then forming, there was hardly any rank to which they might not aspire.

One morning, this splendid scoundrel, who might well be called a *Turcaret* in crime, was occupied with a personage of some consequence, in planning a marriage of this kind for his eldest daughter, when a servant came to interrupt him with the strange announcement, *that the Marquis de Brevannes was there, and wished to speak to him.*

To hear a visit announced from a man, the last of his name, whom a few weeks before you think you have sent into the other world, is not a very ordinary case, and one that is likely to have some effect upon your nerves. Morizot therefore made the servant repeat the intelligence, which had occasioned him such disagreeable surprise; and persuading himself, for good reasons, that it was impossible the Marquis de Brevannes should really be in his antechamber, he concluded, that some mistake in the name would probably explain it all.

The little discussion which arose between the master and servant on this question, induced the previous visitor of the commissary to take his leave; and as Morizot, in the ticklish state of his conscience, was somewhat mystified at the perseverance of the servant, in maintaining that he was not deceived as to the name, he allowed his guest to depart with the assurance, that he would soon have the honour of seeing him again, and that they would then resume their conversation. He next ordered, that the new-comer should be admitted.

On seeing a young man of rather vulgar appearance, the commissary felt greatly relieved; and, recovering his usual haughtiness of look and manner, he made a sign to the stranger to be seated, and asked him to whom he had the honour of speaking.

It were vain to attempt to deceive the reader. In this audacious visitor, he has already guessed the depositary of the dark secrets revealed at the *Golden Lamb.* As we said in the first chapter of this story, Chabouillant "had little elevation in his feelings or ideas, but was gifted with the most imperturbable self-possession," and of course he did not think that a secret of this importance should remain an unproductive capital in his hands. Though he knew what a terrible adversary he had come to encounter face to face, he retained as much ease of manner and presence of mind, as if engaged in the most simple and natural transaction; and it was in that jovial and would-be-elegant tone, the use of which we have before observed in him, that the commercial traveller answered without hesitation to the question asked him: "Sir, I am the bearer of a name, that is neither strange nor indifferent to you—the Marquis de Brevannes."

"De Brevannes?" said Morizot, as if not quite sure that he had heard rightly.

"No, Brevannes—Bré, Bré," answered the commercial traveller, spelling the word.

"You astonish me a good deal," said the commissary; "I knew indeed, before the revolution, a Marquis de Brevannes, who was one of the first to emigrate; but I have every reason to believe, that he died abroad, and, in any case, he would now be nearly sixty years of age. It cannot therefore be he, that I have now the honour of receiving ?"

"The person in question, sir, was my father; I am Brevannes, Junior."

The commissary threw a long and searching glance at the author of this communication, and then resumed: "I think I am tolerably well acquainted with the family affairs of the late Marquis de Brevannes, and I never heard that he had a son, much less a son that bore his name; you are doubtless aware that he was never married."

"Excuse me—the marquis had two children: Esther de Brevannes, whom he acknowledged, and myself, the elder of the two, for whom he did that service in foreign parts, to prevent the name from becoming extinct."

"It is possible, sir," said Morizot; "but what then is the object of your visit ?"

"As my father's sole heir, I wish to ask you, sir, in your quality of former steward to the marquis, for some information as to the state of the paternal fortune."

"The marquis was an emigrant; his property was confiscated, and sold by the nation——"

"And bought by you, I know," interrupted the false De Brevannes, "with the evident intention of restoring it to the rightful heirs. It was a noble act, sir !"

"It is impossible for me to accept this praise," answered Morizot, drily, "for the existence of any such heirs was completely unknown to me."

"What ! even that of my sister Esther ?" asked Chabouillant, in a slightly ironical tone, which had its effect on the commissary.

"I speak of heirs male. With regard to Mademoiselle Esther, the marquis entrusted her to my care before his departure, and it would be strange indeed if I had not known of her existence."

"And of her death, also," continued the commercial traveller, in the same tone which had already so much displeased Morizot.

"Ah !" said the commissary, assuming an air of emotion; "we lost the poor child only a few weeks ago."

"That alone, my dear sir, makes another little account to be settled between us; for, to my certain knowledge, my father had left in your hands a considerable sum of money, which was intended for the dowry of my poor

sister. Now, as she died within two months of her marriage, and before you had time to come to any settlement with her, this money must naturally still be in your honourable hands."

"Without denying or affirming the reality of such a deposit, on which subject you may have been wrongly informed, I would just remark to you," resumed the commissary, with a presence of mind which was becoming every moment more necessary, "that natural children, though they may inherit from their father and mother, do not inherit from each other. In any case, were I inclined to listen to your demands, your right to the name you have assumed would require some confirmation."

"That is to say, I must prove to you, by some mode or other, that I am my father's son."

"Why," answered Morizot, who, thinking he could detect some embarrassment in this reply, now assumed an air of indifference, "it is usual to proceed in this manner, between persons who have no previous acquaintance."

"Well," said the young man, with apparent simplicity, "I must begin by freely confessing that I have in my possession no titles or proofs of any sort; but I have reckoned upon you to help me out of this ridiculous position."

"How so ?" asked the commissary, with disdainful curiosity.

"Having managed the affairs of the marquis for a long time, you must have seen papers, or other evidence, proving my birth; and, in default of other proofs, your testimony may be of great service to me."

"But I tell you again, sir, that I never before heard of your existence, and I certainly shall not affirm a fact of which I am wholly ignorant."

"Then," said the pretended marquis, "we must take up the matter in another light. Are you quite sure, sir, that my father died abroad, as reported ?"

This question was asked in a tone calculated to touch Morizot in the depths of his conscience; he answered therefore with some confusion: "I have heard so, but cannot of course be positively certain."

"Well, then, I can inform you that, about a fortnight ago, he returned to France."

"It is impossible," stammered the

commissary; " but, in any case, I have seen nothing of him."

" I will add," continued this terrible visitor, raising his voice, " that certain reports have reached me, which make me suspect that he was the victim of an assassination, soon after his arrival."

" You are wrong, young man," said Morizot, in the utmost agitation, " to believe lightly such reports."

" And you are wrong, sir, not to believe them; for they go so far as to name the assassin—and the person named is *you*."

" Sir !" cried Morizot, pale and trembling, but trying to assume the dignity of injured innocence.

" That is not all. Esther de Brevannes died a violent death, in consequence of a base seduction, of which she was the victim. She was, moreover, robbed of the dowry left by her father in the hands of a faithful guardian. I will add, that the murder I speak of was committed in a solitary house in the Allée des Veuves, by the person who had the chief interest in concealing all these crimes. He was aided by a former valet and a female pander of the marquis, a charming couple who have now taken refuge at Offenburg— and the dead body was afterwards removed by some blind men. Will you now believe, sir, that I am De Brevannes, Junior, or will you give me your assistance to prove it, even if I am not?"

During this long speech the commissary, though much alarmed, had in some degree recovered himself.

" Come, sir," said he abruptly, " you know that I am tolerably rich, and you think, by a tissue of horrors, to make a speculation of me. I will not deny that you have touched my weak point, for I have a great dread of calumny. Speak, then! what do you require?"

" Allow me, sir !" said Chabouillant; " you do me, I think, the honour to offer me a sum of money?"

" Yes, a round sum—provided you are not unreasonable in your demands."

" But I tell you, sir, that I am determined to have my birth acknowledged and certified."

" Your birth, sir ? I am quite sure that you are not the son of the Marquis de Brevannes, and I do not see what interest you can have in this dangerous usurpation of his name."

" I will tell you the interest," replied Chabouillant. " You pretend that I lay claim to a father who is not mine; that is possible : but nothing proves that your excellent friend was *not* my father, the worthy author of my days being hitherto unknown."

" That is to say, you are a natural child—what then ?"

" Well ! here is a man who is dead —for you will admit the marquis is dead ? "

" Go on, sir," said Morizot, impatiently.

" Well then, being removed from this world," resumed Chabouillant, who appeared to take delight in slowly distilling his argument, " the dear man will not be able to disown me as his son; and, on the other hand, nothing can be easier than to believe in his paternity, for he who has had one illegitimate child, may as well have had two. It is plain as the nose on one's face !"

" But what conclusion do you draw from all this ? "

" The conclusion is very simple. I have no family, and have always wanted one. Here I find a family extinct, and am quite ready to revive it ; but to prevent the interference of the public, I must have a respectable man for my security. Formerly steward of the late marquis, you know more about him and his children than any one else ; you have only to proclaim me his son; no one has any interest in contradicting you ; and, in recompense for the sham father that you will bestow upon me, I promise you the most absolute secrecy as to your own *pranks*."

" Allow me to tell you," resumed Morizot, " that all this appears to me very absurd."

Not so absurd," answered the commercial traveller; " I think, on the contrary, it shows a certain power of combination. Because, you see, it is not enough to give me a name and an agreeable title; I must have the means of keeping up my rank, and I anticipate that my little romance will have all the necessary ingredients."

" What do you mean by that ? " asked Morizot ; for this was touching the chord that was most sensitive within him.

" I mean, to be sure, that, in making me a marquis, you will not leave me to die of hunger. You have, first of all, Esther's dowry ; and, secondly, the De Brevannes estate, which you got for next to nothing. It would be the devil, if I were not able to glean a little of all this plunder."

"And pray, what would be the extent of your strange pretensions?"

"You must give me up the sum of money left in your hands, and, with regard to the real property, I don't know exactly what there is—but I should be content with half."

"You are out of your senses, sir!" cried Morizot, in whom avarice was the dominant passion. "You ask me for the bulk of my fortune."

"Do you think it dear? Remember, my dear sir, that your head is at stake, and the honour of your family."

"You think to intimidate me by these threats; but know, that I do not fear your revelations," cried Morizot, who had gradually recovered his assurance. "Even if there were any truth in what you advance, I defy you to bring any proofs; and, to compromise a man of my position and standing, your single testimony will go but a little way, I can tell you."

"Very well! very well, sir!" said the commercial traveller, a little astonished at the mode in which the commissary took up the question. "We shall see how it will finish."

"I have seen it already," answered

the commissary; and, at the same time, he took up a newspaper to read, as if to hint to his visitor that he was not disposed to continue the conversation.

" Is that your last word?" said Chabouillant, rising.

" I will tell you the harm that you *may* do me," resumed the commissary. " You are able, perhaps, to excite against me, for a few days, that public opinion, which, from an instinct of envy, has always been hostile to fortunes made in financial operations. With a couple of grand balls, and a few dinners, I could silence all the clatter. But it would cost me some twenty thousand francs, and these may just as well be expended on you alone. I offer you that sum; you can either take it or leave it."

So saying, he went on with his newspaper.

" Have you well considered it?" asked the commercial traveller.

" Not a farthing more," replied Morizot, continuing to read.

" You will hear of me again, my dear sir," said Chabouillant, moving towards the door.

Following his natural bent, Morizot had already determined to brave it out by impudence. Far from uttering a word, or making the least gesture to detain his dangerous guest, and not even using towards him the ordinary forms of politeness, he kept his seat, and affected to be seriously absorbed in the occupation he had chosen.

More and more disappointed, Chabouillant hesitated as he approached the door of the apartment, and, as if not to be wanting in civility on his side, he exclaimed in a loud voice, before crossing the threshold: " Sir, I have the honour to be your obedient——"

" Farewell, my good fellow!" answered Morizot, in a patronising tone, and without even looking at him.

Innocence itself could not have assumed an exterior of greater calmness and confidence.

CHAPTER V.

It may well be supposed, that, beneath this surface of quiet insolence affected by Morizot, there lurked the most painful anxiety. But, completely master of himself, this man had played his game in this difficult conjuncture, with his accustomed ability. His maxim was, that, in every difficult business, of which we greatly desire the success, one of the first rules to attain our end, is not

to appear anxious about it. He had begun therefore by putting his adversary off his guard, by an assumption of carelessness and disinterestedness, and by this proceeding he was sure of escaping the danger to which superficial observers might have thought him exposed. To go and denounce him immediately, was a fault of which the possessor of his secret would hardly be guilty; by such a false step, the bungler would have crushed the prospect of his own plan of extortion. On the other hand, a second and close rencounter might be easily avoided. Then, and provided that, till then, the affair had assumed no fresh position, it would be time enough to loose one's hold, and decide upon making the necessary sacrifices. In the mean time, there was everything to be gained, in keeping a cool head, and standing one's ground; it is always time enough to get one's throat cut, when nothing else remains to be done.

It happened, that, on the very day that Chabouillant had presented himself at the commissary's, a public dinner was given at the house of the latter. At his table (for such is the world, and such the privilege of the rich) were expected renowned politicians, characters whose names stood high in the financial list, *literati*, artists, men of science, and finally several returned emigrants, who were soon to add the halo of their names to the imperial eagle, which, yet enclosed within the egg, already threatened to break its shell.

For the last quarter of an hour, the guests were all assembled; Garat only was expected, the celebrated singer of the day, who, it was anticipated, would favour the company with several ballads after dinner. In the mean time, they had formed themselves into animated groups in various parts of the saloon; and of these—as might reasonably be supposed—that which had assembled round the mistress of the house, and her two graceful daughters, was by no means the least numerous.

Engaged in a lively conversation with a member of the legislative body, and the secretary of one of the ministers, Morizot showed nothing of the anxious preoccupation, which must nevertheless have been left upon his mind by the dangerous visit to which he had that morning been subjected.

The door of the saloon suddenly opening, the master of the house detaches himself from his two friends, to go and receive the guest, whom he is thus led to expect. At the same instant, the servant announces to the assembly, the name of *Monsieur de Brevannes*, and Morizot finds himself confronted by Chabouillant.

"How, sir!" exclaims the commissary, in a stifled tone, and hardly able to contain himself; "you have dared ——"

"Yes," whispered the commercial traveller; "I looked upon this as a good opportunity of cultivating our acquaintance. Pray have the goodness to introduce me to Madame Morizot."

The name of Brevannes, known to several that were present, had excited attention, and it was necessary at once to initiate the usurper in his assumed post, or suffer him to perform the office for himself. On the other hand, the insolent gait of this man marked the degree of his resolution, and, if urged, he could easily be determined, on the spot, to proceed to any extremity. Further parley was impossible. Cost what it might, an outbreak must be avoided; and, to gain the ground thus lost, must be a matter of after consideration. With an effort to maintain his serenity of demeanour, Morizot advanced towards his wife, followed by the daring knave, and presenting him to her: "Emilie," said he, "Monsieur is the son of my old and esteemed friend, the Marquis de Brevannes; he had not positively promised me to be here this evening, therefore, I did not warn you to expect him."

While Madame Morizot exchanged with the newly-arrived visitor a few polite words, the last expected guest made his appearance; and almost immediately after, the *maitre d' hôtel* opened the folding-doors of the saloon, and dinner was announced.

Placed at the farthest end of the table, Chabouillant had wit enough to keep in the background, and made but few blunders by which he could in any way commit himself. Notwithstanding the distance to which he had been removed, he was not forgotten by the mistress of the house, who honoured him several times by her particular attention. To be brief, everything went off capitally, and the commercial traveller might have been, in good earnest, the man he was representing, for aught to the contrary which marked his *début* in high life.

After coffee had been served, Garat, who happened that day to be in a good-natured vein, consented to sing, and the part of Chabouillant, lost in the crowd of auditors, was still easy to play. A little later, he followed out an evil suggestion, and thinking himself called upon to make himself agreeable to the lady of the house, he rather took her by surprise, by some expressions which savoured of his profession, and which only became the more apparent from the care with which he guarded his conversation. He was, however, relieved from his perilous situation by Morizot, who came to beg his wife to arrange the parties for play; at the same time, finding himself *tête-à-tête* with his dangerous adversary, he engaged him to come without fail, to speak to him on the following morning.

There occurred afterwards a comical scene, which we shall here relate in a cursory manner, to illustrate how *farce* mingles itself, at every moment, with the great drama of life.

While, isolated from the company, Chabouillant, to prove himself at ease, was attentively considering a painting of Girodet's, he was accosted by a little old gentleman, dressed with extreme care, and who appeared to have thoroughly rehearsed the part of a *ci-devant* young man.

"Monsieur," began this fop, representative of a former age, "you are doubtless related to the good Marquis de Brevannes, with whom I served in the *fusiliers?*"

"Monsieur," replied Chabouillant, seizing the opportunity of making good his footing in society, "I am his son."

"His son? He married then while an emigrant?"

"No! I was born before his departure, but in rather an underhand manner. He has since recognised my birth."

"Ah! indeed!" said the old gentleman; "my good friend was liable enough to certain fits of absence. I use the expression *my good friend*, because I knew your father very well."

"Monsieur, I am enchanted to have the honour of meeting you."

"Yes," replied the ex-fusilier, unconscious of the terrible meaning which lurked in his words, "the excellent Brevannes was a lover of the fair sex; he had in the Champs Elysées a small house, where he used to make up some nice parties, with the *Dervieux*, the *Duthé*, and others of the same stamp."

Once upon this track, the old man made a long excursion into the past, and gave Chabouillant a number of important particulars about his pretended father; after which, he asked him if his position, as a returned emigrant, was legally recognised, and offered him, in case of necessity, the protection of Fouché,* with whom he wished it to appear that he had great influence. He afterwards invited Chabouillant to come and see him, saying that he should be delighted to become more intimately acquainted with the son of his excellent friend, the *ci-devant* marquis: he then left the room, and his example was speedily followed by the commercial traveller, who had nothing to say for himself, nor even stopped to take leave of the commissary, who was then engaged at one of the card-tables.

When the last guests had departed, and Morizot found himself alone with his wife and daughters, the former, naturally enough, spoke to him upon the subject of young Brevannes, and asked him how long ago this last scion of a house which she had thought extinct, had discovered himself to her husband.

The commissary, who never (and with good reason) initiated his family into the knowledge of his affairs, thought it as well, for the present, to allow Chabouillant to retain his self-assumed rank, and replied, that, on that very morning only, the young man, who has been long absent from France, had made himself known to him.

"He looks rather a strange sort of man," remarked the elder of the two young ladies.

"Yes; probably, in the embarrassed circumstances which attend the life of an emigrant," said Madame Morizot, "his father may have a little neglected his education; he wants the habit of society, but the tone is easily acquired; he will soon be initiated."

"I think him good-natured," said the younger Mademoiselle Morizot, a merry girl; "he is lively and impetuous; he must be of a gay turn of mind."

"So it appears to me," rejoined the commissary, with an irony that could be understood only by himself.

"My dear," said Madame Morizot, with some gravity, "I thought you cold and constrained to the young man; when he came in, and you introduced him to me, you looked so stern! It appears to me, that the son of the Mar-

* The Ministry of the Police had at this time been suppressed, but Fouché, who had long been at the head of this department, still preserved great influence over the direction of the political police.

quis de Brevannes might have been received with a little more warmth of manner."

"I do not see why you should think so," replied the commissary. "I, this morning only, saw the youth for the first time, and immediately asked him to come this evening; he had almost given me a refusal, and then, just as we are about to sit down to table, he makes his appearance. I could not quite understand it."

"I will tell you what," replied the lady, archly; "between ourselves, I think you are a little afraid of ghosts."

"I hardly know," replied Morizot, rather drily, "what you can mean."

"But, my dear," said Madame Morizot, with a slight hesitation in her manner, "is not the son of the Marquis de Brevannes also his heir?"

"Well! and what is that to me?"

"It seems to me, that as possessor of the whole fortune of his father, you might have some account to settle with this young man."

"What account? The nation has made a public sale of the property, and I have bought and paid for it; nothing is more clear than my position."

"Doubtless, according to the letter of the law; but what view does conscience take of the transaction?"

"How now? what next? Do you dream of my stripping my own family, to enrich a stranger?"

"A stranger! Can he be rightly so called? Suppose that, instead of the son, the father in person had presented himself; would you have opposed to his remonstrance, the fact of having made the purchase for a twentieth part of its original value, and would you not have entered into some arrangement with him?"

"With the marquis, doubtless," replied the commissary, whose probity was quickly asserted in a merely conditional manner; "I would have hastened to restore to him his possessions at the purchase price; but to the succeeding generation, this duty becomes much less imperative; and in the case of an illegitimate heir, the obligation is still further lessened, and burdens not my conscience in the least."

"It is singular enough," rejoined the worthy woman, "my innate perception of the two cases recognises no difference between them; however, I am well aware, that, in matters of business, women must not trust to their own impressions."

" Yes, my dear, believe me; let us not be quite so chivalrous. We cannot decide the matter by sentiment, and I have my duties as the head of a family to consider."

" As far as I am concerned," said the younger Mademoiselle Morizot, " I think with mamma, and stand up for high principles."

" If my opinion were asked," added the eldest, " it would agree with that of my mother and sister."

" And so much the more so, dear papa," archly rejoined the latter, " as you might find it possible to make some sacrifice in favour of this young man, without reducing us, as an inevitable consequence, to complete indigence."

" Well, well! that will do, my little romancer," good-naturedly replied the commissary. " We will talk of all that another time; it is past twelve, and we must to bed."

Upon these words, the family separated, and all betook themselves to repose, as their several consciences might permit them.

CHAPTER VI.

THE next morning, punctual to the *rendezvous* which had been given him, Chabouillant presented himself before the commissary. The ideas of the latter personage had apparently undergone some strange revolution, for he received his guest in a smiling, and almost friendly manner, and seemed inclined to support his new pretensions.

" How," said he, " does the marquis?"

" Charmingly, my dear Amphitryon," replied Chabouillant. " Well! are we this morning more reasonably disposed?"

" I have reflected much upon our concern," answered the commissary, with a thoughtful air. " You committed yesterday, a piece of audacity, by which you have gained considerable ground. You are a clever man, sir; more so than I thought."

" Nay," said the commercial traveller, modestly; " there is not so much to boast of, either. On leaving you yesterday, I observed a good deal of commotion in the kitchens, and met two of the scullions, carrying some made-dishes. ' Very good!' said I; ' I shall invite myself.' One way is as pleasant as another, to get into good society. Any body else would have done the same."

No! I assure you, few would have hazarded so bold a stroke, which, I now declare to you, forces me to come to some terms."

" So, then," said the commercial traveller, rubbing his hands, " we are in a fair way of cementing the bonds of harmony between us."

" That now depends upon you; and if you will accept a proposal——"

" Let us hear; I am all attention."

" You were telling me, yesterday, were you not, that you felt the want of a family?"

" Yes; I have always felt annoyed at finding myself thrown upon the surface of the earth, without knowing by whom or wherefore."

" Well! instead of one family, I offer you two."

" The devil you do! That's plenty, at any rate. But how?"

" You saw, yesterday, my two daughters," continued Morizot, purposely suspending his idea.

" Yes! by Jove! I compliment you upon their appearance. They are really two Graces."

" The eldest," resumed the commissary, " is in all probability destined to make a very good match, which I have already in view. As to the second, she is equally of an age to be taken into consideration; what should you say now, if I were thinking of marrying her to you?"

" I should say—I should say," answered Chabouillant, " that you were not talking seriously."

" Pardon me! I always treat seriously of serious business; and I offer you, in a formal manner, to become my son-in-law."

" Certainly," replied the commercial traveller, with some slight embarrassment, " this offer is most seductive; but in the first place, we must consider —you, my dear father-in-law, may— possibly—at some future time—have some slight misunderstanding with the laws; in short, you must comprehend, that one would like to transmit to one's children a fair name."

" Especially, when that name is stolen," rejoined Morizot, without, however, infusing into his tone of voice the bitterness of the remark. " You are a child," continued he; " you attach to a fact, with which you believe yourself acquainted, and upon which you are quite misinformed, an importance which it does not deserve; and even, admitting the worst, do you believe that you are yourself committing a praiseworthy action, and one to which no blame can be attached, in appropriating to yourself a parentage and a fortune ?"

"Allowing that we are equals on that head," rejoined Chabouillant, " your proposal is lame in another quarter, because, in truth, I see not the necessity of it."

" Yet hostilities are commenced between us. They must either come at once to a violent termination, or find an end in amicable treaty. I offer you the latter mode of procedure."

" Very good ; but to see a father offering to sacrifice his daughter to an unknown individual, when he might do otherwise, is to me unaccountable."

" My young friend, I begin to think I have too highly estimated your powers of understanding, which I conceived to be of the first order. How can you fail to comprehend, without my entering into any further explanation, the interest which I have in allying you to my family ?"

" No ! your idea surprises me ; and whatever your opinion of me may be, it seems to me, as the author says, that *a father after all is a father*, and would hardly make up his mind to throw away his right of progeniture to the first-comer."

" But you are not the first-comer, since we accept you for the Marquis de Brevannes. I begin, therefore, by conferring upon my daughter a handsome title."

" Be it so," said Chabouillant ; " but, with your immense fortune, you would have no difficulty in finding an equally desirable alliance, elsewhere."

" Doubtless ; but I should have some difficulty about the dowry, which this desirable alliance might render it necessary for me to bestow : whereas to you, I should give the possessions which you claim from me, on behalf of your father. I thus prevent any further proceeding on your part, on the one hand, and on the other, I procure for my daughter a suitable establishment. Is not that killing my two birds with one stone ?"

" Hear, hear !" cried Chabouillant ; " there is certainly some diplomacy about that idea, it must be confessed."

" And I come in for the benefit of having ascribed to me, by the world at large, a kind of disinterested heroism, in restoring to you, by this delicate proceeding, your paternal inheritance."

" Good father-in-law !" exclaimed Chabouillant, with a kind of half-conviction, " you talk of my being clever ;

the term is better applied to you. By the powers ! what foresight !"

" In short," added Morizot, " the stars having thrown us into strange contact, the best thing for both our interests, is, indubitably, a good understanding between us. How can this be better established than by linking our fates together ? This is as clear as it can be."

" Faith !" returned the commercial traveller ; " your reasoning teems with ingenuity."

" Now," resumed the commissary, " let us take the contrary view of the subject. We cannot agree ; you are determined to do me as much mischief as you can ; I, of course, cannot make up my mind to have my throat quietly cut ; in short, if I were the sanguinary wretch you take me for, you might also run some risk."

" As to that," replied the commercial traveller, " you may suppose, that I am not destitute of the means of defence. I have confided to the ears of a particular friend, the whole history of our connexion. In case of any disappearance, he has orders to let the cat out of the bag, and place the whole affair in the hands of justice ; on that head, therefore, I am easy, and you have no interest in getting rid of me."

" That's all right," replied Morizot, coolly ; " you have provided for your own safety. But suppose your accusation once laid against me, how are you the better for it ?"

" You are right ; I never said I should be."

" Besides, might I not, at first sight of danger, decamp, and carry into foreign parts valuables to any amount ? At the worst, have I not the resource of every man of spirit, of escaping infamy by a voluntary death ? and amongst these various hypotheses, how do you come off a gainer ?"

" Neither," said Chabouillant, " do I intend to bring about these unpleasant *finales*. You have just made me a most agreeable proposal, but you must let me have the day to consider of it."

" Take your time," replied the commissary ; " while you commune with yourself, I will sound my daughter upon the subject, and at our next interview, you will most probably find everything settled."

" Very well ; to-morrow at this time, if you like."

" Agreed : to-morrow."

And Chabouillant rose to go. He

was already at the door, when Morizot called him back.

"One word more, my dear son-in-law. Young people are not always well supplied with money; would you like a little in advance from the dowry?"

"If I must speak the truth, I am not particularly well stocked at present. I have lately returned from a journey."

"Very well," said the commissary, opening an iron casket, at the sight of whose contents, both in gold and bank-notes, Chabouillant was completely dazzled; "take what you want."

"Oh! a mere trifle. This roleau of fifty louis."

The sum was immediately handed to him.

"Shall you give me a receipt?" asked the commissary, carelessly.

"To be sure; but what name shall I sign?"

"That of Brevannes, as a matter of course, by which you introduced yourself yesterday to the public."

"That of Brevannes," repeated Chabouillant, musing aloud; "no! upon second thoughts, I would rather not take your money. I do not know how it is; signing this name, which I have hardly had time to get used to, seems rather odd."

"The scruple is worthy of you," rejoined Morizot. "But you can take the money without a receipt?"

This Chabouillant refused, and a slight contest of generosity ensued, in which he had finally the victory, and went away empty-handed; which was decidedly the most reputable, as well as the most prudent thing to do.

CHAPTER VII.

COULD it be the serious intention of a man like Morizot, thus to throw away his daughter, upon a person of whose name, it may be remarked, by the way, he was yet ignorant? It might be possible, that, hemmed in as he was, in this narrow defile, he might feel it his last resource. At all events, he certainly meant to carry out his singular proposal in some shape or other, since, on the day that the above-mentioned conversation had passed between him and Chabouillant, when the family were assembled after dinner, he publicly broached his idea of the marriage, representing it as an honourable and delicate means of restitution to the young marquis.

Chabouillant had not that about him which inspires strong interest; but the young girl to whom he was now offered as a husband, had been, to a certain extent, prepossessed in his favour: moreover, although the republic yet existed, there was in essentially monarchical France a strong feeling about the ancient splendour of a good name, and women, especially, have always been most vulnerable upon this little point of vanity.

Finally, to be made the instrument of an act of probity and justice, which must draw down upon her father and family universal approbation, was a prospect in itself sufficiently attractive to be embraced without hesitation. Mademoiselle Morizot at once decided upon accepting it, and gave her father full power to treat with the marquis upon the subject, as soon as he thought proper.

Chabouillant, on his side, needed little reflection, to assure himself, that, in a temporal point of view, he had a very good prospect before him, and that there was perhaps no other means of profiting by his discovery, Morizot appearing resolved not to submit to be despoiled of his wealth in any other way. As far as the morality of such a proceeding was concerned, he had settled that question in his own mind, before taking any other step; it was evident enough, that the act of stealing a name and appropriating to one's self a fortune, was, as far as any feeling of self-respect went, still more disgraceful and compromising than that of becoming the son-in-law of a murderer.

On the following day, Chabouillant arrived at Morizot's house, and in a formal manner announced his consent to the proposed arrangement.

It was agreed, that after a short delay, the marriage should take place, and that Mademoiselle Morizot should bring, as her dowry, the half of the possessions, both real and personal, that would have fallen to the heirs of the Marquis de Brevannes, if that succession had been open at the time of his exile from France.

Chabouillant, with loose principles and incorrect morals, had, in the groundwork of his character, some good qualities. As a proof of this, he expressly stipulated, that, as some amends for the injury which had been done to Chevillard, whether of sound mind or the contrary, the unfortunate man should be put in possession of a part of the sum which had been destined for Esther's dowry, and of which he had been deprived. Thus would be verified the impression which Chabouillant had given to Mademoiselle Lebeau, of their common interest, and which the long-sought discovery of his beloved family was at last to confirm.

Morizot accepted all the conditions, and that evening was fixed upon for the presentation of the pretended Brevannes, on the footing of a future son-in-law. We will spare our readers the detail of the meeting, having already had a similar subject to treat of, at the time of Chevillard's marriage.

Chabouillant had on the preceding day maintained a prudent reserve of deportment, but on this important evening he was anxious to please, and enlisted all his zeal in the cause; the consequence was, that he became ridiculous and vulgar. Things, however, went off just as well. Notwithstanding his bad figure and awkward manners, he had not proved disagreeable to her who was to be his wife. A little more or less trouble in bringing about a reform proved no obstacle to the young lady, and she quite determined that her husband should become an accomplished gentleman.

Besides, if the suitor showed himself upon this occasion a little underbred, he was not the less lively and amusing. The conversation turning upon the subject of the emigration, in which he was supposed to have followed his father, he brought to his aid many real facts of his life as a commercial traveller, which, by the addition of a little gloss, became in his skilful hands the materials for a most entertaining Odyssey; an excellent story-teller, like most of his calling, he managed to keep alive the attention of his new family during a great part of the evening.

A sprinkling of military exploits could by no means come amiss in his new character of the lover, as the *penchant* of women for heroes is a well-known fact; so he enlisted himself, without any ceremony, in the army of Condé, and related, with profuse details, the history of a number of hot engagements, in which he had, more or less, enacted a glorious and honourable part.

While he was in the heat of his narrative, a servant had entered and given a letter to Morizot. The latter had immediately withdrawn from the circle; the rest had seated themselves round a work-table, on which lay, in graceful disorder, the boxes, embroidery, and worsted-work, with which Madame Morizot and her daughters employed themselves.

Approaching the candelabras on the mantel-piece, the commissary perused with eagerness the note which he had just received. When he had finished it, an exclamation of " At last, I am saved!" burst from him, which, owing to the distance at which he was standing from Chabouillant, passed unnoticed by the latter.

With the exception of this slight manifestation of what was passing within him, he remained externally calm, threw the letter into the fire, as some trifling thing, and resumed his place by the side of the narrator, whose departure he carefully avoided hastening. However, after making an appointment for the following day, Chabouillant took his leave. Then Morizot, pleading a headache from the effects of listening to the eternal rhapsodies of his hopeful son-in-law, pretended to retire to his own room, where, having shrouded his figure in a cloak, he hurried down a back staircase, out of the hotel, and throwing himself into a hackney-coach, he directed the man to drive to the further end of the Faubourg Saint-Martin, and into one of the least frequented streets of this obscure quarter.

CHAPTER VIII.

HE stopped at some distance from the place where his business lay; then, proceeding to a house of mean appearance, he knocked three times, at regular intervals, at a private door.

At this signal, a window opened from above, and some person appeared, who seemed desirous of recognising him who had thus announced his arrival. After these several precautions, steps were heard in the passage, and the door was shortly after opened, to give entrance to the commissary, who, in a few minutes' time, was ushered into a chamber, where he found himself in presence of Legros and his female associate.

Morizot's first words to Legros, on entering the room, were: " You have not yet had time to receive my letter. At all events, it has had no hand in deciding your return."

" What letter?" demanded the man of parchments; " that which you wrote to us, about a week since, in which you told us that everything was hushed up?"

" No! another, which I sent off the day before yesterday morning, to say that it was all up with us."

"There! did I not say so?" cried the Saint-Martin; "you would return to France: it is positively throwing ourselves into the lion's den."

"It would not have been so very strange," said Morizot, bitterly, " if, after having, by your indiscretion, compromised my safety and betrayed our secret, you had taken yourself off and left me here embarrassed and alone."

"What indiscretion can you mean?" asked Legros. "We have not spoken to a living soul; your letters have been burnt as soon as received; we never, except in the evening, left the obscure lodging which we occupied in a second-rate hotel at Offenburg; how could we betray any secret?"

"That I don't know; but one thing you may be sure of, which is, that, the day before yesterday, a man thoroughly acquainted with every fact connected with our affairs, came to my house, giving out that he was the son of Brevannes, and setting an enormous price upon his secret, threatened to reveal the whole, if I did not accede to his conditions."

"How very strange!" said the lawyer.

"Not at all strange," replied the

Saint-Martin, turning to Legros; " you never will believe me. I felt quite sure that I heard something move one morning in the closet adjoining our room, and in which our host had promised to let no one sleep. You persisted that I was dreaming, and would not go and see what the noise was; now we are in for it, and you choose this very time to return to Paris."

" However, the mischief is done now," said the lawyer, sharply. " What kind of man was he who came to your house ?"

" I can hardly tell; an underbred fellow, heavily made, with reddish hair. He looked like a *roué*."

" And so he took it into his head to pass for the son of the marquis? He is a dangerous man," remarked Legros, who always looked at a subject in a professional point of view; " the part he has chosen is not badly hit upon."

" The gentleman is not very exorbitant," continued the commissary; " he simply demands the restitution of the half of his pretended father's fortune."

" Well, give it up; for, in point of fact, the fortune is not yours," said Madame Saint-Martin, " and so shut the accuser's mouth, lest he get all our throats cut."

" Fear makes you wander, my poor dear," answered the lawyer. " But, about this man; his name, his residence; where is he to be laid hold of ?" added Legros, turning to Morizot.

" I have not the least idea," returned the commissary; " he may be the devil, for aught I care. My only object was to keep him in check till your return. This I managed by offering him the hand of my youngest daughter, which he was fool enough to accept. We are now the best friends in the world, and ten days at least will thus be secured, to see what is the best thing to be done."

" And why should you not give him your daughter?" said the Saint-Martin; " there is nothing very derogatory about that. Our safety must be the first consideration."

" Now," said the lawyer, seizing with no gentle touch the arm of the speaker, " will you have the goodness to sit down in this corner, and hold your tongue, with a view to our having a little quiet consultation upon the subject? As regards yourself, my dear Morizot, what is your plan? Have you thought of any course you should like to pursue with this knave?"

" Faith! the first idea which naturally occurs, since he makes a point of being the son of the marquis, is to send him to keep his father company."

" Ever for deeds of blood," said the Saint-Martin, as she shrugged her shoulders, with a slight shudder.

" But it is altogether out of the question," resumed Morizot. " By a piece of truly infernal ingenuity, he has put himself under the protection of some unknown friend, in whose hands he has deposited a narrative of the whole transaction."

" An undoubtedly clever fellow," interposed Legros.

" In case of his disappearance," added the commissary, " the said friend has instructions to make himself master of the contents of the narrative, and to lay the whole affair open to justice; thus his death, far from being of any use to us, only multiplies the perils of our situation."

" Here is the sum-total," said Legros. " In the first place, to discover the spot in which these dangerous papers are concealed; to take possession of them, and at the same time to get his person into our power; this is the only means of saving ourselves."

" To be sure," said the Saint-Martin; " it is all to be done by talking about it."

" Let us see," asked Legros; " when do you expect to meet this dreaded individual ?"

" To-morrow morning," replied Morizot; " he is to come to my house, I believe at about ten o'clock."

" Very well; take this opportunity of obtaining the information we require relative to himself; as he might, however, be reluctant to give it, when he is about to leave you, find a pretext for accompanying him out of the house. I will prowl in disguise, about the precincts of the hotel, track his steps, and not lose sight of him for a minute. The very devil is in it, if I do not get at something in this way."

" Not badly planned, that," said the commissary.

The Saint-Martin could not repress the rejoinder which rose to her lips. " All very fine !" muttered she.

" By my faith !" replied the commissary, impatiently; " you may boast, my dear Madame Saint-Martin, of making yourself, by all this opposition, eminently disagreeable."

" And you ! how benevolent and amiable ! To think of having, by the miserable stipend of ten thousand francs, remunerated us for taking a part in this pretty business."

"Come! we have had parley enough," said the lawyer, silencing the matron; "you understand, my dear Morizot," continued he, "you are to obtain every possible clue ———"

"Yes; and I then take him out, for you to take note of."

"Exactly so; but as I shall not lose sight of him, till he gets home at night, and shall thus be unable to see you during the day, you must send to me, here, the details which you have obtained by your conversation with him. If we should then find it necessary to confer any further upon the subject, I will give you a *rendezvous* somewhere, early in the morning of the day after to-morrow, as it will be prudent to vary the place of our meetings."

"Very good," said the commissary, putting on his cloak; and without taking leave of Madame Saint-Martin, who seemed no more disposed than he was, to bestow upon him this mark of politeness, he was conducted by the lawyer to the door of the house, which he left with rapid strides.

———

CHAPTER IX.

THE scene above related took place on the 16th of February (1804). We take note of this date, because two days later occurred a political event of some importance, which (as will be hereafter seen) influenced, to a certain extent, the sequel of this narrative.

According to agreement, Legros set out on the following morning, and stopped in the Rue de Provence, at a little before ten o'clock, a few steps from Morizot's hotel. Clothed in a smock-frock, and bearing on his arm a basket containing eggs and fruit, by which means he represented a countryman, who had come to Paris to dispose of his provisions, he could, without exciting any observation, easily take his stand, and thus turn spy *upon systematic principles*, as the police have it.

Naturally a keen and shrewd observer, the accomplice of Morizot had already recognised his man, merely by his figure and the colour of his hair, the very moment Chabouillant entered the commissary's house. Immediately on his arrival, the pretended Brevannes was subjected by his father-in-law to a close and circumstantial investigation upon the subject of his name, his family, his position in life, and his connexions.

Morizot's inquiries were perfectly natural, and Chabouillant, confident of fair play, saw no interest in affecting any concealment; he mentioned his name, his ignorance of his own origin (which circumstance had, in fact, suggested to him the idea of taking up the part which he was now acting so successfully), and then, with praiseworthy self-respect, and desirous to free himself from the imputation of being a mere adventurer, or swindler, he explained how he had gained by traffic an honourable livelihood. This led him to speak of the house of the *Tricoloured Prism*, for which he was traveller, of Chevillard, whose acquaintance he had made there, of his last excursion to Germany, and lastly, of the night spent at the *Golden Lamb*—that lucky night, in which he had, by means of the thinness of a partition-wall, overheard the secret to which he owed his power, and to which he was also to be indebted for his happiness.

To all this information, Morizot sought to add that of his son in law's dwelling-place, which it was highly important for him to know; but Chabouillant, who had been perfectly open upon every other point, did not feel such unlimited confidence as not to withhold some few particulars. He reflected, that, in case his father-in-law should meditate foul play, ignorance of his residence would always form some obstacle to his designs; he cleverly evaded an answer to the inquiry, by pretending that he looked upon Morizot's question as the prelude to his intention of paying him a visit, and remarked, that, being shabbily off for lodgings, he wished to avoid company, and never gave his address.

Having thus procured all the information which it was possible to obtain, without awakening suspicion, Morizot told the commercial traveller, that he was anxious to have a thorough understanding respecting the final regulation of their respective interests, but added at the same time, that, as he was under the necessity of going out upon business of importance, he should be obliged to put off this conference to the following day. Chabouillant said, that he was at the command of his father-in-law.

"Very well," said Morizot; "if you will come here to-morrow, about twelve o'clock (but this must not prevent your joining our circle this evening), we will shut ourselves up for the afternoon, and look into the title-deeds and papers of the Brevannes family, in order to see exactly what comes to your share."

" Agreed then, to-morrow," replied Chabouillant, and he was about to take his leave.

" Wait for me," cried Morizot; " we will go out together."

" By the bye," asked the bridegroom elect, " can I not see the ladies ?"

"Half-past ten," said the commissary, looking at the time-piece; " they are hardly up; you would not be admitted."

" Very well; I shall do myself that honour in the evening," returned the bridegroom; and, having again refused fresh offers of money courteously made to him by the commissary, he soon passed out, watched by Legros, who, observing him in Morizot's company, soon recognised his man, much to his own satisfaction, as this incident confirmed his opinion of his own talents in the character of a skilful spy.

Chabouillant had scarcely walked ten paces, when Legros, who had secured to himself the services of a poor clown, to look after his goods, under pretence of being obliged to go into the neighbourhood, divested himself of his smock-frock, and leaving his basket with his substitute, set out in pursuit, keeping a measured distance from the person whom he intended to dodge during the rest of the day.

It may be remarked, that Legros' lucky stars here interposed their saving influence in his behalf. He had hardly left his stand, when an agent of the police came up to the man, who had taken his place, and asked him for his licence as a vender in the public streets. The poor fellow explained, that he was not there on his own account; but the police was at that time unusually strict, by reason of the general excitement created by the invisible presence of George Cadoudal, who was concealed somewhere in Paris, with a band of sixty men, bent upon making an open attack on the First-Consul: thus, the mere fact of his being unable to produce his licence, was a sufficient excuse for hurrying Legros' unfortunate substitute to the police-station, and from thence to a fortnight's imprisonment in La Force; thus furnishing a fresh and lamentable example of the petty blunders which at times are committed upon the plea of regard for the public safety, amongst civilized people.

But to return to Legros. Tracking unobservedly the footsteps of Chabouillant, he saw him first go and make a good breakfast in one of the *cafés* on the Boulevards des Italiens, and then call for the public papers, which he read with marked interest.

After his breakfast, he loitered out upon the boulevards, enjoying the sunshine, and coming suddenly upon the little old gentleman whose acquaintance he had made at the dinner-party at Morizot's house, he listened for three-quarters of an hour to a shambling detail of his love-adventures, duels, and achievements, as far back as the year 1789.

A blooming *grisette* at this moment passed them. The commercial traveller, under the impression that he was soon to take leave of the delights of bachelor-ship, started upon the track of the young Hebe, and as he followed her to a less frequented part of the boulevards, ventured to address to her a few soft words. Whether she were really virtuous, or only experienced an innate aversion for red hair, the young milliner repulsed him somewhat harshly, and he found himself, after his lost trouble, as far off as Frescati's gardens, at about which spot Parisian civilisation arrives at a terminus.

Luckily for him, a girl of less questionable prudery, and of whose attractions no doubt could be entertained, crossed his path at the moment when he received his dismissal from the other. Ever prompt in making the best of an opportunity, Chabouillant considered that her company might form an agreeable diversion in retracing his weary steps back to the centre-point whence he had started. He hesitated not therefore to address her, and his good-humour and the eloquence he derived from his profession, being on this occasion quite in place, he had soon reason to flatter himself on having made an undoubted conquest, when his companion suddenly turned to him, and with terror depicted in her countenance, " Bow to me," she said, " and begone; here is the general."

The unfortunate adventurer, following mechanically the instructions which had been given him, found himself, after taking a few steps, almost thrown into the arms of an immense man, with grey hair and frightful-looking moustachios. Armed with a tremendous stick, and buttoned up to the chin in an enormous blue surtout, this disagreeable *Marplot* shot a pulverising glance at Chabouillant as he passed him; nor was the expression of this pleasing look in any degree changed, when he turned at a distance of ten paces, to see whether it was withdrawn.

Finding himself decidedly out of luck in the affairs of Cupid, Chabouillant, who recollected the old proverb, and was fond of dabbling in forbidden pursuits, thought that the gaming-table might prove more fortunate, and passing to the back of Favart's theatre, still followed by the lawyer (to whom, as our readers must perceive, he gave plenty of work to do), he entered a *hell* situated in the Rue de Marivaux, of rather a higher order than the No. 113, where we have seen him figure on a former occasion.

After sitting for some hours, and becoming winner of thirty louis, he went to acquire an appetite in a *café-estaminet,* * where, to use his own elegant expression, he proceeded to *wet his whistle,* and then adjourned to dinner with the air of a man who had made a good day's work of it.

On leaving the *restaurant's,* tolerably *well lined within,* as we should have said in former days, he found that he had yet some time to spare, before the anticipated hour of meeting his bride elect; and therefore determined to show himself at Mademoiselle Lebeau's, whom he had not seen for some days past. He was most anxious to tell her of the splendid match he was about to make, and the generous proviso made in favour of Chevillard. He got into a hackney-coach, in which he was quickly imitated by his *double,* who never for one moment lost sight of him, and drove to the Rue des Deux Portes Saint-Sauveur. Arrived at his destination, he looked round to make sure that he was unobserved; nor did he perceive Legros, who was too great an adept in the game he was playing, to allow his moves to become visible. Still, from an extra sense of prudence, Chabouillant judged it best to execute a series of serpentine movements in the labyrinth of small streets which constitute the quarter of Saint-Denis. This manœuvre was regarded by Legros as a conclusive index; nor did he fail, during the visit which the commercial traveller was paying, minutely to observe the door, and to inscribe on his tablets the number of the house.

Mademoiselle Lebeau received her guest smilingly, and was in far better humour than on a former occasion. She had had good news from Charenton. The doctor had written her word that day, that a decided change for the better had

* A tavern where smoking is allowed.

taken place, since the preceding one, in the state of Chevillard's health; and he begged that she would visit the patient on the morrow, as it was possible that her presence might have a desirable influence. The happy always listen gladly to the detail of the happiness of others. Without going into particular explanations, Chabouillant remarked to the young tradeswoman, that things were going well with him. According to all appearance, the hostile proceedings, which he had in the first place had reason to dread, were now coming to an amicable termination; and when he should be allowed to speak out, she would be quite astonished at the part which Chevillard was to have in the unexpected good fortune which was to realize the day-dream of his existence.

Mademoiselle Lebeau expressed as much sympathy as she could, in the yet clouded prospect that was thus disclosed to her; after which, Chabouillant, begging her to keep for some days longer the casket he had confided to her care, took leave of her, and proceeded on his way.

The rest of the evening was passed at Morizot's house, and the bridegroom elect was all attention to his intended bride. In the mean time, Legros was almost petrified, waiting for him in the street. About ten o'clock, Chabouillant left the commissary's hotel, and proceeded to the little Rue Saint-Pierre Montmartre, where he entered a furnished house of rather mean appearance.

Through a hole in the door of the passage, the spy observed him come out from the porter's lodge, with a key and a lighted candle in his hand. Here then abode his man, and the duty of the spy terminated after his long round. Rich in his newly-acquired information, Legros relieved himself from mounting guard, and set off to return to his own house.

CHAPTER X.

ON reaching home, after his vigorous pursuit of Chabouillant, the lawyer found a letter from Morizot, containing the information which he had picked up, in the morning's conversation with his intended son-in-law.

Being thus enlightened on the former connexion which had subsisted between the mistress of the *Tricoloured Prism,* Chevillard, and the commercial traveller, Legros, who had already drawn his own inference from the precaution used by Chabouillant, in paying his visit at the Rue des Deux Portes Saint-Sauveur, now doubted not but that he had scented out the hiding-place of the deposit; he therefore sat down, and wrote the following answer to his accomplice and friend:

" I have made a successful campaign, and, to all appearance, the day will not pass over, before I get hold of the much dreaded manuscript. As soon as this is done, I will give you notice; but it will be important to have Chabouillant under your own eye, during the whole day, so that we may have the means of disposing of him, when he is once stripped of his armour. Besides, it is more than probable, that we shall not be able to carry off the papers before the evening; but it all depends upon circumstances, and as I can at present say nothing decisive, you must be ready for action at any time, come what may."

Morizot had finished reading this letter, when Chabouillant entered his room. According to the directions he had just received, he expressed to the commercial traveller his intention of keeping him the whole day, and begged him to stay dinner.

He then shut the door, and immediately submitted to the inspection of the commercial traveller the title-deeds, which it was understood were to be given into his possession. To his great satisfaction, he perceived that the pretended Brevannes gave to these papers, from which he was to derive his knowledge of his family and fortune, much more serious attention than might have been anticipated. Time soon slips away in handling parchments, and it was five o'clock, and night had drawn in, before Chabouillant had got through half the documents.

After four hours' close attention to this hard work, the commercial traveller got tired, and spoke of putting off the rest till the next day.

Morizot managed to keep him at it a little longer, but at last Chabouillant was thoroughly knocked up, and intimated his desire to return home—in the first place to dress, as he was to dine with the ladies, and in the next to take a breath of fresh air; his head was quite bewildered, he observed, with such a rigmarole of writings.

The commissary feared that he might awaken his suspicions, by pressing him any farther, and though he would have preferred not to lose sight of him for a moment, in order to adhere to the letter of Legros' directions, he was obliged to let him go, with particular injunctions not to keep them waiting, and to be back by six o'clock precisely.

The guest was punctual; it had hardly struck six, when he reëntered Morizot's room. He came with the news of the arrest of General Moreau; he had been seized that morning, at eleven o'clock, on returning from his estate of Grosbois. This event gave the commercial traveller the opportunity of discussing some deep theories, upon the nature of politics, which we may be excused from quoting, as they are not essential to the thread of our narrative.

The commissary, having received no news from Legros, became a prey to the most cruel anxiety, which he was soon unable to conceal from Chabouillant. He began to stride hastily across the room, carried on the conversation in broken sentences, and gave every token of a harassed and preoccupied mind.

At last, the commercial traveller asked him the cause of his uneasiness, and begged to know whether he was in any way implicated with Moreau, in the conspiracy of Pichegru and George Cadoudal.

Morizot perceived that he was betraying himself, and seizing the idea suggested to him by the question, he skilfully covered his want of self-command, by answering, that, far from being compromised by Moreau's arrest, he hoped to reap some benefit by it; for upon the news of the political movement, which had affected the state of the public funds, he had attempted some speculations, and the uneasiness which he now suffered, arose, added he, " from the delay of his agent, in forwarding to him the results of this operation."

The explanation carried with it the appearance of truth, and was fully believed by the commercial traveller. Out of respect for his father-in-law's disturbed state of mind, he troubled him no farther with questions, but turned to a mirror, with a view of making some slight improvements in his toilet, which had been rather hastily performed.

At last, a servant came in, and gave Morizot a letter, saying, that the man waited for an answer.

At sight of the handwriting, the commissary hastily unsealed it, and read with eagerness.

While he was thus employed, Chabouillant addressed him.

" Well," said he, " have you had a letter from your agent?"

" Yes ! yes !" answered the commissary, without looking up.

" And are things turning out according to your wishes ?"

" Quite so," returned Morizot, taking up a pen to write a few lines in answer.

" That's all right," good father-in-law," said the commercial traveller, in a jocular tone ; " make the most of your little speculation, so that we may come in for a share of the benefit."

Morizot having written a short note, went to deliver it himself, to the man who was waiting.

He was back in an instant.

" By the bye, my dear fellow," said he to Chabouillant, " we are in for rather a foolish affair."

" What now ?" exclaimed the commercial traveller.

" In my confusion, I omitted to mention to the ladies, that you dined here to-day, and now they have just sent to tell me not to wait for them, as they intend to stop to dinner at a house where they have been paying an afternoon visit."

" It can't be helped ! it is a little disappointment," replied Chabouillant ; " we shall be obliged to dine *tête-à-tête*."

" No doubt ; but you will not like that so well. But, stay !" added Morizot, carelessly ; " a thought strikes me : since we are to be put off with bachelor's fare, let us make the best of it, by going to a *restaurant !* From thence, we will proceed to the Opera, where we shall find the ladies."

" Willingly ! it is a bright idea," replied the commercial traveller.

" Very well ! if you like, we will set off at once. I have been too much harassed during the whole day, to think of eating anything, and I now begin to feel hungry."

Chabouillant made no objection, and in less than a quarter of an hour, the carriage of Morizot had measured the distance which divides the Rue de Provence from the Palais-Royal. Our fashionables stopped at the *Perron*. Inflated with the sense of his newly-acquired rank, Chabouillant a little overacted his part, as he traversed the crowd of gazers, attracted by the sumptuous appearance of their equipage.

The *restaurant Robert*, the scene of the dinner so fatal to Chevillard, was then one of the very few places at which a man who had any regard for his reputation, might consent to dine. Thither the commissary accompanied his son-in-law ; but although there only remained, in the room in which they established themselves, some few scattered guests, on account of the then generally prevailing habit of dining between five and six o'clock, Chabouillant was careful to avoid the low familiarity of manner, which we have observed as marking his conduct upon a previous occasion. Although a self-constituted gentleman, he had soon come to a perception of what was due to his name and birth, and Sbrigani, who had been attracted towards Porceaugnac* by the dignity with which he ate his bread, would have certainly entertained the same profound respect for the smuggled marquis, could he have witnessed the perfect decorum of all his gastronomic proceedings.

It is, however, incumbent upon nobility to be divested of the sense of thirst, and Chabouillant, under the enlivening influence of the sweet gifts of Bacchus (as the songs of the day have it), soon began to invest the future with the most attractive colours. He got quite into a sentimental vein.

" Most certainly," said he to his father-in-law, " there was something adverse in the outset of our acquaintance, but it strikes me, notwithstanding, that we shall understand one another uncommonly well."

" Faith ! I believe so too !" exclaimed Morizot. " As far as I am concerned, I shall do my best to preserve the atmosphere between us from the shadow of a cloud."

" I may now say," continued Chabouillant, " that I had started with some prepossessions against you ; besides, you looked far more disposed to collar me, than to extend the right-hand of fellowship."

" Faith ! my dear fellow, you must confess, on your own part, that the manner of your introduction was anything but conciliatory."

" A true picture of mankind !" philosophically rejoined the commercial traveller ; " to-day at daggers drawn, and to-morrow all hail-fellow-well-met ; and all in consequence of coming to an understanding upon the subject of filthy lucre."

" Provided," said Morizot, assuming an air of melancholy, " that the happiness of my daughter and yourself may be secured by this marriage !"

" This marriage !" retorted Chabouillant ; " it cannot but turn out well. I certainly have my foibles, but setting

* See Molière's comedy of that name.

aside the circumstance of my unknown descent, which rather soured my temper, I do not believe myself on the whole destitute of some sterling qualities, and boasting apart, I might have turned out a very good sort of fellow."

" Fortunately," replied the commissary, " the void is now filled up."

" Doubtless; I begin already to feel myself a different man; family ties, the domestic hearth and fireside enjoyments, constitute my delight. At a later period, the idea of lightening your labours, looking after the education of my children, and finally strewing a few flowers in your path to the grave, forms, let me tell you, my friend, a not unpleasing perspective. And if," added he, with unlucky allusion, " some bitter retrospect might, at times, trouble the peace of your declining years——"

" Alas!" exclaimed Morizot, in a grievous tone, " the most unblemished career cannot be trod without some fearful trials."

" To be sure, I know that; but there is pardon for every transgression: we are often the creatures of circumstances, especially in times of great political commotions. By the bye," continued Chabouillant, " what became of those people at Offenburg, in whose company I passed that queer night, before I knew anything about them? Their feeling towards you was anything but friendly. Did I ever tell you so?"

" Oh!" replied the commissary; " I keep them in check by means of occasional bribes."

" I know that you have a hold upon the man, but the wife is a regular snake in the grass. You must take care of her."

" That will all come right enough," returned Morizot; and, dinner being over, he called for the bill, and looked at his watch.

The account being paid, the two guests left the dining-room. Easy and familiar by nature, and at the present moment especially, influenced by the most cordial feelings of good-fellowship, Chabouillant passed his arm within that of his father-in-law, and they proceeded to the entrance-door. But instead of the equipage of Morizot, which they had expected to find in waiting, to convey the son and father-in-law elect to the Opera, nothing was to be seen but a shabby-looking hackney-coach, which seemed to have stopped at some paces' distance from the restaurant's.

This disappointment was the more vexatious, as the pavement was just wetted by some heavy drops of rain, and one glance at the sky was sufficient to show the proximity of one of those deluging downfalls to which the atmospheric temperament of the Parisian climate is peculiarly liable.

While the two fashionables, still on foot, in vain looked after the expected carriage, and Morizot was storming at his coachman's want of punctuality, the figure of a man emerged from the mass of shadow, which was cast by the crazy vehicle standing in the middle of the street, and walking straight up to Chabouillant, addressed him in a tone of the most marked politeness.

" Have I the honour," said he, " of speaking to the *ci-devant* Marquis de Brevannes?"

Chabouillant, as we have before observed, had not quite made up his mind publicly to use the title which he had assumed. He was therefore disagreeably taken by surprise, at finding himself thus designated by an individual unknown to him, and whose appearance was altogether, as far as he could judge, unprepossessing. The tone of his answer partook of this impression.

" What business is that of yours?" said he, with some asperity.

" You must try and persuade yourself," returned the unknown, " that I have an interest in putting the question to you, and I beg that you will have the goodness to give me an answer, which indeed I have the right to enforce."

" The right?" retorted the commercial traveller, raising his voice to a higher pitch. " What the devil can you want? I don't know who you are."

" We need not make a noise about it," replied his tormentor. " Your reluctance to give your name removes all doubt; you are the *ci-devant* Marquis de Brevannes; your name yet figures on the list of emigrants, and you are moreover accused of being concerned in the conspiracy of Pichegru and George Cadoudal. I," continued he, throwing open his cloak, and discovering the tricoloured scarf, " have the honour to be an officer of justice, and summon you to follow me, in the name of the law."

It was a critical juncture. If Chabouillant denied, in the presence of a public functionary, his identity as the marquis, he overturned, as connected with Morizot, the whole superstructure of the marriage-plot; if, on the other hand, he maintained his assumed name in the face of justice, before whose

tribunal he was apparently about to be dragged, he incurred double peril, since that name was implicated in a serious accusation of treason. Some suspicion did indeed cross his mind, of a trick on Morizot's part, but it was soon destroyed, by the commissary's addressing the officer of the peace, in the following terms :

"I think, my dear sir, that you are under some mistake; this person is indeed the *ci-devant* Marquis de Brevannes, and, as you observe, his position as a returned emigrant, has not been legally recognised ——"

"Precisely so," replied the officer; "there is no mistake."

"Permit me," resumed Morizot. "This gentleman is on the eve of becoming my son-in-law; it is hardly probable, that I, as commissary-general of the republican armies, would give my daughter to one engaged in a conspiracy; I further add, that the position of this young man precludes the idea of his having any part in the attempts of people without a name, and of no recognised class in society. I therefore repeat, that there must be some mistake; your order of arrest must have reference to Monsieur's father, who was indeed a pensioner on the bounty of England; but he has been long since dead, although it was falsely rumoured by the police, that he returned to France, about six months ago."

"I am exceedingly sorry, sir," rejoined the police-agent, "that it should be out of my power to pay any regard to your explanations; but I must beg to inform you, confidentially, that it was after a dinner which took place at your house a few days back, that the *ci-devant* Marquis de Brevannes' name was mentioned at Monsieur Fouché's. The distinction between the father and son has been perfectly well marked; Monsieur is the person with whom I am concerned."

"You have at least a warrant, which you will be good enough to show me," resumed Morizot, with some haughtiness of tone.

"Certainly; and although the urgent and serious nature of the circumstances, authorises my slighting your request, I will show you the warrant," replied the officer of justice, drawing from his pocket a paper, which he handed to Morizot.

The latter, followed by Chabouillant, approached the carriage, which retained its station at a few steps' distance, in order to peruse, by the glare of the lamps, the document which he held. The commercial traveller, while examining the warrant, signed "DUBOIS, Counsellor of State, Prefect of Police," and which appeared perfectly correct, glanced at the inside of the coach, where he distinctly perceived military uniforms. While he thus acquired the painful certainty, that all resistance would be in vain, he was convinced by another circumstance, that the dangerous encounter to which he was subjected, was really the consequence of some political crisis. Whether there was any foundation for such a report, it was believed, at the time of the Consulate, that the returned emigrants were often employed by government, in affairs of the most delicate nature, and were generously remunerated for their services. Chabouillant remembered that the old fop, the former companion of his pretended father's pleasures, had, in the course of conversation, several times mentioned Fouché, and coupling this circumstance with the half-disclosure, which had just been made to them by the agent of police, he soon came to the conclusion, that he was the victim of a denunciation on the part of this cursed little man.

He was making up his mind to the sad necessity of inevitable resignation to his lot, without even daring to put the question to himself, of how the affair was to end, when Morizot, having attentively perused the document, which he held in his hand, returned it to the officer of justice, saying, in an imperative tone: "Very good; the warrant appears correct. You will now be good enough to conduct this gentleman and myself, to the house of the prefect of the police, with whom I have the honour of being acquainted."

"I should be delighted to accede to your request," replied the officer of justice; "but it is impossible. My orders are to arrest Monsieur de Brevannes, and no one else."

"It will not be incumbent upon you to keep me a prisoner," replied the commissary; "I wish you merely to allow me to accompany my son-in-law to the prefect's house, where I feel convinced that my explanation will be heard."

"I understand; but I have positive directions not to disturb the prefect upon any pretext. He is to-day overwhelmed with business; you may suppose, that you are not the only one who desires an interview."

Upon this, the commissary's temper failed, and his anger was so well feigned, that it completely precluded any idea of an understanding between the colloquists.

However, without taking any further notice of the commissary's remonstrance, the myrmidon of justice, turning to Chabouillant, desired him to take his place in the carriage.

The commercial traveller hesitated, and asked where it was their intention to take him?

"You will know that afterwards," was the answer given him; "get in now, and on the road, I shall have time to answer your questions, if I think proper to do so."

Morizot still insisted upon accompanying his son-in-law, and seemed almost inclined to excite him to open resistance.

"Come," said the officer of justice, "we must be off; and if Monsieur does not choose to follow me with a good grace, I have the means of compelling him to submit."

Thus obliged to consent to what was required of him, the unfortunate Chabouillant decided upon getting into the coach, where he found himself in the agreeable society of two of the municipal guard* in full dress, who maintained the strictest silence and decorum. While placing himself on the back seat, he heard the functionary still maintaining a sharp dispute with Morizot, from whom he parted apparently on the worst terms. The vacant place was then filled by the officer, and the windows of the coach were carefully drawn up. The horses, urged to their utmost speed, started at a pace which their appearance would have forbidden the idea of supposing possible, and which would have shamed many more brilliant equipages.

The journey continued in silence, until Chabouillant demanded with eager curiosity, where he was being conducted in such haste? No answer was made him. He then tried to take cognizance of the road by which he was going; he was roughly desired not to put down the glass, and the thick mist by which it was shortly covered, from the effect of the breath of four people within, soon rendered it impossible for him to acquire the desired information.

Without any very clear ideas upon the nature of the danger with which he was threatened, the poor fellow began to reflect seriously upon the perilous intrigue in which he was involved, and would have gladly renounced the name and fortune of all the Montmorencies, provided he might only have resumed his character of Chabouillant, the jolly commercial traveller, and once more have found himself at liberty to swagger on the road, in all the importance of tinsel and finery. Already heartily disgusted with the dark aspect of his grandeur, he was pondering upon the best means of returning to the enjoyment of his real name, without being subjected to the consequences of his fatal flight into the higher regions of existence, when his rolling prison stopped, and thus prepared him for the *dénoûment* of his adventure, by warning him that the journey had come to its close.

The rain, now falling in torrents upon the roof of the coach, impressed the mind with the most forlorn sense of melancholy, by its monotonous sound.

The officer of justice got out, and having carefully closed the door of the carriage, knocked at the door of a house situated at a small distance. Through the thick fog formed on the inside surface of the glass, and the rain darting upon it from without, Chabouillant discovered the glimmer of a light; almost directly after, the police-agent returned, and desiring the guards to get out, directed Chabouillant to follow their example, and placed him between them.

Scared by the solitude, silence, and thick darkness which reigned around him, the commercial traveller felt his anxiety reach to a climax, when he thought that he recognised the trunks of several trees, whose dark outline bore a resemblance to misshapen giants, and recollecting the fearful Alleé des Veuves, he almost felt himself falling into a man-trap.

He then made an attempt at resistance, and in a voice which was immediately stifled by his jailors, who took hold of him by the throat, he screamed out: "Help! murder!"

But in that fearful weather, and in a place almost destitute of inhabitants, it was not likely that any one should come to his aid; roughly urged on by three strong men, who were evidently regardless of the pain they might inflict upon their captive, he felt, after the lapse of a few moments, the door of the house closed upon him—and Heaven only knows the kind of hospitality, which he was likely to meet with in such a place!

CHAPTER XI.

In the half-lighted room into which Chabouillant was now forced, instead of the magistrate, before whom he had expected to appear at the time of his arrest, he found only a woman, who had not at all the air of a servant; nevertheless, the supposed peace-officer said to her: "Let us have a little fire, for I am wet through; and see if you can find a bottle of good wine, to amuse these gentlemen who are waiting outside."

The woman immediately went out, to execute these orders.

"Sir," said the commander of the expedition to Chabouillant, "you have been pleased to take some interest in a painful event, the knowledge of which you obtained somewhat indiscreetly, in a tavern at Offenburg. I thought it might be agreeable to you, to complete your information upon the subject. It was there, in the next room, now occupied by my honourable friends, that the unfortunate circumstance happened. It was in this apartment, that the unhappy

* The municipal guard was then in existence, and has since been restored upon the old system.

gentleman was afterwards deposited, and he was seated in this very arm-chair, still standing in the same place—for the house has not since been visited —previous to his ultimate removal. You see, that I tell you everything."

This impudent and ironical confidence was evidently intended to fill the soul of the captive with terror; but it did not produce the anticipated effect. Cha-bouillant was a brave man, and, once recovered from the first shock, was re-solved, that, if he must die, it should not be like a coward. He therefore answered boldly: " It is then probably to one of the gentlemen-murderers, that I have the honour of speaking?"

" That is hardly the word," replied Legros, without any emotion; " and since you have taken the trouble to lis-ten to my conversation with my wife, you must know, that the affair took place against our will, and that we were only accomplices after the fact."

" It is indeed a distinction worth noting," returned the commercial tra-veller.

" No doubt, it is of importance; and I will add, that, for a man who intended to turn a discovery to advantage, you have really acted with very little skill. Instead of going to Morizot, who is a very difficult person to deal with, you should have come to me, and informed me of your ideas and pretensions. By means of an alliance offensive and de-fensive, and by uniting all our resources of action and influence, we should have been able to do wonders with the capi-talist, and you would not have been brought to the difficult pass in which you now are."

" Really," thought Chabouillant, " in-stead of seeking my life, this good man seems to wish to make me some pro-posal."

" But," continued Legros, " the affair has taken its course, as you would have it; you have publicly announced your-self as the son of the marquis; you have entered on a negotiation of marriage with Morizot; all that is imprudent, rotten, badly constructed—and I must now look to my own safety."

" And to secure your safety, what do you mean to do?" asked Chabouillant, hastily, for he was impatient to know the fate reserved for him.

At this moment, the Saint-Martin re-entered the room, bringing with her all that was necessary to light the fire. Displaying extraordinary self-possession —which made him appear a very dan-gerous adversary—Legros quitted the conversation, to give his accomplice some directions as to the best manner of laying the wood, so that it might burn well. After this, placing a chair for Chabouillant, and taking one him-self, he resumed: " If I were a sangui-nary brute, like Morizot, your business would soon be settled. We are the strongest; a stab with a dagger is soon given; and a hole dug in the cellar, with a cask placed over it, to hide the spot, would keep everything snug."

" Those things are discovered sooner or later," answered the commercial tra-veller; " and you see, that even in this affair of the marquis ——"

" Once bit, twice shy," replied the lawyer; " we should know how to take our precautions. But, all things con-sidered, it does not enter into my views, or those of this lady, to go to any cruel extremities."

" Well! leaving my interests out of the question," said Chabouillant, anxi-ous to urge this consideration, " I think you are right in treating me with some forbearance. I told Mr. Morizot, and I now tell you, that I have deposited in the hands of a friend certain papers of a very delicate nature, which my death would almost immediately bring to light."

" Ha! by the bye," resumed the law-yer, as if he had just thought of some matter of trifling detail, " I knew that I had something to tell you on that head." And therewith he thrust his hand into the pocket of his great-coat, and said to the commercial traveller, as he drew out a small casket: " Do you know this?"

Chabouillant remained staring with stupefied amazement. The casket which he had entrusted to Mademoiselle Le-beau, was in the hands of his adversary.

" This surprises you," resumed Le-gros, " and you did not expect such an apparition; but another time, my dear fellow, you will learn from experience, that when one has something concealed which one wishes to visit, it is best to proceed straightforwards, and without making windings and turnings in the neighbourhood, which are likely to put anyone who is watching you on the scent. And now," added this cunning man of business, who took pleasure in displaying the resources of his inventive genius, " if you are curious to know the manner in which I extracted the venom with which you wished to infect us, I can inform you that the operation was neither long nor painful. In the same dress, and with the same friends that have been useful to me in carrying you off, I had previously made my appearance at the *Tricoloured Prism*, where I gave out that I had come to search the premises, in consequence of Moreau's arrest, which has put all Paris in commotion. Heaven, which sometimes protects innocence, permitted the mistress of the establishment, who, I had been told, was capable of making a very troublesome opposition, to be absent when I presented myself. I was under the painful necessity of putting her furniture and cupboards in a little disorder, for I must do her the justice to say, that your deposit was carefully concealed; but at length, here it is, and I am inclined to think, that you are from this moment my very humble and obedient servant."

"Admitting me to be in your power," said Chabouillant, with nervous volubility, "what do you expect from me?"

Legros rose from his seat, fetched a small table, which he placed before the commercial traveller, and put a light upon it; he then felt in his pocket, and drew forth a pistol.

"I have made a mistake, that is not what I want," said he, replacing his weapon where he had taken it from; and to the pistol—for his pocket seemed to be a true magazine—succeeded a peaceful horn-inkstand, similar to those used by schoolboys, a packet of pens ready mended, and some rumpled and yellow-looking sheets of paper, all which articles he placed within reach of the prisoner.

"Now, my young giddypate," said he, "you must write, and that too in the legible, bold hand with which we are already acquainted, from your amiable attention in setting down our edifying little history."

"But what do you want me to write?" inquired Chabouillant.

"I am going to dictate to you, and you will not have to draw in the least degree upon your imagination. Well, are we agreed?"

"I must yet know what you intend ——"

"My dear friend," said the man of law, "you do not thoroughly understand the question, and I must place it clearly before you."

Then, producing his pistol again, he said, at the same time raising his voice: "This is an instrument which, in one moment, can open for you the gate of the other world. I have close at hand," added he, "some obliging friends, to whom I need say only a word, in order for them to take part in the tragedy, as they have already figured in the little introductory piece. We are armed, and (including the lady) four against one; moreover, the scene is laid in a certain house in the *Widows' Walk*, of which you have heard speak, and where you know people are got rid of without fear of interruption. Thus I am master of your life: this, I think, is well understood."

"Well, what then?" resolutely cried Chabouillant.

"I do not want your life, or at least I do not want it but at the last extremity; but I want my safety. What I am going to dictate, will insure it. It is now therefore for you to choose; do you prefer a bullet in your head, or to write what I tell you?"

Having considered within himself, that there would always be time to choose the other alternative, Chabouillant took the pen, and placed himself in a posture for writing.

"I am ready, sir," said he, looking at Legros.

"Date from Offenburg, January 9th, 1804."

"So far, there is nothing to frighten my modesty," said the commercial traveller, affecting a careless coolness.

"Well, go on," continued the man of law; "'My dear Mr. Morizot,'—it is to Morizot that you are writing."

"I would rather write to anybody else," replied Chabouillant, in the same tone.

"Yes, but we have no choice," said Legros, resuming his dictation:

"'My dear Mr. Morizot, I have done more than procure information respecting the *ci-devant* Marquis de Brev——, who has not had sufficient friendship for you, to die, according to the first report. I have seen him, I have spoken to him, and, by reason of the terrible account that you would have to settle with him, there is no choice left for you, unless you cleverly get rid of him——'"

"I will not write that," said the commercial traveller, laying down his pen; "you wish to prove me your accomplice."

"I flatter myself that I shall do so," rejoined the man of law; "doubtless, you did not fancy, that I conducted you hither with so much ceremony, in order to write love-letters."

As, notwithstanding the incontestable

justice of this observation, Chabouillant still appeared to hesitate, Legros said to the Saint-Martin: "My dear, be kind enough to beg those gentlemen to walk in, for Monsieur begins to make me impatient, and we must come to a conclusion."

These words, uttered in a concise and resolute tone of voice, appeared to poor Chabouillant to imply the serious menace of a sentence of death, and, impelled by the instinct of self-preservation, he again prepared to write.

Taking up the sentence where it had been interrupted, Legros, who recommenced dictating, said: "' Cleverly get rid of him. I further inform you, that the said marquis intends, very shortly, returning to France by way of Strasburg. Now, what prudence and good policy counsel, is this: to wait at the frontier with a good conveyance, to bring him to Paris without allowing him to alight, and, under the pretext of procuring for him an asylum until his position as an emigrant can be settled, to conduct him to your charming little house in the *Widows' Walk*, where he will find someone with whom he will have to do. Finally, I hope that, should this information appear to you of some value, we shall find no difficulty in coming to a settlement, for I shall not exact much, if you are generous. I send this letter by a private opportunity, it being of a very delicate nature for the post.

"' Heartily yours, and hoping soon to see you.

"' Your affectionate ——'"

"Now sign your name," added the man of law.

"I am to sign that?"

"Undoubtedly; is it more difficult to sign than to write it?"

Chabouillant not appearing to have made up his mind, Madame de Saint-Martin now interfered, saying: "Sign your name, sir—sign; otherwise, I assure you that this affair will terminate badly."

Chabouillant, in despair, pressed his head between his hands, and Legros presenting to him the pen, he decided upon affixing his name.

Legros immediately took possession of the letter, folded and sealed it, and, after having obliged the commercial traveller to address it, he carefully shut it up in his pocket-book.

"Now," said Legros, placing before the singular secretary he had chosen, a fresh sheet of paper, "we will proceed to another exercise, and it is with me you are going to correspond."

"What! another letter?" impatiently exclaimed the commercial traveller.

"Undoubtedly; there are several of us interested in the business, and every one must have his right."

Chabouillant could write nothing which would compromise him more than did the letter which was already in Legros' hands. Not having then any great interest to offer resistance, he took the pen, and, being also desirous to see the unravelling of his adventure, he wrote as follows, without once stopping or interrupting himself by any observation:

"Paris, January 30th, 1804.

"My dear Legros,—Your friend Morizot is a terribly stingy fellow. Guess what he offers me for having hunted down the game for him which you know of? The miserable sum of ten thousand francs. But I will be even with him yet, and I have a rod in pickle for him. I have formed an audacious little plan, which is neither more nor less than to make myself his son-in-law; and he may reckon himself fortunate, if he gets out of the business for four hundred thousand livres. You were wrong to take fright and exile yourself, for everything here is very quiet. Return then, to assist me in my charming design, of which your cooperation will insure the success. I need not tell you, that I know better than Morizot how to be grateful for a good service rendered. The friend who will deliver this letter to you, will further inform you how I intend settling our common interest. Hoping we shall soon meet, believe in all the friendly sentiments of your very affectionate

"CHABOUILLANT."

The letter was already folded and ready to be sealed, when Legros changed his mind, and, returning it to the commercial traveller, said: "Write as a postscript, 'The chances of the *roulette* are very pernicious this year; I have all the odds against me. I never once play without losing, and I have great need of refeathering my nest.'"

"Do you see, my boy," said Legros, whilst sealing the letter (upon which Chabouillant afterwards wrote, *Mr. Legros, lawyer, Offenburg*), "this little postscript is designed to explain our acquaintance. And now," continued the adroit practitioner, apparently taking much pleasure in the contemplation of his skill, "understand well the mechanism of this combination. By means of a skilful and happy coincidence, with certain evident facts, which have publicly taken place, the two epistles which you have just finished, establish, in a most satisfactory manner to your profit (as well as on every other point), that you are our accomplice. Should it please you to inform against us, you can gratify your fancy; but then we should bring forward these two papers emanating from yourself, and with the explanations with which they would be accompanied, if we did not prove you to be one of us, you would, in faith, be not a little expert."

" But, my dear," remarked the Saint-Martin, and her observation, on a superficial view of the case, seemed a very judicious one, " you do not consider, that the letters of this gentleman, in compromising him, are at the same time an additional proof that the affair in question has taken place."

" You have really found out that!" disdainfully replied Legros, " and you imagine that this did not enter into my calculation; but the more these letters are against us, the less appearance have they of being written by our influence, and the greater belief they must obtain in the eyes of justice."

" It is perhaps possible," rejoined the matron, who appeared to be but partially persuaded of the truth of this argument.

" Besides, our success will entirely depend upon the manner in which we make use of them, as well as upon profiting by the right moment to bring them forward. For example, if you, sir, were to try to get us into trouble, you might fancy that we should assuredly produce them immediately?"

" By Jove!" replied the matron, " I think it is useless having a weapon, unless one makes use of it."

" Well, for my part, I should conduct the affair quite in a different manner," replied the profound diplomatist. " Should this gentleman dare to accuse us, I should let him go on, and defend myself as well as I could, without making use of recrimination. But should our sentence be pronounced, and we be found guilty, I should then ask to make some disclosures; I should produce these letters, and it would be thought that I had purposely kept them *in petto*, because they contained accusations against myself, then we should see how the informer, who had so impru-

dently stepped forward, would extricate himself from this cunningly-laid trap."

" Here is a great deal of ingenuity thrown away," said Chabouillant; " I assure you that I have had quite enough of this marquis-business, and I shall not breathe another syllable about it to any living soul."

Thinking that his adversary was now completely subdued, Legros became considerably softened; he judged that things had taken a different turn, and regarded Chabouillant as being dependent upon him. Returning then in a friendly manner to the idea that he had started as a feeler at the beginning of the conversation, he said: " Well, my dear fellow, you are wrong to throw away dirty water, before you get clean, and you always run into extremes. It was all very fine, no doubt, to wish to profit by the secret you had discovered, in order to procure yourself a good position in the world, and cast your net for a fortune; but there were a thousand difficulties in the way of this project. You must not let the goose squeak out too much, whilst you are stealing its feathers."

" I repeat," rejoined the commercial traveller, " that I give in my full and complete resignation."

" And I also repeat, that you are wrong to do so, for Morizot is not altogether invulnerable; he has a certain way of behaving towards his associates, which makes him deserve a rap over the knuckles, and if you were in a reasonable mood, I do not say but that a little society might be formed for working a mine ——"

Several loud knocks at the street-door interrupted Legros in the midst of this sentence, and one of the honourable friends whom he had posted in the hall, half-opening the door of the drawing-room, informed the man of law of the alarming noise which was heard without.

Informed of the rapping at the street-door, Legros exclaimed: " It must be Morizot; not finding us at the Faubourg Saint-Martin, where I appointed him, he suspected that we were here. I am sorry that we were not already gone, for we shall be obliged to have a set-to with him. And it was your fault, my dear fellow," added he, addressing the commercial traveller, " for not making an end to your resistance—by my troth! so much the worse for you, if you meet with any misfortune."

Chabouillant might, with a very good

grace, have retorted the accusation, and told Legros, that the verbose and subtle manner in which he had made known his plans, was in reality the cause of the delay which he so much regretted; but the poor fellow's attention being principally occupied by the lawyer's last words, which led him to fear a fresh complication of things, and new dangers, he thought it better to remain silent, and summon up all his courage.

In the meantime, the knocks at the door continued, and bespoke furious impatience in whoever was without.

"Shall I open the door?" asked the Saint-Martin.

"Yes, go," replied the lawyer; and as the matron left the room, he said to Chabouillant: "Do not utter a word; do not contradict what I advance, and leave all to me."

The next moment, the commissary entered. His clothes were streaming with water, for he had been unable to procure a coach, and had been obliged to walk the long round he was compelled to take, in the midst of a pelting rain.

Pale with cold and anger, he was frightful to look upon, and a shudder passed through Chabouillant's heart, when Morizot, after having regarded him with the look of a tiger, said in a hollow voice to the lawyer: "You will doubtless explain to me, sir, the meaning of the pleasantry, which I have just been subjected to."

"There is no pleasantry in the matter," replied Legros; "I had assured you, that we did not want your assistance, and you should not have come."

"But what do you mean by telling me that you intend going to one place, and then going to another?"

"Not at all; it was my intention to drive where I told you; but, on reflection, I thought that this place was nearer, and that we should be more at our ease here."

"More at your ease, and for what?" said Morizot, without taking the trouble to conceal that his thoughts were bent upon murder; "this man is still in the land of the living, when an end ought already to have been made of him."

"But everything is now settled," tranquilly rejoined the lawyer; "I must even own that this gentleman has behaved in a very accommodating and delicate manner."

"Accomodating in what?" demanded the commissary, in a sharp tone; "you well know, that there is but one way of treating with him; either he or we must disappear from this world."

"That is your opinion," said Legros; "but you know, that neither I nor this lady think so."

"What great security then has he offered you? Will he marry your mistress instead of my daughter? Perhaps, you have obliged him to take some terrible oath, which he will laugh at, as soon as he is out of our hands?"

"Oh! an oath?" said the lawyer, shrugging his shoulders; "you must think me very green!"

"In short, you have done something since you have been here, and I think you may deign to inform me ——"

"This is what I have settled," replied Legros: "a letter addressed to you, and one to me;" and he gave the two letters to his patron to peruse.

One valuable quality possessed by Morizot, was, that, letting business take the preference of everything else, he was able to keep cool, even in the most excited state of mind, in order to make himself master of a case, and then to decide accordingly.

He therefore now seated himself near the chimney-piece, took up his eyeglass, for his sight was somewhat impaired by age, and began to read with much attention.

Having satisfied himself as to the nature of the contents, he made a movement, as if he were going to throw the letters into the fire, saying at the same time: "Is it on these pieces of paper, that you intend building our safety?"

"Assuredly," replied Legros, snatching the letters out of his hand; and he recommenced in nearly the same terms, the commentary which he had already delivered for the edification of the Saint-Martin.

"You were speaking just now of being green," exclaimed the commissary; "you ought to have called yourself completely raw."

"Then this arrangement does not suit you?"

"Not at all," replied Morizot; then, addressing himself to Madame de Saint-Martin, he added: "Tell those people who are waiting, to come to speak to me."

"Those people did not come to do what you are meditating," replied the lawyer, "and they will not comply with your wish."

"Why not? do they not follow the same trade every day at No. 113?—and if I pay them accordingly!"

GREENAWAY & WRIGHT

"I tell you they will not do it; and, at all events, I oppose its being done."

"Ah! I see you are crossing over to the side of virtue."

"The question is not of virtue, but of prudence. Already, once before, without consulting us, and contrary to our opinion, you proceeded to violence. To what has that led us? To oblige us to begin afresh."

"It is to be hoped, that, this time, you will be able to hold your tongue."

"Yes; amongst five accomplices, that we should be, a secret is so easily kept!"

"This is foolish talking," resolutely exclaimed Morizot; "happen what may, this gentleman must be made away with."

It must be acknowledged, that the situation in which Chabouillant was placed, was a strange one: no other than Morizot, thirsting for revenge, could speak with such horrible coolness concerning a man's death in his presence.

The commercial traveller experienced a moment of terrible agony, for his defender at first remained silent, as if bending to the authority of these imperious words; but Legros seemed suddenly inspired with a thought.

"You must, however," said he to his accomplice, "renounce your design, and you will yourself acknowledge the necessity of doing so."

"You will never persuade me," replied the commissary, "that, if I meet with a mad-dog, I am to caress instead of destroy him."

"But if this gentleman had a friend, who kept watch over his life, and in whose hands some dangerous papers ——"

"You wrote to me yourself, that you were master of the deposit."

"Yes, of one; but not of two," replied Legros, with most perfect composure.

"How!" said Morizot, addressing Chabouillant, with comic fury; "you have had the precaution to provide yourself with another confidant?"

"With your permission," replied Chabouillant, giving proof of great presence of mind, "I knew you, Mr. Father-in-law, and acted accordingly."

"Malediction!" exclaimed Morizot; "to think that I cannot revenge myself upon this scoundrel!" and, with disappointment difficult to describe, he strode hastily up and down the room.

Profiting by the moment when his accomplice, whom he was deceiving, was still under the influence of his surprise, Legros said to the Saint-Martin: "Get him out"—and, at the same time, he found means to whisper to the man, whose escape he was favouring: "I will see you to-morrow; we have to talk over many things."

When the commissary saw the intention of setting his enemy at liberty, the fear of losing his revenge made him suspect that Legros was playing him a trick, and he started forward, exclaiming: "You will not let this man go ——"

"But what the devil will you do with him?" replied the lawyer, interposing to favour the escape of the fugitive.

Without answering him, Morizot rushed after Chabouillant, and on his part Legros did all in his power to detain his accomplice; so that a real conflict took place between them, and they collared each other, offering the strange spectacle of what might be termed a civil war.

Fortunately, a few seconds after, the house-door was heard to shut, and the entrance of the Saint-Martin unaccompanied, into the apartment, showed Morizot the inutility of offering any further violence.

Breathless from the rough conflict he had just had with his accomplice, Morizot threw himself into an arm-chair, where for a moment he took breath. Then, addressing himself to Legros in a tone which testified lively resentment: "After what has just taken place," said he, "you must understand, that everything is at an end between us."

"And why?" asked the lawyer, without seeming to care much for this menace of a rupture taking place.

"There was evidently some connivance between you and that man; your conduct is infamous."

"You are mad," replied Legros; "I have saved you from an abyss into which you were going to throw yourself, and you wish to quarrel with me for it!"

"You are right; I am mad for having given my confidence for so many years, to a scoundrel of your stamp."

"Ah! let me tell you though," said the lawyer, much moved by this gross abuse, "I begin to be tired of all this, and as the occasion offers, we must come to some explanation. I am a scoundrel, you say? it is possible that I am; but I should like to know, by whose means and for whose sake I became one? You coveted an unhappy girl—we gave her up to you; a fortune which you required, sprinkled with blood—we still were faithful to you. For twenty years, the tool of all your base acts, of your exactions, of your usuries, I prostituted in your service, skill which I might have employed honestly on my own account; and now, what is my reward? When probably on the point of being exiles from our native land, you threw us a paltry alms. Do you call this probity or justice? and are you not a greater scoundrel than I am?"

"But you well know, that I should not have let you want," rejoined Morizot, assuming a milder tone; for this vigorous sally had taken him by surprise.

"That is not the question," replied Legros; "and I do not need your charity. We are not master and servant, but accomplices; only according to your account, the one is to have all the benefit, and the other all the loss."

"Well said!" exclaimed the Saint-Martin, encouraging the lawyer to raise the standard of revolt.

"Well then! for the future, it shall not be thus," rejoined Legros, becoming more animated. "If you wish to murder, as you like dabbling in blood, you may murder alone; and with regard to other matters, which may be more to my taste, and which we shall undertake in common, we will divide the profit, Mr. Potentate; or I am your humble servant, and make not one of the party."

"Be it so," replied the commissary; "you wish to essay your skill alone, and we shall see what you can do without me."

"First though, with your permission, we will close a little account of arrears. When a partnership is dissolved, the affairs are liquidated."

"What do you mean?" proudly demanded Morizot.

"I mean to say, that the paltry sum of ten thousand francs, which you allotted to us at the death of the marquis, can only be regarded as so much on account."

"You jest, my dear fellow, and I have done more than you could justly expect."

"According to your idea, perhaps; but, according to mine, I am far from giving any receipt."

Morizot contented himself with shrugging his shoulders, and, taking up his hat, prepared to depart alone.

Persons who for a length of time have been subjected to a rough yoke, go to greater lengths than others, when they have once broken their chain.

This was now the case with Legros; running to place himself in front of the door: "You were speaking just now," said he, "of calling in the men, who are waiting in the next room, and I maintained that they would not execute your orders."

"Well!" exclaimed Morizot, with a resolute air.

"Will you call them in now," rejoined Legros, "and submit to them the dispute between us? With the high sense of justice which I know them to possess, I wager that they will decide the cause in my favour."

"If not for my sake, at least for your own, you will not admit a set of gallows-birds into matters of so secret a nature."

"You no doubt understand by that term, men of resolution, ready to do anything. The greater reason to depend upon them. Suppose I were to propose to them a good hit; for example, the pillage of a commissary-general; do you think they would refuse?"

It so happened, that, at the moment when Legros was uttering this menace in pretty clear terms, one of his satellites, partly opening the drawing-room door, said: "Now that you have plucked your bird (meaning Chabouillant, whom he had seen go out), have you not soon done with your confabulation?"

"Wait a moment longer," replied the lawyer; then turning to Morizot: "You see, my dogs are getting impatient, and it is my opinion, that, if I were now to let them loose, they would bite hard."

"Ah, Legros!" exclaimed the commissary, in an affecting tone; "I should never have expected this from you—you whom I have always considered a model of delicacy and probity."

"What can I do? one gets tired of everything, even of being a dupe; and then, with Chabouillant at large, our trade is now worth nothing, and I wish to retire from business."

"But, in short, what do you want?" said Morizot, who knew that his dear Legros was capable of anything; "you certainly have not the intention to ruin me and my family?"

"Madame de Saint-Martin," answered the lawyer, employing this evasive manner of speaking, in order to fix a certain sum, "has always been of opinion, that the service rendered to you in the last affair of the marquis, if worth a farthing, was worth a hundred thousand francs."

"Madame de Saint-Martin," replied Morizot, "is really not reasonable."

"A rich man like you, worth millions," said the lady whose name had just been brought forward, "to bargain about such a trifle!"

"Well, shall we conclude at this price?" said Legros; "or must I call in the arbitrators?"

Morizot, thus driven into a corner, replied: "I must needs consent, for you negociate with a pistol at my throat."

Then, like a drowning man trying to find any straw to take hold of, he continued: "Your mistress at one time wished for this house; it is worth more than the sum you name."

"This house!" eagerly exclaimed the Saint-Martin; "after what has happened here, I would not have it, were it worth three times the amount."

"And besides," replied Legros, "for people whose affairs may call them, from one moment to another, into a foreign country, property that can be removed is more convenient."

"But you know, my dear fellow, that I have not the money about me, and you must be satisfied with my word."

"Oh! you are good for this sum, and for many others besides; but everyone has his little whims, and you know that in business matters, I like to have security."

"Well! shall we sign a private agreement, which we can afterwards get legalized before a notary?"

"Pshaw!" exclaimed Legros; "I would rather settle the matter at once." And Providence at that moment putting into his mouth the words which, on a former occasion, he had addressed to Chevillard, he continued: "And in fact, being yourself engaged in trade, you can have no objection to the formality—the purely commercial formality—of a bill of exchange——"

"I like to pay ready money," replied Morizot, in a tone of pleasantry, "and do not choose to have bills drawn upon me."

"What can be done?" rejoined the lawyer, taking from his pocket-book some stamped paper, of which he always carried a good supply about with him, as other people carried their watch or their handkerchief. "I see, that we shall run aground just as we have arrived at port, for those men in the next room are getting impatient."

"Well, let us make a finish to it," said Morizot, in a tone of feverish decision; "what must I write?"

"Why," quietly rejoined Legros, "you know the form: 'Please to pay at sight, on this bill of exchange ——'"

Swallowing the bitter draught, the commissary took the pen, and signed the engagement.

Legros examined it carefully, to see that nothing was wanting; then, after shutting it up in his pocket-book: "It is to be regretted," said he, in a sentimental voice, "that old friends like we are, whose interest in so many instances is the same, and who are, after all, united by ties almost indissoluble—it is, I say, grievous and afflicting to see them part on bad terms."

"Ah! cruel man that you are!" exclaimed Morizot, in the same tone—for he felt that their mutual safety demanded, provisionally at least, that their union should continue—"how could you think of acting such a scene, in so critical a moment, and beneath the enemy's fire?"

"Well," said Legros, "let us mutually forgive any foolish words that may have passed between us."

"You know that I bear no rancour," said the commissary.

"And I, no malice," said the lawyer.

"Ah! you obstinate creatures, embrace one another!" exclaimed the Saint-Martin; "for you have just had a lovers' quarrel, and, like lovers, you must put an end to it."

The two friends fell into each other's arms, and gave a fraternal embrace, with feelings which one may well conceive.

This formality over, Legros opened the drawing-room door, and, addressing himself to his friends, the redressers of wrongs at No. 113, said: "We are at your service, my brave fellows. I beg pardon for having detained you thus long; but our business is now settled, and we are ready to go."

He then reentered the apartment, and gave a look round, to see whether he had left any papers about, and if everything was in order.

This done, they all left the house, and, before packing his followers into the hackney-coach, the lawyer said, addressing Morizot: "Will you profit by our conveyance?"

"Thank you," replied the commissary, "the rain has ceased, and I require a little fresh air."

He accordingly proceeded alone, whilst the coach regained the interior of Paris. Legros took his friends to the Rue de Valois, where he set them down at some distance from their head-quarters.

From thence, he caused himself to be driven, together with the Saint-Martin, to his apartments in the Rue des Moulins; and on the road, he said to that honourable lady: "Are you at last satisfied?"

"Yes, it is not so bad, if the bill of exchange is paid."

"Rest satisfied; to-morrow morning, I am to meet the other one."

"What other?" demanded the Saint-Martin.

"Why, Chabouillant. He is a resolute fellow, who in faith hazarded a bold stroke. I think, that, by coming to some understanding together, we shall find Mr. Commissary plenty to do."

CHAPTER XII.

WE have already seen that Chabouillant, almost immediately after his arrest, had begun to get out of conceit with the enterprise in which he had engaged.

Carried away by an ardent desire to fix a parentage for himself, on some one or other, he had, immediately upon discovering the secret at Offenburg, rather thoughtlessly conceived the plan which we have beheld him put into execution; and, although the exaction which he practised was culpable in itself, yet as he was only to take in very wicked people, who were enjoying with impunity the fruits of a horrible crime, the immorality of the act he was committing was not sufficiently apparent to him.

Willingly regarding himself as a kind of instrument in the hands of Providence, for procuring the indirect punishment of crime, he had not scrupulously reflected, that to steal a name, even when it belong to nobody, and to rob thieves and assassins, was conduct to be condemned, and of which the law might take cognizance.

But death, which he had seen so near to him, having suddenly enlightened his conscience, he regretted that he had so imprudently embarked in the undertaking; and, notwithstanding the friendly disposition and proposals of Legros, he only thought of extricating himself, with as little damage as possible, from this dangerous affair.

In this perplexed state of mind, his thoughts naturally turned towards Mademoiselle Lebeau, with whom he had already made an approach towards confidence, relative to the affair which occupied his attention. He knew her to be a woman of excellent understanding, and capable of giving good advice, and doubted not that he should derive advantage by confiding in her. He had also to beg the poor girl's pardon, for the annoying occurrence of which he had been the involuntary cause. All these reasons determined Chabouillant, as soon as he was restored to liberty, to repair to the *Tricoloured Prism*, where he expected to find still prevailing the agitation and terror always occasioned by a visit from the officers of justice.

On Mademoiselle Lebeau's returning rather late from Charenton, where we know she had to go, she had found her shopwomen in the greatest consternation, her locks forced, her cupboards in disorder; and to complete the matter, she was given to understand that the object of this visit of justice being to seize upon some treasonable papers, which had been found in her possession, she might expect to be arrested from one moment to another.

In consequence of this menace, those around her wished to persuade her to quit her house, and to seek an asylum with one of her friends. But strong in the support of a good conscience, and thinking that this step would be the first proof of her guilt, the courageous young girl peremptorily refused to do so, and she was just occupied in opposing the urgent entreaties poured forth from all sides, that she would consent to a temporary but needful absence, when Chabouillant arrived at the house.

Without showing any anger, and rather with the air of a person who was hurt at having been made a dupe, than frightened at the danger with which she thought herself menaced, Mademoiselle Lebeau reproached the new comer, with the culpable subterfuge he had made use of with regard to her.

" In a case of pressing danger," said she, " I never refuse my assistance to whoever asks it; but I consider it perfidious to obtain a service under false pretences, and to leave those who render it in ignorance of the possible consequences of their kindness."

This grave accusation of abuse of confidence just brought against him, made Chabouillant still more anxious to tell the whole truth; and, having asked Mademoiselle Lebeau to grant him a private interview, he began by assuring her that the threatened danger was imaginary, and then proceeded to relate to her, word for word, the conversation at Offenburg, the dangerous use which he had thought to make of this discovery, and the terrible manner in which, an hour before, this finely-conceived enterprise had been on the point of terminating with regard to himself.

During this long recital, the young shopkeeper, notwithstanding her sagacity, at first seized but imperfectly all the bearings of the case, the details being so complicated, and the links by which they were united, so difficult to follow.

She was especially struck with the part which related to Chevillard, and this, from not being well acquainted with it himself, was exactly what the narrator explained most imperfectly. At length, after several questions calculated to elucidate this frightful mystery, she succeeded in obtaining a clear insight into the part which her former book-keeper had played in this terrible drama.

" Poor fellow," she exclaimed, " into what a fearful abyss he threw himself!"

But as in no case it formed part of the character of this charming girl, to think long of herself and her own interest, she soon gave her attention to the singular and dangerous situation in which the narrator of this history had placed himself, and applying her upright mind and strict probity to the right appreciation of this difficult subject.

"Monsieur Chabouillant," she said, "your conduct has been very imprudent; I knew you to be dissipated, and a little too free on the chapter of morality; but from this point, to so serious a forgetfulness of what an honest man owes to himself, there was a wide space!"

"Say no more, I beg of you, mademoiselle," replied Chabouillant; "do not cover me with confusion. I know, without your telling me, how much I have lowered myself in your esteem; but what must I do to repair my fault? Whatever you command, I will do immediately, so much confidence have I in your good judgment."

"In my opinion, there is but one way for you to act. Providence has placed you on the track of horrible crimes; you ought to reveal all you know to justice."

"My conscience has already, a short time ago, suggested to me to take this course; but only think of the appearance of guilt which these wretches have contrived to hatch up; those dangerous letters which remain in their hands!"

"It is just this which induces me to advise you as I have done. If, on your return from Germany, you had told me the secret which you had discovered, I should have felt embarrassed to give you my opinion, because it is always painful to become an accuser, even in the case of the greatest criminals."

"Certainly," said Chabouillant, readily acquiescing in this opinion, "thus to send a whole party to the scaffold!"

"But in the present state of the case," replied Mademoiselle Lebeau, "you have no longer any choice. By the culpable step you have taken, in wishing to profit by the crime, you have become morally a kind of accomplice. By means of the letters which you have written, your fate is henceforward bound up with that of these wretches, and every moment of delay will strengthen the tie; an immediate confession, and prompt repentance, can alone free you from this responsibility, of which the extent is incalculable."

"But leaving the accusation of murder out of the question, the law has perhaps a punishment for those who assume false names. It will be allotted to me, and I shall be dishonoured."

"I know not how that may be," rejoined the young shopkeeper, "but hitherto you have not profited in any way by your imprudent proceeding."

"No, indeed," replied the commercial traveller; "all the benefit I derived, was, that I had nearly lost my life by it."

"Moreover," continued Mademoiselle Lebeau, "you will, by your revelations, render a great service to society; in short, by going to denounce yourself, you will show, that, having acted from levity and thoughtlessness, you were desirous to make reparation, as soon as you became conscious of the immorality of your conduct——and I think, that there are many reasons for indulgence."

"Yes," said Chabouillant, after having reflected for a moment, "it is perhaps the most simple and safe plan to reveal all to justice; but only think, I, a single witness, against three guilty persons, who will stoutly deny everything! I feel convinced, that you are giving me good advice; but I am playing a very hazardous game, mademoiselle."

"You will say, that I see things in a singular point of view; but, in your place, I would rather rejoice in any danger that might accompany my determination, for the more hazard incurred to yourself by your avowal, the greater repentance and courage it will indicate, and the better it will tend to procure for you the sympathy and esteem of all honest men. With regard to another witness, whose absence you regret, who knows but that Divine Providence may not reserve him for you!"

"How so? what do you mean?"

"Yes; to-morrow, perhaps, Chevillard will be restored to reason, and if he were but to affirm the infamy of which he has been made the victim, do you not think, that this alone would be strong presumptive evidence against the guilty parties?"

"But what makes you hope for the astonishing miracle of his recovery?"

"The medical men, whom I have seen to-day at Charenton, and who for some days past have been much more satisfied with his state. A little while ago, after having had iced water poured upon his head, a most favourable symptom has declared itself; he has fallen into a deep sleep, which had not been the case for a long time; and, according to the opinion of the doctors, it is probable, that, when he awakes, he will have recovered the entire use of his faculties."

"Oh! should this prove so, then the hand of God is in everything that happens," eagerly exclaimed Chabouillant, who, in his character of commercial traveller, was, generally speaking, a follower of Voltaire, and a free-thinker.

"He is here," added Mademoiselle Lebeau, lowering her voice, and with the air of confiding a great secret.

"What! my poor friend is here, in this house?"

"Yes; the doctors think, that the sight of the scenes which might remind him of better times, may be favourable in the crisis which we expect. So I brought him back with me, and have caused him to be carried into his former chamber, which he used to like so much; and what gives us great hope is, that all this movement has not awakened him. It seems as if Nature, feeling the need that she will have to-morrow of all her strength, is collecting her power in this profound slumber."

"Mademoiselle!" exclaimed Chabouillant, with enthusiasm, "Chevillard will be restored to us; it is more than a presentiment, I am now sure of it."

"May God grant it!" rejoined the amiable girl, joining her hands, and raising her tearful eyes towards heaven.

"My resolution is taken," continued the commercial traveller; "not to-morrow, but this evening, this very instant, I will go and declare all to the magistrate."

"Go, Monsieur Chabouillant," said Mademoiselle Lebeau; "and depend upon me to assist you to my utmost ability, in this courageous struggle."

Then, as if the criminal had by this resolution begun to clear himself in her eyes, she held out her hand to him, which he, on his side, always gallant and alert, endeavoured (although this favour was not granted him) to carry respectfully to his lips. They then separated, Chabouillant to repair to the government-commissioner, attached to the criminal court,* and Mademoiselle Lebeau, to go up-stairs to inquire after the sick man, at whose bedside a zealous and skilful nurse was to keep watch all night.

* This, in 1804, was the title of the *procureur-général* attached to the criminal court. There was also a similar officer attached to the civil court of appeal (now *cour royale*). The civil and criminal jurisdictions were then entirely distinct from each other.

CHAPTER XIII.

ALTHOUGH it was rather an unreasonable hour to present himself at the magistrate's, our penitent did not wish his resolutions to cool, and, contrary to his expectation, he was readily admitted; for the state of great excitement into which Paris had been thrown in the morning, by Moreau's arrest, was a motive for the functionaries appointed to maintain public order and tranquillity, to display great vigilance. Thus Chabouillant had scarcely mentioned, that he had some important communications to make, than he was immediately ushered in, and very courteously begged to explain himself.

Whilst walking from the Rue des Deux-Portes Saint-Sauveur to the ancient hotel Lamoignon,* inhabited by the government-commissioner, Chabouillant prepared his address, and it certainly was not an inexpert manner of beginning his recital, to represent himself as escaping that very moment from an ambuscade, where, under the menace of death, he had written some letters, against any bad consequences arising from which, he had come to claim the protection of justice. So that, if the guilty parties should ever make use of these dangerous writings, the effect of them would have been already weakened beforehand, and the mark aimed at by bringing them forward would be almost entirely missed.

The narrator showed further skill, in being completely candid with regard to whatever might bear against himself. Relating with *naïveté* his strange mania for making himself out a branch of some good family, he explained how he had been led by this fixed idea, to assume a name which had terminated with the unfortunate marquis who had been assassinated, and how, from one step to another, he had come to treat with the great criminal Morizot. It must be acknowledged, that Legros and the Saint-Martin, who, by saving Chabouillant's life, had perhaps thought to open for themselves a side-door for escape, found in him a grateful adversary; for he took care to point out the shade of their particular guilt, which was that of being only passive accomplices. In short, his recital was clear, concise, and free from exaggeration, so that it at once gave the impression, that it contained true and conclusive information; and if he was not successful in representing himself as

* Rue Pavée, au Marais.

a person entirely worthy of esteem, he at least passed for one of those every-day characters, who, having but a superficial idea of right and wrong, yet know where to stop in the career of evil, and, when necessary, how to retrace their steps.

The history of the blind men had given to the murder in which they were mixed up, an uncommon degree of notoriety, and public justice, which has also its self-love to satisfy in seeking out and prosecuting crime, had seen with much dissatisfaction its inability to discover the authors of an assassination which had been so much talked about. For some time past, having, as we have said, its attention fully engaged by its political *surveillance*, it had almost entirely given up all researches with regard to this mysterious outrage ; but it may well be imagined, it saw with pleasure, the clue found which was to lead it on the track of the criminals.

Taking up the cause with ardour, the magistrate sent to awake the head of that department, at the prefecture of police, which had the care of certain written information concerning a great number of individuals, who, without having had precisely any disputes with justice, have nevertheless placed themselves in such a position, that it has its eye upon them. When the registers were brought, Legros figured in them as a man frequenting dangerous haunts, as a supporter of hells, and as being strongly suspected of making usurious loans, and other vicious practices. His wife was also mentioned, as habitually pandering to the bad passions of the commissary Morizot. The article regarding the latter, consisted of the deposition made by the doctor who assisted at Esther's death ; in this deposition were related the circumstances of the suicide, and the motives which were supposed to have caused it.

These accounts containing nothing in favour of the accused, and answering besides exactly to the information given by Chabouillant, decided the magistrates to grant an order of arrest against Morizot and the two Legros', and they commanded a commissary of police to see it put into execution on the following morning at daybreak. With regard to Chabouillant, there was no ground for detaining him, for the attempt at extortion (of which he had been guilty) not having been carried into effect, and therefore detrimental to no one, it was doubtful, in a legal point of view, whether it constituted a crime. Besides, the magistrates, who wished to keep fair with this valuable witness, would have been very careful to alienate or intimidate him by any severe measure. They contented themselves therefore with making him write down and sign his denunciation, and, after they had taken his address, and warned him to hold himself in readiness for any summons, he was allowed to return home, where, without his having the least idea of it, a discreet, but at the same time a very active and strict watch, was kept over all his movements.

The night had passed, and Chevillard had never in his life had a more calm and refreshing sleep.

Very early in the morning, and before she had gone up-stairs to inquire after him, Mademoiselle Lebeau had an agreeable surprise. The doctor, who had been the most assiduous in his care of the patient during his illness, did not live at Charenton, but had his residence in Paris. He was of a compassionate disposition, and had taken much interest in the poor madman ; besides, in his character of a man of science, he had found some curious observations to make, in a case which presented rather uncommon symptoms.

As soon therefore as it was light, he arrived at his patient's, in order to be present at the return of his senses, and with the intention of indicating the first assistance to be rendered, and the best steps to be taken, in order to bring about a happy termination to the favourable crisis which he anticipated.

Accompanied by Mademoiselle Lebeau, who affectionately thanked him for his benevolent attention, he ascended to Chevillard's chamber, where he learnt from the woman who had watched all night, that the sleep continued to be calm, but light. He then caused the window-curtains to be gently undrawn, so that a beautiful ray of the morning sun penetrated into the apartment, and shed there a bright and joyous lustre. Then placing himself with Mademoiselle Lebeau and the nurse, in such a position that they could observe the countenance of the patient, without being perceived by him, he recommended perfect silence, and awaited with curiosity what would take place.

After the lapse of several minutes, a deep sigh heaved the breast of Chevillard, and sitting up in bed, he stared around him in great astonishment.

He appeared to recognise, one after the other, the objects by which he was surrounded, and which had been carefully disposed in the same order as they had formerly been.

"Ah! good heavens!" he exclaimed at last; "it was then a dream. But how long and painful a one!"

Having been placed on his bed in his clothes: "Well! what could I have been about last evening?" he asked himself, "thus to fall asleep, without taking time to undress myself?" At the same time, slowly raising himself, like a man who is collecting his ideas,

and who is doubtful of himself, he appeared to have the intention of getting up, and walking about the apartment.

"All goes on well," said the doctor; "but he must not see us yet."

Having taken care to keep the door partly open, he went out with Mademoiselle Lebeau and the nurse, without making any noise; and remaining outside, listening to what was going on, he heard Chevillard occupied with arranging his ideas, and saying to himself: "Yes, I dined with Chabouillant; he made me drink a good deal: yes, it must be so; I must have returned home rather gone, and must have thrown myself on my bed; but what happiness, that all I have seen in this dreadful nightmare was only a dream!—A dream—however—but no, it must have been real—Mon Dieu! I have suffered so much—Oh! yes! all these horrible things have happened to me. And," added he, looking at himself in the glass, " could I have become thus thin in one night?"

At this moment, the doctor, not wishing that he should resume the chain of his cruel recollections, before his head was sufficiently strengthened to support the painful blow, ordered the nurse to speak from outside the door.

" Well! Monsieur Chevillard," said she, repeating the words which the doctor whispered to her in a low voice, " do you not mean to get up to-day? It is past nine o'clock, and Mademoiselle is waiting for an invoice, which is wanted in a hurry, and which you forgot to make out last evening."

" Very well! I am coming," replied the book-keeper, resuming his soliloquy. " Decidedly then," said he, " I must have been dreaming; but never before has a dream left such an impression upon me."

He then occupied himself with his toilet, as he had always been accustomed to do in getting up, and as, during the first days of his illness, Mademoiselle Lebeau had sent to the furnished house in the Rue Copeau, for all that he had left there, he found all the articles for his use in their places, which was an additional reason for making him think that he had been subjected to the powerful influence of a frightful delusion.

When he had gone down stairs, this illusion was continued by Mademoiselle Lebeau, who was in the room when he entered, and who said to him : " It seems, that you and Monsieur Chabouillant have behaved in a fine manner yesterday. How pale and ill you look this morning! Now, was I wrong in telling you, that dining out did not suit you?"

" Yes, I think we have not conducted ourselves very well," replied the book-keeper; " and another time, I will listen to you."

Having said this, he repaired to his desk, where everything was arranged according to custom, and as if he had quitted it only the previous evening. Mademoiselle Lebeau followed him, re-minding him of the invoice on account of which she pretended that she had sent for him, and the illusions of the drama were for a moment transported to a place where they are very seldom met with. If Chevillard could perform the calculations which were asked of him, his reason had evidently returned; but the question was, would his head be capable of the combination of ideas necessary to solve an arithmetical problem? Therefore, although betraying no outward emotion, it was with terrible anxiety, that the young girl watched the progress of this decisive trial.

Chevillard acquitted himself honourably, and without making one false step; he made the addition of several columns of figures so successfully, that Mademoiselle Lebeau, transported with joy, quitted him to join the doctor, who was waiting, concealed in an adjoining room, and announced to him this new symptom of a confirmed cure.

But, as soon as he was alone, the memory of this poor young man, which for a moment had been put on a wrong scent, and was at fault, was again at work. He laid down his pen, shut his eyes, pressed his hands against his forehead — in short, appeared to make a strong effort to recollect himself; then he suddenly burst forth into words : " Yes, yes," said he, starting up, and thrusting his hat upon his head, " there, I shall satisfy myself ——" then, with a rapid step, he descended the staircase, and immediately left the house.

Informed of this in time, the doctor, after having reassured Mademoiselle Lebeau, set off in pursuit of the deserter, walking behind him so as not to be observed, but also taking care not to lose sight of him.

Without a moment's hesitation, respecting the road he had to take, Chevillard traversed all Paris, from the Rue des Deux-Portes Saint-Sauveur to the Rue d'Aguesseau, Faubourg Saint-Honoré, where the mayoralty of the first district was situated, and there, repairing to the office containing all civil records, he asked for and was shown the certificate of marriage, proving that Esther de Brevannes had become his wife.

After obtaining this singular confirmation, he did not seem so much agitated as might be expected; the contention of mind, and the bodily exertion he underwent, in order to recall to his memory past events, served to divert his attention, and thus contributed to disguise from him the bitter effect which it must otherwise have produced.

Having appeared to deliberate with himself for a short time, he left the mayoralty, and rapidly pursued his course to the northern cemetery, where he proceeded straight to Esther's tomb, which he contemplated some time with a mournful look, but without shedding tears, or manifesting any outward sign of grief. The doctor, who continued to follow him, became uneasy at his cold demeanour; and in order to give a shock capable of reviving the unfortunate man's sensibility, which seemed still benumbed, he approached, and, looking at the tombstone, said: " Yes, Esther de Brevannes, a poor woman who died very young."

Chevillard looked at him from head to foot, then, shrugging his shoulders, appeared to take no further notice of him.

" Did not the unfortunate woman die from poison?" exclaimed the doctor, raising his voice. "A victim to the infamous passion of a man named Morizot!"

"Morizot!" exclaimed Chevillard, in an accent impossible to describe; " did you say Morizot?" And, thus speaking, he convulsively pressed the doctor's arm; then, trying to drag him away with him: " Come," added he, " I know the spot; horrible things have taken place there."

"Let us go!" said the doctor, indulging his wish.

But Chevillard, pushing him back, eagerly rushed upon a rising ground, situated near the spot. There he stopped, and looked towards heaven; then, raising his arms above his head, and letting them fall again towards the earth, with a gesture as if he were invoking a curse: " Morizot! Morizot!" he exclaimed, in a voice of thunder. "Take care; I recollect!" and this time, taking a start too rapid for the doctor to follow him, he soon disappeared from his sight.

CHAPTER XIV.

A QUARTER of an hour later, he arrived out of breath at the door of the house in the *Widows' Walk*, and knocked repeatedly.

A neighbour, who was passing, officiously said to him: " You are losing your time, my good sir; nobody is there; that house has been uninhabited for nearly two months."

"Except when murder is committed there!" exclaimed Chevillard, with irony.

"Ah! I cannot tell you anything about that," replied the woman, continuing her road.

At this moment, a singular procession appeared at the further end of the avenue, bordering on the Champs-Elysées. Two hackney-coaches, escorted by municipal guards on horseback, advanced, followed by a crowd of people, and stopped before the door at which Chevillard was in vain trying to gain admittance.

At first, he looked tranquilly on, whilst several persons dressed in black, and carrying papers under their arms, alighted from the first coach. But when, from the second conveyance, he beheld Morizot, Legros, and the Saint-Martin issue, preceded by two individuals wearing tricoloured scarfs, he rushed upon the commissary, who turned pale at sight of him, and seizing him by the throat: " It is he, the murderer!" he exclaimed; " the others are his accomplices; arrest them!"

It was, as may be conjectured, a judicial visit of inquiry, which was going to take place. After having been interrogated and confronted with Chabouillant, whose sudden determination had been to them a blow as unexpected as it was terrible, the accused, in spite of their utter denial of the charge, had remained under the weight of the most serious suspicion and impeachment. The warrant of arrest issued against them, had been immediately converted into a detainder, and now the deputy of the justice of the peace, and the foreman of the jury,* attended by the registrar, had come to reconnoitre the premises, pointed out as the scene of the crime, and conducting with them the accused, in whose presence, according to law, the search was to take place.

The action and words of Chevillard were of a nature to excite, in the greatest degree, the attention of the magistrates. They accordingly invited him to explain himself with more calmness.

"This man is mad," said Morizot, who had recovered from the agitation caused by the sudden appearance of his mortal enemy.

And, in fact, the disordered dress and

* *Jury of accusation*, which took the place of what we call the *tribunal of accusation.* The functions of foreman of the jury answered to those of the present *juge d'instruction.*

excited appearance of Chevillard gave to this allegation an appearance of truth, that insured its ready credence.

But just at this moment arrived the doctor, who had followed in the track of his patient. Knowing the place that the house in the *Widows' Walk* must hold in his memory, he had hoped to find him at this spot. Piercing the crowd, and seeing indeed the unfortunate man, who was gesticulating and speaking with great warmth, scarcely restrained by the police-officers, who were endeavouring to pacify him, he approached the magistrates, made himself known to them, and conversed with them for some time in private.

The magistrates, remembering the madman who had been arrested on the night of the murder, at a short distance from the house in which it was now supposed that the crime had been perpetrated, and the doctor affirming that this unfortunate man had recovered his senses since the morning, and was now only affected in all appearance by the force of his recollections, they considered it their duty to profit by the light which he seemed able to throw upon their researches, and, having entered the house with the doctor and the accused, they summoned this strange witness to appear before them.

The following scene passed in the saloon in which we have beheld so many events take place. The magistrates having seated themselves round the table upon which Chabouillant had written the evening before, whilst the accused were standing surrounded by the municipal guards and police-officers, Chevillard was introduced, having at his side the doctor, who, in case of need, was to serve as a sort of check upon him; the foreman of the jury then asked him, if he knew anything regarding the crime, of which they were trying to find the authors.

"Anything?" disdainfully replied the book-keeper. "I know all."

He began by relating the arrival of the man (it was thus he designated the victim), and the cry that he had uttered in the hall; then he recounted, how Morizot, with the aid of his accomplices, had brought in the dead body; he also pointed out the arm-chair in which the unfortunate man had been placed, whilst he was being plundered; detailed even the circumstances attending the division of the spoil, and all this with a clearness and force of expression, which, with the exception of a little excitement in his manner of speaking, excluded all idea of alienation of mind.

He was naturally asked to give an account of the manner in which he had been able to witness all that he had related.

Running to the window, Chevillard opened it, strode over the window-seat beneath it, then crouching down in the same manner he had done before: "I was thus," he said: "there was a light in the room, out of doors it was quite dark, and I saw everything through the curtains, which were a little open."

At this moment, Morizot, recalling to mind the tardy precaution he had taken with regard to the curtains, which had so badly fulfilled their office, could not help showing, at the recollection of this fatal imprudence, a sign of anger, which did not escape the searching looks of the magistrates.

"But how," asked the foreman of the jury, "were you able to penetrate into the house? What brought you there?"

Taking up his story at a more remote period, Chevillard began the recital of the infamous matrimonial fraud of which he had been the victim; he then related the death of his wife, in consequence of the persecution of Morizot, and at this instant the cold insensibility, which had excited the uneasiness of the doctor, gave place in this poor young man to a burst of the most lively feeling, for his voice faltered, and his disjointed words were accompanied by a flood of tears.

Touched by his grief, the magistrates begged him to rest awhile, and they remarked among themselves, that the account of the doctor, who had attended at Esther's death, perfectly coincided with all the circumstances related by the witness.

Soon after, Chevillard resumed his deposition, and gave the explanation required of him, stating the pious interest which had led him to the house, of which he had a key in his possession; and the probability of this account was soon confirmed by a visit, which was paid to Esther's chamber, where in fact were found many things that had belonged to her.

He was next interrogated on the subject of the blind men.

"I did not see those men," replied Chevillard; "I saw Morizot, who came towards the window, as if he were menacing me; then I became frightened. ——After having fled from the place, I remember nothing more until this morning, when I awoke in the chamber which I occupied before my marriage—and at first, I thought I had been dreaming."

The foreman of the jury then addressed the doctor in an impressive tone : " We adjure you," he said, " on your oath, and on your reputation as a medical man, to give us your opinion as to the mental state of the witness, and to state whether his words appear to you to emanate from a man possessing a healthy brain, and the entire use of his faculties."

The doctor, having taken his oath, explained in detail the progress of the disease, the treatment of which had been confided to his care, and he declared, on his soul and conscience, that, with the exception of a little nervous excitement, occasioned by the renewal of so many horrible recollections, the object of this investigation appeared to him to be restored to his normal state, and to have recovered entirely the use of his reason.

" You will be kind enough to continue your care of him," said the magistrate, " in order to give an account of his state from day to day, until the moment when he is likely to be called to renew his deposition before the jury."

The doctor promised to give the most attentive and strict consideration to the case, and he was then allowed to retire with Chevillard, as other judicial formalities had to be gone through, during which their presence was not required.

The doctor, foreseeing that they should be objects of indiscreet curiosity to the crowd, which continued to obstruct the entrance to the house, begged one of the police-officers to protect them as they went out. The man willingly complied with this request, and as he knew that the magistrates would still be detained there for several hours longer, he placed at their disposal one of the coaches standing at the door, with the condition that it should be sent back immediately after it had conveyed them to their destination.

Chevillard at first showed some repugnance to enter the hackney-coach, saying that he did not wish to return to that horrid house, where they threw iced water upon his head, for, even after they are cured, mad people entertain an invincible horror of the place where they have undergone medical treatment ; but being informed, that they were returning to Mademoiselle Lebeau's, in order to relieve the anxiety which she must have experienced since his hasty departure in the morning, Chevillard made no further opposition ; and soon after, the motion of the vehicle, the long round which he had taken, together with the reaction consequent to the violent emotions he had just experienced, threw him into a state of drowsiness, which the doctor regarded as a blessing of nature, and which he took care not to disturb.

He even wished that his sleep might be prolonged ; but the moment that the hackney-coach stopped, Chevillard awoke, and his cure appeared to have made a great progress in a short time, for he presented himself before Mademoiselle Lebeau with great serenity of countenance and manner.

"Ah ! mademoiselle," said he, in an affecting tone, being now in full possession of his senses, " how can I ever acknowledge all your kindness ?"

" You must not thank *me*," replied the amiable girl ; " it is to our good doctor that you owe your cure."

"Ah ! without you, mademoiselle," rejoined the doctor, " we should never have obtained so speedy a result. Your assiduous visits, and the happy influence which you succeeded in gaining over the patient, were of the greatest assistance to us in promoting his recovery."

" What, I am indebted to you for this also !" said Chevillard, with astonished gratitude ; " I, who was speaking only of your charitable assistance on another occasion."

" Let us not think of the past," answered Mademoiselle Lebeau, interrupting him ; " you are now restored to health ; the place which you occupied here is still vacant ; suppose, as you fancied for a moment this morning, that you only left us yesterday."

As she finished these kind words, a new personage, who always announced himself in rather a hasty manner, entered the apartment. As soon as the commercial traveller, whom we have already recognised, perceived Chevillard, he ran up to him with open arms, and affectionately embraced him. But the convalescent, remembering the fatal influence that Chabouillant had exercised over his destiny, received his advances with some coldness.

Chabouillant, who paid but little attention to slight distinctions, did not perceive the formality of his reception ;

besides he was fully occupied with one subject.

"Well, mademoiselle!" said he, "I have acted according to your advice. Justice is informed of everything, and the guilty parties are now in her hands; I absolutely pulverized them, when I was confronted with them this morning, and I can assure you, that Master Morizot was not sitting upon roses whilst listening to me."

"Morizot!" exclaimed Chevillard, whose eyes became animated at the bare mention of this name.

"Even so, my dear fellow," rejoined Chabouillant; "the very man, of whom you have had so much cause to complain—Morizot, the murderer."

"What! you know of the crime?" said Chevillard.

"And from the first source too; for the accomplices, although contrary to their intention, informed me of all the particulars."

"I have been told of nothing, but I have seen all, and I also have informed justice of it."

But, whilst the commercial traveller jumped for joy, and exclaimed: "Then we are two witnesses; victory! all is safe!" Mademoiselle Lebeau, not knowing, as yet, what had happened at the house in the *Widows' Walk*, became very uneasy at these words of Chevillard, and she made a sign to the doctor, giving him to understand that she feared a relapse.

Upon this, the doctor approached the young shopkeeper, and told her, in a low voice, that, in fact, Chevillard appeared to be fully acquainted with many of the circumstances, and that he had just given the magistrates most conclusive and circumstantial information. "However," he added, "it would be advisable to break off this conversation, which is of a nature to excite dangerous emotions in the patient."

Mademoiselle Lebeau now said: "You have taken nothing to-day, Monsieur Chevillard, you must stand in need of some refreshment. We were waiting breakfast for you, and, with the permission of these gentlemen, we will sit down to table."

"The lady is right," said the doctor to Chevillard; "tasting is not good for you, and you must fare well, in order to regain your strength."

The mistress of the house invited Chabouillant and the doctor to keep them company; but Chabouillant was not a man to fast until past twelve o'clock in the day, and was therefore unable to do honour to the invitation. As for the doctor, he excused himself, on account of his patients, whom he had to visit, and whom the incidents of the morning had caused him somewhat to neglect. They both, therefore, took leave.

Directly after, Mademoiselle Lebeau and Chevillard repaired to the dining-room, where the latter was received with lively congratulations by the shopwomen, who had greatly regretted his departure.

"Take your usual place, Monsieur Chevillard," said Mademoiselle Lebeau, with a gay air; then addressing herself to the other guests, she added: "Now, ladies, we shall no longer be so much embarrassed, since our *carver-in-chief* has returned to us."

CHAPTER XV.

WE are not of the opinion of those who regret the deplorable end of the unhappy daughter of the Marquis de Brevannes.

With a stigma on her birth, with a stigma on her life, and, according to all appearances, destined to have a stigma cast upon her death, she, in the last case, proved this fatal logic to be false, by her devotedness and expiation; and thus gloriously raised from her disgrace, she carried away with her the regret of the small number of honest hearts by whom she had been known.

But beyond the tomb, a real misfortune awaited her; she did not remain long in the memory of him for whom she had died.

It is, however, very easy to justify this quick and involuntary forgetfulness.

In the first place, Chevillard is absolved by the moral philosophers, those merciless dissecters of our feelings and instincts. They number forgetfulness amongst the miseries and infirmities of human nature, which is limited and weak in its griefs, as well as in its joys.

According to Montaigne: "A little thing turns us aside; for few things hold us fast."

After Montaigne, Labruyère says: "For certain losses, the heart ought to possess an inexhaustible source of grief. But it is neither by virtue nor strength, that we recover from a great affliction; we cry bitterly, and we are sensibly affected; but we are so weak and so frivolous, that we console ourselves."

Vauvenargues is more bitter and more explicit. He says: " Constancy is the chimera of Love.

" We do not regret the death of all those whom we love.

" There is no loss which we feel so acutely, and for *so short a time*, as that of a beloved wife."

In short, the most illustrious writer of our time* did not recoil from the afflicting words which are put into the mouth of Father Aubry, when the man of God is trying to console Atala on his death-bed: " If, some years after his death, a man were to revisit this world, I doubt whether he would be received with joy, even by those who have shed most tears to his memory; so quickly are other ties formed, so easily are other habits acquired, so natural to man is inconstancy, and of so little worth is our life, even in the heart of our friends!"

Behold, then, Chevillard absolved by a kind of general law, which, according to good authority, is said to exhaust and dry up in the heart of the greater part of mankind, the source of the most pious grief; but we must also allow, that the husband of Esther had some peculiar reasons for *feeling but for a short time*, as Vauvenargues says, the loss *of the beloved wife*.

It was chiefly the surpassing beauty of this young girl, which had given rise to the sudden passion of the imprudent young man; and love, caused by the senses, is more likely than any other to fade quickly away, or (if we may be allowed the expression) to become *volatilized*.

During the first period of his grief, the deceived husband had generously pardoned the fraud, of which he had been the victim; but, a little later, his self-love had made itself heard, and, without holding the memory of Esther in contempt, Chevillard could not help perceiving that the illusion had faded, and that, in losing its crown of purity, the angelic face of this woman had also been deprived, in his eyes, of part of its charms.

Besides, we must not delude ourselves; physical causes have a strange influence over our feelings and disposition. The least unforeseen event, a fortunate or an unfortunate occurrence, a change of place, and especially an ill-

* Chateaubriand.

ness, may deeply affect our moral being. Now, after the terrible shock which the reason of the poor madman had undergone, is it difficult to conceive, that a great revolution must have taken place in his heart and in his ideas?

With regard to his grand dreams of ambition and fortune, he had for ever dismissed them. And a great change had also taken place in his manner of regarding the character and person of Mademoiselle Lebeau.

Loaded with benefits, received like the prodigal son, continually experiencing the most considerate and attentive care, an exalted feeling of gratitude, which every day seemed to increase and develop itself, had succeeded in his heart to that dull malevolence, with which he had been formerly animated against his young patroness. Aware at length of the moral beauty which displayed itself throughout the conduct of this charming girl, he finished also by perceiving, that she was void neither of grace nor external attractions; and to see sometimes his look fixed on her with interest, and, taking pleasure in following her slightest movements, one might almost fancy (to make use of his own words on a former occasion), that he was now not quite so exclusively *for the fair girls*.

In this state of mind, he never let drop a word, which, in the remotest degree, had any reference to the unfortunate Esther; and, as may well be imagined, nobody, according to the express request of Mademoiselle Lebeau, ever thought of reminding him of this mournful subject.

It happened, however, once, that this sorrowful remembrance was awakened, and the conversation, which then ensued between Chevillard and the young shopkeeper, will show better than anything else, the great change that had taken place in the former.

The day on which the poor madman was arrested, it may be recollected, that, besides the letter which was found upon him addressed to Mademoiselle Lebeau, he had in his possession, that odious sum of five thousand francs, which Morizot had sent as the price of the seduction of Esther, and which Chevillard intended to return to him. This money had been deposited in the hands of the steward of Charenton, in order to be restored to the patient after he had recovered his senses, or paid over to his family, if his madness became incurable, or was greatly prolonged.

The cure being no longer doubtful, the doctor, who, according to the promise he had made to the magistrate, visited Chevillard almost every day, gave him one morning, in the presence of Mademoiselle Lebeau, the bank-notes which he had undertaken to deliver to him.

Chevillard coloured up, but took them without saying anything; and as soon as he was alone with his patroness, he hastened to acquaint her with the impure origin of this money, and with the scruple which had prevented him from employing it to liquidate the debt, which his imprisonment at Sainte-Pélagie had been the cause of his contracting with her.

Mademoiselle Lebeau greatly commended his manner of acting, and she undertook to profit by the first opportunity, to deliver the five thousand francs into the hands of the magistrate, who, according to his judgment, would either restore the sum to Morizot, or bring it forward as additional proof against him, in the criminal proceedings which were now in preparation.

Matters being thus settled, Chevillard continued thoughtful for a short time, and then said to the young shopkeeper: "Nevertheless, mademoiselle, I do not know but we are yielding to an idea of exaggerated delicacy; for, after all, this money is really mine; I have paid dear enough for it, and I so much desire to discharge my debt to you!"

"Why do you so much desire it? Do I appear to you to be a very impatient creditor?"

"Undoubtedly not; but in less than a year I have caused you the sacrifice of eight thousand francs, and, notwithstanding the prosperity of your establishment, it is a large sum."

"Monsieur Chevillard," said Mademoiselle Lebeau, "I am sorry to see you make a noble and honourable feeling give place to an interested one of self-love or of money. Your first impulse was good and generous; believe me, do not alter it; I am the more urgent in requesting this, as I feel quite happy to take part in this act."

"Ah! mademoiselle," said Chevillard, much affected, and in a tone which showed how truly he rendered justice to his patroness, "I know you are capable of everything that is noble, but this is just the reason why I should not abuse your kindness."

"Speaking of noble acts," said Mademoiselle Lebeau, "there will never be so great and fine a one, as the virtuous suicide, which placed this money in your hands; and when I reflect," she sorrowfully added, "that, through a bad impulse, to which I at first yielded, I perhaps contributed to render it necessary!"

"It was necessary in any case," coldly replied the book-keeper. "It was undoubtedly a noble act of self-devotion; but it was also an expiation."

"You are severe, Monsieur Chevillard, you must not recall to mind the fault; you must only remember the repentance; almost every woman, under the same circumstances, would have fallen like this poor girl, but how few would have raised themselves as she did!"

At this moment the conversation was interrupted by the entrance of a customer, and Chevillard, as he returned to his books, said to himself, with a feeling of disappointment: "Perhaps it will again be asserted, that Mademoiselle Lebeau is in love with me! I do not breathe a syllable to her concerning her rival; but it is she who speaks of her to me, and in her praise too!"

Through pique, and in order to revenge himself for the disdain of which he believed himself the object, he thought of Esther rather more than usual during the rest of the day; and recollecting, that, since he had been restored to liberty, he had but once, and then in haste, visited the spot where the miserable creature was buried, he repaired to the cemetery a little before dusk, and there he perceived something, which, in the agitation of his last visit, he had not observed. Although it was winter, flowers, newly gathered, and garlands, showed that the tomb, which he had neglected, had been recently visited. He had no difficulty in guessing whose was the pious and charitable hand which had been occupied in repairing his faulty negligence.

But Chevillard, instead of being grateful for this attention, was almost angry about it. "Why does *she* concern herself about it?" said he, with foolish anger; "*she* wishes to give me a lesson." And, under this false impression, excited by his indignation, he for several days gave way to the sour humours for which we have seen Mademoiselle Lebeau formerly reproach him.

As his ill-temper, however, now proceeded from a totally different cause, it did not hold out against the mild patience with which it was met by her

GREENAWAY & WRIGHT.

who was the object of it; and a continued exchange of mutual consideration and attentions, did not fail speedily to establish the most perfect harmony between the clerk and his patroness.

However, this peaceful state of things was still very far off from a more tender connexion, if such were ever to take place.

Chevillard would not acknowledge to himself, that he was in love; and truly he did not think that he was, and only fancied himself grateful. On the other hand, Mademoiselle Lebeau looked upon the good she had done as a thing of course, and she had never calculated that her generous conduct could have any influence in triumphing over the coldness which the object of her secret predilection had always evinced towards her. Besides, provided that Chevillard was there, that she saw him every day, that he tranquilly played his part in her active and busy existence, that he was not ill-tempered, that he did not talk of leaving her, or of dining out with Chabouillant, she asked for nothing more, and pursued her even course of life, without anticipating the future, in which she neither saw nor sought for the anticipation of anything fixed or certain.

Nevertheless, Chevillard would have done well to be on his guard; gratitude towards a young and amiable girl, full of intelligence and good feeling, soon turns into love: and, when about this time, his friend the commercial clerk and Chabouillant urged him to make himself lord and master of the *Tricoloured Prism*, if his real opinion were, as he stated it to be, that there was no foundation for their view of the case, that Mademoiselle Lebeau had never even thought of him, and that he was in every respect unworthy of her—it was very foolish of him not to stop, when about to be carried forward by a new passion, after having gained the victory over his old one.

But another subject of interest must now occupy our attention: what was going to be done with the great criminals who were already in the hands of justice!

The case had been very actively followed up; so that, in the newspapers of the 7th of March, or the 28th *ventôse*** (according to the style of that period), appeared the following paragraph: "A verdict of the jury of accusation has just sent up before the criminal tribunal now sitting at Paris, the two men calling themselves Morizot and Legros, and the woman Saint-Martin; the said parties being accused of committing murder on the person of the late Marquis de Brevannes. The trial of this strange affair, which, on two former occasions, has already so strongly excited the public attention, will commence on Monday the 10th instant. The small space which is left us in our columns of today, prevents us from publishing at length the act of accusation, but we intend giving some important extracts from it to-morrow."

It is needless to say, that this intelligence created an immense sensation, and that Paris was in a state of excitement.

On the day following that on which the first announcement appeared in the public papers, a shower of applications, couched in the most pressing terms, assailed the judge who was to preside at the trial; and all the choice spirits and elegant women of the time applied

to him for tickets of admission to the reserved seats.

Notwithstanding their republican austerity, the magistrates of that period were neither less gallant nor less open to amiable solicitations, than are the magistrates of our day. The president, therefore, did his best to comply with the pressing applications which were made to him; but, in spite of his willingness to satisfy all demands, and after he had distributed a much greater amount of tickets than the hall could contain, he made an infinite number of discontented persons, and drew upon himself much fierce enmity, which continued to pursue and harass him during his future career.

Not that the affair of Morizot and his associates fully realised, with regard to certain exciting details, all that some imaginations might have conjured up. For instance, the head of the marquis was not preserved in spirits of wine, and brought into court in a glass globe; neither were his intestines chemically analysed; nor were any of those pleasant interludes, half medical and half legal, introduced, which sometimes give to the criminal courts so much *piquant* interest.

But it is impossible to have everything; and, with the exception of the anatomical attraction, this case still promised some exciting scenes.

The special objects of interest were the poor blind men, by whose assistance the singular experiment had been hazarded, which we recounted in our prologue; and, although in fact they were kept from figuring in the trial, not having been able to be found, it was precisely from their presence, that those persons, who were the most outrageously curious, expected the most overwhelming excitement.

On the evening which preceded the opening of the trial, some tickets, which had either fallen into avaricious hands, or had been appropriated by some of the servants of the court, were sold in the neighbourhood of the Palais-de-Justice; and so great was the competition, that three or four louis were obtained for some of them.

A last example will depict the incredible effrontery, and the mad extremes, in which some people indulge, in order to gratify their inclinations. A woman, whom we could name, took upon herself to write to Madame Morizot, who, she thought, might have at her disposal some of these so much

---

* The republican epithets still continued, although the saints had resumed their places in the calendar, and had driven out the vegetables and instruments of husbandry, which had given their names to the days of the ex-*decade*.

coveted tickets; and she mentioned some former connexion, that she had with this afflicted lady, in order to obtain from her the favour of being admitted to witness the terrible trial of her husband.

In the next chapter, and at less cost, our readers will accompany us into the criminal court, where, by a fortunate combination of events, they will behold reunited in the same assembly, and divided into two equal groups, almost all the important actors in the drama which we have related to them.

CHAPTER XVI.

IT would be superfluous to relate how, at an early hour in the morning, an impatient concourse of people had assembled in the vicinity of the court of justice, and how they tumultuously rushed forward as soon as the doors began to revolve on their hinges. It would be equally superfluous to mention the crowd of elegantly dressed ladies, which the trial of capital crimes never fails to assemble. We must suppose, however, that the gathering of the fair sex on this occasion, presented even more than its usual share of elegance and charms, for a newspaper writer of that period, who was rather of the anacreontic school, did not hesitate to compare this brilliant assembly " to a delicious basket of flowers, which had been transported by mistake into the sanctuary of justice."

Evident marks of republican austerity were still manifest in the court of justice, from whence was excluded the figure of the Saviour, which, in all our judicial assemblies of the present day, is placed over the president's seat, in order to impress the sanctity of an oath upon all those who are called as witnesses.

About a quarter of an hour before the entry of the judges, an eager excitement, which prevailed in the assembly, announced the presence of the accused.

Morizot had dressed himself with the greatest care, and notwithstanding a livid paleness, which betrayed his inward agitation, he affected a sort of careless ease in his manner. Gazing round with audacity upon the assembled crowd, he sought to distinguish those persons with whom he was acquainted, in order to inflict upon them the malicious favour of a bow.

Madame de Saint-Martin, who was attired with much pretension, and had her face shaded by a veil, in the style of the portraits of Isabey, was seated by his side. Then came Legros, who was occupied in making notes of those points of the case, which had been communicated to him, and he took from time to time, with remarkable tranquillity, large pinches of snuff from the richly-wrought gold box, which we have already seen in his possession.

Chevillard had been frequently visited by the doctor, to whose care his mental state had been confided; he had also several times given his deposition before the foreman of the jury, and he continued to display a sound and ready judgment; consequently, he had received, at the same time with Chabouillant, a summons to appear as witness at the public trial.

It had also been thought, that Mademoiselle Lebeau might be able to furnish some information, which would be useful in discovering the truth, and she had been likewise summoned to be present.

Seated on the witness-bench, these three pillars of the accusation excited no less curiosity and attention than the accused.

The judges having taken their seats, and the indictment having been read, the interrogation of the arraigned persons was commenced.

During the interrogation, Morizot was haughty and hasty, and contradicted with audacity the charges brought against him; Legros evinced much cunning, and showed himself to be a skilful reasoner, and an adroit liar; whilst his mistress confined herself to a course of denial, which she abundantly accompanied with tears.

When it came to the turn of the witnesses, Chabouillant obtained the palm of gaiety, by his assurance, by his style, which he had specially adorned for the occasion, by the frankness of his confessions, and finally by the merit of invention, which could not fail to be recognised in the rather questionable combination through which he had nearly gained a family-name. It is true, that, when he had finished his deposition, he received a pretty severe reprimand from the president, with regard to the rather irregular manner in which he had tried to make himself out a Brevannes; but, on the whole, he was not seriously compromised: it was universally looked upon as a good trick, that he had been going to play on a set of wretches; and the odium attached to the character of his adversaries procured for him a corresponding degree of sympathy, and a sort of mirthful approbation.

Chevillard, having to relate his misfortunes, was in possession of too touching a theme not to excite general interest, and the pathos of his evidence, which he delivered in very appropriate terms, brought tears into the eyes of many of his hearers. A great sensation was also produced by his answer to Morizot's advocate, who, hoping to make the circumstance of his insanity tell in favour of his client, imprudently endeavoured to throw some ironical doubts on his perfect restoration to reason. "Sir," he replied to the lawyer, with an energy which he derived from the strength of his position, "since the question between us is concerning a sound judgment, and a right state of mind, you, of the two, might be rather considered as the insane person: for if you are honest, and convinced of the justice of the case, as I suppose you to be, you must be subject to terrible illusions, to hope in the success of the cause which you are defending."

The sensation produced in the assembly by this happy and sharp retort, had not yet ceased, when Mademoiselle Lebeau was brought in.

The simple but tasteful style of her dress, her reserved and modest air, without any appearance of affectation or timidity; the charm of her face and voice, which revealed intelligence and goodness; the impression which had already been made in her favour, by all that had been stated in the evidence, concerning her character and strong mind — all contributed to attract the sympathy of the auditory towards her.

The ladies, especially, feeling that their sex was honoured in her person, were the most enthusiastic, and the more readily so, as, from the mediocrity of her rank, she could not excite any sentiment of jealous rivalry.

Mademoiselle Lebeau knew, personally, but very little concerning the facts which were the foundation of the articles of accusation; but she was the first person to whom Chabouillant had confided them, and it was she who advised him to make them known to justice; and she could testify better than any one else, as to the mental state and moral conduct of Chevillard. She had therefore been cited by the judicial administration, in order to confirm the evidence of the two clerks, both of whom, on different accounts, presented a vulnerable side to the defence.

The accusing party, having built great expectations upon the striking virtue of this charming girl, consulted its interest in bringing forward all the great and noble points of her general conduct; and, by adroit questions, the government counsel obliged her to state all the good that she had done. Whilst undergoing this species of violence, to which her modesty was subjected, the young shopkeeper spoke of her good actions with such perfect reserve, and so much graceful simplicity, that universal signs of esteem and admiration accompanied her, as she seated herself on the witness-bench, after having given her evidence.

The rest of the sitting was employed in receiving evidence of a secondary order; and, on the following day, when the court met again, the counsel for the accusation began his address.

Taking up the history of the crime at the moment of the discovery of the blind men, he began by regretting the absence of these two witnesses, who, a very short time after their adventure, had suddenly quitted the hospital of the Quinze-Vingts, since which period, not the slightest trace could be discovered of them. Uniting the murder of the marquis with the odious history of the trap laid for Chevillard, the orator did not perhaps use suitable discretion, when he described this unfortunate young man giving himself up to a deplorable fascination, and neglecting a treasure of grace and virtue, which offered itself to him, in order to rush headlong into a series of horrible mischances.

In speaking of Chabouillant, the advocate endeavoured, if we may so express ourselves, to gloss over the defective part of his conduct, by representing him as an instrument of divine justice, as a sort of living remorse following the footsteps of crime; to any unpleasant prepossession that might be entertained against this witness, he opposed a horrible picture of the morals of the accused, which were of the most repulsive nature, even when viewed apart from the accusation of murder: he represented Morizot as a debauched and avaricious man, who had appropriated to himself the fortune of his former master; he showed Legros to be a usurer, a gambler, and one who complaisantly and readily undertook any dark and ignoble intrigue; whilst he described his mistress, the girl Loison, who called herself Madame de Saint-Martin, as having passed her life in following the detestable trade of a *female Mercury*.

The representative of the law wound up his discourse by an elaborate peroration, in which he placed in relievo the evident interposition of Providence, which, at first, seemed to have confided the secret of the murder to the protection of all kinds of human infirmity, but which afterwards, like the sun piercing through the clouds, had cleared away all the obscurity which it had been pleased to shed over the crime.

We must, however, acknowledge that the effect of this discourse was partly lost from the want of skill displayed by the orator, in his arrangement of the vast accumulation of detail, with which the case was burdened. He too frequently substituted a formal and logical discussion for the breathings of eloquence, at the same time evincing a sort of personal animosity against the accused. A decisive proof also of his commonplace and limited mind, was, that, having chosen for his peroration the sublime theme which we have already related, he did not know where to stop, but spoilt everything by introducing the never-ending topic of the pillars which support society being shaken to their foundation, if the jury pronounced the acquittal of the criminals.

Rich, and having his head at stake, Morizot had retained for his defence one of the most celebrated ornaments of the bar ; and, if the client was hideous, it must be confessed that the cause (in spite of the opinion expressed by Chevillard) was a fine one for the advocate to plead. Accordingly, the counsel for the defendant was most eloquent, and produced the greatest effect.

In the first place, he represented Morizot as a victim of the unjust prejudices which were then entertained against commissaries, and which arose from jealousy, excited by the large profits they made, and by their princely fortunes.

Encouraged by these prejudices, Chabouillant had no doubt formed a plan of extortion, and there was nothing to show why Chevillard, scarcely restored to reason, should not have looked upon the romantic tale, which had its birth in the imagination of a clever sharper, and which might very well have been related to him, as a real event in which he had been mixed up.

It had been said, that some letters had been extorted from Chabouillant, by violence, which the accused of course would have kept in their possession : how then was it possible, that they should now have the magnanimity not to produce them ? In short, all was cleverly explained in favour of the innocence of the accused ; whilst all the contradictions and obscurity appeared to be on the side of the accusers.

We must mention one more detail.

The privileges of arraigned persons are so sacred, that their advocates think they cannot extend them too far. Thus, they occasionally allow themselves to be transported beyond due bounds, and do not always pay sufficient respect to that which is most respectable and most worthy of esteem. Accordingly, the defender of Morizot, in order to weaken the effect produced by Mademoiselle Lebeau's evidence, thought he might indulge in some *piquant* insinuation, regarding the singular goodwill which this young lady evinced towards her book-keeper. But the public had already formed their opinion respecting the young shopkeeper, and whilst Chevillard, moved by a feeling of indignation, which his patroness immediately hastened to repress, rose to call the orator to account, murmurs, proceeding from all parts of the court, warned the calumniator that he was making a false step in opposing a general sentiment, which had taken a course diametrically contrary to the one he intended. Accustomed immediately to perceive the opinion entertained by his hearers, the advocate swerved from his original intention, and, retracing his steps, changed into a strong encomium on the noble girl, the perfidious piece of defamation which, without the attitude assumed by the public, he had meant to launch against her. Thus, on all sides, and in spite of every obstacle, Mademoiselle Lebeau obtained universal esteem and praise ; offering the rare example of simple and unpretending virtue unconsciously commanding admiration, and gaining that unanimous sympathy which is usually reserved for the alluring and unstable illusion of more brilliant qualities.

After the counsel for the two other accused parties had been heard, concerning whom there is not much to say, for they only repeated the arguments which had been advanced by Morizot's advocate, the sitting was suspended for a short time; and it was easy to perceive, from the conversation which was going on in all parts of the court, that the general opinion was, that the criminals would be acquitted. Not that they had succeeded in gaining the least degree of sympathy, and indeed they were generally regarded with the utmost disgust; but in the first place, the basis of the offence was not even established, for there was nothing that proved (besides the affirmation of Chabouillant) that the murdered man was really that Marquis de Bravannes, on whose death Morizot and his accomplices had so much interest at stake. Secondly, could sentence be passed, and three heads sent to execution, on the sole affirmation of an adventurer, and of one who had been confined as a lunatic at Charenton? It appeared, therefore, extremely probable, that the accused would be acquitted for want of sufficient evidence, and the manner of the jury in particular seemed to lead to the anticipation of this result.

When the judges had resumed their seats, the government counsel was called upon for his reply, and he had been speaking for some minutes, when a noise, proceeding from the further end of the court (which was the part reserved for that portion of the public who were not provided with tickets), soon overpowered the voice of the orator.

A constable who was sent to ascertain the cause of the tumult, and to repress it, soon returned, and addressed to the president a few words, which did not reach the ear of the public. Soon after the constable had gone out again, a noise, as of sticks striking against the floor, was heard in a covered passage, which led from the room reserved for the witnesses into the body of the court; and, at the same moment, to the great surprise of all present, there entered our old friends Michel and Corniquet, *arm in arm, and supporting each other*.

At the sight of the two blind men, the countenances of the accused turned of a deadly paleness, and curiosity was on all sides excited to a point which it would be in vain to describe.

When asked why they had not obeyed the judicial summons, the two *virtuosi* began to speak together, so that it was absolutely impossible to understand the explanation they gave.

As Michel, according to custom, displayed great pretensions, the president was struck by his confident and capable air, and he allowed him alone to speak, whilst he ordered Corniquet to keep completely silent.

Michel then related, that, after their unfortunate adventure, they had become the objects of the continual jokes of their comrades of the Quinze-Vingts, at which they had been very much annoyed; and that, about this time, a stranger had presented himself at the hospital, and had proposed to them to enter into a speculation. The speculation consisted in accompanying the said stranger to Bordeaux, where he intended establishing a *Café des Aveugles*, in imitation of the one at Paris. He thought, by announcing that the two members of the Quinze-Vingts, who had obtained so brilliant a popularity in the newspapers of the capital, were to be seen at his establishment, and that they directed the orchestra there, he should be sure to attract numerous and constant visitors.

The conditions which were offered appearing advantageous, the two friends had accepted them, and, without mentioning their intention to anybody, they had followed the speculator to Bordeaux. But theirs was not a happy move, for, scarcely had they arrived at their place of destination, when they found themselves deceived in their expectations. The mayor of the town would not permit the projected *café* to be opened, and this because he feared it might be *too close a copy* of the one at Paris; and, after experiencing numberless difficulties in their negotiations with the person who had engaged them, and who (to use Michel's expression) was *a beggarly rascal*, our two *virtuosi*, ill-treated by him, and without receiving any remuneration, were obliged to beg their way back to Paris on foot, in order to try to be readmitted into the asylum which they had left. They had been a fortnight on their journey, and had arrived only that same morning in Paris, where, hearing of the grand trial which was going on, and in which they were much concerned, they had hastened to offer their evidence to the court.

This explanation could not fail to be favourably received, and the question now was to learn from our two friends, all they knew concerning the affair in which they had been mixed up.

It being important to ascertain whether their evidence would agree, Corniquet was reconducted into the witness-room, whilst Michel remained in court to speak first.

Before making his deposition, he had to swear to speak *the truth, the whole truth, and nothing but the truth;* but when he was told to raise his right hand, he did not fail to raise the left, and then, in his anxiety to repair this blunder, he let fall his hat and stick, which he next began to grope about for on the ground.

Having once more obtained possession of these precious objects, by the assistance of one of the audience, he no longer knew on which side was the bench, which he had to address. According to his old mania of always maintaining that he knew perfectly well where he was, he roughly repulsed the constable, who was going to place him in the right direction; then, facing the company, and turning his back to the judges, he raised his right arm above his head, high enough to put it out of joint.

They at last succeeded, amidst the laughter of the assembly, in placing him in the right position, and he related with endless details the part he had played in the events of the famous night of the Avenue des Triomphes, as he called the place where the scene had been laid, for he would not yet believe that he had been conducted to the *Widows' Walk*, and he had continued every day to hold lively discussions with Corniquet upon this subject, saying, that it was the police who had spread the latter report.

The important point now to be ascertained, was, whether he would recognise by the voice, one of the accused parties to be the man who had imposed upon him and his comrade: Morizot had to speak first, and Michel declared, that he had never heard his voice before in his life.

So far he was right, as well as respecting a municipal guard, who was made to pronounce a few words; but he began to get rather confused in his ideas when he affirmed, in listening to Legros, who spoke in his turn, that he was not the man, and when he designated, as the right party, the recorder of the court, to whom the president had made a sign to take part in the trial.

This blunder was received by a general burst of hilarity, in which the accused themselves joined, for it told greatly in their favour; and the prevailing opinion began to be, that nothing would be gained from these poor devils, when Corniquet in his turn was brought in.

He began, however, by giving a pretty good proof in favour of the possible utility of his intervention, by the clear and concise manner in which he gave the account of his nocturnal adventure.

The testimony by sound now commenced; he listened to Morizot and the municipal guard with unchanged brow, and made only a negative sign with his head; but as soon as Legros had spoken, he exclaimed in an indescribable accent of truth and conviction: "This is the man who spoke to us!"

This declaration produced great commotion, whilst Legros changed countenance, and almost fainted.

In order to test the infallibility of this terrible allegation, the president caused a great number of the officers of the court to speak, designedly mixing the sound of their voices with that of Legros; but not once did the unshaken Corniquet hesitate, and not once did he fail to detect the accusing accent and organ, although the fearful anxiety of Legros contributed to change his tone.

This proof was already very conclusive; but Corniquet himself suggested the idea of another trial of skill, which he felt himself competent to accomplish, by remembering that the voice of a woman had uttered moanings, and he engaged to recognise this voice if he heard it.

Many of those present did not conceive to what a delicate point the sense of hearing can be carried in a blind person, and were ignorant that the observations of science have brought to light almost miraculous examples* of this kind; they therefore feared that Corniquet, intoxicated by his success, had taken upon himself an impracticable task; and curiosity, which, in this affair, revived every moment, saw before it a new cause of excitement.

There was at first some difficulty in putting Corniquet's idea into execution, for none of the women present much relished the idea of performing in this kind of *puerperal* comedy. At last some matrons of the company, in round caps, made up their minds to render to justice the service required of them, and the trial began.

The countenance of the blind man was in itself a spectacle; the lively characteristics of profound attention, and intense powers of memory, being depicted in it.

Three times, and under a different

* See, among other proofs on the subject of this *memory of the ear*, two excellent articles which were published in 1831, in the *Revue de Paris*, by Monsieur Dufau, now director of the Institution of the Juvenile Blind.

form, the moaning of a woman in travail struck upon his ear, and he remained in the same posture; but Saint-Martin being heard in her turn, Corniquet appeared to listen still more attentively; he then made a sign with his hand, that the woman should begin again; and, on this repetition, he declared it to be the voice that he remembered.

After the president had done all that the strictest sense of justice demanded, in order to test the sincerity of these two experiments, the government counsel was called upon to continue his speech; but the latter, in rising, declared that, after what had just occurred, all oratorical persuasion appeared to him useless, and that, in his opinion, the fate of the accused seemed decided.

For the last moment or two, Legros and his mistress, in the midst of the consternation into which they had been thrown, seemed to be concerting together, and Morizot cast some uneasy glances towards them.

As soon as the menacing words of the accusing officer had fallen from his mouth, the woman rose and said with volubility: " Mr. President, Legros wishes to speak, but dares not."

" Well, Legros," said the president, " you have the truth ready to escape from your lips; let it have free passage, and, by the sincerity of your avowal, merit the indulgence of the court."

" Well, then! Mr. President—" exclaimed the unhappy man.

With a rapid movement, Morizot rose, and, casting a terrible look towards Legros, demanded to be heard.

Legros, who had also risen, fell back again upon the bench, hid his face, upon which was depicted the conflict that was taking place within him, in his hands, and contented himself with saying in a stifled voice: " We are innocent, Mr. President; that is what I wished to say."

Perceiving that Morizot exercised over his accomplice a moral authority, which would be an invincible obstacle to the evident desire of the latter to make confession, the president commanded that the commissary should be taken out of court; and, from this moment, Morizot regarded himself as lost.

In fact, as soon as the lawyer felt himself released from the fascination which this man exercised over him, he rose, and, with a calmness which always accompanies a firm determination, said: " Mr. President, will you have the

goodness to require the witness Chabouillant to repeat the scene which took place with him in the *Widows' Walk*, and to ask him if he does not owe his life to myself and this lady?"

" It is useless to recur to these details; they are placed to your advantage, especially if you acknowledge them."

Without making a direct reply, Legros continued: " Is it also well understood, that, in the conversation at Offenburg, Monsieur Chabouillant was able to deduce, from the words overheard by him, that this lady and myself disapproved of the murder of the marquis, and that we only took part in the means necessary to conceal the affair?"

" That was clearly expressed," replied Chabouillant, before he was called upon; " and it was repeated in my presence, without being contradicted by Morizot, when I was ensnared, and forced to write the letters."

" Now, Mr. President," rejoined Legros, " you see what we have been guilty of, and whether we have not been shamefully calumniated."

" But Morizot?" asked the government-commissioner, with much warmth.

" Mr. Counsel, it does not belong to me to accuse an absent friend; I can only say, that, if he had followed my advice, he would not be in his present situation."

After this evasive avowal, the cunning lawyer sat down again, and if any doubt could have attached itself to the motive which, independently of his horror of blood, and of his views upon Chabouillant, had decided him to save the life of so dangerous a witness— this motive, we think, is now fully explained.

The president then commanded, that Morizot should be brought in again; but, at the same moment, much confusion was heard outside; and the constable, returning in a state of excitement, asked for the assistance of a doctor; the accused, he said, had just stabbed himself to the heart, with a small penknife which he had about him, and which he had successfully concealed from the vigilance of those appointed to watch him.

Two minutes later, the doctor of Charenton, who, being present as a witness, had replied to the call of the constable, informed the court that the blow had produced instant death; thus the accusation became null in the person of the

GREENAWAY & WRIGHT

commissary, who, by this means, at least, succeeded in rescuing his name and family from the disgrace of a capital condemnation.

The painful feeling caused by this terrible and unexpected event, suspended the proceedings for a moment, but impassible justice soon resumed its course.

The president concisely summed up the evidence, and, after the jury had consulted together for a short time, Legros and his mistress were declared to be accomplices in the murder which had been perpetrated on the person of the *ci-devant* Marquis de Brevannes.

The fact of *nonpremeditation* being admitted, they were condemned to hard labour for life; and they thus received the benefit of their clemency towards Chabouillant, and got off as cheaply as if *attenuating circumstances* had been introduced into the judicial practice of that period.

When sentence had been passed, the president addressed some kind words to the blind men, and to Corniquet in particular; and he promised to take all the necessary steps for procuring their readmission into the national institution of the Quinze-Vingts, where for the future, it was probable that they would be anything but objects of derision to their comrades. A collection was also made for them on the spot, among the company present in court, and towards which Mademoiselle Lebeau most generously contributed: by this means they obtained a considerable sum, and were put in immediate possession of it; and it is pretty generally known, that a well-furnished purse has considerable influence over the consideration of mankind in general.

With regard to the *strong-nerved* and *elegantly-dressed* ladies, we are of opinion that they must have been perfectly satisfied with their day, and must have found it sufficiently rich in excitement. It must, however, be confessed, that Morizot cheated them in some degree, by killing himself in an adjoining room, instead of performing the deed publicly before the assembly; it was the verbal account at the end of the old *tragedy*, very disagreeably substituted for the lively and stirring action of the modern *drama*.

CHAPTER XVII.

Mademoiselle Lebeau, who did not pride herself in the strength of her nerves, had no taste for those terrible scenes, which end with the executioner; therefore, when the president declared the pleadings to be over, and was about to sum up the evidence, she asked for and obtained permission to retire. The same indulgence could not be exercised with regard to Chevillard, as the important part which he had acted throughout the affair, might render his presence necessary; he was therefore unable to accompany his patroness, and remained in court with Chabouillant; the latter promising Mademoiselle Lebeau to watch over the convalescent, and to accompany him home, as soon as the trial was ended.

The sentence was not passed until late in the evening, and the sitting had lasted without interruption, since twelve o'clock in the day, so that the auditory, including the two clerks, had been kept fasting, and left the court almost dying with hunger.

Chabouillant reminded Chevillard, that the doctor had expressly prohibited, in his presence, a spare diet for his patient; and he therefore proposed, that, before going home, they should take some refreshment together, at the first *restaurant* they came to.

Chevillard shuddered at this suggestion, for he remembered that he might date all his misfortunes from the dinner which the commercial traveller had given him some months before; but considering, that he still owed a return for this politeness, and being now convinced, contrary to his former ideas, that, in the greater part of the misfortunes of life, our imprudence is as much to blame as fate, he did not perceive any particular objection to the proposal that had been made to him; he only stipulated, that they should sup in a moderate style, and that he should exercise his right of being, in his turn, the Amphitryon. These conditions were too reasonable not to be accepted.

Behold, then! after the most cruel and unexpected vicissitudes of fortune, our two friends placed in the same situation in which they were found at the commencement of this story; but misfortune having matured their minds, this meeting in no point resembled their former one. The repast was simple; they drank only to satisfy their thirst, and their conversation was as serious as it had before been empty and trifling.

Chabouillant learned with lively regret (for until this moment, they had not had an opportunity of being alone together, for Chevillard to impart it to him), the cruel influence which his imprudent introduction into the gambling-house had exercised over the life of his friend. The eye of the commercial traveller indeed sparkled a little, at the thought of all the gold which had been for a moment the property of their joint-stock concern; however, whilst he heaped energetic maledictions upon the head of Legros, for his fatal interference, it was less from regret for the loss of the fortune which had so quickly vanished under this man's detestable advice, than from the recollection of the cruel deceptions to which the unfortunate Chevillard had been subjected. He even maintained that, as they had agreed *to marry*, he ought to pay half of the sum which had been employed to the prejudice of Mademoiselle Lebeau, and it was with great difficulty that he was induced to abandon the idea of this honourable reparation.

When they had exhausted past events, they began to speak of the future; and Chabouillant seriously announced to his friend, that, in consequence of the false position in which he found himself placed by his imprudence, he had decided upon taking a resolute step, and upon expatriating himself. "Yes," said he, "after what has passed, I can no longer live in France with any pleasure; I intend to go and try my fortune in America; at the end of some years, my folly will be forgotten; or, should it be still remembered, the money which I shall have in ballast, and of which I shall make an honourable use, will gain me consideration; unless, before that time," added he, in a melancholy voice, "rattlesnakes or the yellow fever ——"

"Ah! you think of going to America!" said Chevillard, meditating; "indeed, that suggests an idea to me. And when do you go?"

"As soon as possible. I intend, tomorrow, paying a visit to our excellent patroness, to see if she will furnish me with some orders; after which, I shall repair to Bordeaux, to embark."

"Well! my friend, you shall not go alone."

"What do you mean?"

"Yes, I will also make the voyage, and accompany you."

"Nonsense! why do you take this desperate course?"

"I, like yourself, have lost all claim to consideration. An object for public derision, through my foolish marriage, and having been known as a madman, what kind of reputation can I now have?"

"But you have so sweet and peaceful a retreat at Mademoiselle Lebeau's; and, as I told you the other day, you have only to say a word, to obtain the highest place in her heart and house."

"Do not let us touch on that subject; you are striking a very sensitive chord, and the ideas to which you allude are perhaps the original motive for my departure."

"How now! I do not understand you. Mademoiselle Lebeau is not a girl to force herself upon anybody, and if, decidedly you cannot reconcile yourself to the notion of becoming her husband ——"

"I, her husband!" exclaimed Chevillard, with great emotion; "an unfortunate, vile wretch like myself; I, who am no longer capable of exciting anything but pity!"

"Chevillard!" said the commercial traveller, looking at him full in the face, "have we experienced a revolution in our ideas? has the little roguish god,

who has often played worse tricks than this, at last opened your eyes to the eminent merit of a certain person?"

Chevillard for some time did not make any reply; then, suddenly allowing his secret to escape from him, he said: "I do not conceal it from you, a great change has taken place in my ideas!"

"Then I congratulate you; you are at least approaching to the desired point."

"Yes, my friend, I love her; and I love her so, as almost to cause again the loss of my reason."

"The deuce, my dear fellow! it was a long time coming, but I now see that we are slightly hooked!"

"And what sort of man should I then be," exclaimed the book-keeper, with enthusiasm, "were I not ready to kiss the print of her feet! a woman whom I treated with ingratitude, and who has only revenged herself by kindness; who released me from prison, and who, during my illness, came every day to sit by the side of my bed; a woman, whose virtues have just obtained public homage, and before whom calumny itself has been obliged to retreat!"

"Whence you conclude," said Chabouillant, with a sly look, "that you must set off for America, and leave this angel of a woman behind you?"

"Without doubt, honour obliges me to do so."

"You argue very justly, my dear fellow," rejoined the commercial traveller, "and I shall look upon you as a great scoundrel, if, in three days from this time, you are not already on your road; but make yourself easy," added he, rising, "I will undertake to arrange the affair, and will make all the necessary preparations for the honourable exile which you are meditating to enter upon. Let us now retire to rest, and we will talk more on the subject tomorrow morning."

Chevillard was a little astonished at the eagerness with which Chabouillant embraced his project of expatriating himself; he thought he might have made some objections to it, and have entered into the subject a little more fully. He would not, however, allow his opinion to be perceived; but, in reality, he quitted his friend, regretting that he had too readily confided to him, as a decided project, what was in truth only a sudden resolution, the bearings and consequences of which he had not given himself time to consider.

Early on the following morning, Chabouillant entered the office of the book-keeper, and asked him if he still kept to his resolution. Chevillard answered, with an embarrassed air, that he had been reflecting on the matter, and that he wished to speak more seriously concerning it.

"Very well!" replied the commercial traveller, "we will talk of it again;" then, with the manner of a man who had no time to lose, he asked: "Is our patroness within?"

"Yes, in her private room," answered Chevillard; "but do not say anything to her yet, about my projected voyage; it is more proper that I should be the first to inform her of it; and the more so, you see ——"

"All right!" said Chabouillant, leaving the office, without hearing the end of this sentence; and he immediately repaired to the presence of Mademoiselle Lebeau.

"Mademoiselle," said he, after the customary forms of politeness had been observed, "you see before you, a man who has come to take leave of you."

"You are going away, Monsieur Chabouillant? and pray where are you going to?"

"I perceive, and you will, I am sure, see it in the same light, that, after what has happened, I cannot with propriety remain in France. I have therefore decided to seek in another hemisphere the family which I have looked for in vain in this."

"Then you meditate taking a very long voyage?"

"I intend, mademoiselle, to go to Rio de Janeiro, and probably to establish myself there."

"It is very painful to see our friends thus depart; but I cannot disapprove of your project. It is certain, that you might here meet with many things which would be disagreeable to you."

"Undoubtedly," replied Chabouillant, "it is a determination which I ought to take; besides, I have a great consolation in my misfortune, and the company of a friend, who is going with me, will render my exile more easy to bear."

"Who then is going with you?" demanded Mademoiselle Lebeau.

"I think he must have spoken to you on the subject," rejoined Chabouillant.

"To me! no; do I know him then?"

"Know him, indeed! Mademoiselle, it is Chevillard."

"Monsieur Chevillard!" exclaimed Mademoiselle Lebeau, with sorrowful astonishment. "You cannot be speaking seriously."

"Very seriously. The poor fellow has the same reasons as myself, for finding himself here rather out of his right position; his foolish marriage, his insanity ——"

"But these are only misfortunes," eagerly replied the young shopkeeper.

"I well know," answered Chabouillant, without appearing hurt by this remark, "that there is a certain shade of difference between our two positions; but besides all this, he has a strong motive for going away."

"And, may this motive be known?"

"Ah! he makes no secret of it; he says, that, if he does not take his flight beyond the seas, he shall go mad again; and having already had a taste of the thing, he does not feel any particular inclination for more."

"But what can cause a relapse? He has a very quiet post here; I shall take care, that he is not too much burthened with work, and it is very certain that nobody will tease him."

"That is true; but there are so many causes for driving a man mad! There is the madman through ambition, the madman through money, the madman through music, *Il fanatico per la musica*, which I saw performed this year at Berlin; we have also *Nina, or la Folle par amour*."*

As Chabouillant had laid particular stress upon this last species of madness, Mademoiselle Lebeau observed: "I thought, that, without being absolutely consoled for the loss of his wife, he did not entertain so sorrowful a remembrance of her as would be likely to affect his reason."

"His wife?" replied Chabouillant; "the question is not of her!"

"But of whom then?" asked the poor girl, with the utmost anxiety; and, as the malicious clerk remained silent, she added, overstepping her usual reserve: "Speak then, Monsieur Chabouillant; you seem to take pleasure in partly revealing secrets, which you will not afterwards disclose."

"Not so, but I am seeking how to express myself; in short, mademoiselle —— do you think any one can become mad through gratitude?"

Mademoiselle Lebeau looked at him with some curiosity, and replied: "Gratitude has always appeared to me a

* Mad for love.

tranquil sentiment, which could not produce such dangerous effects."

"Eh! eh! that depends on persons and circumstances. For example, if you, mademoiselle, had done the quarter for me that you have done for Chevillard, do you think that I should not adore you as a divinity, and that my senses would not be in danger whilst near you?"

"Perhaps *you* might," gaily replied Mademoiselle Lebeau; "but Monsieur Chevillard!"

"Well, mademoiselle, this is just where you are deceived: Chevillard no longer recognises himself; he tells everybody, that formerly you had a liking for him ——"

"How!" exclaimed Mademoiselle Lebeau, with dignity; "he tells everybody ——"

"Pardon me, I get confused; I meant to say, that everybody remarks to him, that formerly you appeared to have a liking for him, and that he, stupid and blind ——"

"But, in correcting yourself, I do not see that you improve the matter."

"In short, mademoiselle, it is very difficult to explain, particularly when I am always being interrupted; but this is the plain state of the case, in two words: you loved Chevillard, when he did not know it, and now he does not know whether you love him when he loves you."

"In any case," said Mademoiselle Lebeau, half laughing and half angry, "if he has commissioned you to speak for him, I do not congratulate him upon the choice of his ambassador; you have so confused the matter, that it is impossible to make anything out of it."

"I sum it up then," rejoined the commercial traveller, "and to speak in plain terms, I ask you this question: Must I tell Chevillard, that you command him to remain?"

"But, Monsieur Chabouillant, your friend is free, and you well know that I have no right to command him."

"No *Jesuitism*, mademoiselle! Chevillard is determined to go, if you do not love him!"

"Well then, as I said at the beginning of this conversation, I do not see any reason why he should go."

"Ah! divine! divine!" exclaimed Chabouillant, taking Mademoiselle Lebeau's hand, which he covered with kisses; and as the latter drew it away in some confusion, he added: "I am

only taking the earnest money;" then opening the door, he called out: "Chevillard! Chevillard!"

Astonished to hear himself called with so much eagerness, Chevillard soon after made his appearance, and perceiving the countenance of Chabouillant beaming with joy, and that of Mademoiselle Lebeau of a deep crimson, he looked first at one and then at the other, with no little surprise.

"My noble friend," said Chabouillant, going straight up to him, "did you not tell me last night at supper, that you had become madly in love with Mademoiselle?"

"Well, I am sure!" replied Chevillard, very angry; "it is you who are mad to talk thus."

"Permit me to speak," rejoined the commercial traveller; "these are your own expressions: 'What sort of man should I then be, were I not ready to kiss the print of her feet! this woman whose virtues have just obtained public homage!'——"

"I might have said this, without attaching to it the same meaning which you do."

"Take care! no denial, or you will spoil everything."

"But, really ——" answered the book-keeper, much embarrassed.

"The question is this," said Chabouillant, cutting short all equivocation: "Is it agreeable to you or not, to become the husband of the *tricoloured fairy?*"

"Monsieur Chevillard," said Mademoiselle Lebeau, seeing that the poor fellow had fixed upon her a look which asked for the confirmation of this sudden hope, "I have reflected much concerning my situation; we have been publicly declared to entertain for each other sentiments more or less true, but which do not render it the less difficult for me to choose a husband; in this embarrassment, an idea occurred to Monsieur Chabouillant, which he submitted to my attention, and which it appears that I have not sufficiently combatted, since he conceives himself authorised to speak to you of a marriage. However, nothing shall be done without your assent, and if you like better to go away ——"

"Ah! mademoiselle!" exclaimed Chevillard, throwing himself at her feet; "what have I done to deserve so much happiness?"

"You have been unfortunate," answered the amiable girl; and she extended to him her hand, which he bathed with tears of joy.

"Behold," said Chabouillant, "it is thus that:

'After a storm, we see fine weather!'"

"Now, mademoislle," added he, "should it suit you to appoint me your agent for the Brazils, I tender you my services, and I shall set off this evening at the latest."

"But why this sad resolution?" said Chevillard.

"I should doubtless have much liked to witness your happiness," replied the commercial traveller; "but is it not true, mademoiselle, that I am obliged to leave France?"

"I wish I could detain you," answered Mademoiselle Lebeau, "but my real opinion is, that your departure is necessary. With your intelligence and activity, you cannot do otherwise than succeed; and as much as depends upon me, I will assist you to my utmost ability. In a few years, you will return to us; by that time all will be forgotten, and this voluntary exile will have been an expiation for your past fault. Go then; but think sometimes of us, as we shall think of you, and let us often hear from you."

"At least," said Chabouillant, "let me be allowed to kiss the bride; it will bring me good luck."

The young girl blushingly presented to him her blooming cheek.

"My friend," said Chevillard, embracing him, "if you have ever in any way been the cause of my misfortunes, you have now insured my happiness."

"Well," rejoined the commercial traveller, taking a hand of each, "think sometimes of the poor exile;" and, feeling that his courage was failing him, and that tears were starting into his eyes, he hastened away.

CHAPTER XVIII.

FOUR years later, from the top of a terrace planted with linden-trees, and which belonged to an elegant habitation, a young woman, leaning upon the arm of her husband, was contemplating with delight, on a fine autumn morning, the magnificent view formed by the valley of Montmorency, below the village of Sannois. At a few paces distant from the happy couple, two charming children, a boy and a girl, were wholly intent upon filling a little cart with the dry leaves, which began to cover the walks; the sudden sound of a carriage, passing rapidly at the foot of the terrace wall, drew the little labourers from their attractive employment, and soon occupied all their attention.

Their curiosity was not disappointed, for a coachman in a yellow livery and blue plush breeches, was driving two beautiful cream-coloured horses, and behind the carriage stood a magnificent negro, in the most splendid and picturesque costume.

Whilst the children were exclaiming at the beauty of this equipage, in which the taste that had been displayed might however be deemed rather equivocal, one of the two persons who were seated inside, leaned his head out of the window, and bowed.

"Why, it is Chabouillant!" exclaimed the husband of the young woman, who proves to be Madame Chevillard, formerly Mademoiselle Lebeau.

The latter at first expressed some doubt as to her husband's having seen aright; but directly after, a servant came to announce, that some strangers were waiting in the drawing-room; and the married pair, hastening to receive them, recognised indeed the enterprising and jovial commercial traveller, in the personage, decorated with several orders, who threw himself into their arms. Finding that they no longer resided in the Rue des Deux-Portes-Saint-Sauveur, he had hastened to their country-house to embrace them.

He was accompanied by a young Brazilian lady, a beauty of rather an olive complexion, whom he presented to Monsieur and Madame Chevillard as his wife. The stranger responded with gravity, but at the same time with affectionate politeness, to their attentive and cordial reception of her.

It was not necessary to put many questions to Chabouillant, in order to have an explanation of the metamorphosis, which had taken place in him. He was scarcely seated, when he related, that, having obtained a situation in the establishment of one of the principal bankers at Rio de Janeiro, he had been fortunate enough to touch the heart of his only daughter. Seeing only with the eyes of his beloved child, the worthy Brazilian had consented to the marriage of the lovers; and dying soon after, he had left his son-in-law at the head of one of the richest banking-houses in the country.

In order not to make any change in the commercial firm, Chabouillant, whilst going through the necessary forms relating to the subject, had taken the name of his father-in-law : so that, after all his anxiety to procure for himself family consideration, he had become the legitimate proprietor of one of those fine strings of harmonious and high-sounding names, with which the Portuguese aristocracy proudly adorn themselves. He called himself, therefore, Joseph - Melchior - Maldonado - Saraïba d'Enserrabodès.

"Good heavens !" exclaimed Madame Chevillard, in a tone of anxiety; "you have now so many names, that I much fear I shall not be able to remember them all."

"This is provided against," rejoined the ex-commercial traveller in the same strain ; and adopting a style which was certainly quite first-rate for that period, when an address was written down without ceremony on the first stray card, he presented one to his hosts, richly engraved and ornamented, in order that they might study at their leisure, and class in their memory, his new and encyclopædical denomination.

One of the grand means of seduction, by which Chabouillant had succeeded with the inflammable person who had become his wife, was the flowery style which characterized his conversation. He was not therefore altered in this particular ; on the contrary, the language which he made use of, warmed by the rays of a tropical sun, and loaded with metaphors borrowed from the picturesque nature of the country which he had lately inhabited, had risen to the wildest style of poetry, and might aptly be compared to those virgin forests with which the Brazilian soil is covered.

If Chevillard and his wife were pleased at the good success which had followed the courageous determination of their old friend, Chabouillant was no less satisfied in learning from them, that, having already retired from trade with a respectable fortune, their union had been productive to them of true happiness, which no mischance had hitherto imbittered.

The first visit of the American banker was rather short ; but, having promised to pass at least a week with his old friends, he arrived a few days after with a cargo of monkeys, parrots, and other birds of magnificent plumage, which he presented to Madame Chevillard, and which formed the delight of her children.

One evening, when Madame Cha-

bouillant had retired early to rest, her husband related to Chevillard and his wife, that, having arrived by the way of Rochefort, he had visited the hulks, where his nerves had been considerably shaken by an accidental rencounter.

In the dress of a galley-slave, and chained by the foot, he had recognised Legros, notwithstanding the change which hard work and mental suffering had produced in the features of this wretched man. In a short conversation which they had together, the latter informed him of the death of the woman who had been his accomplice. In obedience to that fine christian maxim, which enjoins pity for every sin, Chabouillant had put an end to this interview with an old acquaintance, by bestowing a considerable alms upon Legros, accompanying it with all the words of consolation which the occurrence had suggested to him. The good heart of Madame Chevillard applauded this deed of charity, and consequently her husband also approved it highly. An agreeable habit which he had formed, and one which he found answered very well, was always to be of the same opinion as his wife.

After a week had passed in sweet intimacy, the friends separated with the hope of meeting again, for Chabouillant confessed that France was always courting him back, and that he could not abstain from paying it a visit from time to time.

At a much later period, we find Chevillard invested with municipal functions, and his wife honoured with the title of *the mother of the poor;* her inexhaustible benevolence, and the establishment of an *asylum* and a *work-room* for young female orphans, loaded her with the blessings of the surrounding country.

The fearful house which we have so many times entered, did not meet with a better end than its ancient proprietors. Abandoned for a long time, and falling into decay, it was sold by the family of the Morizots, which had quitted France. Bought by a retired sutler, in order to be let out in furnished apartments, and to carry on a sale of brandy and beer, it presented a most dilapidated appearance, and was at last destroyed by a conflagration.

With regard to the *Widows' Walk*, it has now lost much of its deplorable notoriety.

Although lighted with gas, and enclosed by respectable habitations, which have greatly increased there of late, some prejudice still continues to be cherished against it; but it advances a forcible protest against its past reputation, by its being the site of the celebrated Jardin Mabille, a chorographical and rural establishment, of which Chabouillant, in the merry and impetuous years of his youth, would certainly have formed the principal ornament.

THE END.

E. APPLEYARD, 86, Farringdon Street, London.

www.ingramcontent.com/pod-product-compliance
Lightning Source LLC
Chambersburg PA
CBHW080832250626
47160CB00008B/2913